Mikael Lun

# R/N/A

## Deadly Sequence

**MIKAEL LUNDT**
AUTOR & SELFPUBLISHER

**Imprint:**
© Mikael Lundt 2023
Publisher: Michael Gückel, Gartenstr. 15, 95191 Leupoldsgrün, Germany
Editing & Proofreading: Michael Macdonald
Cover design: Michael Gückel
Photo credits: istockphoto.com - nevodka/anusorn nakdee

Print: Amazon KDP
ISBN: 9798859385782

Contact: mikael@mikael-lundt.de
On the web: www.mikael-lundt.de

# 1

Somewhere in the snowy forests of Romania, January 8.

The skin of Test Subject 109 offered no resistance whatsoever to the needle, which was barely half a millimeter thin. Thanks to its nanocoating, the needle slid into the arm as if it were gossamer silk. But silk was nowhere to be found in the sterile laboratory where Number 109 lay. Here, there were only sterile synthetic fibers, the whiteness of which was so brilliant that it almost hurt the eyes.

Just about everything in this room was white: the masks and gowns of the staff, the medical equipment, the beds to which the test subjects were tied with belts, the walls, the floor and the ceiling with their sensors and cameras. Only the dark skin of the six anesthetized women on the medical tables resisted the dictatorship of the pale interior. In contrast, their complexions seemed all the blacker.

Suddenly, a red light broke into the monochrome still life. A shrill alarm followed. Both came from the neighboring laboratory, which could be reached through a glass door.

A selection of employees in protective suits let go of their test subjects and turned around. One of them went to the door and peered over into the lab, from which the blood-red light was still shining. He pressed the call button on the intercom next to the connecting door.

"Control Room, do you read me? This is Dr. Stewart, we've had an alarm in Lab 6, and they should all be sound asleep in there." He released the button and waited.

The speaker crackled, then came the answer. "We have the situation monitored. Continue your proceedings."

Stewart looked back and forth between the intercom and the glass door. Just as he was about to turn around to continue his work, he heard a rumble and clatter from next door.

Not a second later, a bloodied fist pounded against the window.

Stewart flinched. Truthfully, he knew this wasn't necessary. The door was made of laminated glass and was not permeable without a key card.

Then a face pressed against the glass.

Those eyes - fiery red!

All the blood vessels in them seemed to have burst. The eyes fixed Stewart.

Other employees approached and watched as the woman now threw herself against the door with full force, as if she had no regard for her own body.

Again, Stewart pressed the intercom button. "Emergency in Lab 6," he reported. "This series is a total failure."

"Stand-by," came the reply.

Agonizing seconds passed.

Stewart exchanged glances with the staff around him.

That's when the voice from the loudspeaker spoke up again, "Execute Protocol Delta, we're enabling the decontamination process, acknowledge!"

On the other side of the passageway, a bright orange emergency switch lit up, set into the wall behind a glass cover.

"Acknowledge!" repeated the voice from the intercom.

"Procedure is ready," Stewart replied tersely.

"Confirmed. Trigger procedure and monitor."

Stewart walked over to the switch, flipped up the cover and pressed. The button clicked into place, changing color from orange to green.

A loud hiss was heard from beyond the door, then screams, animalistic grunts. After a few seconds, there was dead silence.

No one stirred; none of the subjects in Lab 6 and none of the staff in Lab 7. The red light from beyond the door went out, and the glaring white overhead lights came back on.

Stewart avoided looking through the glass; he knew what

the gas did to living organisms. Rarely had he been so glad that the doors between the laboratories were absolutely airtight. Briskly, he went to the intercom.

"Lab Number 6: decontamination complete," he reported and turned around. Satisfied that he'd done what was required, he noticed that his colleagues were already getting back to work, taking the last samples from Subjects numbers 108 through 114. He had sworn to himself not to let this work get to him, to suppress his feelings, but he realized that he was increasingly succeeding in this only with ever-mounting difficulty. The sooner they were done here, the better.

Stewart returned to subject Number 109 and looked at her for a while. Could the same thing happen to her as to the woman in Lab 6? Why didn't they tell him what he was injecting the subjects with? He knew the answer. All of this was highly illegal. With the best will in the world, he could not convince himself that these experiments had ever been approved by any authority. But now he thought of the numbered account that had been set up for him, which by now must hold almost a million euros.

"Hang in there for just a while and then retire," he said to himself in reflection. He turned his gaze to a display next to the medical table and skimmed the readouts. An update had just come in: the analyses of the first series of samples from numbers 108 to 116 were there.

Stewart sucked in the air in a sharp inhale. There they were! Exactly the parameters they were supposed to achieve. He suddenly felt warm all at once under his smock. He scrolled through the results, then waved to Daniels, his colleague standing over at 111. "Look at the data, 109 is responding!"

Daniels also dealt with the display in his place. "Acknowledged. 111 responds as positive – no, wait. The whole row!"

The other employees checked the displays. One by one, they confirmed success.

"This is it!" exclaimed Stewart joyfully.

"I'll start the verification," Daniels said, making a few inputs. "We'll save all the results and report the breakthrough to headquarters. We can start packing our bags, colleagues," he announced.

"At last! How I hate this shabby country!" replied Stewart.

"After today, I can't wait to say goodbye lab, hello field study," Daniels commented, and then reported, "Results are validated and submitted. Headquarters confirms receipt."

"Very well, then we'll do some more ..." Stewart continued, and was interrupted by a loud crackle from the intercom.

A sober, cold voice was heard. A different voice this time. "May I congratulate you on your success, gentlemen. Your work is bearing fruit that will go down in the history books."

Stewart and the others looked at each other in puzzlement. No one had expected such a quick response from headquarters. But to whom did this voice belong?

Stewart and Daniels walked up to the intercom. Stewart pressed the button. "Thank you, we're delighted, sir ..."

"Let's cut the chatter. I'm sorry to inform you that in light of this recent success, we need to tighten security measures immediately."

Stewart looked over at Daniels, his face suddenly concerned. "What do you mean?" he asked.

Stewart was about to press the intercom button to pass on the question when the icy voice spoke up again. "I thank all my colleagues for your service. Unfortunately, we are now parting ways."

"I don't like the sound of this!" shouted Daniels and hurried over to the lab exit. There he held his access card up to the reader. Nothing happened. "Shit, what the hell is this? Are they locking us in here?"

Unrest started to spread among those present – until the door to the neighboring Lab 6, where the incident had occurred only a few minutes ago, slid open very slowly.

Stewart stepped back, startled. He pressed his face mask over his nose and mouth, rushing forward to press the intercom button. "Hello, hello, Lab 6's containment door is opening – the gas hasn't neutralized yet, it's going to ..." The rest of his sentence was suddenly lost in a fit of coughing. Stewart sank to his knees, slumping to one side and hitting his head on the way down. He couldn't move. As he stared helplessly ahead into the swollen and bloodied face of Subject 106, he heard the muffled sound of bodies falling to the floor behind him.

Then there were screams, bloodcurdling, shrill. His mind was already too disorientated to realize that they were his own.

# 2

WHO Camp Endurance, Southern Mali, Africa, September 26.

Dr. Laura Delille pushed aside the dusty tent canvas and peered out into the shimmering midday heat. The line of people was hardly getting any shorter, and that despite the fact that she had processed dozens of patients in piecework since this morning. She shook her head in resignation. It was no wonder when there was only one doctor for every 10,000 inhabitants.

A hand gently rested on her shoulder. Laura didn't need to turn around to know it was Kimara, one of the faithful souls here, one of the nurses and caregivers she had personally trained. Laura knew what Kimara wanted: to remind her of the meeting. She sighed heavily. "God knows I have better things to do," she said, turning to the nurse.

"I know," Kimara replied, smiling in her usual disarming way, "but we can manage without you for an hour."

"I still don't see the point."

"You know what they wrote in the letter, it's for the good of the project! We need attention and positive coverage. If only for their sake." She pointed to the tent entrance, behind which the line of patients waited.

"Have I ever told you that I hate reporters?" asked Laura and continued without waiting for an answer: "So-called journalists! My grandfather used to say that they're a bunch of scribblers - and he was right. They twist everything to suit themselves, put absurd statements in your mouth, and cut the things that really matter because they're not exciting enough. What good are these guys?"

All that came back from Kimara was a wry look and a shrug. "To answer your question, yes, you've said that before.

Not just once. Are you done now?" That smile again.

"Alright, I'll wait over in my tent for this guy." She left the treatment tent and made her way through the refugee camp. She walked between the countless rows of semi-circular foil tents and filthy barracks. With each step, a little more of the dusty, bone-dry ground was kicked up.

She had not yet reached her private tent when she heard the loud rattle of a motorcycle coming roaring up the driveway at high speed.

Laura immediately guessed – this would be that reporter who just wouldn't let up. And he obviously knew who she was, too, because he stopped right in the middle of her tracks, braking hard and bringing the motorcycle to a grinding halt next to her. In the process, he created a massive cloud of dust. The man was wearing no helmet, no other protective gear, just a white shirt, blue jeans and oversized dark sunglasses with a narrow silver rim. In addition, his skin was so heavily tanned that it was hard to believe the guy was supposed to be English. He looked out of time, like watching a movie from the 80s.

When the dust had settled a bit, he got off the bike and chuckled at Laura.

She didn't return his smile. "Tell me, by any chance, have you maybe watched Top Gun a few too many times?" she asked casually.

The man cooly took off his glasses. Piercing deep blue eyes gleamed at Laura. "Feel free to call me Maverick!" he said, grinning mischievously.

Laura suppressed a groan. She would have her fun with this guy. It bothered her how effortlessly he'd happily shrugged off her dig. "All right, Mr. Stevens, let's get this over with."

"Please, Dr. Delille, do call me Hugh. No one calls me Mr. Stevens."

"Fine, Hugh it is. This way please, I don't have very much time."

She walked past Hugh's motorcycle and led him into her

tent, which contained a worn desk, two chairs, a camp bed, and lots of boxes.

Laura sat down behind the desk and pointed to the chair on the other side.

Hugh took a seat. "May I?", he asked. Without waiting for an answer, he placed a digital voice recorder on the table.

Laura cocked her head, hesitating, but then nodded.

"Thank you, Dr. Delille, for taking the time to have this conversation. Since I've had to wait three weeks for this, it's pretty clear how busy you are." Hugh made a grand sweeping gesture that seemed out of place in the stuffy tent, then continued. "So let's get down to business. You're here in Mali researching the effects of malnutrition and trying to identify possible solutions, is that correct so far?"

"If I'm honest, I don't often get to collect data for my study because day-to-day medical problems take priority. There are nearly 200,000 internally displaced people from the north living in southern Mali. And since word got out that there is a doctor here in the camp, people have been coming in droves. This morning I had a mother who walked 90 kilometers here with her feverish child because there was nowhere else to take care of them. I don't need to mention that the child was obviously glaringly malnourished."

"What did you do?"

"A. V. P."

"Meaning?"

"Antibiotics, vitamin supplements, peanut paste. It's not much. But we're doing everything we can to mitigate the effects even a little bit."

"You sound unhappy with things? Is this a case of trying to swim against the tide?"

"Let's stop with the silly idioms. Why do journalists always have to dig into the cliché box?"

"Well then, since it's myself, I'd like to state the matter more comprehensively, Doctor."

Laura put on a smile, but her counterpart ignored it.

"The rampant famine in Africa is no coincidence – two years of failed harvests in a row, skyrocketing world market prices for food, the massive consequences of climate change through drought and heat. And you're here doing research on the symptoms. Do you think that's really an effective approach? Where does that get us? What does that do for the people here?"

Laura gritted her teeth and swallowed the venomous retort that was on the tip of her tongue. "Look, Hugh, the thing is, everyone does what they can. We strive for goals we can realistically achieve. Journalists like you are chasing a big story, trying to get the big break and explain the world to your readers. At least, that's what I would expect of you. Of course, more often than not, that expectation is disappointed. Often enough you're just chasing. Short term viral circulation. Do I blame you for what makes the media world tick?" She paused for a moment, waiting to see if Hugh would respond. But he didn't. Then she continued. "So, you want to talk about my work here, fine. But please, without the polemics and without the sensationalism."

Hugh nodded silently for a long moment. "Okay, point taken. Sorry. Shall we start again?"

Before Laura could answer, her cell phone, which was lying on her desk, rang. She looked at the display and recognized the number of the WHO office in the capital, Bamako. "Will you excuse me for a moment? I have to take this," she said.

The reporter sighed.

"And would you turn that off, please?" asked Laura, pointing to the voice recorder.

"Sure," Hugh replied, reaching forward and pressing the stop button.

Laura picked up. "Delille."

She spun around in her chair and turned her back to Hugh as she listened to the caller.

"Dr. Delille, good to reach you. I am Peter Brauer, a

colleague of yours in Bamako. I was told you would be just the person for my problem."

"Not like I don't have enough problems of my own," Laura said, casting a quick glance over her shoulder at Hugh, typing away on his cell phone, pretending not to listen. "Okay, Peter, how can I help you?"

"You published a field study on fertility and external factors three years ago, didn't you? It could be that there are troubling new findings on that front."

"You're right, that was my last area of research, but I'm working on a very different area of study now, Peter."

"It's not just an academic issue, I think we may have an acute problem here in Mali."

"I'd love to help you, but ..."

"I'm glad to hear that!" interrupted Brauer. "I've already requested you through official channels, and it's all been approved by headquarters."

Laura didn't know what to say for a moment. "I ..." she began.

"Can you come here today?"

"Today?" asked Laura in surprise, looking at her wristwatch. It showed half past noon.

"It's important. The Mali authorities have officially asked for help. In return, I can offer to relieve you with additional staff so that you have more time for your project."

Laura pondered, thinking of the ever-lengthening line of patients in front of the medical tent. Brauer's offer sounded too tempting. "All right, I'll come," she said finally.

"Wonderful, I'll inform the minister right away. I'll meet you at the Ministry of Health, call me when you're in town." Brauer hung up.

Laura turned back to Hugh and saw that he was eyeing her with interest.

"Problems?"

"I'm afraid we'll have to postpone our interview, there's an urgent matter I need to attend to immediately."

Hugh frowned for a moment, then lit up. "Then I'll go with you! We can continue the interview on the way, and we might just get some nice reporting along the way."

"Sorry, I'm not allowed to take anyone in the Jeep, regulations, you know how it is," Laura said. It was a small lie, but it must have sounded half convincing, because Hugh's expression dropped. Laura had not the slightest desire to drive three hours in the afternoon heat on dusty roads all the way to the capital, but she consoled herself that at least this way she would be rid of this troublesome reporter. "You'll excuse me? I have to go in a minute."

Briskly, she rose from the chair and pointed to the exit.

"All right. When will you be back?" Hugh asked, standing up as well.

"I'll call you," Laura said.

"Heh, sure thing, sure thing," Hugh retorted. "Don't get too excited, Charlie. You're not rid of Maverick yet."

# 3

### Bamako, Mali capital, Central Laboratory of the Ministry of Health

"Surely this is a mistake?" Laura Delille sounded alarmed. She finally looked up from the monitor and sought eye contact with Peter Brauer.

He sat leaning back on a swivel chair and slowly shook his head. Behind him, half a dozen lab employees in white coats scurried around. "Well, at first we thought the same thing. If it had just been this one sample, that assumption might be plausible, but we're talking a good two dozen by now. We can rule out a mistake."

"You mean the ovaries of more than 20 women look like this?"

"Yes, 27 so far. Who knows what the number of unreported cases is."

"Your working hypothesis? A virus? Poisoning?"

"I called you because neither I nor any of the doctors here at the ministry have a viable hypothesis. All we know is that these young women, most of whom have already given birth to two or three children, suddenly became infertile and had miscarriages. And this happened due to a cause that is completely unknown to us."

Laura sighed. "You were definitely right, that is indeed worrisome. Are the patients all from one region or are they spread across the country? Is there a connection between the women?"

"Partly. Some are related, others have never met. There are 16 cases from Bamako, but 11 from completely different regions. The distribution so far doesn't provide a logical pattern."

"Can I examine one of the women myself?" asked Laura.

"Sure, if that helps. Most of them live here in town. We've collected their addresses and, as far as possible, phone numbers. But what do you expect to get out of it? Our diagnostic capabilities are limited - and those of the local authorities even more so." Brauer pointed to the lab area behind him, whose equipment was obviously not the latest.

"I want to talk to the women first and foremost. Find out more about their medical history, if there were any pre-existing conditions, contact with toxic or contaminated materials."

"I will go through the contact data and look for suitable candidates. But it's probably not going to happen today. Will you stay overnight? I can recommend a safe and clean hotel."

"Thank you, I already have my regular accommodation here. Can I take the data with me and study it further?"

"Yes, I've already cleared that. The authorities are grateful for any help." The overwhelming pressure was written all over the man's face. "By the way, he sends his apologies, he has to inaugurate a new health center somewhere."

"It doesn't matter at all, politicians have never been much help with this kind of thing. They shy away from actual tangible work." Laura chuckled, with Brauer joining her.

"You're right about that." Brauer handed Laura a USB flash drive. "This is a copy of all the results so far. Some are from labs outside Bamako, but most were done here. Maybe you'll find a clue to the common origin of ... well, this phenomenon." Brauer tightened the corners of his mouth. "Although I secretly hope there's a harmless explanation for all this."

"We'll see, I'll do my best. Did you also send samples to the central lab in Geneva?" asked Laura.

"Not yet, but I'll make the necessary arrangements if that's what you want. Let's just hope the logistics decide to play along."

"Thank you, that would be a great help in getting more

accurate data." Laura pocketed the USB stick and rose. "Shall we have a coffee?"

"Sorry, I have a mountain of paperwork on my desk. This job as office manager is hell. And now, on top of all that, now we have this to deal with. I appreciate your support."

"No problem. Just don't forget your promise about the staff. Go ahead and fill out the paperwork for two new positions in my camp." She winked at Brauer.

"Of course. They're at the top of my paper pile."

The next morning, Laura sat in the café *La Boulangère* near Bamako's largest marketplace. Outside the window, the usual hustle and bustle of the market was taking place. Women in brightly colored robes streamed home from shopping - balancing baskets and bowls on their heads. Men at stalls hawked their wares, overladen mopeds rattled by. It was a completely unremarkable Wednesday morning.

Laura had deliberately decided against having breakfast at the hotel, although the buffet didn't look bad. The coffee, however, she knew from experience, was worlds better in this nearby café.

Here you could get an authentic French latte. And if there was one thing she longed for after the last few months in the camp, it was to finally enjoy a real coffee again that tasted like home. She was equally tired of the instant brew and the bear-strength African varieties.

As if reading her thoughts, the café owner Eloise came around the corner and poured Laura a refill without her having to ask for it. Wordlessly, she disappeared again.

Laura took a big sip and then turned again to the files she had pulled from Brauer's USB stick onto her laptop. She wanted to be as prepared as possible and review the latest documents before she left for her appointment with a patient. To do this, she had to go to the other side of the Niger, to the northern part of the city. She was already dreading the thought of plunging into the wild traffic jam of Bamako by jeep. That had already been more than enough for her on the drive last night.

The dusty roads, the endless traffic jams, the vast numbers of motorcyclists weaving through even the smallest gaps. Of course, they all rode without helmets, as was typical for the country. In addition, there were the many museum-worthy vans, patched and rusty by the dozen. In view of the temperatures of almost 40 degrees Celsius, they were mostly on the road with open sliding doors, if they still had any at all.

Laura had become accustomed to such things. This was Africa, and people didn't usually take safety too seriously. There were no official statistics on serious injuries to helmetless motorcyclists in Mali, but the reports from local hospitals spoke for themselves.

She pushed aside thoughts of accidental trauma and returned her attention to the laboratory findings. The results were startlingly similar. The patients' hormone levels were completely out of whack, most estrogens - above all estradiol, estrone and estriol - were barely detectable, and the progesterone level was also far below the normal range. This could be the cause or the consequence of the second major symptom. Laura knew only too well that estrogens were produced in the follicles of the ovaries, but also in the subcutaneous fat tissue and in the adrenal cortices. However, the ovaries of the affected women were downright atrophied. The examination results that Brauer handed over to her showed various degrees of severity of deformation or shrinkage. This may have been because the condition had progressed to different degrees or because the women had been exposed to the cause to different degrees.

What might cause such a phenomenon? The spontaneous appearance was more indicative of a pathogen or poisoning and less of an inherited defect. It was also consistent with the reports that some of the patients had previously complained of flu symptoms or itchy and red eyes. That was the best indication of a virus. However, she was not aware of any virus that caused such a combination of symptoms. Was this possibly a completely new species? She fervently hoped that it was not and that there would be a less frightening explanation.

Laura finished the rest of her coffee, which had become cold by then, and closed the laptop. It was time to get some first-hand information. She put a generous tip on the table, stood up, and nodded graciously to Eloise on her way out. "You really do make the best coffee in town," she said in parting. "Well, see you soon!"

# 4

About 25 minutes later, Laura had made her way through the heavy downtown traffic to the northern district of Korofina, where she planned to meet the patient. Laura once again glanced at the note with the names and coordinates: Zahra Traore, 12.676568, - 7.946147. She was grateful for the accurate data and the GPS system in the jeep, because road signs were nowhere to be found here. She didn't even know if these dusty sandy roads that ran through the low rows of houses had official property names at all; there was no need to look for house numbers.

Peter Brauer had arranged the appointment at very short notice and suggested starting with this patient. She had just completed her training as a nurse at the Bamako Heath School and so was very open to medical research.

The GPS reported reaching the destination and Laura parked the car in front of a clay-brown bungalow huddled in a gap between two slightly taller houses. It almost looked as if it wanted to hide.

She got out and walked toward the house, which had a door painted an unusually dark green. When she had stepped up to about two meters, it opened and a six-foot-five man with short-cropped hair came out.

Laura stopped instinctively. Was it the wrong house?

The man stood up in front of her and silently eyed her.

Laura overcame her rigidity and spoke up. "Excuse me ..." she began and was promptly interrupted.

"How many more are coming?" the man asked.

"Excuse me?"

The man nodded toward the house. "Nobody said anything about photos!"

Confused, Laura shook her head. "I ... want to see Zahra, is she there?"

"Of course! And your colleague is also there and asks loud questions."

"Colleague?" Laura thought about what Brauer had said. She was pretty sure he couldn't accompany her because he had appointments with representatives of other aid organizations. Had he come anyway? But what was that about the photos? "I'm sorry, let's start at the beginning," she said as kindly as she could, giving the man a smile. "I'm Dr. Laura Delille, I'm here because I ... because I'd like to help your wife."

"I'm Moussa," the man grumbled. "Come with me and we'll get this over with. We want our peace." He promptly turned and walked back through the green door into the house.

Hesitantly, Laura followed him in.

The inside of the house seemed all the dimmer in contrast to the bright sun outside. Two children, estimated at five and seven, were sitting in front of a television with cracks in the display, watching cartoons. They took no notice of Laura. Moussa led them through the kitchen to a small terrace behind the house.

There, Zahra sat at a faded, formerly black plastic table, talking to a man.

For a moment, Laura felt as if she had been knocked for six. Abruptly, she stopped in her tracks halfway to the table. She knew the man! But it wasn't her colleague Dr. Brauer - on the contrary, it was someone who had absolutely no business being here.

Hugh Stevens sat there at the table with her patient, chatting as if it were the most normal thing in the world.

Anger crept up from the pit of her stomach, but Laura fought down the impulse to immediately yell at the brash reporter. She glanced at Moussa, who eyed her suspiciously and gestured her towards the table. If she made a scene now, the already annoyed husband would probably throw them both out the door. At worst, he might get physical, which she wouldn't mind with that miserable blowfly Hugh, but at the same time it would certainly rob her of any chance to get any information. So she would take Hugh to task later.

With difficulty, she managed an awkward smile, then stepped forward to the table and extended her hand toward Zahra. "Hello, you must be Zahra, my name is Laura. I'm here to ask you a few questions. You've already met my colleague." She looked over at Hugh, who didn't look remotely bothered or guilty. "I trust he was well behaved?" she asked in a sharper tone.

"Yes, he was very nice," Zahra replied.

Moussa grumbled something incomprehensible. Apparently, he did not share the same opinion.

"By the way, thank you, Hugh, for your preliminary work. But we can manage on our own now. Please wait for me outside, and we'll discuss everything later. Now I need to talk to the patient in private, in confidence as a doctor – you know the procedure."

The right corner of Hugh's mouth twitched ever so slightly. It could be displeasure at being ushered out like that, or it could be a suppressed smile. Laura decided it had to be the former. Otherwise she would have to strangle the cheeky fellow on the spot.

Hugh waited another second before putting his camera in his bag and standing up.

Immediately he was escorted out by Moussa.

"Please excuse the mess and my tardiness," Laura implored.

Zahra nodded. "No problem. I know doctors are very busy."

"I'll be happy to take my time with you. Okay then, we'll just start from the beginning ..."

When Laura stepped back out onto the street nearly 30

minutes later, she found Hugh leaning casually against his motorcycle a few feet down the road. She had wondered if he would actually wait for her so she could give him a proper bollocking, or if he would sneak off again just as stealthily as he had snuck into the patient's house. Anger rose up again in Laura at the thought of it. She stepped up close and glared at him. "What the hell were you thinking?"

"I do believe we've already met, Ma'am?" replied Hugh calmly. "You know, Maverick and Charlie?"

"Don't deflect, you impostor. You can keep the you. I should report you!"

"Ha! What for?" Hugh looked visibly amused.

"Stay the hell out of this!"

"Ever heard of freedom of the press?"

"What you have pulled off here has nothing whatsoever to do with press relations. You are posing as a WHO employee, I really should have you arrested!"

"Wait a minute, I didn't make any claim of the sort. They asked me if I was WHO and I just didn't say no right away. That's all. Then I started asking questions, it was harmless."

"Don't play dumb. You know exactly what I'm saying. You shamelessly exploited the situation. For your story!"

"I'm doing my job here, as you are doing yours. And I'm happy to give you an opportunity to comment so that it's an informed report."

"Save it! I'm not giving you anymore."

"That's too bad, because I'm writing about it anyway, you can't prevent that and you know it. Nevertheless, I'll give you the opportunity to describe things from your point of view. So, what will it be?"

"Nothing. You go your way and never interfere again. Write what you want. I don't know what you've made up here, but no one will believe you anyway."

"Don't you even want to know how I found out about the patient? It's not like I came upon it by accident."

Laura thought for a moment. This point could not be

dismissed out of hand. Hugh had to have informants who had tipped him off. And they would potentially continue to do so. The effort to pursue the matter quietly and without troubling press releases could be severely damaged. "All right! Who did you bribe?" she asked.

"I don't name my sources, of course. Press code of honor."

Laura let out a pointed laugh. "Sorry, but that was too ridiculous, even for you."

"Of course, I can't compete with your high moral standards, Dr. Delille," Hugh said sarcastically. "Look, I don't want to work against you, I want to cooperate. I certainly have some valuable information and countless contacts with important people here in town. You could benefit from that. In return, you provide me with medical insights, how's that?"

"How do you imagine that? I'm supposed to just hand over internal Ministry of Health and WHO data to a reporter? I'd like to keep my job for a while, thank you very much."

"Your job is hardly in jeopardy. From what I hear, you're an ace who definitely won't be thrown out the door. And I mean, this is Africa, there's no GDPR here."

Laura sighed and shook her head. "Let me do my work in peace. And stay out of this."

"What a pity, we would have made a good team. But that can still happen. I'll give you three days to think it over. If I haven't heard from you by then, I'll publish the story. And not to some rag, you can be sure of that."

"Do whatever you need to do. Have a nice day!" Laura left Hugh at the motorcycle, walked to her Jeep and got in. Without hesitation, she started the engine and drove off. First, she needed to get some distance. The guy brought out the worst in her. But what was much more worrisome was that he might well be right in guessing that this could make for a pretty big story. She just didn't know yet if she wanted to read it.

# 5

Keller Villa, Grunewald, Berlin, 27 September

*"To the elect of a new age, the wise and daring, who are willing to rise above!*

*Listen to me, my brothers in spirit, my companions on the path to fulfillment. The time is near when the path of humanity will part. And each of you must ask yourselves the important question: Is he walking with us on the path to eternal light? Or does he wander in darkness until he perishes, forgotten and lonely?*

*I say: Choose wisely, choose the path that the Brotherhood of Light shows you - the path that the Power of Creation has intended for us since the beginning of time. Do not go astray any longer!*

*The perversion of today's world and the decay of the human race must end. They have been poured out on us far too abundantly in recent years. We are born from nature, have lifted ourselves up from it, have made it our subject. But all too often without sense and reason, without goal. What is the point of all this striving? Truly, it is almost too simple. But it needs this small step, which you must still take. Therefore, let it be declared to you: Death is an illusion, an invisible threshold that needs no more than daring and wisdom to overcome..."*

Christian Keller ceased from typing more characters into his computer and skimmed over the last paragraph he had written. He had only been instinctively aware of the words as he had written them down. They had flowed out of him from a state of inner ecstasy.

But the more he read, the more his mind confirmed what his feelings had told him long ago: There was no longer any doubt. This was it! At last he had distilled the pure essence of his idea and put it into words. Before him lay the core of his manuscript, the basis of what he sought to express, the radiant vision of a new world order that he and his kind were quietly and secretly building. Perhaps he should even preface his manifesto with these words? Yes, this would probably be appropriate. Soon his work would be ripe for publication. And then nothing would ever be the same again.

Satisfied, Keller leaned back in his black leather chair at the desk and let his gaze glide over the bookshelves. Heavy dark-brown mahogany cabinets reached up to the ceiling of the library. This was both his retreat and study. On the shelves, Keller had gathered more than a thousand years of literary history, from ancient occult manuscripts to ornately leather-bound first editions from the time of the early mechanical printing presses to current reference books on medicine and pharmacy. It was in this continued tradition that he saw himself, as a classical scholar - but also a visionary and free spirit, willing to break any convention if necessary. How glorious this new age would be! Keller liked to dream about it.

But he was abruptly interrupted - by a soft but definite knock on the heavy wooden door of the library. Keller knew it had to be urgent, because otherwise no one would dare disturb him while he was working on his manuscript. He brushed aside the tinge of annoyance. He had accomplished enough for today and could get back to the tedious business of the day.

There was another knock at the door.

Keller closed the text program and snapped the laptop shut. Then he called out loudly, "Come in!"

The door opened slowly and Spencer entered, Keller's private butler. He liked the old-fashioned term, though it was hardly appropriate for what Spencer did for him and the trust he enjoyed. He knew things that would never be revealed to a mere domestic servant.

"What's so urgent?" asked Keller.

"I'm heartbroken, but they seem to want to notify you immediately of any new developments. Mr. Kruger is here and asks to speak with you."

Keller nodded. "Send him in. And then please reserve a table at *Fin de Siècle* for six-thirty."

"Very well. For you alone?"

"For two."

Spencer raised his eyebrows almost imperceptibly. "I don't suppose you'll be taking Kruger out," he remarked in his typical dry tone.

"You assume correctly, my dear Spencer. That would indeed be unusual. I have an appointment with a lovely lady, of course, and that's all you need be interested in."

"Of course. I'll arrange everything." Spencer offered a bow and disappeared through the door.

Less than five seconds later, Kurt Kruger entered - chewing gum as usual. His haggard face looked even more angular than usual. Not even his half-length hair, some of whose strands had become entangled in his stubbly beard, could conceal this.

Keller detested Kruger's sometimes unkempt appearance. But he knew it was part of his cover. You'd think he was a globetrotter or day laborer, not a professional agent and hit man.

Silently, Kruger closed the door and stepped within two feet of Keller.

"You look exhausted, Kruger. The long stay on this backward continent doesn't agree with you, does it?" Keller looked up and gestured to a second leather chair in front of the desk.

Kruger raised the right corner of his mouth, but otherwise did not address the remark. "Thanks, I'd rather stand. I've been sitting on the plane long enough."

"All right, have it your way. Let's get right to the point, then. What's the urgent matter?"

"My informants have apprised me of a development that would be potentially unwelcome to our schedule."

Keller tilted his head and frowned. "Well, let's not get carried away. What could possibly upset our plan now?"

"The authorities in Mali have turned to the World Health Organization for help."

"Well, what good is that going to do them? Those amateurs down there don't have the intellect at all to grasp what it's really all about. And don't tell me that this impotent association of WHO thinks it can do something?"

"It's unusual for them to respond so quickly, but in this case .... well, an office has recently been opened in Mali, and the new head of the site seems to want to prove himself. He immediately assigned a doctor to follow up on the cases. And from what I have gathered, this woman is very, very good. A French woman named Laura Delille. She has performed several field studies in Africa and has strong connections among the upper echelon of WHO. I don't think we should underestimate her."

Keller waved it off. "She'll be groping around in the dark and won't find anything. And even if she does. It'll be too late by then."

"Yes, it's possible. But part of my job is to visualize the worst case scenario. Anyway, I took care of that office manager Brauer before he left. I came up with something very nice for him."

Keller gave Kruger a skeptical look. "You threatened him?"

"I have put measures in place to make him susceptible to blackmail. In time, he will certainly be dancing to our tune."

"All right. As long as it's discreet. You can take your sadistic streak elsewhere. And remember, next time I want to be fully informed before such decisions are made."

"Of course. But in this case, I thought it pertinent to respond quickly." Kruger paused briefly before continuing. "There's something else. A reporter has been nipping at Dr.

Delille's heels. He writes for a handful of British newspapers. Some online media. The guy is quite a sleuth."

Keller stood up and walked alongside his bookshelves, which were filled to the ceiling. He stroked the spines of the books with his right index finger, feeling the surface of the fine leather and linen bindings. He stopped at a work from 1935, the title read: *Euthanasia and the Sanctity of Life*.

He stared silently at his bookshelf for a while longer, then turned back to Kruger. "We'll stay quiet and not stir up any more dust. Let him snoop around, he'll only scratch the surface, just like that doctor. But anyway, you stay on this and report back to me. And as far as the WHO is concerned, from now on I will put out some feelers of my own. That's where a more diplomatic approach is appropriate."

"So, no further action? I could get rid of the doctor. Or at least the reporter. Just waiting might prove to be a mistake," Kruger interjected.

Keller fixed his counterpart. "It will prove to be precisely the right move. Now do your job and stop lecturing me! I'll let you know if there's anything I need you to do."

"Well, there you go," Kruger conceded defeat. "I guess I forgot I was merely the dim stooge."

"Don't give me the chopped liver act, Kruger. You and I both know that you're neither stupid nor a mere stooge, otherwise I wouldn't employ you - and especially not pay you so damn well. Just remember that I'm the one making the decisions here. The right decisions that need to be made! And now, if you'll please, I have to change. Nothing personal, but I intend to spend the evening in pleasant company."

Keller walked around Kruger and toward the door. Just before he stepped out, he turned back. "Have Spencer give you the keys to the guest house. Take a shower and get some rest. You look like crap. Tomorrow we leave for the new facility, and you will accompany me to coordinate security measures there." With this, he turned again, leaving Kruger alone in the library.

# 6

WHO Camp Endurance, Mali, September 27th

When Laura Delille arrived back at WHO's treatment camp in the evening, she'd had a long, dusty car ride during which to try and organize her thoughts. She had hoped for more from the conversation with Zahra Traore. Although the budding nurse had been very conscientious in reporting what her life had been like in the past weeks and months, it had ultimately not been particularly revealing. The patient had not changed her living situation or her diet, had not knowingly come into contact with toxic materials, and had not fallen seriously ill.

The only thing that had caught Laura's attention was her participation in a vaccination study to test a new malaria vaccine. However, the trial had been completed six months earlier, and according to the report, Zahra Traore had been in a control group that had only been injected with a saline placebo. The same apparently applied to a second student at the medical training school, where Zahra was studying.

Nevertheless, Laura took it upon herself to find out more about this project. Something told her there might be something fishy about it. Some pharmaceutical companies regarded Africa as a kind of free-range laboratory, performing experimental studies for which they would never get permission elsewhere.

It struck her as suspicious that this was a study by a private foundation, and one that Laura had never heard of at that. As far as she could tell, they had no connection to any known university or a pharmaceutical company. But the foundation had to have received the new vaccine from somewhere.

She knew she was clutching at a very thin straw, but at the same time she knew that Hugh Stevens had the same information and would certainly follow up on this lead. She hated to think that there might be some manner of race developing here in which she might lose. Not that she needed to be first, necessarily, but it bothered her immensely not to be in control of all the necessary information. It was more than annoying to have to deal with these side issues instead of fully concentrating on the work at hand.

Laura drove the jeep through the gate of the camp and headed for her tent. Hopefully, no more work had been left behind for her during her absence. After the exhausting day, she had little desire to attend to dozens of patients. As she passed the treatment tent, she was pleased to see that there was no line in front of it.

She parked the jeep right next to her tent and got out. She would try to reach Brauer one more time. Her colleague from Bamako hadn't answered his cell phone all day, and even his secretary couldn't tell her where her boss was. But she had assured her that the requested reinforcements for her camp would arrive in two days. Laura would believe that when she saw it with her own eyes.

As she entered her stuffy tent, she pulled her laptop out of her bag, and tossed the bag onto the bed. She placed the computer in the docking station on her desk and turned it on. A message from Brauer was already waiting for her in the e-mail box. She quickly skimmed the lines. He apologized profusely for not being able to come to the meeting. An urgent appointment in the Congo had interfered. But he hoped that everything had gone to her satisfaction. Laura sighed as she read this wishful thinking. When did anything ever go satisfactorily in this country? They were lucky when the basic things of everyday life went even halfway smoothly.

In the e-mail, Brauer asked Laura to keep him informed of developments and promised to get back to her as soon as he returned from his appointment. What exactly he was planning, however, he did not mention. Laura decided not to worry about that, on top of everything else.

But now that Brauer was unavailable for a while, she could hardly ask him to help her research the foundation in question.

She could forget about the African regional office in Brazzaville, Congo, as well. By the time she explained to them what it was all about, it would be at least two days from now.

Now she probably had to move up to the next level and call her boss at WHO headquarters, to whom her project reported directly. She took a quick look at her watch: 5:35 p.m.. That meant it was now two hours later in Geneva, where WHO headquarters was located. Still, she had no doubt that Johann Engström would answer the phone. There was no closing time for him, she had learned in the years of working together. She pulled her cell phone out of her pocket and dialed his number.

Johann Engström didn't notice the vibration in his jacket pocket at first. And even after he had registered that someone was trying to call him, it still took several seconds before he brought himself to answer the call. Without looking at the display, he answered.

"Engström," he said in a low voice.

"Johann, it's Laura Delille. Am I interrupting something? You sound off."

"Oh nothing, it's fine. What's up?"

"Do you know Peter Brauer? A German, he's recently been running the new office in Bamako?"

"Not that I know of. I'm sure he's been assigned by the Africa Regional Office. What about him, is he giving you any trouble?"

"No, not directly. He asked me for help. It's odd you don't know anything about it. He said everything had already been cleared with headquarters."

"It's possible. I've had so much on my plate lately, it's

possible that one or two things have sailed under my radar here."

"Are you sure everything is okay?"

"Don't worry about it. Why are you calling me now?"

"This thing Brauer came across makes me suspicious. You remember that study from two years ago on factors influencing infertility?"

"The one that cost twice as much as estimated? How could I forget?"

"Well, it seems to me that the data could still become very relevant now. Here in Mali, there have been a number of mysterious cases of sudden infertility. The women are spread all over the country and most of them already have children. I have spoken to one of those affected, and so far there seems to be nothing unusual about her. With one exception: she was in the control group of a vaccination study a good six months ago."

"So ..." replied Engström. "You mean these are side effects? But she was in the control group and not vaccinated?"

"Exactly. According to the records, she was only given saline. But I don't trust this. This study was conducted by a certain Rosenblatt Foundation. The name doesn't ring a bell with me, and I can't establish any ties to universities or pharmaceutical companies. Can you do anything with this info?"

"Not with just that. But do you really have more here than just a bad gut feeling?"

"Not yet. Still, my gut tells me something's wrong, and not just because of this mysterious foundation. A reporter has gotten wind of these cases and apparently senses a big story. I'm trying to keep him away from it. We should definitely avoid causing unnecessary panic."

"It's that serious, you think?"

"The results are very disturbing. I can email them to you if you like."

"Do that. I want to see if we can find out anything about

this foundation. As for the reporter, I advise you to be diplomatic." Engström waited a while for a response, but Laura remained silent. "Laura, I know this isn't your strong suit, but I'll tell you: once the press is on a story, there's hardly anything you can do about it to get them off it. Try to delay the story, or at least influence it in our favor."

Engstrom heard an vexed sigh from the phone, followed by a muttered, "All right."

"Okay, Laura. I have to go now and take care of a personal matter. Keep me posted."

"Take care, Johann. Give my love to the family."

"Yes, I ... See you soon." Engström hung up and pocketed the cell phone.

A soft knock on the door announced the arrival of a nurse. She carried a transparent plastic bag over her arm and stood beside Engström. "It's time for the infusion, Dr. Engström. Do you want me to do it? Or would you like to give it to her yourself?"

Engström stood up and took the IV bag from the nurse. "I'll do it. So that this old desk jockey don't get too rusty."

The woman nodded and began to read the displays on the equipment next to the bed. She turned to Engstrom once again and gave him a smile. "I'm sure your daughter will get better eventually."

Engstrom sighed and forced himself to return the smile. "Yeah, let's not give up hope, huh?" Then he connected the new bag and, following the usual routine of manual motions, adjusted the dosage via the roller clamp on the infusion system.

# 7

### Maya-Maya Airport, Brazzaville, Congo, September 28

Brazzaville Airport was undoubtedly one of the most modern and sophisticated airports in Africa. Curved metal struts spanned the large check-in hall in elegant arches - it looked almost like a snapshot of frozen waves sloshing across a mirror-smooth floor of polished marble. In between, there were repeated patches of glass through which the glistening light of the Congolese sun broke. Compared to the somewhat clunky construction of Bamako Airport, from which Peter Brauer had departed a good nine hours ago, the architecture here represented a quantum leap in terms of aesthetics.

Brauer settled down on a silver mesh bench in the waiting area and fished the laptop out of his wheeled business case. Fortunately, he had landed a good half hour earlier than planned and would be picked up here shortly. He was quite relieved about that, since after all, he had never been to the WHO's African headquarters since he started work two months ago. It wasn't exactly a stone's throw from his location either.

But if the boss called you to him, then you came – even as a newcomer, and even if that meant a grueling day's journey. But he would be very reluctant to fight his way through this unknown city on his own and was grateful that they had offered to pick him up right here.

Brauer was just about to open the mail program when a man in a dark blue chauffeur's uniform positioned himself in front of him and addressed him in almost accent-free English. "Dr. Peter Brauer?"

Brauer nodded and simultaneously closed the laptop again. "Yes, that's me. Are you my cab?"

"Not a cab, no. But I am your driver. If you'd like to follow me, please? Everything has been arranged, I trust, to your complete satisfaction."

"Very well, I'll follow you." Brauer pocketed the laptop and rose.

Outside in the short-term parking lot, the chauffeur walked toward a gleaming white stretch limousine with tinted windows.

When Brauer realized that this was their destination, he gradually slowed his pace and stopped a few meters from the car.

"Excuse me," he asked in the driver's direction. "Is this right? I mean, are you sure? I'm here for a WHO work meeting. This looks like we're going to a gala or something."

The chauffeur stopped next to the rear right door of the car and turned around. "No gala, but as far as I know there will be a private function, someone from the executive floor is celebrating his retirement, I was told," he explained and opened the door. "Get in, it's air-conditioned."

Brauer looked down at his sweaty suit. He was definitely not prepared to attend a celebration. Why hadn't he been told that! However, the prospect of an air-conditioned vehicle was very tempting.

"Are you coming?" the driver inquired.

Shrugging his shoulders, Brauer started moving again.

"Give me your suitcase, I'll stow it in the back of the trunk out of your way."

Brauer looked at him irritated for a second. There should be enough room in the back of this car, but he didn't want to waste any more time. So he pressed the handle into the driver's hand and got in. He closed the door, and a pleasant coolness enveloped Brauer. The dark windows also dimmed the glare of the afternoon sun to a very bearable level.

Brauer leaned back and stretched out his legs. He could probably get used to this unexpected comfort. He heard the trunk being closed and the driver getting in the front. The window separating the chauffeur and passenger area was made of opaque black glass.

The car started moving, and Brauer took his smartphone out of his pocket. He had received a lot of e-mails during the flight and wanted to go through them quickly. Especially if there really wasn't going to be a work meeting today, but a party. First, a message from the Ministry of Health jumped out at him, promising additional data on the infertility phenomenon.

He immediately forwarded the mail to Laura Delille and then skimmed the attachments. They were evaluations of recent statistics that he had supplied. The results seemed even worse than he had feared. Not only was there a sudden appearance of increased infertility, but the rates of miscarriages and stillbirths had apparently exploded in the last six months.

An error message from the e-mail app jolted him out of his data study. The smartphone reported that sending had failed. Brauer cursed the unstable network and started a new attempt.

Then he turned to another message that had come from the aid organization Terre des Femmes. It contained reports from several of the Women's Network's African cooperation partners about rising infertility in the countries of Ghana, Burkina Faso and Sierra Leone.

Brewer suddenly began to feel quite hot despite the air conditioning. The phenomenon had apparently spread to neighboring countries. It had to be an epidemic. That meant he should probably bring out the big guns. Just as he was about to forward the second e-mail to Laura Delille, a text message popped up.

"We're waiting at the airport, where are you? Missed your flight?"

It took Brauer a moment to process what he was reading. The sender was Scott Barksdale, the man he was supposed to meet. Apparently, he was waiting for him at the airport. But if that was the case, where was he going? His gut told him he was absolutely in the wrong place.

At that moment, the limousine slowed and pulled over. The doors on the left and right of the car opened and two women in black vinyl outfits rushed in - one African and one Asian.

Brauer was too taken aback to react quickly. The doors were already closed again and the limousine drove on.

"Can my friend Cindy and I get a ride?" the Asian woman asked in a lascivious tone. "I'm Sheila."

"Shit," Brauer gasped, looking back and forth between the two women. "I ... this ...," he stammered, and was interrupted by a "ping" from his cell phone. "Email transmission failed."

"Now, now, now. That's enough of that," Cindy ordered, snatching the cell phone away from Brauer.

He tried to take it back, but the Asian woman grabbed him from behind and held him tight. "You will comply!"

"Yes, don't be coy. You've been a bad, bad businessman!" Cindy tossed the cell phone into the champagne cooler full of ice water.

Brauer reached for the door handle and pulled on it, but the door was locked. At last he wriggled out of the Asian woman's grip, who clearly had more strength than expected, and pounded on the glass window to the driver's cab. "Hey, open up!" he shouted. He got no response.

Now he felt cold metal on his left wrist and heard the click of handcuffs. He wheeled around. "There's been some kind of mix-up!" Brauer shouted in near panic.

Cindy promptly stuck a strip of tape over his mouth. "Shhh...," she continued, ripping open Brauer's shirt so that the buttons flew off. With her pointed fingernails, she pinched his nipples. "If you don't behave, we'll have to punish you!"

Sheila suddenly ran the needle of a syringe along Brauer's neck. Brauer instantly froze, and Cindy tightened the handcuffs on the grab handle above the door.

"What's in that damn syringe?" gasped Brauer.

"Nothing to worry about, we just want to have some fun together, this will loosen you up," Sheila promised, jabbing Brauer in the neck with the syringe.

Immediately he felt his resistance collapse like a half-baked soufflé.

Hugh Stevens slammed the receiver of the scuffed landline phone down. "Motherfucker!" he growled.

Despite the anger rising inside him, he made sure that the line had been disconnected before he insulted his editor-in-chief. And that was despite the fact that he had a great desire to say what he thought to the pompous snoot for once. Since old Will Davidson was no longer at the helm, but that slimeball Adrian Keen, Hugh had thought dozens of times about quitting. Just quitting the whole thing.

This time it had been particularly bad. Keen had immediately dismissed Hugh's investigative journalism as if it were about the village mayor's 90th birthday, or a clay pigeon shoot in Gloucestershire. The guy was a fantastically misplaced at his post; he had no flair whatsoever for real journalism, for topics with explosive power and scope.

Instead, he wanted more and more tabloid journalism and made no secret of the fact that he thought it was a waste of money to maintain an Africa correspondent at all. Yet his editorial team was already sharing the costs with three other media outlets. And now Keen wanted him to skip research and meet with some tribal chief who had allegedly proclaimed a new era of cannibalism.

Hugh knew it was bullshit, an insane outgrowth of the utterly absurd European conception of the African continent. What was he supposed to deliver to Adrian Keen? Creepy folklore? A brightly painted chief gnawing on pretend human bones? Hugh felt a great desire to write some nonsense just to satisfy his dopey boss. And there was no denying it: Hugh needed the money.

He knew that was how journalism scandals came about.

And ultimately, this decline in professional ethics was also the reason why people of integrity like Laura Delille harbored a latent resentment against members of the press. He could understand that. He hated it himself! That made it all the more important for him to get a really significant story on paper for once. And he just felt that these infertility cases could be just such a thing – a real revelation!

There was no way he was going to let it go. He was too ambitious for that. But he had to somehow manage to get this dismissive doctor on his side. To his astonishment, his usual charm offensive had not yet had the desired effect. Maybe he had to try something else. In any case, he would not give up anytime soon.

Hugh opened the mail with the information on the cannibal chief that Adrian Keen had sent, and shook his head as he read it.

"What a bunch of bullshit! But fine, Mr. Slimeball, you shall have your man-eater." He opened a new text window and began typing an article without further research.

# 8

*Camp Endurance, September 29*

Around 7:00 a.m. the next day, Kimara stormed into Laura's tent at camp. Excitedly, she waved her hands in the air. "Laura, signs and wonders are still happening! The new colleagues are here."

Laura sat at her desk in front of her first cup of instant coffee with a pained expression on her face, unable to take much in of the exuberant joy of her senior nurse.

Kimara seemed to notice this. "What's the matter? Bad night's sleep?"

"Yeah, kind of. I lay awake until midnight thinking about these cases. And now I can't really bring myself to turn on the computer and do any more work."

"You didn't even tell me what exactly was going on in Bamako. Are these infertility cases that bad?"

"Bad? Well, that's a matter of definition. Sure, it's terrible for the women who are told they'll probably never be able to have children again. Miscarriages are also a traumatic experience. But war in the north is a different caliber. Famine and drought may be worse, too. So what can you really say?"

"You're right, of course. Let's focus on the positive. Come on over and I'll introduce you to our two new sisters!"

Laura emptied her cup and rose. "Let's go, then."

Outside the camp, as every morning, there was a hustle and bustle. In the two years that the camp had been in existence, it had become more like a village, with an estimated ten to twelve thousand people living there. Nobody knew that exactly. But some of the residents had been here from the beginning because there was no prospect of improvement in the war-torn areas.

Nevertheless, the camp had not yet advanced beyond the status of a simple tent settlement. The few corrugated iron huts that some of the residents had put together from scrap metal and leftover building materials regularly fell apart, so most of them stayed with the tried-and-true tents, whose supply seemed assured for the time being thanks to international donations.

On the way to the big medical tent, Laura and Kimara passed Gozo's improvised workshop. As it was every day, the man from northern Mali was preparing a recipe for clay bricks.

Laura kept shaking her head, on the one hand at his continued lack of success, and on the other at his almost superhuman persistence that kept him trying. When she passed right by the low tent wall Gozo had erected, she stopped and took a moment to watch him work.

"Yes yes, don't say anything, Madame!" shouted Gozo, without looking up from the vat he was stirring. "Today this will work! Today they will not crumble. I can feel it in my blood!" he declared, turning to face her now after all. He beamed at Laura. "Just think of Thomas Edison and the invention of the light bulb! How many times did he fail?"

"Oh, Gozo! I would so love to help you and get the raw materials you need, but you know how it is here."

"No, no. I will do it alone. And I will prove what man can accomplish with enough ingenuity and perseverance. Even under these conditions!"

"I really admire you. And I really believe in your success. I'd really like a fancy adobe hut like that. So you can go ahead and write down my order, provided it doesn't fall on my head while I'm sleeping."

"No way! I have to move on now, I had an idea in a dream tonight that I have to test."

"Goodbye, Gozo!", Laura called out to him as a farewell and walked on together with Kimara.

"It's not going to work. No way," Kimara said softly,

shaking her head. "If only he were as handy as he is cute."

"You never know. And if there's one thing people here need, it's hope. I think Africa can use more people like Gozo."

"You're right about that!" admitted Kimara.

There was already a small line of people in front of the medical tent. However, it was much shorter than usual at this time. Laura walked past the waiting patients into the tent and was pleased to see that the new nurses were already busy assessing symptoms, treating wounds and administering injections with vitamin preparations.

"Wow, this is going like clockwork," Laura announced appreciatively. "Soon you won't need me anymore."

"There, there," Kimara countered. "Don't get ahead of yourself!" She laughed and pointed to the two sisters. "That's Nana and Fatima, fresh from nursing school in Bamako. And as I've already noticed, well trained."

The two sisters stepped closer and nodded a little shyly.

"Hello, you two, you don't know how happy I am that you are supporting us. I am Laura Delille, the camp's doctor. If you have any questions or problems, feel free to come to me anytime. Just not before my first coffee." She smiled. "Okay, I won't keep you guys from working. Are there any difficult cases you want to show me? You've got the standard stuff down pat, I see."

Kimara took the floor again. "Today is comparatively quiet, no serious cases so far. And I have one more piece of good news. Little Youssouf's fever has finally gone down. The new antibiotic is helping and I think, slowly, he's coming out of the woods."

"Thank goodness, that stuff was hard enough to get." Laura looked around the medical tent one more time, then turned to Kimara. "Okay, I'll leave you here and go over to my place. Maybe I can elicit an insight or two from the Bamako data after all. If anything comes up, you guys call me, okay?"

"Sure, you bet," Kimara replied, grabbing a clipboard from one of the tables.

Laura left the tent with a liberated feeling. At last she had some leeway and was no longer in danger of drowning in the mundane tasks. A touch of cheerfulness almost crept in, but it didn't last long. It was promptly dampened again by thoughts of the mysterious developments in the infertility cases - and by the loud rattle of a motorcycle coming roaring into camp. Laura knew immediately that it was Hugh Stevens' machine. She could just feel it. An agonized groan broke out.

"Every time I think it might be a good day and that things are finally looking up, the next downhill slide arrives!" she growled. What was this guy doing here again?

As she turned the corner and headed for her tent, her premonition became certainty. Hugh Stevens was casually leaning against his motorcycle, as usual, waiting. When he saw her, he pushed his sunglasses down and put on a smile.

Laura did not respond, but stood silently in front of the reporter and crossed her arms in front of her chest.

"Oh, come on," Hugh piped up. "Why do you act so mortally offended?"

"What do you want?" retorted Laura. "Shouldn't you have published your story by now? I haven't read anything of the sort. What's the matter? Didn't anyone want to print your wild story?"

"I haven't finished her yet," Hugh said diplomatically. "Maybe I never will."

Laura cocked her head. "Okay, then I'll ask again anyway. What do you want?"

"Are we going inside?" asked Hugh, pointing to the tent.

Laura sighed. "As if anyone here would be interested in your investigation. In fact, I should have you kicked out after the stunt you pulled on that patient."

"Please, I have really important information. I promise it's relevant to you, too."

The way Hugh had said those words made her wonder. For once, the reporter had sounded neither arrogantly jaded nor overly casual. He had sounded almost concerned.

"All right, let's go in," Laura declared, leading the way.

Hugh followed her and settled into the same chair he had sat in on his first visit.

Across from him, Laura took a seat behind her desk. "Fire away!"

Hugh waited a moment before he began to speak. "As you know, I'm very well connected, not just here in Mali, but practically all over Africa. And when I got a message earlier from a colleague in Congo, I just had to come here."

Laura raised her eyebrows and waited to see what was coming.

Hugh continued. "Your colleague from Bamako, Dr. Brauer, would you say he had a dark side by any chance?"

"What do you mean? He's certainly no Darth Vader. Why do you say 'had'?"

"Because he was found dead in a hotel room in Brazzaville, Congo. Next to a prostitute who was also dead. They both had an overdose of some designer drug in their blood and it looked like they had been playing sadomasochistic games."

"Brewer?" Laura leaned forward, dumbfounded. "Well, I can't believe that!"

Hugh pulled out his cell phone and showed her a picture.

"Oh you ..." Laura gasped. "Put that away! You don't hold anything sacred, do you? Did you publish that?"

"No, who do you think I am? The police sent me the material. But the man is Brauer , isn't he?"

"Yes ... I think so. The dead man looks like him. But why are you telling me this? Do you want me to comment on it for your report?"

"Nonsense! I don't plan on making an article out of this. That's not on my level. I'm telling you this because I don't think this was an accident or a failed sex game - you obviously don't either."

"What are you saying? That someone killed these two? Is that it?"

Hugh nodded. "I'm afraid so. This scene seems too contrived, despite everything. Unfortunately, it also means we're dealing with some pretty dangerous people here."

"We?"

"Well, what do you think? That there is no connection to the findings you and Brauer have made? No connection with my research? We've obviously stirred up a hornet's nest. And whether you like it or not, we're both in the same boat."

"If only half of that theory is true, you and I are not in the same boat, we're in deep shit, my dear Hugh!"

"Oh, really? Well, at least we're on first name terms again now."

Laura eyed the reporter and wondered again what to make of him. The fact that he was so willing to share this information with her and had not immediately made a sensational report out of Brauer's death gave her hope that it might be possible to cooperate with Hugh in some way. And perhaps that was even necessary, given the dicey situation. But at the same time, she knew that her counterpart was a cunning fellow who should not simply be told everything freely.

Laura cleared her throat. "You want some coffee? I only have instant brew, though." She stood up and walked over to the kettle.

Hugh put on a smile. "Sure, why not? There's never anything wrong with a little coffee date among colleagues."

"Don't get carried away, please. I know it's part of your job, but it's not part of mine. So let's keep things on a professional level for as long as possible." She poured two cups of instant coffee and placed one on the desk in front of Hugh. "Well, let's talk in confidence - off the record, as they say. I don't want to be quoted on this."

"Of course. Confidential is my middle name. Well, actually, my third name."

"I get it, Maverick. Now let's get down to business."

# 9

Forest near Lychen, Brandenburg, Germany. September 29

In a nondescript patch of forest north of the eastern German town of Lychen, where sparsely populated Brandenburg borders the almost deserted Mecklenburg-Western Pomerania, Christian Keller and Kurt Kruger got out of a dark green Land Rover. The drive from Berlin had only taken an hour and a half or so, but Keller still felt as if he had traveled to the end of the earth each time. This impression was not by accident. He took another closer look at the camouflage of his facility.

Here in this little forest, which he had bought years ago for a ridiculous price, several inconspicuous buildings had been erected in recent months - a large central hub and several smaller sheds and machines around it. The buildings were just tall enough to serve their purpose well, but still overshadowed by the trees all around. Hidden behind the cheap-looking sheet metal facades - and a second layer of concrete - were highly sensitive production lines complete with tons of sensitive electronics.

This plant could compete with any other pharmaceutical factory in the world or even surpass most of them. It had such a high level of automation that, in principle, only a handful of employees were needed to keep it running smoothly.

Standing in front of the buildings, as Keller and Kruger had just done, one did not have the slightest idea of their one-billion-euro interior. Freshly cut or sawn timber lay around the halls. Transport trailers and forestry machinery were parked on a paved area between the halls. Even if a hiker happened to stray into this place, he would undoubtedly mistake it for a wood processing plant. And that is exactly how it should be.

"Well, what do you say, Kruger? Is this a high-tech pharmaceutical company or a sawmill?" Keller continued.

Kruger lifted the corners of his mouth appreciatively. "Not bad, I must admit. And I'm glad you followed my advice on this one."

"I always follow good advice. Especially when it comes to protecting investments," Keller clarified.

Kruger chewed his gum silently for a while, looking around the halls. After Keller said nothing further, he spoke up again. "Well, you probably should have listened to me about that doctor, too. I did get her supervisor out of the way, but I think he managed to provide her with more information beforehand. Still, chances are pretty good that she won't keep snooping around - once she sees what happened to Brauer."

Keller screwed up his face. "I'm not happy about it. They told me they were going to blackmail him, not kill him."

"You see, the local staff down there are not quite at the professional level we expect. They have taken for anesthesia some drug that is circulating in the clubs right now. The good man's heart couldn't take it. But let's spare the details. It could be to our advantage," Kruger explained.

"It's too much hoopla for me. But so be it. If you say she'll shut up now, everything's fine."

"I said there is a chance. Nevertheless, I still think we should muzzle the doctor for good."

"Just muzzled, or dead?"

Kruger put on a nasty grin. "I'm flexible."

"Sure. It just seems to me that you've been lacking precision lately. We'll take care of it, but not with your crude methods. There's no need for that sort of thing yet. I happen to have a far more discreet idea. How it involves you, I'll explain later."

"Whatever you say," Kruger replied curtly, casually brushing a strand of hair from his face.

"Yes, as I say. Now come on, we'll go inside and I'll show you what we've created, and you can start up the new security system. But before you do, spit out the gum, top hygiene protocols in there."

Keller stepped forward, produced a key and opened a double sheet metal door at the front of the central hall. Behind it, a steel security airlock came into view, secured with an electronic RFID reader and a biometric retina scanner. The airlock was built flush into the solid concrete wall that nestled against the corrugated metal shell. The entire building was a house-within-a-house construction, and the outer hall was literally just a thin facade. The reinforced concrete walls behind it provided protection against all manner of attacks and were seamlessly sealed all around.

Keller rested his chin on the trough mounted under the retinal scanner and waited for the sensors to scan and check the vein pattern inside his eye. After an orange LED signaled positive detection, he held a coded access card up to the reader. The LED changed from orange to green, and after half a second, there was a brief hiss from the door frame. Slowly, the motorized airlock door opened a crack. Keller pulled it open fully with his hand and pointed inside.

Kruger spat his gum on the muddy ground, stepped on it with his boot as if it were a burned-out cigarette butt, and joined Keller in entering the sterile world beyond the protective cloak.

After Hugh Stevens left, Laura Delille had initially distracted herself with the day-to-day tasks of the camp. Re-ordering supplies, medicines, and tent tarps, reports for relief organizations, disbursements for local relief workers, and many more bureaucratic unpleasantries. But an unseen force pulled her back to the data collection from the Ministry of Health after only a few hours. A voice inside her said, "You have to keep investigating".

But she didn't have many concrete starting points. That's why she now sat silently in front of the laptop and stirred with a spoon her cup of coffee that had long since gone cold. The thing with Brauer wouldn't let her go, there had to be more to it. She could still hardly believe that he was dead, so unbelievable did the circumstances seem to her. She had hardly known him and therefore felt less sadness, as much as growing concern.

She had already looked through the data on the USB stick several times, so, lacking other options, she decided to once again check the little material Brauer had sent her by e-mail. She typed his name into the search field of the mail program. As she did so, an e-mail popped up that she had never seen before. Apparently, an overzealous filter had moved it to the spam folder.

Laura swallowed. It almost seemed like a message from the afterlife. Because Brauer was dead and no longer sent new e-mails. The pictures from Hugh's cell phone always lingered with her, even though it had been hours since he had shocked her with them.

According to the date, Brauer's message must have been sent shortly before his death. But since it did not come from his official WHO address, but had been sent via a private mail server, it apparently got stuck in the filter. Or was it the dozen attachments stuck to the message?

She still hesitated to open the mail. Her pulse was rising. She had probably just downloaded something very explosive onto her laptop. Something that had potentially cost Brauer his life. But she knew she had to keep going. Not just for Brauer's sake, but because she sensed that something big was going on here.

Laura shook off the thoughts and clicked on the mail. It contained no note from Brauer, but began directly with the forwarded address lines and sender. Originally, the mail came from the Ministry of Health in Mali and contained further statistics and data on infertility and miscarriage rates. Even at first glance, it was clear to her, they had only scratched the surface so far. If one also added the presumably very high number of unreported cases of women who had never been to a hospital, one could quickly imagine the scope one was dealing with here.

The cases did not appear to be due to a singular triggering event, but appeared to multiply, suggesting a contagious pathogen. A pathogen that had not been found in any of the women. To make matters worse, the case curve in the ministry's analyses did not appear to remain linear, but gradually changed to an exponential curve. This meant that there was no time to lose.

She reached for her cell phone and immediately dialed Johann Engström's number at WHO headquarters. At the same time, she forwarded Brauer's e-mail to him. After only two rings, her boss answered.

"Johann, it's Laura, do you have a minute, it's very important," she gushed.

"Slow down, slow down," he hushed, "I haven't even taken my tea bag out of the cup yet."

"Johann, listen to me. This thing here in Mali is a real disaster. They killed Peter Brauer because of it."

"Wait a minute, what about Brauer?" asked Engström.

"What about Brauer? You don't know yet? I thought the office had notified you!"

"About what?"

"That he is dead, I already told you! He was killed together with a … well, never mind … he was found in his hotel room in the Congo."

"When?"

"Two days ago. Listen, please, as tragic as all this is, I'm calling because he emailed me something just before he died. I just forwarded it to you. In my opinion, we're looking at an epidemic here very soon."

"Epidemic, I beg you. You know we don't use that word lightly."

"I choose it deliberately. Look at the data!"

"I am. But you also know this isn't my field, you're the expert on such cases."

"I don't want you to analyze the data for me, I want you to get me support. More colleagues, more resources, initiate interdepartmental action. We are dealing with an unknown pathogen," Laura urged.

"Pathogens? What makes you think that? I'm just skimming your data and I don't see a pathogen anywhere here. Please keep your voice down!" Engstrom's voice suddenly sounded firmer and more nervous at the same time.

"Johann, this is spreading. Brauer had samples sent to you, have you analyzed them in the meantime?"

"I don't know about that, the labs are pretty overloaded, as you know."

"Give it the priority it needs! Let's not waste time, because I'm afraid whatever this is, it somehow transfers from person to person."

"Infertility? Laura, I beg you!"

"I ... Johann, are you even listening to me? You just said I'm the expert. Then you should already trust my judgment."

"Oh, I do. You know I do. But unless you can give me some solid facts and a hypothesis that makes sense ..."

"I just emailed you the facts. And you know my hypothesis."

"That's not good enough, sorry. Not yet. Because if we start panicking on the basis of a mere guess by a single - albeit very competent - employee, we'll be in hot water. And we don't need that right now."

Laura sat there silently for a moment, not knowing what to say back. Johann had always been her ally and had supported her wherever he could. Now she got the impression he was trying to brush her off. "Okay," she finally said wanly. "I'll get you the data. But don't blame me if it's too late."

"Laura, in my position, I know exactly who is responsible in the end and how uncomfortable some decisions can be," Engstrom remarked cryptically. "And you're going to need to hold back on the scare tactics, too, all right?" His voice no longer sounded collegial at all, but like a boss giving orders.

"All right, I'll keep my peace for now - and you in the loop," Laura said contritely. "Take care, Johann."

Johann Engström placed the receiver on the machine and pulled the tea bag out of his Darjeeling. He put it on the spoon, wrapped the thread around it to squeeze out the last of the liquid, and layed down both on the creamy white saucer. He looked up from the tea to his counterpart. Across the desk, Kurt Kruger sat casually in the visitor's chair, nodding with satisfaction.

After a moment of iron silence, Kruger spoke up. "Well, that sounded pretty convincing. You've earned a reward."

Kruger pulled up a slim aluminum case and placed it on the desk. The locks snapped open, and he flipped up the lid. He removed a large IV bag, inside of which was a pale pink, slightly cloudy liquid. "Let me congratulate you. Your daughter has officially been accepted into our rare inherited disease study program." He slid the bag across the desk toward Engstrom, who carefully accepted it.

"Just administering it like a regular IV – it's foolproof." Kruger winked at him. "I've been told it works quite effectively, but only as long as you don't interrupt the treatment."

"You're a son of a bitch," Engstrom said tersely.

Kruger burst out laughing. "Yeah, you said it. So you shouldn't mess with me. After all, you just found out how Brauer fared." Kruger folded the case shut and rose from the chair. "So, cooperate with us and we won't have any problems with one other." He pointed to the bag. "And there will always be supplies, of course."

# 10

Hugh Stevens' office, September 30

"The money should have arrived, right?" asked Hugh Stevens, facing the screen. He waited a few seconds for the answer from his counterpart, who was connected via video chat.

"Hugh, I could care less about the money. I still think this is a bad idea. If it comes out that my clinic was involved in anything illegal ..." said the woman, her pitch-black short hairstyle contrasting starkly with her white coat.

"On the contrary, it's a good idea! And I've already assured you that I'll keep your involvement confidential."

"I know you, Hugh! If it benefits you, you'll turn anything into money."

"Amy, so far this thing is already costing me more money than I even have."

"Why are you so committed? I have to admit, you almost sound seriously concerned. And this data is ..."

"Right now I can't tell you anything more, I'm just trying to back up my theory."

Amy looked at him in silence for a while, then lowered her eyes and tapped away on her keyboard.

Short time later, a "ping" sounded from Hugh's computer.

"This is the link to the analysis of your data. But I'll say right now that I don't think the whole thing is credible. Someone may have put you on the wrong track."

"All the info comes from reputable sources, I have no reason to doubt that the facts are robust."

"In that case, it's very strange indeed," Amy said. "Of course, it would be best if I could examine these patients myself, but I don't want to fly to Africa, nor can you get them here."

"What did you find out?" Hugh queried.

"As you know, my clinic specializes in reproductive genetics and artificial insemination. We also do modifications to cells and DNA, and I'm pretty good at detecting those, too."

"Modifications? To what?"

"Oocytes. Maybe modification is not the right word here. It sounds too artificial, perhaps 'organic modifications'. Open the file TDX_1b."

Hugh searched the transmitted folders for the aforementioned file and opened it. "What am I looking at?"

"A cemetery. All of this woman's eggs have died. She will never be able to have children again," Amy explained.
"As far as I know, she already has two children and everything went smoothly there. So how is that possible? A disease?"

Amy swayed her head back and forth. "I would hope not. Maybe it's a rare genetic defect, though I've never encountered anything like it. The fact that there are similar signs in other female patients also makes that unlikely. But the files are incomplete, so I can't verify that."

"And do you think there's an external trigger here, a common cause?"

"Possible. Maybe even probable. I can't say more from a distance. And as intriguing as I think it is, we have to leave it at that. I can't go any further out on a limb. If my boss finds out …"

"Thanks, Amy, I appreciate it." Hugh smiled. "Maybe we'll see each other again sometime and drink to old times."

Amy raised her eyebrows and was silent at first. "Oh, Hugh. They've been over for so long. We'd better leave that alone. Take care!"

The video chat ended and Hugh stared at the analysis screen. He had just received further confirmation of his story, an independent third-party opinion that supported his suspicions. But no spark of satisfaction set in, as it usually did when he had mastered a crucial step in the investigation. On the contrary, his apprehension had only grown.

Hugh didn't have time to rack his brains any further, as the aged landline phone rang. He glanced at the twinkling, single-line display. "Shit," he cursed. It was the number for Adrian Keen, his annoying boss. Briefly, he considered just not answering, but that would only make things worse. He lifted the bacon grease-covered receiver from the phone. "Adrian, I was just thinking about you," Hugh said in a put-upon friendly tone.

"Nicely done, my friend," Keen replied. "Not because I buy your bad acting, I know you're probably not happy that I'm calling. I just want you to know that your story is a click magnet. This tribal chief is giving us good ad sales. And we're getting quoted on it everywhere."

Hugh felt his stomach gradually tighten into a lump. He had more or less made up the whole story out of anger and exaggerated it fabulously.

He cleared his throat. "Yes, um ... I'm glad you liked it," he replied as neutrally as possible.

"Why the long face? You've finally understood what I want from you! I thought I'd have to fire you if you didn't finally step on the gas with your articles. But that was a masterclass, I want more of it."

"Hmm, let me see what I can do. But I still want to work on my stories, too. I'm on to something really big, so I need some time and space for that."

"You praise a guy once, and right away he gets cocky! Fine, get me some horror stories and we'll see. What do I know, someone who carves flutes out of the bones of his enemies or something, be creative!"

"I don't know ... You really have a strange idea about Africa."

"I don't give a damn about Africa, I only have one idea, and that's high click numbers and increasing returns, so get to work. I want three new stories by the end of the week!" Adrian hung up.

Hugh sighed. Three new topics - and just as moronic as

the invented cannibal chief to boot. That seemed an impossibility to him, especially since there were far more important matters to attend to now.

Moussa Traore's hand squeezed the handle of the machete as if trying to squeeze a ripe lemon. He tried to think, to fight the unbridled hatred that took hold of him. But every time he tried to tell himself that life went on, it only got worse.

It all seemed to him like a whirlpool pulling him down. He knew it would soon be a whirlpool of blood. Nothing seemed the same anymore. Especially not since his wife Zahra had fallen into a coma. But the disaster had run its course much earlier. It had all started here, after she had taken part in that wretched vaccination study. The bastards had done something to her - and he would beat the truth out of them now.

Moussa stepped out of the shade of a large palm tree and walked across the parking lot toward the Silver Lining Medical Center. The name alone made him furious. Silver Lining! He could not see it.

Some passers-by jumped aside when they saw the six-foot-five man with the huge machete approaching.

Moussa perceived everything as if it were happening on a film in front of him, as if he were only observing and not the one acting here. And even if it were, he didn't care if someone tried to intervene or called the police. By the time they got here, it would all be over. If they showed up at all.

He accelerated and changed into a running stride. With a scream, he tore open the glass door at the entrance to the low-rise building and stormed past the reception desk. He was hell-bent on mowing down anyone who got in his way.

But there was no one here.

Gasping, he stopped. The sterile white corridor was deserted, the doors to the left and right were open.

Moussa wheeled around. The counter at the entrance was unoccupied. The lights were on low.

What was going on here? He started moving again and ran

to hallway intersection in the center of the building and then to the left. All empty!

One by one, he walked down all the corridors, looking into all the rooms. Again, no one! Only a few boxes with disposable gowns, gloves and syringes stood on the floor at the end of the last corridor before the back exit.

The pigs have taken flight!, thought Moussa. He sank to his knees. All strength seemed to leave him in a split second. The giant, who had just been terrifying, suddenly looked like a weak child. He felt as if he were bleeding to death.

His vision clouded, he could no longer hold back the tears. He wept not out of grief or anger, but because he realized that he was absolutely powerless, helpless against an enemy who had stealthily stolen away. His thirst for revenge would remain unquenched today - probably forever. The machete fell from his hand, and a metallic clang echoed through the corridors of the deserted medical complex.


Hugh placed a black plastic bag on Laura's desk and looked at her promptly.

She glanced back and forth between the bag and Hugh. "I fear the Danaans, even when they bring gifts," Laura said, tilting her head.

"Well, there's no antique wooden horse in there, if that's what you mean." Hugh reached into the bag and pulled out a French press machine and a can of coffee. He placed both on the desk like trophies. "If we're going to work reasonably together here, we're going to need some damn good coffee."

Laura lifted the corners of her mouth appreciatively.

"I don't only bring good things, though," Hugh continued, placing a USB flash drive next to the coffee can.

"I thought not. I don't have any good news either. But first, let's make some coffee." She stood up and filled the pot on the stove with water. "Do you want to start or should I?"

"You start, I'll wait until after the first coffee," Hugh replied and sat down.

"All right, first of all, it looks like my bosses don't want to know much about this, which actually surprises me. But at the WHO, they've become very cautious when it comes to pandemics, they don't want to be accused of scaremongering at any cost."

"Typical," Hugh commented, earning a wry look from Laura.

"You press people aren't exactly innocent of this either, you make good money from panic, but let's not go there!"

Hugh raised his hands placatingly. "You're right, I'm sorry. I'd rather not tell you what my boss wants me to do."

"Okay, so that means we're on our own for now. And things are getting more and more mysterious. I told you about this privately financed vaccination study in which many of the patients participated. According to the authorities, the company was recently dissolved, and the Bamako site no longer exists. I hardly think that's a coincidence."

"Surely not. They're trying to cover something up," Hugh agreed with her. "Once it became clear that Brauer and you were on to something, they probably started covering their tracks right away."

"Bad news for us. But I got information elsewhere on that." As she continued, she spooned coffee into the French press and poured the hot water. "Just before he died, Brauer emailed me a whole bunch of records. I just fished them out of my spam yesterday. In short, this thing is spreading. In the message were statistics on miscarriage rates and predictions of infertility. The case curve could go into an exponential trajectory and soon shoot upward by leaps and bounds."

"An epidemic after all," Hugh opined.

"According to the data, yes." Laura pressed down on the filter of the cafetière. "What concerns me most is the fact that the vaccination study, if it's what triggered all this, was done over six months ago."

"But new cases are still popping up, right?" surmised Hugh.

"Quite so, it seems. That speaks to a pathogen that is spreading through the population. It is possible that it is mutating. That could explain the slow, limited spread at first, but at a certain point it suddenly accelerates. There could be a new variant that is spreading from person to person."

"That would really suck, to put it unscientifically."

"Quite so. That sums it up quite well. But the even bigger shitstorm is that none of the patients examined had a pathogen detected. That may be because the labs here didn't look hard enough or looked for the wrong thing. But there is another possibility. Whatever is causing these symptoms may not be detectable by usual methods. I would need actual samples and a high-tech lab, like the one in Geneva."

"Hmm ... well. Speaking of high-tech. I brought you something, too. An acquaintance of mine works in London at a specialty clinic for reproductive medicine."

"Who else do you know?" Laura commented, pouring coffee first for Hugh and then for herself.

"I told you, I'm extremely well connected. Well, on this stick here are their analyses."

"Of what?"

"Of some patient data kindly leaked to me from the Ministry of Health. Now, please, no preaching on data protection."

"You're a lost cause anyway," Laura replied, putting the flash drive into her laptop.

"It's the result that counts. Please open the folder TDX_1b."

Laura did as instructed and got an overview of the analyses. She brooded over the data for a while, shaking her head.

"You want me to tell you what that looks like to me?" asked Hugh.

Laura paid little heed to this, but continued to scroll through the files.

Hugh set his empty coffee cup on the desk and poured himself a refill. "This looks like The Covenant."

"I beg your pardon?" Laura glanced away from the screen and looked at Hugh in irritation.

"The Covenant" is a science fiction film from the 90s. An alien race has secretly introduced perfidious birth control under the guise of charity and is hoarding all the eggs. These are genetically modified and used in a controlled manner in surrogate mothers. A group of humans are in league with these aliens and are cooperating to create a new breed of hybrid beings."

Laura let out an agonized sigh. "Aliens are among us and want to take over the world? That's a little too much for me!"

"I'm not saying aliens are involved in our case. It just reminded me of it."

"Wait a minute," Laura exclaimed suddenly, typing frantically on her keyboard. "Damn, what was that man's name?"

"What man?" echoed Hugh.

"Shh. Quiet, I need to think."

Hugh got up and came around the desk to see what Laura was looking for.

"Dartmouth, Dougall, Dwyer ... it was something with D," she muttered to herself. "Something Scottish." She drummed her fingernails nervously on the table. "McDouglas!" she exclaimed suddenly. "Professor Howard McDouglas."

"Who's that?" Hugh asked.

"A professor they took away the chair from at my university. It was a big deal, there was a lot of fuss, that's why I remember it at all. I didn't know him personally, and it happened in my first semester there, and it's been twelve years since."

"I don't follow you. What does this have to do with us?"

"Yeah, sorry. Cue birth control. Something rang a bell."

Hugh still looked at her doubtfully.

"They were just rumors," Laura said. "But they sounded a little like your sci-fi movie."

"That's why they fired him at the university?" asked Hugh.

"Officially, he had to leave because of discrepancies in

research funding. But behind closed doors, it was said that he had been working on a genetic procedure that could be used to make targeted changes. Of course, something like that already exists today in other forms. But it must have been a little more specialized with McDouglas."

"You mean things like these gene scissors? CRISPR-Cas, right?"

"Exactly. But this process is still very costly, and the areas of application are severely limited. McDouglas, as far as I know, had been researching a therapy with artificial RNA. And in principle, something like this could also be used to interfere with reproduction. In any case, someone must have had considerable doubts about his goals, otherwise one would not have simply dismissed such a highly decorated researcher. But that's probably far-fetched."

"I don't think so," Hugh replied.

"But that doesn't fit. McDouglas was a great theorist; but he never did any laboratory experiments."

"Maybe not while he was in college."

"You mean he went ahead and put his research into practice?"

"Maybe. The guy is suspicious, if you ask me. What was he up to after he got kicked out?"

"I don't know. They said he went back to Scotland and disappeared in the Highlands."

"I'll track him down," Hugh explained. "You can't trust Scotsmen anyway, they'll stab you in the back the first chance they get."

"Calm down, Hugh! We don't know at all if this fits together. We're following a very thin thread here. I want to try to get to his research from back then first of all. I still have some good contacts at the university."

"Yeah, you do that. I'm still going to put out some feelers as to where that nutty professor has gone."

Laura nodded. "Good, that's the cue for the coffee, by the way. Thanks for the machine."

"Just healthy self-interest," Hugh replied, smiling. "I'll swing on my bike and come back tomorrow. Right now, I've got a story to give my boss. Maybe I'll put in some aliens, the idiot might like that."

"Feel free to take your aliens with you. I have more than enough strange things here at camp."

## 11

Keller Villa, Berlin-Grunewald, September 30

The elegant music room in Christian Keller's villa was bathed in bluish dim light. On one of the long sides of the room, which measured a good six by eight meters, stood a low console with hi-fi technology - all devices fully analog. Centered was a turntable with a walnut cabinet and a titanium platter weighing a whopping 2.3 kilograms. To the right of it stood a preamplifier in a discreet champagne-colored finish, and at the ends of the console were four massive silver power amplifiers, each as heavy as a refrigerator and equipped with 800 watts of power. On the very outside were two man-sized speakers in the shape of obelisks, finished in a classy black piano lacquer. Perched on top of each speaker was a sphere of silver wire mesh, with a blue plasma flame flickering inside. Its task was to radiate the high frequencies of the music, and to do so in all directions simultaneously, in order to produce the most natural sound possible.

These two obelisks were real rarities, of which there were only a few left in the world. Also because the plasma technology used enriched the air with ozone and nitrogen oxides to a borderline risky degree.

But this did not matter to Christian Keller. For him, the only thing that mattered was perfect musical enjoyment. The rest would be taken care of by the whisper-quiet ventilation system with microfiltration technology. He sat in his wine-red velvet armchair in the acoustically best position in the room and watched as the lambent of the plasma tweeters gradually became more intense as the orchestra swelled. Atonal chord progressions joined one another, punctuated by rhythmic outbursts. To the untrained ear, it was exhausting music with all sorts of dissonances and irritating moments. But Keller knew the piece almost by heart. Even if he himself lacked the talent to play music at this level, he knew enough about composition that this was a masterpiece for the ages: *The Rite of Spring* by Igor Stravinsky.

Another eruption of music, the orchestra fully exploiting the dynamics and catapulting from zero to one hundred. The subwoofers in the obelisks unleashed their full power and literally made the room quake.

No sooner was this outburst over than the door to the music room opened a crack and a sharp beam of light cut through the dim atmosphere like a knife.

Keller gritted his teeth, swallowing his anger at the interruption and straightened up in his chair. Even at first glance, he recognized who had interrupted his musical enjoyment: Rose Harding, a longtime employee and, for the past three months, the manager of the new operation near Lychen. She was unmistakable with her shaved head and thin eyebrows drawn in with kohl. Keller found such an appearance, if it could be called that, on women simply repulsive. A bald head emphasized the bones of the skull and the face, which in Rose Harding's case was not a good thing. But at the same time, he admired her ingenuity when it came to medicine.

He waved toward the door, and the doctor entered with an aluminum case in her hand.

Keller, meanwhile, stood up, turned down the volume and brought the lights up. "What is it, Dr. Harding?"

"The first test batch of Beta from our new production facility," Rose explained in her usual, almost indifferent-sounding tone. "You said you wanted to examine it right away."

"Right! So I guess everything is going according to plan out there with you guys."

"We are making very good progress on Project Beta, as evidenced by the contents of this case." She set it down on a small table next to the chair and let the two latches snap open. Slowly, she lifted the lid. Inside, in compartments padded with dark gray foam, lay three syringes. A cool haze rose, coming from the cooling system built into the case.

Harding pointed to it with the flat of her hand, as if presenting it on commercial television.

She continued, "We will be ready to go into testing with this soon. But Project Alpha, I think, is still stuck in Phase 2."

Keller pushed Harding aside and reached into the case to take out one of the syringes. He held it up to the light and twisted it between his fingers, as if looking for something. But there was nothing in the slightly milky liquid; it was perfectly homogeneously mixed. Now he turned back to Harding. "You promised to solve the problem with Alpha."

Harding remained unfazed by Keller's reproachful tone. "We will very soon. There were unforeseen complications."

" Maybe we need to make a bigger sacrifice?"

The doctor looked at him for a moment with a touch of irritation.

Keller waved it off, sat back down and very slowly rolled up his left shirt sleeve. "Do you hear that? *The Rite of Spring* by Igor Stravinsky. It's a masterpiece, isn't it? Do you know what it's about?"

Harding just shook her head silently.

"This is a ballet piece describing a spring sacrifice in pagan Russia. A virgin is given to the spring god as a propitiation." Keller took the protective cap off the syringe.

"You want to test the compound yourself, right now?" asked Harding in an unusually concerned tone.

"Why not? You just explained that it's ready!"

"Yes, in principle. But ... I thought we were doing a study before ..."

"No, not with Beta. This project is something special. And the plan has long been set in motion, it's just a matter now of making sure we stay on schedule. And I already said, we have to make sacrifices. But we expect a reward for it, too, don't we?" Keller tied off his upper arm with a rubber band and watched the veins on his arm swell. "Now quiet down, we're about to get into the second part of the ballet, where the virgin dances herself to death in a ritual, isn't that symbolic of our whole endeavor?" He turned up the volume.

Harding nodded timidly, but did not answer. It would have been pointless in view of the thundering music.

Keller plucked the protective cap off the syringe and placed the needle flat on his skin. "May the god of spring grant us eternal youth!" he shouted loudly, stabbing the vein. As he forced the fluid into his bloodstream, he gestured with his head toward the door, signaling Harding to leave him alone.

The doctor did not hesitate, turned around and disappeared through the door.

Keller remained alone with Stravinsky, very gradually approaching an ecstatic state in harmony with the music.

Laura Delille rubbed her temples. She could no longer ignore the throbbing in her skull. For the past three hours, she had been combing through the digitized archives of her old university, the Sorbonne in Paris, to which she had kindly been granted access. But so far with very moderate success. There wasn't much on Professor McDouglas in the files. This could be due to the fact that the digitization had not yet reached the years before his expulsion or that such an alumni's work had been given low priority. It could also be that his unpopular research had been deliberately sidelined. Whatever the outcome, it was frustrating. Nothing more than a one-page thesis paper, only loosely related to McDouglas' work, had been found.

Laura looked at her watch: 10:16 pm. It was high time to take an aspirin and call it a day. Just as she was about to close the lid of the laptop, the icon for a new message appeared with a pop. She clicked on it and the window with the message opened.

The e-mail came from René Dargaud, one of her fellow students at the time. Judging by the address and signature, he was now teaching at the Sorbonne himself. Laura had to admit that she had lost track of most of her fellow students after graduation and didn't even remember the faces of many of them - or vice versa. René, on the other hand, she remembered very well. He was the rocker type who had actually been more busy with his band than with studying during his studies. It was impressive that he had become a professor at one of the most prestigious universities in the country. She shooed away the memories of that time and began to read:

"Dear Laura, I hope you are well! It's been too long! And now the grapevine reports that you're roaming around our archives looking for the legacy of an outcast. Forgive me, I shouldn't joke, but McDouglas is still a red rag to many here. I'm writing to you because I don't want you to waste your time. You won't find anything. All the files from his office have gone to the basement and I wouldn't be surprised if they threw away the key to the room. I don't think they'd let you in there as an outsider either. And before you ask, sure I could do it for you. But I've only had the job for five months and I don't want to kick the hornet's nest, if you know what I mean. Still, I'd like to help you out. I have it on pretty good authority that McDouglas lives in a castle on a peninsula in the middle of Loch Shin in the north of Scotland. And I have something else for you: his phone number. I'll copy it for you below. It's from an old phone list and I don't know if it's still correct, but you can try. If you need anything else, or if you're ever in Paris, I'd love to hear from you.
- René."

Laura scrolled down. There was a number, it started with +44, like all phone numbers on the British isle. If it was indeed valid, that would be the jackpot. She could ask McDouglas directly. Should she try it right away? She looked at the clock again - half past ten. That meant it was an hour later in Scotland. It might not have been a good idea to call

McDouglas in the middle of the night, but Laura knew she would do it anyway.

She picked up her cell phone and typed in the digits. She heard the call sign, so the number was still active.

It rang three times, then a sonorous but at the same time whiskey-swilling voice answered, "Howard McDouglas."

Laura was amazed that it was actually that simple and forgot to answer for a second.

"Hello?" the Scottish voice asked.

"Professor McDouglas, this is Dr. Laura Delille from WHO."

Silence lingered on the other end of the line.

"Professor?" Laura repeated.

"Once upon a time. I haven't been a professor for a long time now. WHO? How did you get this number? What do you want from me?"

"The matter is a bit complicated, but in principle I want to ask for your help."

"With what?" interrupted McDouglas.

"We have a growing number of strange cases of infertility here in Mali and other African countries, and the way women's eggs ..."

"Stop," McDouglas said.

"Sorry, I'm going too fast."

"No. I just don't understand what you want from me, of all people. It's not my field."

"Yes, I think you do. Your work, professor. At the Sorbonne, I remember you ..."

"I'm not talking about that," McDouglas replied gruffly and hung up.

Laura tried to dial the number again, but only got a busy signal. "That went splendidly!" she grumbled.

A few minutes later, a beep sounded from her cell phone. She had received an SMS from an unknown number - also with the +44 area code. Hastily, she opened it and read the few lines:

*"If you can really stomach the truth, come see me: 58.08323148169013 -4.494744889704514. H. McD."*
Laura typed in the coordinates on an online map service. The map showed only various shades of green and blue-colored waters in between, but virtually no roads. She zoomed out. The outlines of northern Scotland became visible.

"Come to me. The nerve of that guy." Laura shook her head. "How does he imagine that?"

The throbbing in her temples had not improved at all. She pulled open the drawer, squeezed two aspirin out of the blister and gulped them down. Now she shut the laptop and shuffled to her bed, knowing full well that she certainly wouldn't be able to fall asleep anytime soon.

As expected, the night had been restless. Laura had been lying awake for a long time, struggling with herself. Was she supposed to fly to Scotland just like that, out of the blue, to talk to McDouglas? Why did the guy on the phone hang up on her and then invite her to his castle? On the other hand, it reinforced her suspicion that the professor knew more. His reaction to her description of the events here had been very strange. Nevertheless, she now stood in her tent in the late morning, packing her bags.

Around 2:30 a.m., she had finally made up her mind to go on a business trip to distant Scotland, even if she didn't yet know how to account for it. But that was probably the least of her problems. If Engström didn't give her any support, she literally had no choice but to pursue the matter herself.

She picked up her cell phone from the desk and pocketed it. Then she hesitated briefly and pulled it out again. She had one more decision to make. What about Hugh Stevens? Was his cooperation trustworthy enough that she should inform him or even take him with her? On the other hand, he would probably show up there anyway, knowing him as she did.

The decision was taken from her. She heard the rattle of Hugh's motorcycle from outside.

Barely two minutes later, he was already standing in the doorway, looking back and forth between Laura and her suitcase with interest. "Where are we going? No, wait, let me guess." He pulled a piece of paper out of his pants pocket and unfolded it. "Loch Shin?"

Laura pulled out the cell phone and showed Hugh the message from McDouglas.

"Ha! Amazing, how did you get his number? I just found the address," Hugh explained. "Now what?"

"I'm going there," Laura replied curtly.

Silence spread while Hugh considered his answer. "I'll go with you," he then said.

"I wonder if this is such a good idea …"

"I'm coming with you!" insisted Hugh. "We're a team, remember?"

"No, I didn't forget. In fact, I was just thinking about calling you when you were already standing in the doorway."

"Then everything is gravy. Now relax. All flights to the UK leave until after midnight now. We won't get one to Glasgow until 2:18."

"Okay, we'll fly together. But don't do anything stupid when we get to McDouglas, I have a feeling we're going to have to tread very carefully if we want information from him."

"Hey, caution is my middle name."

"That line is getting a little worn out, don't you think?" said Laura, giving him a side-look.

"All right, I'm going to go to my apartment and pack. I'll meet you at the airport later."

"All right, I have some things to take care of here anyway, and I have to give Kimara some tasks to cover. I hope she can manage on her own for a few days."

"I've already reserved two tickets, partner-orientated as I am," Hugh added, winking at her. "You'll have to pay for them yourself, though."

"I'm happy to pay for myself. Thanks for the reservation anyway, see you later."

# 12

*Kurt Kruger's apartment, Berlin-Rudow, October 1*

In an outwardly dilapidated factory complex in southern Berlin, Kurt Kruger sat in his spartanly furnished but newly renovated third-floor loft, cleaning one of his guns as he did every day.

Today it was the turn of a special piece: the M40A5 sniper rifle. It was just one of a good three dozen firearms, all neatly sorted and hanging on one of the unplastered brick walls, but Kruger was extremely fond of this rifle. It gave him a priceless sense of power. What was good for the U.S. Marines was good for him.

The M40A5 was a modified version of the standard M40 with a better Schmidt & Bender scope, an additional rail for attaching a night sight and the possibility of attaching a silencer to the barrel. All in all, not a particularly compact gun, but extremely versatile. Just like Kruger himself.

He thought back to the time when he had been interested in training for the Marines. But the drill had not been for him. It all turned out differently, after a slippery slope to jail. A new start in Germany, his father's homeland. Finally, a lucrative career as a professional killer. And he was at peace with himself, no matter what might come.

Kruger finished cleaning the rifle and hung it on the wall with the others. Now it was time for item 2 of his daily routine, checking security updates. He checked to see if there were any messages during the night from his ramified network of informers or from automated spy tools he had unobtrusively installed on one target or another. There were no significant occurrences on the vast majority of channels, but one message from his new AI-based correlation platform showed a hit. A direct link between two targets who were on his grid. Laura Delille and Howard McDouglas. The professor had sent a message from his cell phone to the doctor's.

Kruger didn't know the contents, since he only had access to the mediation data, but still, that definitely marked a red line. He had to hand it to the doctor that she was quite adept at putting puzzle pieces together and tracking down crucial people. Clearly too skillful for his taste.

Now it was clear that they had to take immediate action - firm, clear action! He looked over to the wall where his arsenal of firearms hung. Then he reached for the phone and dialed Christian Keller's number.

With cream-colored protective covers on his shoes, Christian Keller strode across the sterile floor of his production facility. Everything in here was of the highest purity, and no employee was going to change that. The floor was so clean that you could literally have eaten off it - if that hadn't been strictly forbidden inside the production facility. In addition, one had to wear protective clothing and a face mask.

Keller circled a stainless steel tank, a good two meters high, from which hoses, cables and metal pipes ran off in all directions. The whole construct was imprisoned in a kind of cage that provided space for all kinds of metrological apparatus, probes and sensors. This was just one of the computer-controlled synthesis chambers that produced precursors of preparations in a highly complex process. Behind it, in a second row, were several similar vessels of varying sizes. Of one particularly large one, only the gigantic lid was visible, as the tank was mostly recessed into the floor. The ceiling was adorned with a network of cable harnesses, pipes and ventilation ducts. In between, fire alarms, sprinkler systems and surveillance cameras kept an eye on every inch of the plant around the clock.

Behind the oversized steel vat, Keller spotted site manager Rose Harding discussing with a second employee who was a full head shorter than her but gesticulating all the more excitedly.

Slowly and as silently as possible, Keller approached to listen in to what was going on, but the employee, whose name badge read Obermeier, had seen him and immediately fell silent. Dr. Harding noticed Obermeier's glance and turned to Keller.

"Don't let me interrupt," Keller said calmly. "It can be very revealing to a boss when employees openly share problems."

"There are no problems," Obermeier said hastily. "Just minor discrepancies, not worth mentioning. Excuse me, I should get back to my department."

Keller looked at him suddenly for a brief moment, then nodded at him and Obermeier disappeared. Now he turned to Harding. "What department is that again?"

"Quality assurance. Obermeier monitors product quality and compares samples to specifications."

"Ah, right. I should be here more often. So, what could be wrong with our quality control?"

"The production quality level could not be higher. I think we are struggling with the consequences of our haste."

"Explain," Keller demanded.

"You know the process. But I think we should have taken more time in developing the new mRNA products, especially alpha. Splicing the hnRNA should have actually removed all the introns and irrelevant sections of genetic information."

"And we did. Didn't we?"

"Yes and no. We removed everything that was not necessary for our purpose and then inserted the artificially generated sequences. So far, so good, but it is possible that we forgot some remnants that were ... well, let's say, were camouflaged and that could potentially trigger undesirable behavior."

"Are you trying to tell me that Alpha doesn't work properly? Surely not!"

"What Obermeier has told me is that it works ... too well.

Although maybe that's the wrong way to describe it."

Keller looked at Harding, frowning. "What exactly is that supposed to mean?"

"The batches we have tested in Africa show traces of mutations."

"Mutations? Surely I'm not hearing you right?"

"We double-checked it. The reserve samples have changed. And another strange thing is that the case numbers from Mali and Congo are much higher than our projections. There shouldn't be that many. Maybe it is also a statistical error, but we are just at the beginning of the analysis. I'll know more in a few days."

Keller was silent for a moment. He thought about the infusion he had given himself yesterday, after which he had felt almost weightless. Still, he had to ask, "What about Beta? Is it working as planned?"

"Beta is not affected by the phenomenon. It was a separate process and since it is the second product developed with this new technology, we were able to directly implement everything we learned from Alpha. However, the samples we have stored are not as old as those from Alpha. That's why I had advised a slow trial."

"It's too late for that. You may not be aware that we are following a larger timeline in which both Alpha and Beta are essential."

Harding shrugged her shoulders. "I'm just stating what I think. Technically, we can go into mass production with compound Beta very soon. I still recommend postponing the global rollout of Alpha for now."

"We're not going to do that. You just told me it works better than you thought. So, why should we delay it? We might even save money because we'll need fewer doses."

"That ...," Dr. Harding broke off. "I guess that would be a good thing," she finally said, but her face reflected a distinct hint of concern.

"Give out Beta infusions to everyone here on site. As a

sign of my appreciation - and as a quality assurance measure," Keller ordered.

"As you wish, I will arrange it," Harding replied. "So we'll start with Beta in Phase 2?"

"That's right. Get to work!"

After two stopovers, the plane with Laura Delille and Hugh Stevens on board had landed at Glasgow Airport at 14:06 local time. They had wasted no time and immediately organized a rental car.

The sat nav had calculated a good four hours for the drive from the airport to McDouglas Castle, which was now almost over. Laura had slept through most of it, making up for the lack of sleep the day before.

When she opened her eyes again, the view outside had changed quite a bit. A low cloud cover hung over the gently undulating hilly landscape, from which a fine drizzle fell incessantly. The lush green of the hills fought valiantly against the onset of dusk, which would soon turn everything into dull gray.

They were driving on a road that was far too narrow and lined on both sides by low stone walls. It was one of those roads where you constantly hoped that there would be no oncoming traffic. It was good that it was almost deserted here. The villages mostly consisted of only a few small houses, here and there was a farm or croft, and in between sheep, sheep and more sheep. The contrast to African Mali could not have been greater.

"I'm really glad you're driving," Laura said. "This left-hand traffic would drive me crazy."

"Yeah, no problem, I'm used to it. It's just these trails they call main roads here that are a joke. Scotsmen, that's what they are! Always a touch too economical," Hugh replied.

Laura glanced to the side, where the boundary walls passed ominously close. "Can I get the deposit back on the car, or have you put too many scratches in the paint already?"

"Not a single one. They were all in there before." Hugh grinned.

"I see. How long do we have?"

"You woke up on time. Our target should show up just ahead there."

Less than two minutes later, a gloomy silhouette emerged on the otherwise flat peninsula in Loch Shin. Howard McDouglas' castle was apparently the only structure on the otherwise empty headland.

"Whew, this is the perfect setting for a scary movie," Hugh said as he steered the car down the increasingly bumpy dirt road. "We visit the mad professor at his remote castle, where he conducts experiments in a secret laboratory. In the dungeon, he holds his subjects captive. The only question is, are they sheep or people?"

Laura sighed. "Are you tinkering with another lurid fake story for your boss?"

"Don't remind me. I'm dreading the moment I turn in my expense report. I'll probably get fired." Hugh parked the car in a gravel lot in front of the castle.

"You really care about this thing, don't you?" voiced Laura.

"This is it. You know, before they sent me to Africa - and before my faith in real journalism took a severe hit - I really wanted to make a difference. I wanted to do investigative stories, to bite where it hurts the rich and powerful. And for the first time in a long time, I finally feel that fire inside me. This thing here is just the story par excellence!"

Laura nodded silently at first, then said almost casually, "Interesting, behind that casual, motorcycle rebel's hardened exterior is actually someone with principle. Best show your diplomatic side when we talk to McDouglas."

"Diplomatic is my middle..."

"Leave it," Laura interrupted him and opened the door.

Hugh got out on his side.

Fortunately, the drizzle took a break and they arrived dry

at the entrance. Up close, it looked much more compact than they had expected. It was more of a glorified mansion than a real castle. Still, the castle appeared rustic enough to fit into the landscape. Some details revealed that it had probably been very extensively refurbished. The massive double-leaf entrance door, for example, was undoubtedly recent. For an antique wooden door, the surface was too flawless and the frame too perfectly set into the wall. Also, all the windows had insulated double glazing. At the top of one of the small towers, one could even see a satellite dish, which looked rather strange on the old facade.

"Must have cost a fortune," Hugh surmised. "Did he really get such a good settlement from the university?"

"I don't believe it's severance; I'm sure the Castle was family-owned before that."

"You're probably right. After you, please," Hugh said, pointing to the antique gold door knocker.

Laura stepped forward and lifted the metal ring. The moment she dropped it, not only was a metallic clacking sound heard, but also a kind of gong with three tones in a row from inside. The knocker was just an unusual bell button.

The right wing of the door opened a crack, and an older man with a half bald head and a black service uniform appeared. "Whom may I report?" he inquired.

"I'll eat my hat if that guy's name isn't James," Hugh whispered, getting a kick out of Laura.

"Dr. Laura Delille." She looked to Hugh. "With companion."

The butler nodded. "Wait here. I will inquire if you are to be received." With that, he closed the door again.

"He could have let us in, it's cold as shit," Hugh complained, flipping up the collar of his jacket.

After a moment of waiting, the door opened again. An elderly gentleman with a gray beard, traditionally dressed in a kilt, appeared. A pipe hung in the corner of his mouth.

"Professor McDouglas, I am extremely pleased that we

have the opportunity to speak," Laura expressed, extending her hand in greeting.

McDouglas took her hand but did not answer. He looked over at Hugh. "Who's that?"

"He works with me. Hugh Stevens. Actually, he's a journalist, but ..."

"A reporter? You're dragging the press here! From what I've read about you, I had thought you far less stupid."

"Listen ...", Hugh spoke up. But before he could finish his sentence, McDouglas slammed the door.

"What are you doing?" agitated Hugh, pounding on the door.

"Well, I can understand him a little," Laura said. "At first, I would have liked to strangle you, too."

"It's nice that we know each other better by now. But what are we supposed to do now? In this godforsaken place?"

Laura pressed the door knocker again. But this time, no chime sounded from inside. "Professor McDouglas! It's really important that we get to talk to you! I need to know what's going on in Africa."

They stood in front of the castle for a good ten more minutes, but no one opened. When it started raining again, they got into the car in frustration.

"Back over in town, I saw bed and breakfast signs. Let's find a place to stay for the night first, I'm pretty beat," Hugh said, starting the engine. They left the dark walls of McDouglas' castle behind them.

# 13

*Keller Villa, night, October 2.*

It was already shortly after midnight, but Christian Keller was still working on his manifesto in his library. He had felt for some time that it needed a little more precision in places. He probably needed to break away from the sometimes archaic language that he so appreciated and always enjoyed when he found it in the historical manuscripts in his collection. But it became increasingly clear to him that with the completion of his life's work, a turning point in time was at the same time approaching. And it was appropriate to write something less poetic and cryptic.

Keller jumped ahead a few chapters in his book to the section called "Auslese." He changed the heading to "Selection Pressure" and began to write.

*"The human race knows no boundaries. The good thing about this is that it is irrepressibly curious and always continues to learn and increase its knowledge. But this boundlessness is also its greatest weakness, which would ultimately be its undoing. It lacks the limiting factor that stops us and anchors us to the environment. How can unlimited growth work in a world with limited resources? The answer is simple: not at all. Everything is finite, yet humans seem to challenge this law of nature and keep spreading, like an infection in an organism that ruthlessly destroys the tissue that surrounds it. The means to this end is technology, market deference, misuse of resources. But must we stand idly by? Are we supposed to run into ruin with our eyes open? We, who have recognized what is wrong? This answer is also so simple that one is afraid to give it. Nevertheless: No, we should not. And we won't. To do so, we must increase*

*the selection pressure. We will set the limits that nature lacked when it created us. Either we do this now or we are doomed as a race in general.*

*I am not saying that it will be easy, that it will be painless, that it will be possible without sacrifices. On the contrary, these sacrifices are considerable. It means removing gigantic obstacles and starting anew in many places. It also means releasing into darkness all those who are not worthy of seeing the light of this new world. This also applies to many an unfaithful comrade who has decided not to maintain the path to the end. Do not look back, tomorrow is already here, and there will be no more yesterday."*

Keller finished the paragraph and saved the document. Satisfied, he reached for the whiskey glass on the desk, in which deep orange 30-year-old Scotch gleamed.

"To the companions whose path ends today," he said aloud, bringing the glass to his mouth.

At the same time, Howard McDouglas was also sitting at his desk in his study. This had been the center of his work for many years and gave him the feeling of having a place in the ranks of the scientists he had admired all his life. His study was furnished in an old-fashioned way, as befitted a traditionalist like McDouglas, as well as the building in which the room was located. What wasn't covered by dark wooden shelves was covered with brown paneling. The ceiling was also made of wooden panels, but these were covered with paintings. It was almost reminiscent of a church, even if the motifs were entirely different - birds, snakes, trees. McDouglas was not a religious person, rather the opposite.

The castle was quiet and lonely, as it always was at this late hour. Jonathan, his servant, also lived here - downstairs in his own apartment - but he used to go to bed around 10:00 p.m. at the latest. McDouglas was alone with himself and his thoughts. He stared into the flames blazing in the fireplace.

In October, it quickly became uncomfortable up here in

the north, especially at night it was only a few degrees above zero. But McDouglas hadn't lit the fire because he was cold, but rather because of its hypnotic effect. He could stare into it for hours and organize his mind. Normally, at least. Today he didn't really want to succeed. All his trains of thought wandered in circles. What had he done? The image of Pandora's box came to his mind. Would he do the right thing now? Did it still matter?

He pulled an old-fashioned flip phone without a touch display out of the drawer and started writing a message.

He had not yet gone far when he heard a clang from below. He listened, straining into the silence. It had sounded as if a glass had shattered on the stone floor. Probably Jonathan, he wasn't the youngest anymore and was getting a bit scatterbrained. Should he take a look anyway?

McDouglas typed a few more words into the message and pressed send. He put the cell phone back in the drawer.

All was quiet again in the castle, except for the crackling from the fireplace. McDouglas wondered a little, since Jonathan probably would have come up immediately and apologized profusely for making such a noise in the middle of the night. On the other hand, he knew that McDouglas never went to sleep before midnight.

The professor descended the arched stone staircase to the first floor, where, in addition to Jonathan's servant's quarters, there was the entrance hall, the kitchen, and a large dining room with a wide glass front facing the garden.

Everything was quiet in the entrance hall. But the door to Jonathan's apartment was open.

McDouglas crept across the smooth marble floor to the apartment and knocked on the door frame. "Johnathan? Are you all right?" he asked quietly. He opened the door a little wider so he could survey the living area without having to go inside.

Everything seemed deserted. Once again he inquired through the doorway, a little louder, but he received no answer this time either. He turned around and went to the kitchen.

Through the intermediate door to the dining room he could see Jonathan. He was lying motionless on the parquet floor. Had he had a heart attack? Beside him, McDouglas caught sight of the remains of a shattered glass. But there were too many shards on the floor, and some were too far away. His glances followed the trail. One of the large glass doors had a hole in it. McDouglas felt the cold draft blowing in.

Were there burglars here? Was this a robbery?

"Jonathan?" he asked again, kneeling down next to the man lying on the floor. Carefully, he shook his shoulder and turned him a little to the side. A puddle of blood appeared.

McDouglas flinched. A red dot flashed in the corner of his eye, but before he fully grasped the situation, he heard another clang and felt a burning pain on his neck. He wanted to get up and run away, but he felt dizzy. Warm blood flowed down his neck.

There was a third clang. At the same moment, McDouglas felt a brutal crack in the back of his head and then there was only endless blackness.

Laura Delille took a crocheted doily from the chair and sat down at the large oval wooden table in the breakfast room of the bed and breakfast where she and Hugh had stayed. Here, too, there was a lot wrong with the decor for Laura's taste. Just as in the rooms, Harriet, the landlady, had cluttered everything with pillows, doilies, and porcelain dollies. In addition, there was flowered wallpaper and flowing curtains on all the windows. Above all, the mass of dolls, all in flowered dresses, gave the whole thing a slightly eerie atmosphere.

Moreover, the porcelain figurines could not hide the fact that she and Hugh were the only guests here at the moment. The tourist season seemed to be long over, and Harriet's bed and breakfast had been the last one still open for miles around. So they would have had no choice anyway, and had to live with the doily and doll craze.

As if on cue, Harriet came wobbling into the breakfast room. A fluffed skirt with a floral pattern hung over her flared hips.

She smiled at Laura and placed a menu on the table. "Sleep well, child?"

Laura could not get used to this form of address for the life of her, but did not want to start a discussion with the nice older lady about whether adult women should be addressed as such or not.

"Everything is fine," she assured her and picked up the menu. She skimmed what was on offer.

Harriet apparently noticed her frown and spoke again. "If traditional Scottish breakfast isn't for you, I can just bring you toast and jam."

Laura detached herself from the list, which included fish, sausages, sliced cold haggis and baked blood pudding. She smiled sheepishly. "Toast and jam would be great, thanks!"

"No problem, of course I know that local cuisine is not to everyone's taste. Coffee or tea?"

"Coffee, please!" said Laura hastily, and followed up with, "Nothing against tea, but I really need more caffeine."

Harriet nodded and turned toward the kitchen.

Meanwhile, Laura looked out the wide front window at the loch. The bed and breakfast was on the east shore of Loch Shin pretty much level with McDouglas Castle. You could see it quite well from here. Only a narrow strip of water separated the headland from the shore.

In the bright morning light, the Castle looked much brighter than in the dodgy drizzle last night. The sky was still overcast, but it didn't look like rain today, which was very conducive to Laura's mood.

Hugh Stevens entered the breakfast room and joined Laura at the table. "Morning!" he said, plopping down on the chair. Then he grabbed the menu directly and looked at Laura with amusement only moments later. "Let me guess, you're starting the day with Lorne and Black Pudding, right?"

"I don't know about Lorne, but I sure as hell don't eat anything made of blood for breakfast."

Hugh laughed. "Stop it, it's delicious!" He lowered his voice. "If you ask me, it's the only good thing about Scotland."

Harriet returned from the kitchen with coffee and a basket of toast.

"For the young gentleman, what may I bring?"

"Full Scottish Breakfast for the young gentleman. Everything that fits on the plate!"

"Very good," Harriet praised, beaming up to both ears. She put down the basket and coffee pot and disappeared.

"I thought you medical people had stomachs of steel, what with autopsies and all," Hugh said.

"That's the job, but breakfast remains a private matter, so I'm happy to forgo blood," Laura explained.

"Very sensible. You know, my parents both worked in the hospital. My father was a trauma surgeon and my mother was a nurse. They had a habit of discussing the particularly nasty cases at home over dinner, even when I was really little. It definitely toughens you up."

"I can imagine," Laura agreed. "For us, it was about other issues. Powdery mildew or grape aphids."

"Your parents are winemakers?"

"That's right – eighth generation. But I absolutely couldn't get anything out of it. I wanted to get out of the provinces and study. My father thought it was bullshit, but my mother always supported me. Well, let's not go there."

"We don't have to tell each other our whole life story right away," Hugh affirmed, taking a sip of coffee. Then he changed the subject. "We should try to contact McDouglas again right after breakfast. Or have you tried calling him yet?"

"No, my cell phone is dead and the charging cable is in the camp in Mali. But I didn't notice that until I went to plug it in last night. Can I borrow your charger later?"

"Sure, if it's the right connection. Maybe it's better if we go back in person anyway. Or in other words, just you. I'll stay in the car for now so he doesn't slam the door in our faces again."

"I think that's a very good idea," Laura agreed with him and grabbed a slice of toast.

## 14

Around 11 o'clock that morning, they turned back onto the gravel road on the headland in Loch Shin. A good ten minutes later, they arrived at McDouglas Castle. The area in front of the building was very much no longer deserted as it had been the previous evening. There were five vehicles in the parking lot: two police cars, two black hearse vans, and a small civilian car. Three policemen were waiting next to one of the cars.

"Fuck, that can't mean anything good," Hugh exclaimed, automatically slowing down a bit.

"Hearses never mean anything good! Do you think McDouglas is ...?" continued Laura.

"We should expect the worst."

"So what do we do now?" Laura wanted to know.

"I don't know, but I think the cops saw us. So we can't turn back. If they stop us, let me do the talking."

"Don't mind if I do," Laura agreed.

The officers had indeed noticed the approaching car, and one of them approached quickly with his hand raised.

Hugh stopped beside him and rolled down the window. "Good morning."

"This area is blocked. Police action. Please turn off the engine and show me some identification," the policeman demanded.

Hugh turned the ignition key to the off position and flipped open his wallet. He pulled out his driver's license and press pass. Laura handed him her passport, and Hugh handed everything to the officer.

The policeman glanced at the IDs. "I really wonder how you vultures in the press always get wind of this so quickly. Did the cleaning lady tip you off?"

Hugh wrapped himself in diplomatic silence.

The officer shrugged his shoulders. "All right. I'll still have to check it out. Wait here." He moved away and went back to his colleagues. One took the IDs and sat down with them in one of the patrol cars.

Meanwhile, Laura watched the castle and tried to figure out what had happened here and whether her appearance had anything to do with it. The two hearses sent a clear message. McDouglas was probably dead. And someone else, or the second hearse would make no sense. A frightening thought popped into her head: it could just as easily be her and Hugh, now lying in dull tin coffins in the vans.

Through the large door they had knocked on yesterday, a policewoman with red hair tied back in a ponytail now came and joined her colleagues. She exchanged a few words with the officer who had taken their IDs a few minutes ago. He pointed in the direction of her car and the policewoman followed his hand with her gaze. Then she put her head into the patrol car and got their ID cards. With jagged steps she came in their direction.

"She sure looks like she's in a bad mood," Laura remarked.

"Yeah, I know the look on her face. Either she's going to send us packing or she's going to arrest us."

"For what?"

"We'll know in about five seconds."

A short time later, they were sitting in McDouglas' study on two chairs in front of the desk.

Behind it, the policewoman had taken a seat as if it were her office they were in. She had introduced herself to them as Caitrin Broderick, head of investigations. "You'll forgive the circumstances. Our station is in Glenmorangie, three quarters of an hour away. So we'll have to conduct the questioning here, although that may seem inappropriate."

"Questioning?" repeated Hugh. "I must have misheard you."

"Mr. Stevens, please. We're talking about a double homicide here. And I don't buy that you're here just reporting. It's just not possible this quickly, and the cleaning lady is still in shock. You can't have known about the incident. And I don't believe that you were on vacation and just happened to want to take a look at this castle either. So let's get down to business." She looked at Hugh with her piercing green eyes, as if wanting to make herself crystal clear.

Hugh was silent.

"No answer is an answer," Broderick explained. "Okay, let's start simple. What were you doing here?" Broderick looked back and forth between Hugh and Laura.

"We wanted to talk to Professor McDouglas," Laura now spoke up.

"Ah, you can talk too, how excellent!" remarked Broderick. "What did you want to talk to him about?"

"Professor McDouglas used to teach at my university in France. I wanted to talk to him about one of his research projects from back then. I'm a medical doctor, you know."

"Fine," Broderick said. "But that doesn't explain why you have a reporter in tow."

"I follow Dr. Delille's work journalistically," Hugh replied. "Science is a big issue for the readership today."

"Dr. Delille, I have looked at your passport. You were last in Mali. And now you're flying to Scotland to interview your old professor. With all due respect, don't they have the internet in Africa?"

"I ..." Laura hesitated. Should she mention the mysterious infertility, the vaccination study, the dubious research McDouglas had done, or the dead office manager Brauer? What could the local police possibly do with that? If she spouted an unproven conspiracy theory in front of Broderick, with no serious evidence, it would only make her all the more suspicious.

"McDouglas invited me," Laura said. "I'm afraid I don't know exactly what he wanted to tell me myself. But obviously it was so important to him that he couldn't talk about it on the phone or over the internet."

"Finally, something honest," Broderick pulled open the drawer in McDouglas' desk. She pulled out an old flip phone and showed it to Laura and Hugh. "You've been in contact with him lately, it seems. He's been writing you messages."

Laura nodded. "He invited me to come here, like I said."

"And the patents?"

"Patents?" Laura was stunned. "What patents?"

"That's what I'm asking you!" demanded Broderick. She picked up the cell phone and read a message.

*"Follow the trail of patents. Maybe then we'll talk. Alone, without the reporter."*

Broderick looked over at Hugh. "He obviously didn't trust you."

Hugh raised his hands helplessly.

"I didn't even get this message yet, my phone was off, the charging cable ..."

"Yeah, yeah, yeah. All right. You don't want to talk, I know that."

"We don't know anything," Hugh added.

"Where were you last night between 11:00 p.m. and 1:00 a.m.?"

"In bed!" retorted Hugh.

"Together?" probed Broderick.

"Listen here!" exclaimed Laura.

"No," Hugh said all the more calmly. "We were over in Shinness at the bed and breakfast, each in our own room. You can ask the landlady."

"We will. Is there anything else you might want to tell me?"

"I don't see what," Hugh mused. "Can we go now? Nothing's going to come of that interview with McDouglas, after all."

Broderick eyed the two silently for a while, as if considering what to do with them now. "There's something suspicious about you two, I just don't know what it is. But you definitely don't seem like you know how to handle a gun, so I'll refrain from arresting you. It would be troublesome to get you to Glenmorangie. But be on stand by for further questioning. Now get out of here." Broderick rose and pointed to the door.

Hugh and Laura also stood up and responded to the call.

Just outside the door, Hugh turned around again. "Rifle, did you say? I saw the broken windows downstairs. Someone must have fired from outside. And in the dark."

Broderick nodded. "From the circumstantial evidence, yes."

"Surely that must have been a sniper rifle. Who's the second dead man?"

"Jonathan Gowan, a servant."

"And ..."

"That's enough, Mr. Stevens. This is not a press conference here." Broderick again pointed to the door, where one of the other officers appeared. "If you would be so kind. My colleague will take you downstairs and give you back your documents." With these words, she took her seat again and did not dignify them with another glance.

Laura read the text message from Howard McDouglas one more time. It was the exact text that Caitrin Broderick had read about an hour ago:

*"Follow the trail of patents. Maybe then we'll talk. Alone, without the reporter."*

She wondered if she could have done anything if her cell phone hadn't been turned off. Could McDouglas still be alive? But that was nonsense. If she had read the news yesterday, it might have tempted her to pull an all-nighter by researching the patents mentioned, but she still wouldn't have been at the castle sooner. The words 'sniper rifle' resonated in her mind. And she didn't like the sound of it at all. She was a doctor, for crying out loud, not a secret agent.

There was a knock at the door of her room.

"Come in!" she called.

Hugh appeared in the doorway. "I got the WiFi key from Harriet, but the connection isn't very good. We'll have to see how far we can get."

"I still can't believe McDouglas was shot. Just yesterday we were talking to him. He asked me to come here specifically. We were so close to finally finding out something more. And now?"

Hugh set his laptop down on a small table by the window and opened a browser window. "There's a central database of patents we can search. Maybe we can find out why McDouglas was so coy."

"So you mean they killed him for his patents?"

"Maybe, but I doubt it. More likely, he was killed because of what he knew - and because he was about to pass it on to you."

"I don't know if I want that knowledge anymore. This morning was intense. Hearse, police ..."

"I can understand all too well. We have to be careful," Hugh said. "Whoever had McDouglas in their sights - we shouldn't draw their attention to us."

"Speaking of drawing attention ... Isn't it possible that we led the killer to him? That it's our fault?"

Hugh shook his head vigorously. "I'm sure you know that's bullshit. McDouglas was in this a lot deeper than we were, I'll bet. He knew too much. Or he just decided he wasn't going to play the game anymore. And that's why he became a danger."

"You're probably right," Laura agreed with him. "I'm used to war and death and disease, but this situation is completely new to me."

"We have to try to stay focused and keep going. We're following the trail of patents as McDouglas described it." He pointed to the laptop. "And don't worry, this is an official directory that anyone is free to research. It shouldn't raise any suspicions."

"All right. Let's get started," Laura decided.

They spent the next two hours searching the database for patents involving Howard McDouglas. Because of the poor Internet connection, the search dragged on much longer than they would have liked, but in the end it was crowned with success.

"The professor used to be quite prolific," Laura remarked appreciatively.

"That's right. Now I also know how he financed his retirement in that castle. He's given dozens of licenses to pharmaceutical companies, which are probably very lucrative."

"McDouglas seems to have done very little research after his expulsion from the Sorbonne. There is only one patent that is newer than twelve years and that's this one." Laura pointed to an entry.

"MRNA MIXTURE FOR VACCINATION AGAINST MALARIA DISEASE"

She opened the entry and waited for the data to load. Then she read aloud: "The subject matter of the invention for which a patent application has been filed relates to a mixture of substances containing a synthetically generated mRNA sequence for vaccination against malaria. Further, the invention relates to a pharmaceutical composition containing a mixture of mRNAs for the treatment of persons suffering from malaria ..." She paused and looked at Hugh. "The whole document is 158 pages long, but I don't think it will do us much good to read through it all."

Hugh shook his head. "Maybe not that, but ..." He pointed to a section in the side column of the website. "In addition to Howard McDouglas, the applicants for the patent are named as Rose Harding and a company: Keller Pharma S.R.L."

"S.R.L.?" asked Laura.

Hugh typed it into a search engine. "Seems to be the common form of business in Romania."

"Romania is not exactly a stronghold of the pharmaceutical industry," Laura noted.

Hugh started a new search query for Keller Pharma and landed on the corporate website, which showed a good dozen subsidiaries around the world. He clicked through the pages and eventually found a few entries about the company's history and scope of operations. "I guess this is the mastermind behind the whole thing," he said, pointing to a photo.

The caption identified the man depicted as Christian Keller, the sole heir and current head of the Keller Pharma family business. Below that was a photo of the now-deceased company founder Franz Albert Keller. Both had the same put-on minimal smile that was common for posed business photos. Otherwise, the pictures looked just as sterile as one would expect from a pharmaceutical company.

Laura looked at the two photos for a moment. "I don't know these guys personally, but 'likeable' doesn't exactly spring to mind."

"Even if the pictures were sympathetic, their machinations certainly are not," Hugh commented.

"You're definitely right about that. And in order to preserve their German clean-man image, they outsourced the dirty work to Romania. Typical," Laura said.

"I'm sure you're right there. And the malaria vaccine fits the bill, too. After all, that's exactly what they've been testing in Mali at this vaccination center."

"At least in appearance."

"Right. We don't know what they actually did there. But the effect was certainly not the one described in this patent here."

"And now?" asked Laura.

"I'm going to go over to my room and see if I can get any of my colleagues from Eastern Europe on the phone."

"That sounds reasonable, I'll check with WHO to see what they know about Keller Pharma."

# 15

Hôpitaux universitaires de Genève, Geneva, Switzerland, October 2.

Johann Engström entered the University Hospital of Geneva that day with an entirely unfamiliar feeling. Even if it might not have been a completely new feeling, it seemed so long since he had last felt it that he could hardly remember it. Still, he was almost certain it was hope. Real hope, not that desperate kind of sham confidence that he'd often refused to give up.

His heart pounded as he approached the room where his daughter had lain for more than a year - ever since her condition had deteriorated dramatically. For the last two months, she had been in a coma and the doctors' prognosis had become increasingly bleak.

But now everything was different. Engström had secretly connected the infusion bag to his daughter's IV about 36 hours ago at night, hoping that no one would catch him by surprise. It had taken three quarters of an hour for the pale pink liquid to disappear completely into her bloodstream, and Engström had let the empty bag disappear back into his briefcase. Then they had waited another hour to see if there would be any immediate change. But that was not to be expected. Every preparation needed its appropriate time to take effect. As a physician, Engström knew that very well, but no one was immune to irrationality.

When there was no change the next day, he was seriously worried he had been deceived. Well, deceived would have been the wrong word. He had been coldly blackmailed, his personal situation shamelessly exploited! How much trust could one have there?

But when the call came this morning from the audibly

astonished chief physician informing him that Ariane had woken up from her coma and, what's more, had begun to speak, Engström could no longer keep to his office. He canceled all appointments and raced there. And now he hesitated, with his hand on the door handle. Probably because he was afraid it might have been just a dream or a hallucination.

The decision was taken from him when the door opened and a nurse came out. "Oh, I'm sorry!" she cried, "did I catch you with the door?"

"No, it's all right, it's my own fault, why am I standing here in a daze?"

"Dad?" he heard from inside.

A shiver ran down Engström's spine. How long had it been since he heard that voice? Certainly not for four years, since Ariane was 13. "Yes, I'm here!" he said and hurriedly stepped into the room.

His daughter sat upright in bed, beaming happily at him.

"This is a miracle," Engstrom breathed, grabbing her hand. "Are you all right?"

"Yeah, I feel ... I don't know, like reborn. How is that possible? The doctors here won't tell me. Or they can't."

"I'll talk to them later. For now, just stay here. I have so much to tell you."

"And I have so many questions."

"Ask. Anything you want."

The call to the editorial office was far less friendly and uncomplicated for Hugh than he had hoped. Instead of giving him the number of the Eastern Europe correspondent, the editorial assistant first connected him with his supervisor, Adrian Keen.

Hugh was not overly surprised, however, as he had already blocked two of Adrian's calls and clearly angered his boss. Now he had been going on a tirade for five minutes.

"And then the travel expenses!" agitated Adrian further. "I checked the credit cards, Hugh! Why the hell are you booking a flight to Glasgow? I'm not hot on geography, but I know it's not in fucking Africa!"

"Are you done now?" butted in Hugh, who was getting tired of hearing it. "If you'll let me finish a sentence, I can explain why."

"Oh, don't tell me you think I'm being unreasonable? Then I formally apologize!" said Keen in an unmistakably sarcastic tone.

"Adrian, I'm on to something big. Listen, this morning I was at a crime scene. Two men have been murdered, you might say executed. One was a former professor at the Sorbonne in France, a luminary in medicine and a pioneer in gene therapy. He was shot in his chateau, through the window pane. Apparently by a sniper."

"Are you kidding me? Are you seriously trying to get your head out of the noose here?", Keen hammered.

"No, so far no one knows about it, we have the story exclusively. I can send you the report in an hour, along with a photo of the castle. Maybe later I'll somehow get to the cleaning lady who found the scene."

"All right, if this is really a good story, I won't fire you right away. But that still doesn't explain what the heck you want in Scotland!"

"I can't tell you that right now, but I can tell you this much: The dead professor is a puzzle piece in a very big story. The biggest one you can imagine!"

"How many times have I heard hyperbole like that come out of your mouth, Hugh?"

"I'm serious, dead serious."

"Okay, you have a week. I think, Africa wore out anyway. Keep at it, but if you make a fool out of me, you're fired, I swear!"

"I promise it will be worth it. But one more request: publish the story about the murdered McDouglas under a pseudonym. I need to continue undercover research and don't want to draw unnecessary attention to myself."

"You know we're usually very reluctant to do that. But ok. I sure hope that was the last concession."

"I'm sure you will. You won't regret it."

"Sure, Hugh. I regret it already."

Laura nervously drummed her fingers on the desk facing the window in her room. She had been waiting for Johann Engström to call her back for over an hour. His assistant had told her that he was out of the office until further notice, and that his cell phone number only resulted in his voice mail. However, she had already left two messages. Just as she was about to try to reach him again, the cell phone rang. The display showed Engstrom's number. She hurriedly answered it.

"Johann, finally. I was beginning to think something had happened."

"Everything is fine, Laura. Really, everything," Engström explained cheerfully.

"I need to talk to you, do you have a few minutes?"

"Sure, is there any news?"

"I'm in Scotland, Johann."

"Excuse me? Why? What about the study in Mali?"

"We have other problems, I've already explained that to you. I came here to talk to Professor McDouglas, you knew him, didn't you?"

"Yes, Laura, sure. But I don't quite understand, what did you want from him? And what do you mean 'knew'?"

"He was murdered before I could talk to him."

"Murdered, for heaven's sake, is that true?"

"I was at the scene, and he and his butler were shot."

"Laura, this is not good. I don't want you to get involved in something like this."

"Are you not listening to me? I'm in the middle of this."

"It's best we talk about this in person. You shouldn't stay there any longer. And since you're already in Europe anyway - unauthorized, I might add - you might as well come to Geneva to headquarters."

"Does this mean I get your full backing on this now?"

"We'll see. I want to be fully informed first. To be honest, there are still so many things that are a mystery to me."

"I can be there tomorrow. I need to get to the databases anyway, I guess there is actually a link between infertility and a malaria vaccine. The manufacturer of the drug is Keller Pharma."

After a pause that was a little too long, Engstrom said, "Come here first, I'm sure this will all get sorted out."

Achim Obermeier stood at the TX-750E analyzer in the quality assurance department of the secret Lychen Keller site and could hardly concentrate on his work. Sweat stood on his forehead and he stepped restlessly from one foot to the other. Under his protective gear, he was hotter today than ever before. He was not sick, he had no fever. The morning temperature screening would have revealed that beyond a doubt. Nor was the state-of-the-art ventilation system in the production facility malfunctioning. The heat he felt was due solely to excitement. And he had brought it on himself.

The moment he had decided to change sides, when he had devised the plan to smuggle samples out of the plant, knowing full well that this could be extremely dangerous. Scruples was a foreign word to the people who pulled the strings here. He had realized that much too late. By then, he had already plowed along this one-way street for many miles. Now he was trying to find an exit somewhere before the road finally ended in hell. And there was no longer any doubt in his mind that that was exactly where it led.

Obermeier's brain was running an endless loop: just don't attract attention, get out of here in one piece, and then we'll see...

When his employees left for their lunch break in the small canteen of the production plant at 12:15 p.m. sharp, he casually remarked: "You guys go ahead, I want to finish something. And I'm not really hungry anyway.

He waited until everyone was out of the room, then pulled the sample containers out of the analyzer, where they had been lying untouched for hours. With his right hand, he placed the majority of the containers on a support next to the device. At the same time, he quickly dropped two of the samples into the left pocket of his white coat.

As simple as this process was, it felt like a capital crime. In fact, it was the opposite - a desperate attempt to prevent a gigantic crime.

Obermeier pretended to take some notes, then continued to the door and down the hall toward the cafeteria.

In the first basement of the complex, Christian Keller, alerted by Kurt Kruger, entered the facility's security center.

"What is it?" he asked, the visit clearly was an inconvenience to him.

"Something very interesting, I think. At first I thought this AI-based video analysis was completely overrated, but apparently it's worth the money," Kruger explained, pointing to the large video wall that showed two dozen smaller camera views and a large main window in the center.

"What did it discover?"

"Obermeier. The algorithms of behavioral analysis have flagged. His movements, his time spent on apparatus, even his body temperature do not match his usual values. A human being probably wouldn't have noticed anything. Just dismissed it as a man having a bad day or getting sick or something. But you can't cheat this artificial intelligence that easily. So I continued to keep an eye on him. And about five minutes ago, when everyone else went on break - bingo!" Kruger brought up a saved video sequence on the main screen and ran it.

Keller watched the action. "Pretty handy, the good Obermeier. What did he make disappear?"

"Well, we don't know yet, but I'd love to get my hands on him."

Keller watched the recording for another moment, then turned to Kruger. "Seal off the exit first."

"And what do we do after that? Should I drag him out into the woods and shoot him?" A faint smile stole onto Kruger's lips.

"Oh, don't. We can still learn something from him," Keller said. "This afternoon, we'll administer the Beta infusions to all the staff. But there will be an unfortunate mix-up." Now Keller smiled. "Instead of Beta, he'll get Alpha - in tenfold doses. And then we'll watch what happens. You can always shoot him afterwards."

Kruger nodded. "I'm looking forward to it."

## 16

Glasgow Airport, Scotland, October 3

Hugh tossed the car key into the rental car company's return box at Glasgow Airport and turned to Laura. "Well, looks like we're about to part ways. But first, I have something to show you. Please don't rip my head off."

"Can't promise," Laura replied, looking at him skeptically.

Hugh pointed to a magazine store a little further down the aisle, grabbed his suitcase and headed out.

Laura followed him, but waited outside the store while Hugh bought a newspaper inside.

When he returned, he held out today's issue of the Independent Observer to her.

Immediately, she recognized McDouglas' castle in the picture. "What did you do?"

"Sorry, I had to deliver something to my boss to keep my job. But it's not half bad, read it for now."

Laura hesitated to take the paper, obviously disappointed that Hugh hadn't told her about making the McDouglas murder into a story. Then she picked it up and began to read the article.

Hugh waited until she was through. "As you can see, I didn't mention any details, nor did I mention anything about what we found out in Africa. And the article appeared under a different name so it couldn't be traced back to me."

"Okay, I'm not going to rip your head off. But why didn't you tell me before this appeared?"

"I ... I don't know. Stupid reporter's code. Never tell anyone about a story until it's in print," Hugh explained.

"I don't quite buy that."

"Maybe I was afraid you'd talk me out of it. But I wouldn't

have had a choice anyway, I want to keep investigating. And if the paper fires me, it certainly won't be any easier."

"They're going to fire you?" asked Laura.

"No, not anymore. But my boss threatened me with it because I flew to Scotland without permission at his expense."

"I understand. My boss wasn't thrilled either. He probably didn't just summon me to Geneva because he wanted to see me again," Laura said.

"But that's good, you're at the central hub of information, you have access to archives and labs, that's great."

"Yes, this could really be a step forward. And I'm hoping that's how I'll finally move forward with this."

"We'll be in touch?" asked Hugh.

"Of course, partner. But in the future, please be honest with me."

"I promise."

"I have to go to check-in, my plane leaves in 45 minutes," Laura said. "When are you flying?"

"I'm on the 11 a.m. flight to Heathrow."

"All right, let me know when you land." Laura pushed the paper back into Hugh's hand, picked up her rolling suitcase, and put on a smile. Then she headed toward the ticket hall.

The puncture site on the crook of his arm had certainly stopped bleeding long ago, but Achim Obermeier continued to press the sterile absorbent cotton onto it as he boarded the elevator to the lower floors. He knew that he bruised very easily. No matter whether it was when drawing blood or administering injections. If the person wasn't extremely careful, Obermeier had a hematoma the size of a Wiener schnitzel on his arm the next day. And even if all care was taken when injecting, there was a very good chance that it would still happen and his arm would hurt for a week. As a medical professional, he had of course researched the reasons. From vitamin K deficiency to a rare hereditary disease, there were many causes, but none he could prove beyond doubt, so he had to settle for the explanation that it was simply predisposition.

The thoughts about the origin of the bruises came in handy, because they distracted him from the fact that his plan had literally been put a stop to. All of the workers had received an injection of the new Beta agent this afternoon and were now to remain in the plant overnight - for observation. He hadn't made it out of the production facility, let alone into town. Tomorrow he would make up for it and get the samples - and himself - to safety.

Obermeier stepped out of the elevator on the second basement floor and entered the residential floor, where private apartments had been set up for the indispensable employees of the facility. They did not shine with comfort, everything was white and sterile, and personal belongings were not allowed either. Obermeier also hated the thought that there was no window. But what could he have seen? The earth beneath the Brandenburg Forest? Watching moles and earthworms at work was likely to be only moderately exciting.

With his key card, he unlocked the door to apartment 21F and entered. Automatically, the lights turned on, and a man-sized panoramic screen generated an image of a sunset on a tropical island. It was a cheap illusion, but it still worked.

Obermeier finally took the cotton ball from the puncture site and threw it into the wastebasket. He critically observed the arm to see if there were any signs of discoloration, but he knew that it was much too early for that. Tomorrow he would know for sure - about the arm, his plan and possibly his future.

He hung the coat, which still had the samples in its pocket, on a hook behind the door and dropped onto the bed. Only now did he realize how exhausted he was and how much the tension of this day had worn away at him. He was glad that he and his actions in the lab had not been discovered. But as long as he was in this facility, that could still happen at any time.

"One thing at a time, Obermeier," he said to himself and closed his eyes. Actually, he only wanted to rest briefly before brushing his teeth, but fatigue overcame him and after a few breaths he was already fast asleep.

As suddenly as the tiredness had come, it disappeared again. Around midnight, Obermeier woke up in sweaty clothes. It was still dark in the room for a few seconds. The room automation system had dimmed the light and switched off the screen after the motion detectors no longer registered any movement.

Now the lighting was turned up again and Obermeier tried to get his bearings. But his vision was blurred, milky streaks ran through his field of vision, as if conjunctivitis were clogging his eye. His throat scratched, he cleared his throat, producing a hoarse croak. Everything felt swollen, as if he'd had an allergic reaction.

Panic rose in him. Were these side effects of the injection? Obermeier heaved himself out of bed and staggered into the bathroom. The light went on, he looked in the mirror and was startled. His eyes were bloody, as if the vessels in them had burst, his lips were thick and blue. He felt the blood rush from his head to his legs and his vision narrowed to a tunnel. His circulation was failing. He had to report this, somehow get up a floor. There was a drug depot there. But he felt that he would not make it there.

Obermeier got down on his knees, crawled out of the bathroom toward the small desk that stood next to the bed and tried to pull himself up. Somehow he had to reach the phone that was up there. He got hold of the cord and pulled. The phone crashed to the floor with a clang. Obermeier punched in zero; that would connect him to the internal switchboard. A voice came on and Obermeier tried to call for help, but nothing more than a harsh whistle came out of his throat.

He made a second attempt, breathing became increasingly

difficult, his tunnel vision narrowed further. He wanted to call out one last time. He did not succeed. His body convulsed, his arms and legs twitched briefly and violently, then he lay still.

The screen on the wall showed a blooming spring meadow in the morning light.

It was late afternoon when Laura approached the WHO headquarters in Geneva. Her cab just passed the small park on the south side of the building complex and then turned off. At the front, the gigantic logo of the World Health Organization was emblazoned on the facade. An Asclepius staff in front of a world map, entwined with a laurel wreath.

On the plane, Laura had had a lot of time to sort out her thoughts and feelings. Most of all, she had been concerned that Hugh hadn't let her in on his plan before he published the article about McDouglas. But as much as this pissed her off, she also knew that this was just his job. And basically, it was none of her business at all. What would she say if Hugh interfered with her work? Well, actually, he had already done that, if she was honest. And continuing to be honest, she was glad he had. In a weaker moment, she might even have admitted that she missed him a tiny bit now that he had left for London and they were no longer working together on this.

The cab stopped in front of the main entrance.

Laura shooed away the thought, paid the driver and got out. She hadn't been here in a long time and had to get a new ID first. Hopefully, the process had not become more complicated.

Fifteen minutes later, Laura knew that nothing had changed here. Neither was there any less bureaucracy than before, nor had the duty roster become more flexible. Now, at just before 5 p.m., most employees knew only one direction - out the door and home.

Laura swam against the tide and made her way toward the labs. There was no point in going to her own office, where she had spent perhaps a total of two weeks over the past three years. The dusty PC and old files were unlikely to have missed her.

Now there was no time to lose if she wanted to achieve anything today. And at the top of her list was to look at the results of the analyses that she and Brauer had commissioned. It was still a mystery to her why she had not received any information about this so far. Had the samples really been a victim of logistics and never made it from Africa to here?

Finally, someone picked up. "Paul?" Hugh asked into the phone, waiting.

A tortured groan came in response.

"Am I speaking with Paul Friedman? Isn't this his number?" Hugh asked.

"He's dead," said a dull but unconvincing voice. "And anyway, who wants anything from him?"

"This is Hugh Stevens, we're colleagues at the Observer, I'm in charge of Africa."

"That's nice. Is Africa as fucked up as the fucking Eastern Bloc?"

"Don't, Paul, I'm calling because I want to ask for your help."

"Oh ho! That's a new one. Someone is asking instead of ordering. Did they fire Adrian Keen or where did this sudden kindness come from?"

"Um ... no, unfortunately not. But I know exactly what you mean. That's why I'm calling. Adrian's not too thrilled with my research, and I need some info from you, if you have any."

"Oh man, I'm going to make some coffee. I just got back from northern Russia yesterday. Keen had me chasing some damn nuclear waste thing that had absolutely nothing to it. Such a waste of my life. Have you ever stayed in a hotel in the Russian countryside? It's really very special."

"I can imagine, I don't think it's much different in Africa in that respect."

"I guess that makes me feel better, to hear it from a fellow sufferer," Friedman said. In the background, Hugh heard the hum of a coffee machine, which died away after a few seconds. "Okay, coffee's starting, now shoot. What can I do for you?"

"I'm doing some research on a messy issue here. It's a pharmaceutical scandal, if you will. Strange cases of infertility have been documented in Mali and the Congo. And after digging a little bit further, I think there's a medical experiment gone wrong here. There was a malaria vaccination study that may be the cause. The manufacturer is a Romanian subsidiary of Keller Pharma."

"Woah, man. You sure talk a lot in the early morning," Friedman remarked, noisily taking a sip from his coffee cup.

"Paul, it's afternoon," Hugh remarked.

"Yeah, yeah, it's afternoon for you, but I just got up, so it's early morning for me. All right, you say there's some nasty pharma shit cooking and now you want me to put out some feelers in Romania to see if anyone knows anything about this company, right?"

"That's right. That would be a great help to me."

"I can do that. But I'll tell you one thing, Romania is a hot place. Just between you and me, I've heard some rumors there that also have to do with dubious medical stuff."

Hugh wondered if he should follow up. Did he even want to hear the rumors? After all, there were enough inconsistencies in his head already. But curiosity won out. "They would be?"

"As I said, they are rumors. I got them from local colleagues. Strangely enough, though, nothing has ever appeared about it in the local papers."

"Now you've got to tell me!" repeated Hugh.

"You remember the big wave of migrants from North Africa? After they closed the routes to Italy, Greece and Turkey, many bypassed them via Eastern Europe. Somehow they made their way thousands of kilometers through Romania, Hungary, the Czech Republic, Poland or who knows what. None of these countries are known for welcoming refugees with open arms, either sending them back illegally, pushing them on to the next country, or interning them in questionable camps."

"I know the reports, but what does any of this have to do with my investigation?" asked Hugh.

"I don't know. You'd have to figure that out for yourself. But the point is: In Romania, probably more people were admitted to these camps than eventually got out. Of course, there were deaths and some simply escaped because the conditions were so catastrophic. But all in all, there are still several thousand people missing. They say they were taken to a clinic for medical care. But first of all, these people were obviously not sick, and secondly, they were never brought back."

Hugh was silent for a moment, thinking.

Friedman spoke up once again. "Well, it's up to you what you think about it. It just came to me when you told me about the medical experiment in Africa."

"Is there any evidence?"

"Listen, if there was hard evidence of this, don't you think I would have made a story out of it myself by now? It's all hearsay. Of course, it sounds implausible, but in my experience, there's always a kernel of truth to this kind of thing."

"I'm afraid that will be the case."

"Well, the assholes on this planet just don't die out. I'll make a few phone calls later and see if I can find out anything about Keller Pharma. I know a healthcare expert in Romania, he's well connected in the industry. Call me back in a day or two, okay?"

"Thanks, Paul, and keep your head up."

## 17

WHO Headquarters, Geneva, Switzerland, Laboratory C, evening of October 3.

Laura slipped on her gown and face mask and entered laboratory Area C in the basement of the WHO site in Geneva. It was not very busy, and she only saw individual employees in the rooms to the left and right of the corridor. At the end of the hallway, she finally found the lab she was looking for: "C11-2" was written on a sign next to the door. Through the glass, she saw that there was only one lab technician left here. He was sitting at a computer with his back to her. She knocked and then entered.

"Hello, I'm looking for Joseph Lang," Laura announced.

The lab assistant, who could hardly be older than 25, turned around and raised his hands apologetically. "Dr. Lang is already gone, I'm the only one who has to work overtime."

"Maybe I should introduce myself first. How rude. I'm Dr. Laura Delille, and I'm working on a project in Mali."

"Rajah Kapoor," the man introduced himself. "I think I read your name the other day, Dr. Delille."

"That makes sense, I had samples sent over. And call me Laura. We can also be on a first-name basis, everyone does that in Africa."

Rajah looked at her with surprise for a moment, as if caught off guard by the offer, then he recollected himself. "Of course. Just call me Rajah."

"And the samples? They should have ended up here, right?"

"I remember them, yeah. That was strange. Dr. Lang had a discussion with Prof. Engstrom about them. I thought I was imagining things. He's never shown his face down here before."

"I know him well and had asked him to inquire. The analysis was very important to me."

"Yes, well ..." Rajah slid back and forth in his chair. "It didn't look like that, honestly. I only overheard in passing, but it almost seemed ..."

"What?"

"It seemed like Engstrom didn't want us to evaluate the samples."

"I can't believe that," Laura replied, but then began to think. Engström had also been unusually reticent in recent phone calls. But why would he do the exact opposite of what she had asked him to do? That seemed absurd to her.

Rajah continued, "The samples have definitely been here. And most likely they are still in the cold room. But I don't think there are any results yet. I'll check on that. One moment." He turned to the computer and made some entries. "It's like I said: everything is still untouched in storage. And there's a note here that processing is on hold until further notice."

Laura felt the anger rising inside her. What the hell was going on here? With difficulty, she pushed down the feeling and forced herself to smile. "Rajah, my friend," she said in the most adorable tone she could manage. "You're working overtime today anyway, what do you say you stay a little longer today and analyze these samples for me?"

"I ... I would do that, but the note! I could get in trouble."

"You won't. They are my samples and I ordered the analysis. What trouble is there to be had here? This is all a simple misunderstanding."

Rajah still looked at her doubtfully.

"It's really all right," Laura affirmed. "The analysis is very important to me. And if anyone makes a fuss about the note, send them to me. I'll take the blame."

Rajah nodded hesitantly. "All right, then. My evening was over anyway. You'll have the results in the morning."

"Thank you! You're my new favorite WHO staff member

from now on." She slipped Rajah a card. "This has my cell phone number on it. Please let me know when the analysis is done. Now I have to go and clear up the misunderstanding with Engström."

Laura left the lab area and stuffed her gown and mask into a prepared container for used clothing at the exit. She pulled her cell phone out of her pocket and looked suspiciously at the display. Why had Engström still not answered? She had already tried to reach him twice by phone and, on top of that, had written him three messages. No answer so far.

She decided against trying again and instead took the elevator up to the executive floor. She wasn't too hopeful that she would find him there, but perhaps his assistant was in the office. She looked at the clock, it was now 5:50 p.m. and the offices were emptying more and more. Against all expectations, she was in luck. The door was open and Johann Engström's assistant was sitting behind her desk. Apparently she was about to leave, because she was packing up her things.

Laura tried to remember her name. Then she spotted the name tag peeking out from just under a folder. Kimberly Watson. She remembered talking to her on the phone. Kimberly had stuck in her mind as a consistently friendly person.

Laura knocked on the doorframe and took a step into the room. "Hello, Kimberley. Is the boss in? I've been trying to reach him all day."

The blonde woman in her mid-thirties looked up. "Then you must be Dr. Delille. There is an entry in the calendar that you were coming. Unfortunately, Johann isn't here. He called in sick. Which is not like him at all."

"Nothing bad, I hope? I really need to talk to him urgently. He's not answering his cell phone, and he's not answering my messages."

Kimberly looked at her silently for a moment, as if considering whether to tell her more. Surely she knew where Engstrom was and if something was amiss.

Laura put on a smile and repeated her sentence, "It's really important. He asked me to come here. And now I can't reach him."

"All right," Kimberly said, "you didn't hear this from me. I mean, actually, the information can be traced pretty easily. He's in the hospital, but not as a patient. His daughter is there, and from what I've heard, she's finally doing better."

Laura could not remember Engström telling her about his daughter's illness in recent times. She knew that she had had health problems at one time, but in recent years Engström had said nothing more about it, and she had assumed that the matter had settled.

"You wouldn't happen to know the name of the hospital, would you?" she asked, looking innocently at Kimberly.

"University Hospital."

"Thanks, I owe you one," Laura commented.

"How many times have I heard that phrase!" retorted Kimberly, stuffing the rest of her things into her bag. Then she turned off her desk lamp. "Do you want me to give you a ride? It's almost on my way home."

"That would be great, thank you."

"No problem." She got up and left the office with Laura in tow.

About 20 minutes later, Kimberly dropped Laura off in front of the hospital. "She's in ward D3, as far as I know. I don't know the room number. But you'll find it."

"Thanks again," Laura said and got out.

By now, the university hospital lay in the twilight. The last remnants of the rust-red sunlight were reflected in the glass parts of the facade. The glittering stripes were repeatedly interrupted by square blocks that the architect had probably deliberately left out and moved the outer wall inward at these points. Thus, the large main building looked almost like a chest of drawers, in which some drawers were missing.

Laura entered the clinic, took a look at the map and then took the elevator to the third floor, where ward D3 was located. She found the ward room deserted. After a minute of waiting, she peeked in and discovered a current occupancy chart next to the door. She leaned forward and squinted her eyes. She felt like a private detective, snooping into things that were none of her business. She found the line she was looking for in the chart: Ariane Engström, Room 3025.

She pulled her head out of the ward room and walked down the hall. The ascending sorted numbers on the doors finally led her to the room labelled 3025.

Laura took a deep breath. She had no idea what was waiting for her behind that door and how Engström would react when she so suddenly invaded his privacy. But there was no way around a face-to-face conversation, this matter was too important and the events surrounding it too strange.

Twice she tapped her fingers softly against the door, then opened it a crack. Engström was standing at the bedside, taking an empty infusion bag from the stand. Apparently he had not noticed her. He threw the bag into a wastebasket next to the rack and turned back to his daughter, who was asleep in bed.

Laura knocked softly on the doorframe once again and entered. This time she was heard.

Engström quickly turned around and looked visibly surprised. He took a step toward Laura and put on a weak smile.

"Sorry, I've been here most of the day," he said. "She just went to sleep. The IV makes you very tired."

Laura nodded. "I see. How come you never told me she was in the hospital?"

"It's not a pretty story, I've had to learn to cope with it."

"What does she have, if you don't mind me asking?"

Engström sighed: "A special form of transthyretin amyloidosis accompanied by polyneuropathy. This is a very rare, progressive neurological inherited disease," he explained. "As of a few days ago, she is participating in a new gene therapy trial, and the results are very promising. Unfortunately, I've been so tied up because of it, sorry!"

Laura didn't know about this particular disease, but knew that genetic nerve diseases were about the worst thing that could happen to you. At the same time, these were probably the most challenging diseases to treat. In the meantime, there were only effective methods for individual hereditary diseases. Everything else merely alleviated the symptoms and delayed the inevitable.

"You know, Laura, I had almost given up hope. But when she opened her eyes and talked to me the other day after her first infusion, I knew there was still hope."

"I'm really happy for you." Laura stepped closer to the bed and looked at the sleeping Ariane for a while. "How old is she now? 16?"

"Almost eighteen," Engström replied. "The best present would be if she could celebrate her eighteenth birthday at home."

"And this therapy is not yet approved, I assume. A trial?" She casually glanced into the bucket containing the infusion bag. It bore only a blank label on which someone had handwritten "#002" and a cryptic number. The latter was probably a coded project or patient identification number. This was not unusual in the course of anonymizing studies.

"I ... well, there's no point in beating around the bush. We were incredibly lucky that Ariane was able to participate, actually the study was already full," Engström explained. "I'm not entirely comfortable with the idea that I may have put a little too much emphasis on my position at WHO to put pressure on her. But ..."

"It's okay, you don't have to justify yourself," Laura said as she continued to look at the bag. Something about it aroused her suspicion. Then she saw it. There was no manufacturer's name, but she recognized a logo. It was a different color than the one she had seen before, but otherwise it was exactly the same symbol. She had last seen this emblem on the patent application of Keller Pharma SRL.

A thick lump formed in her throat. Apparently, this company had made a real breakthrough in the treatment of Engstrom's daughter, a medical sensation perhaps.

But Laura was doubtful there wasn't an obvious downside to all this. She turned to Engström, still undecided whether to yell at him, shake him, or just leave him standing there wordlessly.

Engström apparently noticed her doubtful look, but misinterpreted it. "The treatment is safe, there are virtually no side effects, except for fatigue."

In her pocket, Laura's cell phone beeped and she hastily reached in to mute it. Not wanting to wake Engstrom's daughter, she headed for the door.

Engström followed her out into the hallway.

Laura picked up her cell phone and read the contents of a text message. It came from Rajah, who apologized that the samples to be analyzed could no longer be found. Strangely, this message did not make her angry, but provided the clarity she had longed for. She now knew where she stood.

"Laura, I ...," Engström continued.

"No, let me start. I want to apologize," she said, amazed at how easily this lie rolled off her lips. "I overstepped my authority and ran into a dead end that is no good for me or WHO."

Engström raised his eyebrows, but continued to listen without interrupting her.

"Maybe I wanted variety and misinterpreted things. It could also be that I'm just overworked. But I promise you, this is the end of it."

"I'm happy to hear that. Take some time for yourself, you haven't had a vacation in two years. We need brilliant people like you, but they also need to be fit and resilient."

"Yes, I may have realized too late that I'm burned out. I'm going to visit my family in France and relax. After that, I'll fly back to Mali and stop chasing ghosts."

"That's good. Because I have to say, you look like you've been through it lately."

"I also feel incredibly tired. The best thing for me to do is go to the hotel and get a good night's sleep."

"Submit your leave request and I'll make sure it's approved first thing in the morning."

"Thank you, Johann," Laura said, smiling wanly. Not because she was actually that tired or burnt out, but because she knew that she had just lied coldly, drawing a line under a friendship that had lasted for years.

# 18

*London, England, October 4*

Hugh tossed and turned on the sofa, trying to find a comfortable position. The clock read 4:46 in the morning. With a sigh, he threw the blanket aside and sat up.

This was not a sustainable state of affairs. He could only be grateful to his old buddy Mitch for spontaneously putting him up in London, but his couch left a lot to be desired. Yet there was no other way. If he ran up his expense bill with expensive London hotel rooms, Adrian Keen would be right back on his tail.

Hugh got up and shuffled into the kitchen. After all, Mitch had a fully automatic coffee machine that could make a first-class cappuccino.

While the machine was heating up, Hugh continued to think. He had been thinking for half the night that the pieces of the puzzle didn't quite fit together. He was referring not only to the as yet unproven and largely unbelievable story of the Eastern European correspondent Paul Friedman, but also to the general motives of the suspected masterminds at Keller Pharma.

What was this all about? If this was all just a case of unexpected side effects, the effort to keep it a secret was simply too much. After all, three people had already been murdered. Who would go to such lengths to cover up a medical problem?

Of course, pharmaceutical research cost vast sums and often proved tedious, but was saving money a sufficient explanation? Moreover, a malaria vaccine was only suitable for a limited market, so the expense of such a conspiracy seemed far too great to him. Everything indicated that there was more hidden in the dark and that they had only scratched the surface so far. He and Laura were probably still alive only for that reason. Up to this point, he had been able to suppress quite well the fact that they were in serious danger, the idea that someone could actually be after them seemed too unreal to him. He had viewed Brauer's death, as well as that of McDouglas and his employee, through the glasses of a press representative, who was trying to maintain the necessary professional distance.

But that was working less and less. Now the realization rose from his subconscious that they could be the next to catch a bullet. And he felt responsible for that - even if he had no more stake in the research than Laura did. He liked her. And he felt he should protect her somehow. But how could that be done if you didn't know from whom? He wondered if Laura had accomplished anything yet. He would definitely contact her later, also to find out if she was all right.

The coffee maker signaled with a green light that it was warmed up and ready to go. Hugh placed a large cup underneath and pressed the button. The grinder started moving with a loud rattling sound. A short time later, the machine began to brew the powder, and fresh coffee aroma unfolded in the kitchen.

Hugh sucked in the scent with a deep breath. Now things were looking up. He would put this horrible night behind him, forget the couch, and fly to Romania. He had already found the address of Keller Pharma's Romanian subsidiary. He was sure that there must be people in the vicinity who knew something. You couldn't run a company out of the ground without leaving traces.

He wasn't going to wait for new information from Paul Friedman. He might as well do his own research on the ground and contact him from the road. Besides, the hotels in Romania were likely to be more to Keen's price point. It was also probably a good idea for him to draw attention to himself and for Laura to stay under cover.

Hugh reached for the coffee cup and took a big sip. Yes, things were truly looking up now.

Christian Keller sat in the drawing room of his villa in the Grunewald district of Berlin and enjoyed his breakfast: black coffee, a hard-boiled egg, whole-grain bread. Unlike so many things, Keller loved breakfast as a minimalist.

Actually, he had only started eating anything at all in the morning again last year, after neglecting the meal for years. Too much stress, too many appointments. But health was a precious commodity, and Keller knew very well that a proper breakfast was definitely conducive to physical well-being.

Much had changed in the last two years since he had started working on his manifesto and vision. If he was honest, this new era had begun when his father died and the reins fell into his hands. He had turned the entire corporation around and streamlined it, aligning it entirely with his goal. A goal that would make him immortal. Nothing and no one could prevent this. Keller was just decapitating the breakfast egg when there was a knock at the door to the parlor.

Kurt Kruger entered the room and stood at the other end of the table. In the meantime, he had cut off his shaggy hair and shaved thoroughly, so that he again looked much more civilized and less Third World. Only he couldn't stop chewing gum.

"What a tidy sight, Kruger!" greeted Keller. "Would you like an egg? I can ask Spencer to prepare one for you."

"No. I already ate two hours ago."

"Fine, then at least sit down. Your constant standing around is really getting on my nerves."

Kruger groaned slightly, but grabbed a chair and sat down at the table to the side of Keller. He slid a newspaper across to him.

Frowning, Keller took it and unfolded it. He began to read. After a while, he put the paper down and looked reprovingly at Kruger. "I'm not at all surprised that McDouglas's death is all over the press. I told you it was completely out of fashion to shoot people. You handle something like this discreetly, how many times do I have to repeat that, Kruger?" Keller had grown louder and louder with those last words. He pushed aside his breakfast plate. "You can really ruin a great day, you know that?"

Kruger, who had been silent until now, now spoke up. "Just let me do my job, okay? I know what I'm doing. And it's not to do with anything about McDouglas in the paper, either."

"Then what are you getting at?"

"It's only in this one newspaper. The report about McDouglas has to be firsthand and was not prompted by a police announcement."

Keller picked up the newspaper again. "It says a certain Stephen Humes wrote the article. Have you checked that out yet?"

"Of course, I poked around a bit. It seems to be a pseudonym; the newspaper apparently doesn't employ a Stephen Humes. But who could it have been? Hugh Stevens, he was there with Delille."

"Annoying blowfly," Keller commented.

"Like I said, I would have gotten rid of him and the doctor earlier."

"Don't start that again, I'm really not in the mood."

"The question is what McDouglas told them."

"Figure it out, damn it!" agitated Keller.

"Sure, I will. Stevens has booked a flight to Romania, anyway."

"What does that tell us?" asked Keller.

"That he knows more than is good for him."

"Make sure he realizes that immediately," Keller said.

"It might also be a good opportunity to make him disappear," Kruger added.

"All right, you have my permission to take care of him. But you do it my way. Shooting reporters isn't exactly subtle."

"Still effective."

"Kruger, don't start this again. I'll decide. Maybe this idiot will still be useful to us."

"But I'm advising you, and part of that is asking critical questions," Kruger replied.

"For once, you don't ask, you listen! You fly to Romania and then do exactly what I tell you."

There was a visible layer of dust on Laura Delille's desk at WHO headquarters. This proved that she really hadn't been here for a long time. Why should an unused office be cleaned regularly? In passing, one certainly hardly noticed the dust, but now in the morning light, which shone obliquely through the window, it was particularly noticeable.

Laura took a seat and booted up the computer. She had decided to actually submit a vacation request, if only as a cover. She certainly wasn't going to throw everything away, rush head over heels to France, forget her duties, and end up becoming a winemaker.

She had no aptitude for it anyway.

Instead she opened the database of the European Medicines Agency EMA and started searches for approvals and applications for preparations from Keller Pharma and any subsidiaries. She found all sorts of entries from a wide variety of applications, but not a single note related to the Romanian subsidiary Keller Pharma SRL or to an mRNA-based malaria vaccine. Now the study in Mali seemed all the more suspicious.

Just as Laura was about to check more international directories, her cell phone rang. At first she thought it was Hugh, who should have answered long ago, but when she pulled the phone out of her pocket, she realized it was a Skype video call. The screen showed a photo of her colleague Kimara from the Endurance camp in Mali. She answered the call. The jerky video image took a few seconds to stabilize, then the connection was established.

"Kimara, I'm glad you called, is everything okay with you guys?" asked Laura.

Kimara's expression, however, seemed anything but cheerful. "Laura, it's here! Whatever this plague is, it's reached the camp. The last two days have been terrible."

"Oh damn, what happened?"

"Since you left, there have been three miscarriages. One woman had to go to the hospital, by all accounts she went into a coma. We still have two dozen pregnant women here, I don't know what to do! People are getting restless."

"Slow down, it doesn't mean that everyone will be like this," Laura tried to reassure her colleague, but didn't believe it herself.

"It's not only bad here, I hear nothing but horror stories from Bamako. The rumor mill is bubbling. Have you made any progress? Why isn't WHO doing anything?" Her voice trembled such that it stung Laura's heart.

Yes, why did they do nothing? The thought was unbearable! She swallowed hard. "Kimara, I'm on it. But I don't know how quickly I can get anything done. It remains unclear what's triggering this or how to contain it."

"You have to do something!" demanded Kimara. "I haven't told you yet, but ..." The rest of the sentence was lost in sobs.

Laura guessed how it would end. "You're pregnant," she said.

Kimara nodded. Tears were still running down her cheeks.

"I'm doing everything in my power!" said Laura. "Please believe me."

Kimara calmed down a bit. Then she quietly replied, "I believe you. But I'm afraid that won't be enough."

The connection jerked again and the picture finally froze.

"Shit!" exclaimed Laura, slamming the flat of her hand down on the desk so that the dust just swirled through the air. What the hell was she supposed to do now?

## 19

Iași Airport, Romania, October 4

Hugh Stevens stepped off the Wizz Air plane that had taken him from London Luton to Iași International Airport, far to the east of Romania. The low-cost airline from Hungary did not necessarily shine with the best of comforts, but did offer direct flights from Great Britain to Eastern Europe.

As Hugh descended the passenger stairs and walked across the tarmac to the terminal building, he pulled his cell phone from his pocket and turned it on. He was hoping for a text message from Eastern Europe correspondent Paul Friedman, who had promised to provide more details. But there was no sign of it. The cell phone showed no messages at all. Not even from Laura, whom, contrary to his intention, he had not contacted before his departure.

Probably because he had been afraid that she would talk him out of the tour to Romania or - even worse - insist on coming along. He would not have wanted either. More than ever, he was convinced he'd better keep her out of the line of fire - or at least try. He only hoped that she would not put herself in danger of her own accord.

The compact Iași terminal building was functional and reasonably modern. But the sterile architecture of steel struts and lush glass surfaces betrayed the fact that it must have been built in the early 2000s and could do with modernization again.

Because it was a comparatively small airport, Hugh didn't have to wait long for passport control and luggage. He grabbed his suitcase from the baggage carousel and headed out of the building toward the cab stand. At the very front of the line was the car of a bearded, scowling cab driver who looked as if he would rather eat his passengers than take them to their destination. He also made no move to get out to load Hugh's luggage.

Just then Hugh glanced at the other vehicles farther back in the line to see if their drivers looked friendlier, when the bearded man gave a grunt and asked curtly, "Where to?"

Hugh dug out the piece of paper with the address and showed it to the driver.

"Get in," he grumbled, starting the engine and activating the meter.

While driving downtown, Hugh tried to reach Paul again, but for the umpteenth time got only a voicemail reply. What a work ethic he had! Adrian Keen should take a look at this guy instead of always being on him.

The disgruntled driver drove seemingly haphazardly crisscrossing the city, and Hugh suspected the guy was trying to rip him off by taking the dumbest possible route from the airport to the train station. But there was little point in arguing with this grumpy bear, especially since he didn't know the city.

After about 25 minutes of driving, they stopped in front of a tall office building north of the main station.

Hugh paid the driver and got out. At the entrance to the office complex, he found a conspicuous number of corporate signs. It almost looked like an address for mailbox companies. In any case, Hugh could hardly imagine that a pharmaceutical production facility or even a secret laboratory had been housed here.

At least he spotted the Keller Pharma SRL sign relatively quickly, according to which the company's rooms were on the sixth floor. He entered the building through a large, automatic sliding door and headed for the elevators. What to do once he reached the top, he did not know, but he trusted in his skill to seize the moment.

The entire sixth floor of the building consisted of separate one-room offices, most of which appeared unoccupied.

Through the frosted glass doors, one could see that only a few had lights on. That might have been because it was early afternoon - but even apart from that, everything here more or less underlined an impression of cover addresses and dummy companies.

A feeling of relief spread across him, when he reached Keller Pharma's office at the end of the corridor and he saw that a shadow was moving inside. So at least he hadn't come for nothing.

Hugh knocked on the door, heard an "Intrați!" from inside, and guessed that this was the Romanian word for "Come in." He opened the door and spotted a woman, about mid-20s, sitting behind a gray formica table. She was the only person in the sparse office, which, apart from the desk and two gray filing cabinets, contained only a silver clothes rack.

"Good afternoon, my name is Stephen Humes," Hugh said, putting on a smile. "I've come for the interview."

The young secretary frowned and looked at Hugh in irritation.

"Do you understand me?" added Hugh.

"Yes and no," the woman replied. "I understand what you're saying, but it doesn't make sense. Who did you want to talk to?"

"With your boss, of course! This is Keller Pharma, isn't it? My assistant has made an appointment. I came all the way from London. Now don't tell me that was in vain! You see, I am the editor of the largest British medical journal. You must be familiar with the Medical Times, right? This interview has been planned for a long time!"

"I ..." the obviously startled secretary continued. "This must be a ridiculous misunderstanding. There's no one else here. My job is to answer the phone when it rings and empty the mailbox."

"Then, where is everybody? Are you telling me Keller Pharma has no employees?"

"Yes, of course. But ..."

"But what?" Hugh's voice became sharper.

"Not here," the secretary said meekly.

"That's just great!" exclaimed Hugh further, and began pacing up and down the small office. "I think this is going to make for some really lousy reporting about you. Let the world know what a dump this is!"

"Wait a minute, now listen!"

Hugh stopped and fixed the woman. "I'm listening!"

"There ... there's another location. I've never been there, but I happened to see plans in the mail once. But I don't know if I'm allowed to tell you that." The woman seemed visibly intimidated by Hugh's assertive performance. She hesitated to speak further.

"Get on with it, I don't have all day! I have a deadline to meet and I want to fly back today."

"I ... Wait!" She dug out a notepad and wrote something down. "This is the address, the facility is southeast in a village almost on the border with Moldova. But I can't tell you who you'll find there. It's probably better if, because of the interview ..."

"That's enough for me!" Hugh interrupted her and grabbed the note. "Many thanks, at least Keller Pharma seems to have a competent employee after all. Maybe there's hope yet." He nodded at her, turned around and disappeared from the office.

He hurriedly walked back down the hall to the elevator and headed downstairs. He knew that after this questionable performance as an impostor, he had to leave quickly, before the secretary had time to think about what had just happened and possibly warn someone. Now all he had to do was find a cab - and if possible one with a friendlier driver.

After half a dozen failed attempts, the internet connection to Mali was finally back up. Laura had been struggling for the past three quarters of an hour to establish a stable video chat with the camp. She knew that the reception there wasn't very good and that the network was always unstable. But did it have to break down at this precise moment?

Finally, the client signaled that Kimara was available again. Laura pressed the call button and waited anxiously. It took a few seconds, and then, with a jolt, the face of her African colleague appeared on the screen again.

"Kimara, thank God I'm reaching you. Are you feeling a little better?" asked Laura.

"Yes, I've calmed down. It was all just too much this morning. The situation here is still serious, but I'll be fine."

"Okay, Kimara, that's good. Because you have to do something for me. I know that the conditions in the camp are not ideal for this, but there is no other way. It's really important that we act as soon as possible. Please get me fresh samples from all the women who are showing symptoms of infertility or who have had recent miscarriages. I need blood samples, swabs, and anything else you can do on the fly. There should be another pack of dry ice in the bottom of the freezer in our specimen refrigerator. Pack everything in a Styrofoam box. And express it to me directly at WHO headquarters - addressed to me personally. It's extremely important that this happens today."

"Of course, I will take care of everything," Kimara replied.

"I will personally supervise the analyses. Hopefully, we'll get to the bottom of this mysterious phenomenon," Laura explained. "And please include a few samples from healthy women who have had contact with the patients in question. I'd like to pursue a theory."

Kimara nodded hesitantly. "Sure, I can do that. But why from healthy women? Do you think this whole thing is actually contagious? That it's a plague and it's just a matter of time before we're all infected?" Her voice now sounded more concerned again.

"I really don't know, it's just a theory of mine so far. We need to be extra thorough. Although time is of the essence. Anyway, I will do my best, I promise you."

"I know that. I just don't understand why you don't have a whole department working on this," Kimara replied.

"Well ... the situation here is ..." Laura faltered. "It's a little difficult right now, and not just because of the usual red tape. I think there's something going on here that I don't quite understand yet, and that I can't control. It sounds like something out of a movie, but I don't really know who to trust. It can scare the crap out of you, but I don't have time for that."

"It just sounds crazy," Kimara said. "The whole world has gone crazy. People are nuts, and sometimes it seems to me that nature has now ganged up on us to get rid of us. No wonder if we're wrecking the whole planet."

Laura sighed deeply. "I sincerely hope that's not the case. We'll find a solution all right. Please get to work on this now. Time is short."

"Yes, I'll get right on it. I'll get back to you with the shipment number for the express service. I hope I can get everything to Bamako in time."

"Thank you. And stay strong!", Laura wished her, looking at her colleague silently for a few seconds.

"See you soon," Kimara said. Then the connection was terminated and the video window closed.

Laura glanced at the half-completed leave application still on the screen. She closed the file and pressed delete. They could forget about it. Now was not the time for vacation, but for overtime - in the lab. Once the samples arrived, she would just wait until the regular lab staff had gone home and set about evaluating everything herself.

## 20

Moşna, Romania, October 4

After a cab ride of a good hour, Hugh Stevens arrived in the small town of Moşna, which lay southeast of Iaşi. The driver, who had been almost as taciturn and grim as Hugh's first driver, dropped him off in front of a plain, shabby boarding house. One looked in vain for hotels outside the larger towns, and you had to be glad if you found a place to stay at all.

Before going in, Hugh wanted to get his bearings. He picked up his smartphone and tried to determine the direction. He'd entered the address he'd snagged from the secretary into his map app and found that only a forestry road led there. He turned once in a circle and followed the compass needle on the display to estimate the direction. His destination was in a large patch of forest to the west of here.

By now it was after 4 p.m. and Hugh was considering whether he should leave for the Keller Pharma location today. He would have to walk several kilometers through fields and meadows, since the cab driver had refused to take him to the address mentioned. It would probably be evening by the time he reached the destination.

He wasn't particularly comfortable with the idea of wandering around a Romanian forest at night, but on the other hand, sneaking up on the facility in the dark without being seen would have its advantages.

Hugh pocketed the cell phone, took his suitcase to the boarding house, and checked in.

A white-haired man of about 70 welcomed him with a smile. "Hello, hello, come in!" he called out to Hugh.

To Hugh's delight, the landlord was a lot friendlier than the local cab drivers.

"Good afternoon, I'd like a room," Hugh explained.

"But of course!" said the man, spreading his arms as if to embrace Hugh. "You're in the best accommodation far and wide. Gheorghe will take care of you like a son," he assured him, beckoning Hugh closer. "Follow me, please, and I'll give you the nicest room."

Hugh walked behind the old man and past a dreary breakfast room. He hoped that his room was more attractive than that.

His hopes were dashed, but thanks to his long stay in Africa, Hugh could get along with just about any accommodation. "It's quite wonderful!" he lied and threw his things on the bed.

"Dinner? Gheorghe is a good cook."

"No, no. Thank you. I'm about to leave for another hike. I want to see the beautiful nature. I probably won't be back until late."

"No problem. I'll give you the key to the front door, come back whenever you want. But please be quiet, Ileana is a light sleeper."

"Of course. Quiet is my middle name. You won't hear a peep."

Gheorghe looked at him doubtfully, then dug a bunch of keys out of his pocket and fumbled for one of them. He handed it to Hugh and pointed to the door. "Your room key's there. Breakfast from 7 o'clock, all right?"

"Don't wait up for me. I'll probably sleep a little longer."

"Yeah yeah. Sure. You're on vacation, after all! Let me know if you need anything" Gheorghe turned and left the room.

Hugh packed a light jacket, a notepad and pens, a camera, two water bottles and a couple of candy bars into a backpack. He walked out of the room. He was sure it would be late at night when he returned.

Less than fifteen minutes after checking in, Hugh was already on his way toward the forest, stubbornly following the directions of the navigation app. As a result, he reached the edge of the forest at about 5:45 pm. There was still some distance to go and he estimated that he had sunlight for another hour and a half. The scenery was really beautiful and the weather was a pleasantly dry 22 degrees. Hugh almost forgot for a moment that the purpose of his stay was far less enjoyable than the surroundings suggested.

One question circulated incessantly in his mind: what would he find there in the forest?

He had not yet advanced 500 yards into the interior of the wooded area when he noticed a shadow flitting through his peripheral vision a few rows of trees away. Hugh turned his head slowly in the direction from which he had perceived the movement, but saw no one. Perhaps it was an animal? Hopefully there were no wolves or bears around.

A crackling sound made him spin around.

There was someone standing back there. A man in dark clothes. About 100 meters away.

Hugh's pulse quickened, his mind raced, but he didn't move. Was this a guard? A hunter? Or just a walker after all? With difficulty, he forced himself to remain calm. Nobody knew him here, nobody knew why he was in this forest. So why should this guy want something from him or pose any danger?

On the other hand, the secretary from the office in Iași had possibly warned the colleagues on site.

"Hello, how are you?" the other man called over. Hugh immediately noticed that this individual didn't have a typical Romanian accent, but spoke a much more American-sounding English.

"Um, good. I guess," Hugh replied, feeling ridiculous for making such small talk in his present situation. He was far too energized for that.

"Wonderful day, isn't it?" the man said, coming slowly toward Hugh. "Are you on vacation?"

"I ...," Hugh stopped, wondering if it was too late to run.

"What's the matter, you seem flustered?" inquired the man, who was only 50 yards away.

Hugh realized that he was not wearing a uniform, but a dark green vest with all sorts of pockets sewn on it, and black trousers to go with it, also with extra pockets on the sides. He had a shoulder bag over his shoulder.

"Who are you?" asked Hugh freely now. "You look like an angler.",

The man grinned. Hugh saw that he was chewing gum incessantly as he came closer and closer. "I'm Peter Shanks, and you are?"

"Stephen Humes," Hugh said.

"Ah ha, then we've been officially introduced." Shanks stopped.

For a while, the two men looked at each other.

"So, what are you doing here?" Shanks enquired.

"Vacation. Just time to relax."

"Seems like a good idea to me; you seem pretty stressed."

"I ... have to get going," Hugh explained, pointing down the forest path.

"Yeah, no problem. Let's walk together for a bit." Shanks fiddled with his shoulder bag.

Hugh's instincts told him loud and clear that there was something wrong with this guy, but he just couldn't put his finger on it. So he continued on his way and Shanks walked beside him.

"What are you doing here?" asked Hugh finally.

"Same as you, I guess ... I wander around a bit here and there, enjoying the sunny autumn. Just seeing what I can find. And that's when I find you, isn't that strange?"

"Yes, strange," Hugh repeated.

"A little farther ahead," Shanks began, pointing down the path. "There's an abandoned hall a few hundred yards down. Really spooky. I can't find it in my book, but it's interesting." Shanks now opened his bag, took out a beefy SLR camera with a telephoto lens, and showed it to Hugh.

"A book, you say?" echoed Hugh.

"A coffee table book rather - Abandoned Soviet Heritage. I'm looking for old bunkers and military installations from the time of the USSR. I'm told there was something like that here at one time."

Hugh relaxed slightly. "There's a bunker up ahead?"

"No, no. That's way too new. I don't know what it is. I haven't been in it yet. Before I did, I wanted to get my other lenses out of the car first. But if you want, we can look at it together. That would be a nice change of pace."

Hugh nodded, though he still didn't quite buy Shank's story.

"Sometimes I sell pictures and stories to magazines. There are a lot of people who are interested in old installations from the Cold War days." He looked at Hugh as if he meant him.

"Oh, uh … yes, I would think so," Hugh said.

"Don't you?" asked Shanks.

"Well, maybe a little. I'm not that knowledgeable about history," Hugh lied.

"Never mind. It's just around the bend," Shanks explained, pointing ahead.

They reached a low, almost square building that had been erected in a clearing. It had a side length of about twelve meters and had no windows, only a front door and some ventilation grilles on the sides. On top of the flat roof of the dark gray painted building, one could see outdoor units of air conditioners and a satellite dish.

"This is definitely not a Russian bunker," Hugh said.

"No, they look different. They're so overgrown and dilapidated that sometimes you can barely find the entrance. This may have been an intelligence site, but it's actually too new," Shanks said.

"And it's abandoned?" inquired Hugh.

"Yes. I knocked and went around. No one there. But the door's unlocked." Shanks pointed to the entrance, which had a massive steel door.

"That's pretty strange," Hugh muttered, stepping closer. "Why would someone put in a high-security door and not lock it?"

Shanks shrugged his shoulders and continued to chew gum silently. Then he took a second, smaller lens out of his pocket and attached it to the camera instead of the long telescope. "A wide angle is better inside," he explained, walking past Hugh toward the door.

He stood indecisively a few steps away from the building and thought about what he should do. This was certainly the exact location of Keller Pharma that he had been looking for. However, this strange fellow claimed it was abandoned. Hugh had hoped to surreptitiously gain some knowledge here or find a new lead. If the facility had been abandoned, however, the chances of that were slim. Unless something useful had been left behind. That was one possibility. The other was that this was a trap. That this Shanks had led him here deliberately.

"What is it?" inquired Shanks, who must have noticed Hugh's hesitation. "Nothing will happen. I do this kind of thing all the time," he assured him, opening the door. "There, you see. All dark and quiet. No one here to complain if we look around a bit." He took a flashlight out of one of his many vest pockets and shone it into the hallway.

Hugh took a step forward to get a better look inside.

"Alright, I'll just go in first and check out the situation." Shanks entered the building and the door slowly closed behind him.

Once again Hugh looked around. The forest lay silent and deserted around him. This place seemed deserted indeed. Slowly he walked toward the door and pulled on the massive handle. A strange smell came to him from inside, sweetish and pungent, as if one had tried to fight rot with disinfectant.

He entered the building and saw Shanks standing a few feet down the hall at a box. Then small lights came on in the ceiling.

"I found the emergency lights," Shanks said, waving Hugh over.

Hugh took a few steps toward him. Behind him, the heavy metal door slammed shut, making him wince.

"It's all right, my friend!" shouted Shanks to him. "There's really no one here."

They walked down the hallway, which had locks to about a dozen rooms to the left and right. Some doors were open, others could only be seen through the glass.

Shanks took photos here and there. In most rooms were hospital beds, IV stands, a few low consoles, but all were empty. Some of the adjoining experimental rooms were connected by glass doors or panes set into the wall.

On the ceilings in each room were numerous sensors, vents, sprinklers, nozzles, and even video cameras. A room at the very back looked like a former laboratory, from which all inventory had been removed except for the tables.

In this room, Hugh discovered another filing cabinet with several drawers on the far wall. If there was anything useful here, it might be in there. Hugh took a step inside. Just as he was about to ask Shanks to follow with the flashlight so he could see better, it went pitch black. The lights had gone out.

"Shanks!" shouted Hugh.

No answer.

"This is not funny! Turn the lights back on." Hugh listened tensely into the silence, but could hear nothing but his own increasingly rapid breathing.

"Shanks!" he shouted again, fumbling for his cell phone to activate the LED light on it. But before he had fully pulled it out of his pocket, a violent blow struck him on the back of the head. Hugh saw only flashes of light dancing on his retinas. He staggered, hit a wall, and sank to the floor.

Christian Keller put the fish cutlery aside and dabbed the corners of his mouth with the fine cloth napkin. "Did you also enjoy it?" he asked his counterpart.

The petite blonde nodded and brushed back a strand of her almost unnaturally golden hair. "You have fabulous taste in all things. In restaurants, in cars, in fashion," she said.

"And with women, dear Rebecca. More wine?" He reached for the bottle that stood ready in a cooler.

Again Rebecca nodded, and Keller poured her another glass. The bottle of Château d'Yquem cost almost 500 euros at Keller's favorite posh Fin de Siècle restaurant, but he thought the wine was worth it. And that still made the bottle cheaper than Rebecca, who was truly well compensated for her services. Whether her fee was really appropriate would become clear after the meal.

A vibration in Keller's pocket snapped him out of his thoughts. "Sorry," he said, picking up the cell phone. The display showed a message from Kruger.

"Mission accomplished according to plan, awaiting further instructions."

A smile crept across Keller's face.

"Not another woman, is it?" asked Rebecca in a playfully offended tone.

Keller laughed. "No, no. Just the work. But don't worry, we won't be bothered again tonight." He pocketed the cell phone. "A dessert? Or do we want to skip that?"

## 21

Former Keller Pharma site, Romania, October 5.

Hugh awoke in absolute darkness. His head was pounding and his mouth felt as if it had been filled with sand. He lay on his side in a contorted position and took a while before he could stir himself to some extent. His limbs ached and were stiff from lying on the hard floor for so long. He was freezing cold.

Only slowly did the memory creep back, where he was and what had happened. He reached for his cell phone, which was still halfway in his pants pocket. With shaky fingers, he pulled it out. It slipped from his hand and slammed to the floor. The thud echoed eerily through the empty plant. Hugh groped around on the floor, finally sensed the device and picked it up. The display came to life and seemed so bright after the long darkness that Hugh had to squint his eyes. He opened the menu and activated the flashlight function.

The room lit up in spots and Hugh was able to get his bearings. He was still lying in the lab he had last entered and had been knocked out in. The back of his head throbbed and he felt for the spot. In the back right he found a large bump and felt dried blood in his hair.

"Son of a bitch," he growled, examining himself for more injuries. It was hard to establish how he was doing, because somehow just about everything hurt. But it seemed the rest of him was fine.

Upon examination, he discovered that the sleeve of his sweater had been pushed up on his left arm. This one was particularly painful. And now Hugh realized why. Right in the crook of his arm, a bruise had formed around a small puncture. He felt it.

"Shit," he breathed. It looked as if blood had been drawn from him. Or even worse: he'd been injected. Had he been drugged? No, the bump on the back of his head proved that he had been knocked out. But what had happened then? And why this puncture? What had this Shanks, or whatever his name was, done to him?

Hugh struggled to get to his feet. Dizziness overcame him, and he had to hold on to the door frame. Then he stuck his head out into the hallway and called out, "Hey, is anybody there?"

No response.

He looked at his cell phone again, the clock showed 11:22. Almost 18 hours since he had entered this building! He had been knocked out in an exemplary manner.

On the floor next to him was his backpack, the zipper was open. Hugh checked the contents, which still seemed intact. He grabbed one of the water bottles and drank it down greedily. The sticky, dry feeling in his mouth improved somewhat, but the chill in his body remained, as did a slight dizziness. He should probably see a doctor. He'd have had caught at least one mighty cold after that night on the cold floor - if not worse. But for now, he had to get out of there. Hopefully the door of this bunker was open! If not, he'd been dealt a bad hand.

His eyes fell on the filing cabinet that had caught his attention before the lights had gone out. Hugh crossed the empty lab and pulled open the drawers one by one. They were all empty.

"What a bloody mess!" he cursed, slamming the drawers shut with all his might and kicking his foot so hard he almost lost his balance again.

The cabinet bounced a few inches to the side and Hugh caught sight of a white corner peeking out from under it. He got down on his knees and pulled at it. It was a single sheet of paper that had probably accidentally ended up under the cabinet instead of inside.

He couldn't do much with the contents; they were obviously lab results with all sorts of values that meant nothing to him. However, there was a line at the top of the sheet that he understood: "Keller Pharma SRL - Project Alpha, Phase 1 - Findings Day 16, Subject 109."

Hugh folded up the sheet and stowed it in his notebook. Then he closed the backpack and put it on. Let's get out of here!

Gheorghe looked at Hugh as if he were a ghost. The landlord of the boarding house even crossed himself. "What on earth happened to you?" he asked, visibly concerned.

Hugh slowly approached the small counter in the front room of the boarding house. After the previous night, the way back had seemed three times as long and arduous as the way there. He had to look pathetic, even more so with the bloody wound on his head.

"It's all right," he assured. "I fell in the woods and passed out. It's not so bad, I just need to rest a bit."

Gheorghe nodded tentatively, but did not look convinced. "But ..." he started and fell silent again. "I'll ask Ileana to make you some soup. We can also call a doctor. But you'd better lie down first. I'll bring you a double-brined tuica in a minute, it's our national drink and helps against everything."

"Thanks, the doctor thing definitely doesn't sound bad," Hugh said. "I'm pretty knackered." He shuffled upstairs to his room and closed the door behind him. His eyes fell on the mirror of the laundry nook, which was next to the door, and he shuddered. Now he knew why Gheorghe had reacted that way. His skin was deathly pale and his eyes were blood red, as if various veins had burst in them.

"Shit, I look like a fucking alien zombie," Hugh whispered.

The parcel service took its time - an unbearable amount of time, which Laura basically didn't have. All that morning, she had repeatedly checked the tracking information of the overnight express online and begged the driver to please hurry. But the shipment from Mali had been sent in the "Express 17" variant, which meant that the package had to be delivered by 5 p.m. at the latest. In this case, the driver seemed to mercilessly push the deadline to the last minute.

If Laura hadn't been so eager to finally get some results, she could have just sat back and waited, but she was too busy for that. The fact that she wouldn't have had a chance to hijack the lab before the regular staff had gone home couldn't change that. Her tension was growing with every hour, and doing nothing was slowly driving her crazy. Besides, she had been careful all day not to accidentally run into Engstrom. He might ask why she hadn't taken a vacation as arranged. Or why she was still here at all. After all, her current place of work was Mali.

Laura's thoughts drifted off while she now - shortly before 5 p.m. – wandered a little through the entrance hall of the WHO headquarters. The sad face of Kimara from yesterday came back to her mind. She simply had to accomplish something. She owed it to her and to the other women who had fallen victim to this insidious phenomenon.

At 16:57, the parcel service finally turned the corner. Laura stepped out the door and intercepted the driver, who was just getting out. "A package for Laura Delille?" she asked, holding out her arms.

"Yeah, right. And sorry, the traffic was hell!", the driver apologized and scanned the barcode.

"Yeah, yeah. That's all right. Give it here."

"Here you go. Sign here." He held out the scanner and a display pen to her.

"Sure." Laura scribbled her signature on the device, turned and left the driver standing there.

Shortly after five, the flow of employees going home for the day swelled again in the building. Laura got into the elevator with the package under her arm and rode down to the basement, where Lab Area C was located.

There, too, the mood was one of departure, with the lab technicians and doctors getting rid of their coats and slipping into their everyday clothes.

Laura waited impatiently in the hallway until the hustle and bustle died down and then grabbed the prescribed equipment herself to work in the lab.

Room C11-2, where she had asked for the results of the first samples two days ago, she found deserted. She placed the package on a stainless steel table in the center and took an overview of the available equipment and utensils, which were placed on work consoles all around the walls. She should have found everything she needed to evaluate the samples.

Then she grabbed a pair of scissors and cut open the package along the adhesive strips. Inside the cardboard package was a sealed Styrofoam box. Again, Laura loosened the tape and removed the lid. Several flat plastic jars, sachets, and different colored blood collection tubes were revealed. All of them were numbered and additionally labeled with the patient's name and age.

She took out all the containers and sorted them on the table according to the respective sample type so that she could then analyze them in the most time-efficient way possible.

"Excuse me, please," she heard a voice and was startled. She turned to the door.

"What are you doing, if you don't mind me asking?" It was Rajah, the young lab assistant whom she had met here the other day.

Laura tilted her head. "What does it look like to you?"

"It looks like you're trying to do some kind of analysis here."

"What if it were?"

"Then I guess I'd have to tell you that's not allowed. You're not allowed to work independently in the labs. If Dr. Lang finds out!"

"You're not going to rat me out, are you? After all, I had to fly in new samples especially because you lost the old ones in a very unusual manner!" Laura's voice now sounded blatantly reproachful.

Rajah put on a pained expression. "It really wasn't my fault," he defended himself. "Our department has never lost anything before."

"Then the case is all the stranger, isn't it? So, what is it now?" Laura inquired.

Raja looked back and forth between Laura and the stacks of samples on the table. His face reflected a mixture of discomfort and regret. "So ... then there is only one correct solution. I have to do the analyses. But I'm only doing this to restore the department's reputation."

Laura didn't really want to involve Rajah in this, now that she knew how dangerous this was. But on the other hand, the analysis would be much faster and more precise if he helped her. Not only did he have a better routine, but he was also more familiar with the available equipment.

"Thank you," she said, pointing to the arsenal of samples. "That's going to be some overtime."

"Oh, I'm used to that," Rajah said, picking up a bag of blood samples. "We'd better get right to it."

## 22

Hôpitaux universitaires de Genève, Geneva, Switzerland, October 6.

Johann Engström sat next to his daughter's bed in the university hospital and watched the rain pattering against the window panes from outside. It was late morning, but the sky was so gray that it might as well have been just before sunset.

Last night, he had given Ariane the third and, for the time being, last infusion of Keller Pharma's experimental gene therapy. How many more would be needed later was written only in the stars. His contact had made it very clear that they would be necessary. Engström hated this state of affairs. He hated the dependency he had gotten himself into. Basically, they were blackmailing him by putting their finger in the most painful of wounds. Ariane was now so much better that she would be released in a few days.

That should have been reason enough for Engström to rejoice. But deep inside himself, he realized: The pain was still there. It had only changed. At what price had he bought Ariane's health?

The analyses of Laura Delille, of which he had learned this morning, suggested that the price was very high. Much too high! He was guilty, and for personal reasons. It was unforgivable.

How far would Laura go? And how much further was he allowed to go? It had been a convenient illusion to believe that she would give up now and stay out of it. He knew her far too well to take that seriously, but he had probably just hoped that it would be so.

He could not protect her if she sank deeper and deeper into this swamp, in which he himself had no idea exactly what monsters were hiding. He only knew that these monsters had long since sunk their claws into his flesh and were not thinking of letting go.

The sinister plot he had been drawn into turned out to be much bigger than he could have ever imagined. It had been a huge mistake to get involved with these people, but on the other hand, his heart told him: How could it be wrong to want to save his own daughter from a creeping death?

Engström turned away from the window and now realized that Ariane had long been awake and was looking at him.

"What's wrong?" she asked, "And please don't lie, I've been watching you for a while and I can see that something is bothering you."

"Oh, just work!" said Engström. "So much has been left undone, it weighs on me."

He saw the skeptical expression in her eyes, but was grateful that she did not inquire further. It seemed completely impossible to him that he would tell her what he had done. He put on a smile. "So, now I'm back to you. Let's plan your birthday!"

Laura had been busy all morning evaluating the results of the lab tests from yesterday's late shift. She and Rajah had been working on the equipment until shortly before midnight in order to be able to perform as many analyses as possible while the samples were fresh.

Even before the final results of all the tests were available, it had only confirmed what she already knew, namely that they were dealing with something as mysterious as it was dangerous. Not because they had discovered a highly contagious pathogen, but because there was still no trace of one. However, judging by the increasingly rapid spread of the disease, there should be one.

Only the analysis of a sample of breast milk that Kimara had spontaneously packed in the package provided the decisive clue. In addition to the usual components, it also contained unusual lipid nanoparticles that were well camouflaged but could only be of artificial origin. Now the detailed analysis of these apparently self-decomposing particles was available. They contained mRNA strands and virus-like DNA components.

Laura knew immediately where she had last read about such a combination: in the patent documents Keller Pharma SRL had filed for its malaria vaccine. Residues of such a vaccination in breast milk or blood would have been explainable if the women whose samples she was analyzing here had participated in the still obscure study in Mali. But none of them had been involved in it as subjects. It should therefore be impossible that traces of the active substances used were found in them. But that was clearly the case, as has now been shown.

Laura had been waiting for hours for the results of the extended analyses she had initiated last night - on the one hand a breakdown of the mRNA strands and on the other hand a PCR-based analysis of the remaining samples for traces of the mRNA found in the breast milk. They were not yet available, and Laura would have preferred to join Rajah downstairs in the lab, but she couldn't do that if she didn't want to come under the scrutiny of the lab manager, Dr. Lang. So she had to wait, hanging around, at least until 5:00 p.m.

In the meantime, Laura had already reviewed several studies that showed lipid nanoparticles to be "non-cytotoxic" and thus considered cell damage to be very unlikely. She was also able to find several other preparations and vaccines that used such lipids as transport vehicles for the substances that were actually effective. These so-called adjuvants made it possible for the vaccine to reach its target and achieve the desired effect. The nanoparticles helped to cross cell membranes without the active substances being degraded in the process.

Now Laura asked herself the all-important question: Was she dealing with the disastrous side effects of a vaccination study that had gotten out of hand, or was it just a cover? She suddenly remembered the old science fiction movie Hugh had mentioned at the Mali camp about human birth control by aliens. That was exactly the kind of thing that could be accomplished with a compound like this – assuming you could control the effect. Had Keller Pharma really brought something so monstrous into the world?

The fact that the cases seemed to spread relatively uncontrollably suggested against this, but this impression could well be deceptive.

Her thoughts slid back to Hugh. She felt bad that she hadn't contacted him in so long. On the other hand, he could have contacted her.

She jumped up. Hopefully nothing had happened to him! Hastily, she picked up her cell phone and dialed his number. It rang for a long time, then a sleepy, raspy voice that Laura almost didn't recognize answered.

"Hugh? Is that you?" she asked.

"Yeah, who else? Sorry, I was asleep, I feel pretty bad."

"What's going on? Where are you?"

"I have a confession to make," Hugh said.

"That would be? Tell me!"

"I flew to Romania to track down this company that produced the vaccine."

"Are you crazy? You know what happened to McDouglas."

"That's why I flew alone," Hugh explained.

Laura didn't answer immediately, trying to understand what he meant. Then she piped up, "Because you didn't want to put me in danger? That's thoughtful, but I can already take care of myself!"

"Be glad you weren't there."

"What happened?"

"I was at the facility where they apparently developed this stuff. Or at least tested it."

"Shit, Hugh!"

"It was abandoned, but ... I still can't believe I was so stupid ... There was this guy, a guy named Shanks. Supposedly a photographer. He was at the facility, too. And then... I think he knocked me out."

"Are you hurt?"

"A laceration to the back of the head and ... I don't know, I feel sick. I was lying on the cold floor for ages. But that's not all, I have a puncture on my arm, like they drew blood. Either that or they injected me with something."

"Have you been to the doctor?"

"The landlord of my boarding house brought in a country doctor who looked half dead himself. He gave me aspirin. That doesn't help much. But I'll be all right," Hugh assured her.

"I hope so! The best thing would be for you to go to a hospital or come here right away, the University Hospital in Geneva is top-notch. And we'd best discuss what to do now. I have some new findings."

"I also want to show you something urgently. It's a document I found in the facility. I guess it's a lab report from the series of tests they did here. I can't do anything with the values, though."

"Send me a picture of it, please! I had samples come in from Mali and now I know what to look for." She paused for a moment before continuing. "Hugh, I think we should warn people. The situation in Africa is getting worse all the time, and this thing is spreading. I know I was totally against publishing at first because I didn't want to start a panic, but now ..."

"You mean we have enough to nail these pigs?"

"I hope so. But that's not the point, we have to make sure this doesn't spread any further."

"We can try, but my feeling is that we're trying to catch up to events that are already ahead of us."

"Then we'll just have to run faster and overtake them. I'll go back to the lab right after this to do the rest of the evaluations and validate the results. After that, we'll take it to the public."

"Okay, I'll try to get a flight for tomorrow morning. Hopefully I'll still be alive then," Hugh said.

Laura knew it was meant jokingly, but the way Hugh had said it scared her. What if they had injected him with some kind of poison? She reflected. "I don't think there's any question about that. Get your butt over here, Maverick!"

"As you command," Hugh replied. "Until tomorrow!"

Kurt Kruger sat in his sparse factory loft in Berlin and zoomed in on the photo on the screen that had just been transmitted. It showed a white sheet with laboratory values.

Then Kruger started playing a phone recording that also came from the spy software he installed on Hugh Stevens' phone yesterday.

Until just now, he had been quite satisfied with how the operation in Romania had gone. That idiot Stevens had let himself be easily lured into the trap out of sheer curiosity. Thus he was able to implement Keller's orders effortlessly.

But as it now turned out, something had been overlooked in the liquidation of the site in Romania. This gave Hugh Stevens an advantage that had not been calculated. How big it would be, Kruger could not judge, he could not do anything with the laboratory values on the note, but he would have to report it to Keller.

And he certainly wouldn't be holding back on his opinion that none of this would have happened if, instead of injecting Stevens with a double dose of Alpha, he had simply picked him off in the woods and buried him.

He continued to follow the recording of the telephone conversation with Laura Delille. Kruger did not particularly like its content either. They would have to act immediately if they didn't want the plan to falter at the last few meters. That things were as sound as Keller always affirmed, he did not believe. Doubt and skepticism were as much a part of Kruger as his innate senses. And Christian Keller, despite - or perhaps because of - his brilliance, also tended to overestimate himself. But one was never allowed to tell him that if one intended to continue in his service. And that was what Kruger intended to do.

There was no turning back in this endeavor. Either you were on the right train and would soon be able to enjoy all the comforts you wanted. Or one sat on that train which would drive through, without stop, to its final destination in the forecourts of hell. Getting off the speeding train was no longer an option in either case.

## 23

WHO Headquarters, Geneva, Switzerland, evening of October 6.

Laura was just about to turn off her computer in the office and go down to the lab floor when there was a knock. She called out, "Come in," and the door opened.

Johann Engström entered, followed by a second man with a half bald head in a white coat. She did not know his name, but she had seen him briefly yesterday in the corridor outside laboratory Area C. He and Engström both had the same unhappy, annoyed expression on their faces.

"What were you thinking, Laura?" asked Engstrom reprovingly.

"About what? What's going on?" she replied, feigning innocence, but suspected that it was about her secret night shift in the lab. That other man was most likely lab manager Dr. Joseph Lang.

He spoke up. "Our security policies are there for a reason!" he blurted out angrily. "Do you think it's a joke that Rajah Kapoor had to be quarantined?"

"Slow down, slow down," Engström intervened. "Let's talk this through calmly." He pointed to two chairs.

Dr. Lang puffed contemptuously, but sat down.

"What do you mean, quarantine? What for? We've taken all safety precautions," Laura stammered, defending herself. "I know I shouldn't have been involved, but time is of the essence. Especially after the first samples disappeared in a strange way, Dr. Lang!"

"Stop deflecting," he replied. "This is about Ebola."

"Ebola?" repeated Laura in amazement. "That's absurd! The samples are from my camp in Mali. If there was Ebola there, we would know about it."

"Nevertheless, there was a contamination alert in lab C11-2 because of your samples!"

"When? There should have been an alarm much earlier."

Lang looked at her with narrow eyes. "There was. I'm accusing you of ignoring it. No, that you suppressed it even!"

Laura looked confused in the direction of Engström, who had lately just been sitting silently. "What's going on here?" she asked him.

"The documentation of the lab's systems support that conclusion," he said tersely. "It was a false alarm. Otherwise, we'd hardly be sitting here without protective suits."

"It's still bullshit!" agitated Laura. "Of course we don't have Ebola in the building. But there was no alarm either. We're dealing with something else entirely."

"With what, may I ask? What were they so secretly analyzing down there? And what did you tell Rajah to keep him so persistently silent?"

"He had nothing to do with it. I asked him to work overtime and he couldn't say no. That's all."

"That doesn't answer the question," Lang insisted. "That's my lab you've been messing with."

"That's enough! We haven't done anything wrong."

"I don't see it that way!" objected Lang.

Engstrom slowly raised his hand to stop the argument. "Okay, we'll have to talk about this again. But for now, we're glad it was a false alarm and Rajah is not infected. Still, I'm going to have to ban you from the lab. You will now take a few days off, no arguments. And after that, we'll discuss possible consequences."

"We don't have a few days, Johann," Laura said. "And I think you know that! Why are you interfering with my investigation?"

"That's enough now," Engström replied sharply. "You're overworked! And now on leave until further notice, for at least two weeks. I don't want to see you here after tomorrow." He stood up and walked toward the door.

Dr. Lang followed him with a barely suppressed victorious smile on his lips.

Laura didn't care what the idiot thought. God knows she cared about other things than the ego of a pedantic lab director.

After Engström and Lang left her office, she dug a USB stick out of the drawer and plugged it into her computer. Then she copied all the lab results that were available. These would now have to suffice, because she could not get to the results of the detailed analyses that had recently been initiated. Lang had blocked her access to them. And now that Rajah was also under observation, there was no chance to get them any other way.

While the data was being transferred to the stick, she once again picked up the smartphone that contained the image file Hugh had sent her. On the small display, the contents of the photographed sheet could not be seen very well, so she now connected the cell phone to the computer as well. She transferred the photo to the PC and opened it there in full size with an image viewer.

It was now 7 p.m., and Laura's office was the only one on the entire floor that was occupied at this time. She was still poring over the data Hugh had sent her and comparing it to the lab results. The document from the Romanian facility not only proved that the site did indeed belong to Keller Pharma, but it finally gave the whole thing a name: Project Alpha. That was probably little more than a cryptic code name, but it allowed certain conclusions to be drawn.

Why should there be such secrecy if this was a regular research project? Also, the tests conducted by the laboratory at the facility did not fit a malaria drug or a vaccination that was supposed to protect against infection with the associated pathogen. Such tests would have looked quite different.

Here, fertility factors had been searched for, the efficiency of various mRNA fragments had been determined and these had been compared with target values, the origin of which Laura could not exactly assign without further data. It was clear, however, that the test subject, whose results were noted on the sheet, had reached these target values and even exceeded them in parts.

Above all, the fertility markers that were searched for, all of which were at the lowest level, allowed only one conclusion. The main purpose of the drug used in Romania was not to vaccinate someone against a disease, but to make them infertile. This was exactly the proof they needed. The definite proof which would be the core of the publication. As soon as Hugh Stevens arrived here tomorrow morning, they could set everything in motion.

Hugh pushed up his dark sunglasses and waved at the stewardess. He had bought the glasses before departure in a small store at the airport in Iași so that his zombie eyes would not be seen. He was too irritated by the looks he received - from passers-by, from vendors, even from the usually impassive cab drivers. It had gotten a little better since yesterday, but it would be quite a while before the burst veins disappeared.

The stewardess came to his seat and Hugh ordered an orange juice. He had an unquenchable thirst. At least the fever he had suddenly developed last night had disappeared by the morning, so he could actually start the trip to Geneva.

Apart from the red eyes, the symptoms reminded him strongly of those he had received during his first flu shot. Those had also been short and severe, rather than long and sluggish as in a real infection. This suggested definitively that he had been injected with something in the plant to which his body reacted with defensive measures.

If he could get his hands on that wretched Shanks, he would love to beat that information out of him. But honestly, he had to admit that he felt too groggy for that.

Now the stewardess returned and placed the juice on the

small folding table in front of Hugh. "Is there anything else I can get you? An aspirin, perhaps?" She smiled.

"Thanks, I've already popped enough Romanian aspirin. But feel free to bring me more orange juice, I'm in desperate need of vitamins." He drank the cup in one go and handed it back.

The stewardess nodded and walked back down the aisle to the service area.

He hoped vitamins would help restore him, but doubted it would do much good. Whatever they had given him was certainly a pretty nasty thing. He was probably lucky he hadn't met the same fate as Brauer or McDouglas.

Nevertheless, there had to be a reason that he was still alive. Because, as he realized more and more, the opportunity to make someone disappear had been ideal there in that remote Romanian forest.

Hugh shooed the thought away and opened his laptop instead. Immediately he started the word processor and began to write.

He had gotten away with it once again for now, but an uneasy feeling inside him told him he'd better hurry up with his story anyway.

A cell phone ringing jolted Laura out of her sleep. With difficulty, she rolled over in the hotel bed and looked at the alarm clock next to the bed: 9:32 a.m.

So late already! That meant she had slept far longer than intended, but the two late shifts of the last few days had taken their toll. She fished the phone off the nightstand and looked at the display. It showed that the call was from Howard McDouglas.

Immediately she was wide awake. That couldn't possibly be! Laura overcame her initial confusion and answered the phone. "Dr. Laura Delille," she answered hesitantly.

"Yes, hello," a woman's voice came forward. "I'm not sure where to begin. Well, I'm Nicole ... McDouglas. Maybe you already know, but my Uncle Howard passed away, and the funeral is in two days."

"Hello ... Nicole," Laura said now. "I'm so sorry for your loss. Your uncle was a great man. I didn't know him particularly well, but it's a tragedy."

"That's definitely true - still a very mysterious thing. You know, I can't understand all this," Nicole commented. "The police just gave me back his cell phone, and I'm informing everyone who's in it. And you're the last person he spoke to. Well ... I don't know. Actually, I just want to know why this had to happen ... Who killed him."

"Nicole, I'm terribly sorry about this. I don't know what to say. He was murdered, there's no question about that. And it's true, I did talk to him. We were still with him the night before he died, and the next day the police questioned us - me and Hugh Stevens, a journalist I work with."

"You were there?" asked Nicole in surprise.

"Didn't the police tell you that?"

"Oh, you can forget the police! First they don't tell you anything, supposedly for investigative tactical reasons, and then they quietly stop working."

Laura thought for a moment about what she could say to Nicole that might help or be a comfort to her, but she couldn't think of anything better than, "We'll get these guys."

"What do you mean you want to get those guys? I thought you were a doctor, a colleague? Do you know who's behind this? You have to tell me!" Nicole now sounded visibly agitated.

Laura continued with emphatic calm. "I'm a doctor, that's true. But I wasn't a colleague. I came across your uncle by chance because he ..." She paused for a moment. "Because, from the looks of it, he was actually involved in something bad. I couldn't believe it either because Professor McDouglas taught at my university and was considered an outstanding mind, but the facts are stacked against him. His work ..."

"What did he do? You know?" Nicole interrupted her.

"Not exactly, no. He was killed before he could explain it to me. But he wanted to tell me. Apparently, doubts had come to him about the project. But now everything he was working on seems lost."

Laura waited for an answer from Nicole, but only silence came from the phone. "Nicole? Are you still there?"

"His work, you say? If it's really about that, maybe there's something ..." she continued.

"What do you mean?"

"In his will. I am the sole heir. He left me his castle, his savings and investments, but also his life's work."

"You have his research?" asked Laura in surprise.

"No, I don't. I have a key card. It belongs to an archive where he apparently stored everything he ever created."

"Nicole, this could be insanely helpful! We need to see if there's anything in there about the last project. It's very dangerous, and time is of the essence."

"I'm standing here in a house with blood stains on the floor that can't even be completely wiped away. So I can guess that it's dangerous. If it wasn't, I wouldn't be in this situation. And yes, it can scare the crap out of you! Luckily, I'm a Highlander."

"I'm sorry, I know this is all extremely difficult. But time is getting short. Will you give me access to his work?"

"It's not that easy. This particular archive is in Iceland, I know that by now from Wikipedia. It says it's part of a global science project run by a foundation. They've built a self-sufficient facility there with a digital library, research archive, cold rooms and computer center. Everything is completely powered by geothermal energy. The scientific heritage of mankind is to be stored there in a disaster-proof manner. In his will, my uncle wrote that he wanted to preserve his entire work for posterity and keep it for all time."

"Then this seems to me to be the best place for it. And this key card gives you access, I assume?"

"That's what the will says."

"I have to go there," Laura insisted.

Silence spread again, so Laura continued, "Nicole, I know we don't actually know each other. I can only ask you to trust me. People's lives literally depend on it."

"I'll fly there, after the funeral," Nicole said. "If you promise me that's how we'll find out who killed him, I'll take you with me."

"I can't promise that. And I won't lie to you. But I promise that I will do everything I can to see that you get justice. The same people killed a colleague of mine. All the clues lead to a company called Keller Pharma, which filed patents with your uncle. But it all seems to have been a cover. What is clear is that if we don't find a way to stop this, more people will die."

"Okay, I'm going to let you go to the archives and you can look for what you need there. Whatever Howard did, I hope we can do something about it."

"I hope so, too. Thanks. Let's talk again later, okay?" Laura said goodbye, hung up and went to the window to pull aside the curtains. Outside, the sun was shining again after yesterday's rainy day.

Laura had about two hours until she had to pick up Hugh at the airport. Then they would go on the offensive.

## 24

Keller Villa, Berlin-Grunewald, October 7

Christian Keller had just injected himself with the third infusion of the Beta agent and was now clearly feeling the invigorating effect - stronger even than after the last two injections. He was almost intoxicated by his own invention.

"Come closer, try Dr. Keller's miracle elixir!" he shouted, as if he were at a fair, and finally burst out laughing. Too bad there was no audience in his library to applaud him.

Keller almost felt like he was in an old novel. But this was reality. There in the syringe that still lay on his desk had been no alchemical concoction, no magical tonic with which to extract money from the pockets of gullible idiots.

This was a milestone in medicine! A real miracle elixir, except that it was produced on the basis of the most modern medical procedures. Nevertheless, it would make people money - a lot of money, in fact. And his preparation would deliver on its promise. No more aging, but a multiplication of life expectancy, if not immortality. Who wouldn't give away their entire fortune for something like that?

It had been a long, arduous journey until this exclusive preparation reached maturity, and this had to be rewarded accordingly.

Keller thought of Howard McDouglas, whose doctoral student he had once been and who had discovered, as if by chance, the mechanism that had made this triumph possible. He almost regretted a little that his former professor could not live to see a new world order take shape. But there was no place in it for doubters, pessimists and prophets of doom. And just as little for fools. It was good that this old fool could no longer stand in the way of the final goal. Nothing and nobody could! There was a knock at the door and Keller turned. "Come in!" he called loudly.

The door swung open and his butler, Spencer, entered. "Dr. Harding is here. Are you willing to see her? The lady gets quite enervated if you keep her waiting. I can send her away, though."

"It's all right. I'm expecting her."

"Whatever you say. Would you like me to dispose of that for you?" Spencer pointed to the empty syringe.

"Please."

Spencer grabbed the syringe with two fingers of his gloved right hand and carried it out of the room as if it were a delicate object.

Keller was amused by his servant's old-fashioned English manner, but he also appreciated it. A few moments later, Dr. Harding appeared in the doorway. In her hand, as last time, she carried a small suitcase.

"It's commendable that you always deliver the supplies personally," Keller greeted his site manager.

"Indeed. I'm an exemplary employee, very conscientious," Harding explained in a tone that was hard to interpret. It could just as easily be ironic as serious.

Keller hated this quirk in her, preferring clarity in his counterpart's expression. "Put it on the table," he instructed her. "I'll put everything in the freezer myself."

"Well, you can guess that I'm not just coming to drop off some shots."

"Didn't we have this conversation last time? Judging by the look on your face, you're trying to talk me into it again."

"To do that, I would have to assume that you have a conscience, but that would certainly be a mistake."

Keller had to grin. "Point taken. So, what's up?"

"I wanted to talk to you earlier, but you haven't been to the facility in days."

"Well, I've been busy, I run a corporation after all. That's why I have you, to take care of the site."

"I do. But as you so often point out, you make the decisions. And one such decision is about to be made. Since the Obermeier thing, we've lost our best analyst. Quality assurance is suffering and we need a replacement."

"I'm not comfortable bringing someone new on board at this critical stage. That would be an unnecessary risk. You will have to make other arrangements, Dr. Harding."

"It's not just that. It's also what Obermeier had mentioned. Although it's very unusual and contrary to all predictions, the Alpha compound does seem to continue to mutate. We need to know how it evolves to make sure it doesn't affect the efficiency of Beta." She pointed demonstratively at the case.

"Do you think that's possible?" inquired Keller.

"In any case, reactions to Beta are very mixed in the workforce. We would have to do more testing. But ..."

"What is it?", Keller impatiently inquired.

"We don't have any subjects. The sites in Romania and Mali have been closed."

"Because they were no longer needed, those were the conclusions you drew yourself, or am I mistaken?"

"You know that assessments like this are always just a snapshot of the time and that we're dealing with a technology that is largely experimental and constantly evolving."

"Revolutionary, I think you mean."

"Sure, yeah. But let me be clear right now: something is wrong. Something that was outside of our focus, that we didn't consider, and that is now beyond our control."

"I will not tolerate this pessimism!" replied Keller coolly.

"Fine, that's your right, of course. Still, I'll ask you one thing: What makes us so sure that Beta protects against something that is constantly transforming and also spreading differently than we thought?"

"Nothing is certain in this world. Except that the doubters and fools do not die out," Keller announced in a theatrical tone.

"But ...," Harding began.

"No more buts. You analyze the mutations and continue researching Beta. Make the appropriate adjustments! Then I'll see to it that I get you the necessary resources for that. Now get out of here before you ruin my day completely. I have an appointment with Kruger in a few minutes, and I'm sure he doesn't have any good news either, if I know him."

Harding left the library and Keller was left alone. The mood that had been so euphoric just a moment ago had faded. He sensed that they were facing a serious problem. Alpha's high-handed behavior was a risk, for it prevented the unrestricted control over dissemination that Keller had wanted. And his plan was based on two basic elements. Alpha was one of them, Beta the second. They acted as opposites in this complicated game. There was no provision for suddenly changing the rules - unless it was Keller himself who saw to it.

Now it was time to tighten up the schedule. Keller was glad that he had already started buying up book and magazine publishers more than a year ago. These would now ensure the dissemination of his manifesto and secure the necessary media attention.

He would have liked to revise his manuscript before the whole world read it, but there was no time for that now. He just had to swallow this small drop of bitterness. No plan was perfect, not even this one.

"I can't lie in a sick bed and twiddle my thumbs now!" protested Hugh.

But Laura pulled him along by the arm toward the cab stands. Immediately after Hugh's arrival at the Geneva airport, it had become clear to her that she would not get him to the hotel as planned, but straight to the hospital. He looked rather worn out, sweating, complaining of dizziness and freezing cold, although it was a thoroughly warm autumn day. When he had taken off his sunglasses for a moment and she had seen his blood-red eyes, she had been sure that detailed examinations would have to be made as soon as possible.

"We're going to the university hospital, doctor's orders!" she determined.

"I have to finish the article, you know yourself how important it is," Hugh replied as they took seats in the back of a cab.

"How far along are you?"

"I got quite a bit done on the plane, but then my eyes closed and I didn't wake up until the plane touched down. Nevertheless, I've already incorporated most of what you sent me. The final touches are still missing, though, and the story has to hit like a bomb."

"I don't think we need to worry about that. If you've described the situation as half as dramatic as we think it is, it's going to cause quite an uproar."

"You're probably right, maybe I'm too critical and can't see the forest for the trees. Or maybe it's this damn buzzing in my head! Here, read over it to make sure I've got it medically right." Hugh pulled the laptop out of his backpack and handed it to Laura.

During the 20 minutes or so it took to drive to the clinic, Laura worked through the text, adding notes and a few additions.

Hugh, meanwhile, closed his eyes and leaned back. He was still sweating and exhausted from working on the text.

"This is a really good article," Laura said as the cab pulled into the parking lot in front of the hospital.

She handed the laptop back to Hugh, who smiled faintly at the compliment and slid the laptop into his backpack.

Laura continued, "I just highlighted a few places for you where you could maybe make it clearer as far as the medical facts go. But otherwise the text is top-notch. Could be left as is if you're too weak to continue."

"It'll be fine. I definitely want to send the article to the editor today," Hugh explained.

After Laura had paid the driver, they both got out. "Your

best bet is to go straight to the emergency room, then they should admit you as an inpatient and give you a thorough check-up," Laura suggested.

"Oh man, how I hate that word," Hugh grumbled, following her to the entrance.

"It'll be fine! You're in good hands here."

There was a kind of coordinated chaos in the emergency room. Patients streamed in or were delivered by ambulance. One by one, they were registered, pushed into treatment rooms or directed to waiting areas. A display board next to the entrance showed an estimated waiting time of 80 minutes.

Laura and Hugh got in line at the registration desk and waited. "I've got to go sit down somewhere in a minute," Hugh said. "The dizziness is coming back."

"Give me your insurance card, I'll handle it," Laura replied.

Hugh dug out his Global Health Insurance Card, which he had been issued by the British NHS for working abroad, and handed it to Laura.

She watched him walk to a row of chairs, sit down and pull the laptop out of his backpack again. She had to hand it to him: he was extremely passionate about his job - and about this article in particular. Hopefully, this one had the necessary effect as well.

As Hugh typed, she waited patiently until she could check him in. The staff member from the patient reception apologized for the rush, but explained that they were currently at full capacity due to two serious accidents on the highway.

When Laura joined Hugh a good ten minutes later with a waiting number, Hugh had finished revising the article and emailed it to his editor.

He folded the computer shut and stowed it away. "So, now I can die," he joked. "I'll get the Pulitzer Prize posthumously."

"I don't want to hear that!" protested Laura. "They'll get you back on your feet here."

Hugh gave an agonized sigh and then toppled forward

from the chair so suddenly that Laura almost couldn't get a grip on him.

She immediately got down on her knees next to him and felt for his pulse. "Over here, quick!" she shouted toward the registration desk. "He's unconscious, we need to get him to the shock room."

Two orderlies in pink and white gowns rushed over with a wheeled gurney. One of them checked Hugh's pulse and breathing, and then together they hoisted the unconscious man onto the stretcher.

"He has complained of dizziness and fever. He may also have come into contact with a toxic or infectious substance," Laura explained as the nurses started moving with Hugh toward an automatic sliding door.

"We'll take care of everything," assured the nurse to the left of the gurney.

"I'm a doctor. Can I help?" asked Laura.

"No, you have to wait here. Access for staff only!" the other man explained, pointing to an inscription on the glass door.

This opened and Laura watched as they wheeled in the unconscious Hugh on the stretcher and took him into a room on the left. She was still standing there when the doors had long since closed again. "Hang in there, man!" she said quietly, returning to the waiting area.

She realized that she was afraid for Hugh, afraid that they didn't have the proper means at hand to treat him. Who could say what he had come into contact with in Romania? The standard laboratory tests were unlikely to be sufficient to expose Keller Pharma's perfidious means.

Anger rose in Laura. After all, these bastards would soon have their asses handed to them by the press. Now she had to take care of the rest.

Johann Engström's office on the executive floor of WHO headquarters was in twilight. The sun had set about half an hour ago, and only a little gray residual light filtered in through the windows. The computer monitor had also switched to energy-saving mode some time ago and showed only deep black.

Engström could, of course, have switched on the office lighting, which was optimized for the best working atmosphere, or at least the small desk lamp in front of him. But he didn't feel like it. Dark was the hour and darkness gradually settled on his mind.

A "ping" from the PC speaker broke the silence. The screen came back to life and bathed everything in bluish light. The mail program reported an urgent message. It was the status report he had requested from the WHO's African regional office. For a moment, Engström hesitated to open it. What could it contain? Did he really want to know? Ignorance was bliss, after all. But it wasn't. It increasingly tormented him. It was crystal clear to the WHO chief that he would have to live with the consequences, no matter what he decided now.

With a double click, he opened the mail and read. The report from the Brazzaville office in Congo was frightening. Cases of miscarriage, infertility, and sudden death or coma were skyrocketing, and the prognosis did not bode well for the future.

Why hadn't he listened to Laura Delille when there was still time to act? Why had he put his personal feelings above the welfare of so many? Engström knew the answer. On the one hand, because he hadn't realized - or didn't want to realize - the connection or the magnitude? And on the other hand, because he was a father who had grasped at the last straw to save his dying daughter. But how many of the victims were also fathers? Or daughters? He felt his stomach contract to the size of a golf ball.

What was his daughter's future going to be? Who decided who would have a future, and what future, anyway?

If he was going to do something, it had to be now. This epidemic could not be concealed much longer anyway.

Engström saved the report from Africa on a USB stick and logged into the lab server. There he opened a password-protected zip archive called "Delille_Mali_Findings_v2" and extracted the entire contents into a separate folder on the stick.

The first step had thus been taken. Engström only hoped that it was not too late to take the other steps.

# 25

Hôpitaux universitaires de Genève, Geneva, Switzerland, October 8.

"Well, that doesn't make sense to me, there's got to be more, surely?" asked Dr. Jean Guyot, Hugh's attending physician, looking piercingly at Laura.

"Look, I've said it twice now, but I'll gladly repeat it a third time: I don't know what he was injected with. Everything I can say is based on speculation. It could be that he was given an experimental mRNA vaccine that's officially supposed to help inoculate against malaria."

"Malaria? In Romania?" Dr. Guyot's tone lapsed back into sarcasm.

Laura sighed heavily. She knew all too well from her own experience that some physicians had a tendency toward an oversized ego and reacted a bit oddly when they had to admit that they had no idea. And if her instincts did not deceive her, that was exactly the case here. After the restless night she had spent half of in the clinic, however, she couldn't have an unproductive argument with Guyot, especially since Hugh remained unconscious and unresponsive to any medication.

So she tried diplomacy again. "Dr. Guyot, we are colleagues after all. And we both should care a lot about the patient's recovery, so let's just work together as best we can."

Guyot nodded tentatively, then the previously stiff features of the gray-haired man in his mid-fifties relaxed somewhat. "You are right. But the case is very strange, you must admit, and your explanation seems abstruse. Of course, these symptoms could be side effects of a vaccination, but could just as easily be something else entirely. The fact that a WHO doctor, of all people, brought this patient to us also makes me wonder."

"I know, but it has nothing to do with my work at WHO, at least not directly. We just got to know each other through it."

"I see. Very well, if you assure me that this is not a case of some exotic tropical disease that will cripple my entire hospital."

"Certainly not. We were in Mali until a week ago, it's true, but there were no exotic diseases there, and I'm perfectly healthy. Hugh Stevens was, too, until this trip to Romania. Can we maybe deal with the findings now?"

Dr. Guyot still didn't seem satisfied with the story, but left it at that and picked up a tablet instead. "The blood work is actually fine so far. Here, look." He turned the tablet so Laura could read the results. "A few inflammatory markers are elevated and the liver values are not ideal, but that doesn't surprise me if the man is, as you said, a reporter. They like to have a few too many."

Laura left the jab at Hugh unchallenged, but calmly finished reading the lab report.

Dr. Guyot continued, "In any case, I don't see in the findings any explanation for this profound unconsciousness - it's almost a kind of coma. Is there perhaps a chance that he was not inoculated, but poisoned with an unknown substance?"

"What do you mean? Polonium or something?" asked Laura.

Dr. Guyot shrugged his shoulders. "Maybe, I'm speculating the same way you are."

"No, I think such a poisoning is rather unlikely," Laura replied.

"Then I guess it really is an extreme form of side effect. You mentioned an mRNA vaccine. Now not just any pharmaceutical company makes something like that. Do you know where the drug comes from?"

"It's just a theory, but ... Okay, from the beginning. I recently had to deal with some mysterious cases in Mali, infertility, miscarriages, occasionally comatose states. However, women were affected without exception. Whereas ..."

Laura paused and considered. "I honestly didn't look for affected men at all. Maybe the symptoms are different in them."

"That could be possible; even medications sometimes work better or worse based on gender," Dr. Guyot interjected.

"Correct. In any case, our research led us to a malaria vaccination study conducted by Keller Pharma. The drug used came from a Romanian subsidiary of the corporation. And when Hugh Stevens went on site to investigate, they ... well, knocked him down and gave him an injection. That was about two days ago."

"So if it was this vaccine, but I can't think why it would be administered, you might find residues of the specific mRNA in his body," Dr. Guyot said. "But without a clue as to what exactly to look for, it would be quite a bit of rummaging in a haystack."

"That's right," Laura affirmed. "It's a complicated procedure, I've done it myself."

"Well, I don't know if we can do that here either," Dr. Guyot admitted. "And who's going to pay for it? Health insurance is likely to refuse to pay for expensive special tests. Why don't you do it at WHO?"

Laura did not react immediately. Partly because she didn't have a sensible answer. Yes, why didn't she actually do that? Because her hands were tied, damn it! "Dr. Guyot, it's like this," she began, but was interrupted by a knock on the door.

She turned around and saw Johann Engström poking his head into the room. "Speak of the devil," Laura said softly.

"Do you have a minute?" Engstrom asked.

Laura looked again at Hugh, who continued to lie motionless in bed. "We'll talk more later, all right?" she said to Dr. Guyot, then joined Engstrom out in the hall.

"Shall we walk a bit, perhaps?", Engström asked, gesturing down the corridor.

"I don't really feel like walking," Laura replied dismissively.

"Please, Laura, I'm trying to apologize right now. Don't make this so hard for me."

"All right, let's go and talk."

"I really don't know how to start. It's complicated."

"Start by explaining why you obstructed my work and left me out in the cold by myself!"

"They made me do it."

"Who? Who made you do it?"

Engström stopped and turned away.

Laura saw a tear glisten in the corner of one eye. "Oh, damn! It's because of Ariane, isn't it?"

Engström nodded, but did not make a sound.

"You don't have to say anything else. I saw the IV bag. It was from Keller Pharma."

Again, Engstrom nodded. "I did this on my own, even without letting the doctors here in on it. But she ... she absolutely had to be in this study. I swear to you, I had no idea what was really behind it. You have to believe me. When I finally grasped the full magnitude and consequences, it was far too late."

"You realize the price we're paying?"

"Now, yes. But Laura ..." He took her hand and squeezed it tightly. "We will do everything in our power from now on." Engström let go of her again.

Laura felt something in her hand and looked down. It was a small silver USB stick with the WHO logo on it.

"I hope ...," Engstrom said. "I pray it helps!"

"Johann, but what about ..."

Defensively, he raised his hands. "I don't even want to think about that." He swallowed hard. "I have to go, there's so much I have to take care of right now."

"Wait a minute. What about my lab ban? I really need to analyze more samples. Hugh Stevens is lying there in that room, and I need to find out what's wrong with him."

"Sure, Laura. I'll talk to Dr. Lang. Maybe you can come in tonight."

"At the very latest! Tomorrow I fly to Iceland."
"Iceland?" Engstrom looked at her, frowning. "I'd better not ask why."
"It's all about the McDouglas research. As it stands, there's a full back-up."
"Laura, please be extremely careful. These people will stop at nothing."
"I know that all too well. I'll be careful."
"Good luck ... to all of us," Engstrom said, turning and walking quickly down the hall.

Kimara pushed aside the tarp of the large treatment tent in the middle of Camp Endurance and took a cautious look outside. Dense black smoke was still rising from the east end of the settlement. It reeked of melting tent canvas, smoldering foam, and burned flesh. It was a disgusting mixture that rose to her nostrils, but she knew there was nothing she could do about it. Conditions in the camp were becoming increasingly chaotic. People were panicking, wanting to leave the camp, or taking out their fear and anger on others. There were fights, even attacks on the staff, which is why Kimara had ordered the staff to stay in the medical tent and only treat emergencies that were brought to them.

She never thought that the situation could escalate like this, but she could understand people. She herself sometimes felt like smashing something, screaming loudly and raving. But she couldn't do that, she was in charge here while Laura was away. She wished it were different, and that she didn't have to carry this burden.

She closed the tent entrance again. The smell was simply unbearable. The residents had arbitrarily decided that the dead had to be burned to prevent further spread. Kimara could not prevent this, or perhaps did not want to. What could she have suggested as an alternative? How could she and her handful of nurses have intervened? It would have been completely pointless.

Apart from the 48 deaths, there had been 27 cases of comatose males, 13 miscarriages, and dozens of cases of unusually heavy menstrual bleeding in the previous ten days. It was all too understandable that panic was spreading. Although the majority of the unconscious men had recovered after no more than three days, three showed no sign of improvement even after more than a week. In addition, there was no clear pattern in the spread of the disease. Cases were not concentrated among families or tent neighbors, but were scattered more or less randomly throughout the camp. Kimara began to suspect that everyone here had been infected for a long time, but that not everyone showed symptoms or that this had happened across multiple time periods.

If only Laura were there to care, Kimara would feel a lot better. But what could Laura do here? She knew that it was best if she worked on a solution in Geneva with all the means at her disposal.

A loud bang snapped Kimara out of her thoughts. It had almost sounded like an explosion. She stepped back to the tent entrance and looked out. The previously rather smoldering fire was now blazing far beyond the tents in the foreground.

"What the hell are they up to?" she said, aghast.

A woman with burns on her arms came running up to the medical tent yelling at them, "Do something, they're throwing gas cans on the fire!"

Johann Engström steered his Renault Twingo E-Tech through Geneva's rush-hour traffic. In his position, he would have been entitled to a much larger and more comfortable company car, but Engström had deliberately chosen this agile and economical small electric car - on the one hand to set a positive example and on the other to make it easier to find a parking space.

The compact car usually paid off even in heavy morning traffic, as was the case at this moment, but it was no match for the traffic jam on the Avenue de France, through which Engström had been struggling to make progress for ten minutes. Finally, the end of the construction site responsible for the traffic chaos became apparent, and the jam began to dissipate.

Engström moved to the right lane, which was now free again, and stepped on the gas. On the left, as usual, the speeders and tailgaters rushed past. Engström was also in a hurry, but this speeding was completely pointless and dangerous. Why should you increase your risk many times over in order to arrive 30 seconds earlier?

He had barely finished that thought when he saw a beefy black SUV roar up from behind and soon completely fill the Twingo's rearview mirror.

Another one of these idiots who tailgated, pulling into the left lane at the last moment as if they thought the car in front was a terrible traffic hazard.

But the SUV did not pull into the left lane. It rammed Engström's small car, which lurched forward and skidded.

Engström just about brought the Renault under control when the SUV shot up from behind again. "Shit!" he yelled and was immediately drowned out by the impact.

This time, the black car hit him on the left rear corner and pushed him onto the shoulder. Engstrom's Twingo swerved to the right, rolled over several times and crashed into the guardrail at still high speed. The SUV accelerated and sped away.

Around noon, Laura opened her laptop and looked up the number of laboratory director Dr. Lang in the WHO telephone directory. Engström had not contacted her again, and now she wanted to ask in person what the situation was regarding free lab time. She typed the number into her cell phone.

It rang for a little eternity until Lang finally picked up. "Lang!" he said gruffly, as if he had answered the phone only reluctantly.

"Dr. Lang, I'm glad to reach you," Laura said gently.

"Glad? You've got a lot of nerve! What more do you want, I thought you had been sent on vacation."

"I can't take a vacation now, the situation is serious."

"You can say that again, all hell is breaking loose here. I don't have time ..."

"Has Johann spoken to you? We cleared up the misunderstanding. He offered me the prospect of lab time."

Silence lingered on the line as Lang did not answer. "You spoke to him today?" asked Lang finally.

"Yes, this morning at the hospital, we talked about everything and cleared the air."

"Then you're probably the last person to talk to him. He had a terrible accident on the way here."

"What? How?" stammered Laura, feeling her stomach tighten.

"On the expressway, a collision. He crashed into the guardrail and overturned. The battery then malfunctioned and the whole car was ablaze when help finally arrived."

"You ... You mean he's dead?"

"Yes, unfortunately. So you can imagine that there's a lot going on here."

"I don't even know what to say."

"Then say nothing and hang up," Lang said.

"But the lab time?" stammered Laura.

"You can forget that! As far as I'm concerned, you still behaved irresponsibly. I don't want to see you in my lab."

"Dr. Lang!" Laura objected.

But the lab manager had long since hung up.

Laura put the cell phone away and looked at the screen of her laptop again. For now, the lab data she had collected was all she could work with. She had to trust that the university hospital would do its best to help Hugh.

Tomorrow morning she would check on him again before leaving for the airport. She was not comfortable leaving him here alone and flying to Iceland on her own, but she knew she had other priorities. Tomorrow afternoon, she would meet Nicole McDouglas at the Reykjavik airport. That was an appointment that couldn't be rescheduled - even if it hurt not to be able to take care of Hugh in person.

That was simply impossible. First, because they were running out of time, and second, because she was lucky that Nicole was letting her get ahold of her uncle's data at all. With that, perhaps a therapy could be developed. And it could ultimately benefit everyone, including Hugh. She just hoped it would succeed in time. In any case, the prospect of finally fitting the missing pieces of the puzzle together had never felt better.

## 26

*Hôpitaux universitaires de Genève, October 9*

First there was this scent – delicate, floral, yet so distinctive. It led Hugh's consciousness up out of a leaden blackness - first into a dark gray sea of clouds without a hint of outline, then into a light mist of swirling vapor. Finally, around him was pure white. White walls, a white ceiling, white bedding. But there were also the glorious colors of a bouquet of flowers on the table beside his bed. That was where the fragrance came from.

Hugh shook off the mental paralysis of long unconsciousness and tried to reconstruct recent events. He had been hospitalized. But he remembered little of what had happened after he and Laura had stepped through the door. Laura. Where was she?

Now Hugh looked around the room. He was alone, in the company only of flashing apparatus and the bouquet of flowers. There was no clock to tell him what time it was. And through the window he saw only gray sky. In fact, he didn't even know what day it was.

On the back of his left hand, he discovered an IV hanging from it. Above him dangled a gray remote control with a bright red nurse call button in the center.

He put his right hand up, pressed, and a light next to the door came on, signaling that the call had arrived at the nurse's station.

Hugh waited and concentrated on his body. He felt like he had thrown up, like he had partied the night away. But he still felt worlds better than when he arrived there. He even noticed that his stomach was growling. That was a good sign in any case. They must have been treating him. Maybe they even knew what had triggered his symptoms. Whatever it had been, he certainly had a lot of questions.

After a few moments, a nurse came in, her name tag identifying her as 'Cecille'. She stepped up to the bedside and smiled. "Slept in, did we, Mr. Stevens?" she asked. "How are you feeling?"

Hugh tried to speak, but only a cough came out. His mouth was too dry.

Cecille poured him a glass of water and handed it to him.

Hugh drank it down in one go. "Thank you, I'm fine," he said. Speaking was a lot easier now.

Cecille checked the IV and Hugh's vital signs. "Everything looks good," she explained. "We're glad you're back with us."

"How long was I gone?"

"I don't know for sure, but you've been here on the ward for two days now," the nurse explained.

"What ... I mean, how did you treat me?"

"Basically not at all, we don't even know what you had." She pointed to the IV. "That's just saline, you were dehydrated. But the doctor can explain all that to you better, I notified him as soon as you hit the call button."

As if on cue, a gray-haired man in a white coat came in; he had hard features and piercing blue eyes. "I'm Dr. Jean Guyot," he introduced himself. "I'm glad to see you've regained consciousness, Mr. Stevens. Indeed, your case presents us with some puzzles."

"I'm sure it does. Didn't Laura, excuse me, Dr. Delille, tell you?"

"Well, the colleague's explanations were not necessarily satisfactory - and despite all her effort, not very helpful. We did all sorts of tests while you were unconscious, but we couldn't find a definite cause. She said you had come into contact with an unknown vaccine?"

"Yes. That is, maybe. I don't know what it was, but most likely it was something like that."

"Well, whatever it was, you reacted to it with severe side

effects. But now those seem to have almost completely subsided, don't they?"

"I feel relatively good, the dizziness, the cold, the shivering, it's all gone. I still feel a little run down, but I'm sure that can be cured with a proper meal. I'm starving."

Sister Cecille nodded. "Then I'll see what I can do about that." With that, she disappeared from the room.

"Well, Mr. Stevens," Dr. Guyot resumed, "I still have to tell you that we haven't found out what exact reaction was triggered in your body and whether there might be further consequences. If it was a vaccination and your immune system just reacted unusually strongly, we may assume that the acute phase is over by now. But there may still be effects later. This should be medically monitored and clarified."

"I understand. Forgive me for asking so directly, but when can I get out of here? You need to know that Dr. Delille and I are working on something very important."

"Yes, that's what I was told. Of course, without being given specific details. But to your question, my advice would be to stay here for at least another 48 hours for observation."

"I don't have that much time."

"As I said, it's medical advice. You can, of course, leave at any time. But I would be reluctant to let you go unaccompanied."

"Maybe Dr. Delille can come get me?"

"Of course, if a medical professional is taking care of you, that would be my preference. Mr. Stevens, your case was very exciting, but still, I have enough patients to take care of. Let me know if you have any further questions. Only I won't promise that I can provide answers."

"That's how we all feel, Dr. Guyot. There are always more questions than answers. One more thing: where are my things? I really need my laptop."

Dr. Guyot pointed to a narrow cabinet next to the bed. "Everything's in there. Nothing gets lost in our house." He nodded to Hugh, then turned and left the room.

About 20 minutes later, Hugh had eaten. The remains of lunch, which had actually been over for two hours, had been cold, but Hugh didn't care. As his stomach filled with meatloaf, potatoes, and peas, he felt his strength gradually returning.

He swung his legs out of bed and went to the closet. From his backpack he took out the laptop and flipped it open. All he saw was a blinking icon with a battery crossed out. The battery had been only 15 percent full when he had gotten off the plane, and after the two days on standby, it now seemed completely drained.

Hugh also dug out the charging cable, plugged in the computer, and sat down with it at a small table to the left of the bed.

The computer booted up and the first thing Hugh did was check his newspaper's website. He had expected his article to be prominently placed at the top. But he did not find it there. He used the search function and entered his name, but the results page showed only the articles he had written while still in Africa.

Hugh reflected for a moment. The pseudonym! He probably hadn't mentioned it in the rush of sending the manuscript, but that didn't matter now. Perhaps Adrian Keen had independently republished the second text under the same name. Now he tried Stephen Humes, but the search spat out only the text about McDouglas's death. Hugh tried keywords like Keller Pharma, malaria, and infertility, but nowhere did his article show up. It just wasn't online.

Then he checked the newspaper's e-paper, which contained all the printed texts. But here, too, there was no trace in the last two issues that had appeared since his hospitalization.

"What the hell?!" cursed Hugh. Hadn't that bungler Keen given his article the priority it deserved? Surely it was obvious that this was a time-sensitive story that couldn't be put on the back burner!

Then another thought occurred to Hugh. Had his mail

arrived at all? Had he sent it or had he already been too befuddled? Had he made a mistake?

He opened the mail program and found his message neatly filed in the Sent folder. There was no error message in the inbox, but there was an out-of-office note from Keen's address. So the email had arrived. Hugh knew that his boss always read his messages anyway. He might otherwise miss a profitable opportunity. So it seemed all the more strange that he hadn't replied yet.

Kurt Kruger looked out the floor-to-ceiling window at the barren Icelandic landscape. He could not understand why people lived here. Why the last inhabitants had not already fled. Everything was somehow flat and stony, gray and brown. Hardly any vegetation, just some green-yellow lichen between the rocks. Kruger had the feeling that civilization ended just behind the airport.

This here was an enclave - or the last outpost before the wilderness. He knew, of course, that every year tourists flocked to the island through this very airport near the capital, Reykjavik - voluntarily. He just didn't understand what they wanted here. Maybe there were beautiful corners, maybe the breathtaking nature with its geysers, glaciers and the like was hiding in the hinterland.

Kruger didn't care. For him, Iceland was a country like any other, just like Mali, Germany or the USA. Countries were an artificial construct, and soil was only a stage for action. Kruger had no sense of beautiful landscapes or leisure activities. He was only interested in his task, and he would use any means to bring about the desired result. And who knows, maybe that would even give him a little pleasure today.

Kruger spat the chewed-out gum into a wastebasket next to the window and took a new one out of the wrapper. Ever since he quit smoking cigarettes, he'd been addicted to that damn gum. But at least it wouldn't kill him too soon. After all, he still wanted to enjoy his retirement - as soon as he had accumulated enough money for it. He opened his suitcase and got a change of clothes ready. Then he checked his cell phone. There were about three hours left until the flight he was waiting for would arrive. That was much more time than he needed to get into character and make final preparations.

On the third try, Hugh finally managed to get his boss Adrian Keen on the phone. He had a murderous rage in his belly and wanted to confront him as to why his story had not appeared.

But Keen was cool about it. "Yes, you know, the last few days have been very turbulent. We have new owners again, this time a holding company from Germany. The Krauts, of all people, they take everything twice as hard! Well, business is business."

"Good for you, Adrian, but that's your problem. And that doesn't explain why my story didn't appear! I had stated that it was extremely urgent."

"Legal is still reviewing it. You make some pretty serious allegations in it."

"Excuse me? You're not telling me that's the reason!"

"There could be immense costs if we go too far out on a limb with this," Keen explained unapologetically.

"Since when do you care if facts are true as long as they get clicks and circulation? Since when did you become such a stickler?" asked Hugh angrily.

"That really hits me hard."

"Answer the question!"

"Well, new owners, new specifications. Every story now goes across the legal counsel's desk."

"This is bullshit! We don't have time to wait for some nitpicker's comments."

"Hey, I'm just doing my job, too. Speaking of which: There's some restructuring planned, and there's no point in keeping you in suspense for long. All correspondents are being eliminated. And as sorry as I am, your contract is up in three months."

Hugh felt as if he had been knocked on his head and at first did not know how to respond.

Keen finally spoke up again, "Nice to finally experience this – Hugh Stevens is speechless," he announced with amusement.

"You can take that job and shove it up your ass," Hugh replied. "Then I'll just publish the story somewhere else; it's too important to let it languish in your archives."

"Where? On your piddly blog?" asked Keen. "You know you don't have comparable reach anywhere. Besides, I wouldn't. We hold the rights to the text, you know the contract. And until you officially leave at the end of the contract, you can't publish anywhere else. The publisher will sue you and any other medium to the hilt if you violate it."

"Did you even read the story? Don't you get what this is all about?" Hugh realized he was getting louder.

"Sorry Hugh, you know I'm interested in business first and foremost. And how we do business is still determined by whoever owns the store. It's as simple as that."

"And who the fuck is that, please?"

"Actually, I wasn't going to tell you, but since we're having such a nice conversation: His name is Christian Keller. And now maybe you understand why your story will never appear."

# 27

*Lodge House 'Zur reinen Wahrheit', Berlin, October 9*

Christian Keller stepped through the burgundy curtains, trimmed with gold edges, onto the stage, which was made entirely of dark tropical wood. He strode to the front, where a narrow lectern stood. On its front was emblazoned the coat of arms of the lodge to whose closest circle he had belonged for ten years and to which his father and grandfather had also belonged. The emblem showed a golden triangle with a sun in the middle, whose rays broke out in all directions from the ordered geometrical forms. To the left of it a tree, to the right of it a human being. Both seemed to absorb the light of this sun and feed on it. Above the coat of arms the name of the lodge was written in golden letters: „Zur reinen Wahrheit" - Towards Pure Truth.

Keller calmly placed both hands on the lectern and eyed his audience. At the dozen or so round tables in the hall sat the assembled members, a total of about 250 people. Just about everyone had accepted his invitation, but Keller had not expected otherwise. It was only early afternoon, but there were already all kinds of exclusive spirits and wines on the tables. Next to them were hand-painted teapots and bowls with pastries.

"Media vita in morte sumus! In the midst of life we are embraced by death," he announced. "This is an old Latin motto, but it could not be more apt today. Or do you not feel how the times are changing? How death and decay lurk around the next corner?" Keller let the words sink in for a moment, then continued, "We are here for a reason. We seek knowledge, the truth. For the truth will redeem us. But the ignorant out there threaten to plunge the world into the abyss.

There are too many of them who heedlessly and recklessly ruin themselves and our world. But what should we do, I ask you? Just stand by and wait while the lie of unlimited growth, of inexhaustible resources, drives us to our doom? You do not have to answer. It would be banal. How could we follow a lie when we are committed to the truth?"

Shouts of approval and taps on the tables signaled to Keller that he had his audience hooked. He raised his hands and gestured to the audience. "You are different than these others. You deserve a better fate. We need to redistribute the roles, we need to provide moderation and balance! And what if we already had the means to do so?"

Again, Keller paused before continuing. "What if death were no longer a black curtain that throws itself mercilessly over us? What if we could push it aside like this curtain behind me? What if behind it lay that endless radiant light which so fascinated the founders of our Lodge 300 years ago? And let me tell you one thing, my friends: these are not empty words!"

Keller pulled a syringe from his jacket pocket and held it up. "If you want to find the Philosopher's Stone, you should first drink from the Fountain of Youth. Forgive me for the worn-out phrases, but it is precisely that Fountain of Youth that I hold in my hands here."

A murmur went through the audience, some whispered.

"I put all my passion, all my intellect, all my fortune into this project. And it has been crowned with success. How long can a person live? 300 years? A thousand years? Maybe forever? We're going to find out. And rest assured, this won't be something you can get on the open market, nothing that just anyone can afford. Life is precious. A long life, perhaps priceless? No, for the right people it will be affordable. For the rest, well ... What do we care about the rest?"

Applause and shouts of approval reached Keller's ears again. He took off his jacket, unbuttoned his left sleeve and took the protective cap off the syringe. A drop glistened on the tip of the needle. Keller put it to his arm and poked through the skin into the vein.

"As you can see, it is completely harmless. This is my fourth injection, and I can say that the effect is ... well, it's indescribable. That's why I won't even try to put it into words." He had pushed the entire contents of the syringe into his bloodstream and pulled the needle out. Once again, he held it up.

"I know you will have questions. You will want to experience it for yourself! And you can. I will be sending each of you an exclusive invitation in the next few days. Under no circumstances should you fail to attend. Soon I will present my book, the true manifesto of a new world order. And I will make this preparation available to you, if you are willing to journey this way with me - the way into the light. Come and you will understand why both are so important."

Keller did not wait for applause or any other reaction from the audience. He took his jacket and walked off the stage. "See you behind the curtain!" he shouted loudly and then had already disappeared behind it.

Keller's driver was already waiting at the rear exit with the limousine. He opened the door for him, and Keller got in. "To the airport," he said as he took a seat. "And tell the crew to load the equipment and get the plane ready for takeoff."

Hugh put the cell phone aside in exasperation. Apparently Laura's phone was turned off, which is why he ended up going straight to voicemail every time. His suspicions grew stronger. She was probably already on a plane - to Iceland. And alone. The thought drove him crazy.

His gaze slid around the room. He had to get out of here. Just as he was about to start packing up his things, he stopped at the bouquet of flowers. Had Laura brought it? Who else could it have been? He didn't care for flowers, but it was still a nice gesture. Only now did he notice that an envelope was stuck between the lush blossoms. Why hadn't he seen it right away? Probably because he was too busy being upset about the doctors and that miserable bastard Adrian Keen.

He took the envelope out of the bouquet and pulled out the card. On the outside were get-well wishes in curved script, along with colorful circles and lines. When he opened it, he saw some handwritten lines.

"Dear Hugh, I don't know when you will read this message. I hope soon. And I hope you'll be feeling better. Maybe I'll be back by then, too. I left for Iceland to meet with Nicole McDouglas. You have to understand that I couldn't wait any longer. It is immensely important that I get to the archive with the research work. This is our only chance to really do something. See you soon, Laura."

Hugh grew hot and cold. His fear had come true. When had Laura written these lines? Today, yesterday? The bouquet looked fresh. It had probably not been here very long. But still, it was too late to stop her. Up there in the remoteness of Iceland, the two women would make a perfect target. Just as he himself had been in Romania. What if this guy who had outsmarted him was waiting for them up there? He had intercepted him in Romania and must have known beforehand that he was headed there. What were the odds, he wondered, that he already knew about Laura's trip? Hugh didn't need to do the math. There was obviously an information leak.

He got up and went to the closet. There he stuffed the rest of his things into his suitcase and backpack.

"Where are you going?" he suddenly heard a voice call from behind him. He hadn't heard Cecille coming.

Now the nurse stood in the doorway with her arms crossed. "You are not yet fully recovered, it is too early to ..."

"On the contrary, I'm damn late," Hugh interrupted her.

"But we had discussed that you would stay 48 hours for observation. Dr. Guyot wants to give you another checkup, and besides, it takes time for them to finish your discharge papers."

Hugh grabbed his suitcase and backpack and stepped toward her. "I'm sorry, Cecille, you're kind, but I couldn't care less about your papers. I don't have time to argue. I'm going to get out of here now."

"But ..." the nurse protested, nevertheless stepping aside as Hugh took another step toward her. He left the room.

"I'll have to make a note of that, at least sign the assignment of risk for me!" She hurried after Hugh down the hall.

About 15 minutes after Laura landed at Keflavík International Airport in Iceland, she had already picked up her suitcase from the conveyor belt and was now walking through the terminal. Keflavíkurflugvöllur, as it was called in the local language, was located about 50 kilometers from the capital Reykjavík on the southwestern tip of Iceland on the Reykjanesskagi peninsula.

Although it was the island's main airport, serving all destinations in Europe, North America and Greenland, it was still a fairly small airport with only a handful of stores.

Laura walked past an outdoor clothing store, a bookstore, a cosmetics boutique, and a stand selling Danish smørrebrød. She headed straight for a Segafredo café. It was lunchtime. Laura wasn't hungry, but the prospect of good coffee actually cheered her up. Maybe she could pass the time until Nicole McDouglas finally arrived in a good three hours.

She grabbed an extra-large latte and a croissant and took a seat in a cozy seating area of black leather chairs.

The coffee was excellent, whereas the croissant was more like a bland milk roll dough. Outside, passengers scurried by, shopping, getting snacks and drinks. There wasn't much else to do here, and Laura wondered what she should spend the next few hours doing, except thinking the same thoughts over and over again, sometimes about Hugh, sometimes about Kimara, sometimes about Engstrom, whose charred remains had long since gone to a mortician.

A man with a piece of paper in his hand peeled himself out

of the crowd and headed for the café. He was tall and lanky, wearing a dark suit and had an almost military-looking short hairstyle that didn't quite match the rest of his appearance. Several times he looked back and forth between his note and her. Clearly, he was looking for someone.

Laura looked around. There were only a few guests in the café, and the man was coming directly toward her table. Gradually, she noticed how she was getting more and more tense. Who was this guy, and why would he want to see her, of all people? No one except Nicole and Hugh knew that she wanted to fly here.

The stranger stopped in front of Laura's table. "Dr. Delille?" he asked in accent-free English that sounded just a touch American.

Laura nodded. "That's me."

"You're the one I was looking for" He showed her the piece of paper. It was a printout from the WHO website, which had a profile page with a photo of her. "You wear your hair differently now, very chic," he explained.

"Yes, well … Thank you. But excuse me, who are you and why are you looking for me?" inquired Laura.

"Excuse me, I'm Franklin Scout, Ms. McDouglas' assistant," he explained. "Shall we?"

"What do you want? I thought she wasn't coming for a few hours."

"Oh, forgive me, I thought you had been informed. Ms. McDouglas chartered a small plane and was therefore able to arrive early. This has the pleasing effect of allowing us to continue our journey right away. This is because the domestic flights depart from another airport directly in Reykjavik and that would entail a transfer there and more waiting time. Ms. McDouglas stressed that we were in a hurry, so I suggested we pick you up here."

"All right," Laura said hesitantly. "That sounds reasonable. So is Nicole here?"

"Correct," Franklin confirmed.

Laura finished her coffee, but left the half-eaten croissant. "Okay, let's go then." She rose.

"This way," Franklin gestured, pointing to a spot at the far end of the hall. "It's all arranged. The plane is waiting outside, we'll fly directly to Fagurhólsmýri, from there we'll take the snowmobile up the glacier to the archives."

"I haven't ridden a snowmobile yet, I have to admit. In Africa, we don't see those things very often."

"Yes, of course it doesn't snow in Mali," Franklin agreed with her.

Laura was nonetheless puzzled by this remark. Her momentarily soothed apprehension promptly returned. This Franklin knew quite a lot. He could just be a super meticulous assistant, but somehow she doubted it. She also couldn't remember mentioning Mali to Nicole. In any case, her WHO profile page hadn't been updated in quite some time, as evidenced by the old photo. The new project in Mali was not mentioned on it either, although she had asked several times to have it listed.

"I have to make a quick stop at the little girls' room," she said, turning toward the restrooms.

"The transport has a toilet," Franklin replied.

"It's urgent, I'm not used to the coffee anymore," Laura explained with a shrug. "Be right back." She entered the ladies' room and squeezed into one of the stalls, suitcase and all. There, she pulled out her cell phone and began typing a message. Maybe it was paranoia, but Hugh's recent experiences had made her wary. She typed, "Nicole, am in Iceland. Meeting on schedule?" Then she hit "send."

A few moments later came the answer: "Just getting on the plane in Edinburgh. See you there. Turning off cell phone now."

"Shit," Laura cursed softly and frantically typed a reply that something was wrong and Nicole had better not come. But she received no more response.

She looked up from her phone and stared at the scribbles

on the inside of the restroom door. Right in front of her was written, "Life's a Heap of Bull." She shook her head. All of this was indeed a giant pile of bull crap. What was she supposed to do now? There was someone out there waiting for her who was certainly up to no good. And she couldn't hide forever in a windowless restroom that offered no escape. So she had to get past the guy. But how? And then where? She kicked the suitcase, which made a dull "plop" sound. It was probably time for the really grand performance.

She stood up, opened the door and pushed out the rolling suitcase. Calmly, she stepped out of the ladies' room a moment later and nodded to Franklin, who was standing a few steps away. She left her rolling suitcase against the wall next to the door and fiddled with the zipper of her jacket. Suddenly she yelled, "There's a bomb in that suitcase!" and took off running, pointing her outstretched arm back at the suitcase.

Immediately, pandemonium arose, people shrieked and ran away in different directions.

"Bomb!" repeated Laura, looking over her shoulder.

Franklin sprinted after her, but tripped over the bag of an older man who crossed his path. He shoved him aside gruffly and chased after her.

*Shit, is this guy fast*, Laura thought and dashed past the Smørrebrød stand and into a side aisle. Back there was a small door marked with an unfamiliar Icelandic word and the English addition "Staff only." She ran toward it and pressed the handle, and the door swung open. Laura rushed through a short hallway with two rooms on either side. Then came to another door, to all appearances an external door. Through this one, too, she rushed. Cold wind blew toward her. She heard the door slam again behind her.

She ran along a row of boxes and garbage cans on the left and disappeared between two large blue overseas containers. Completely out of breath, she squatted down and tried to calm herself.

Where was this Franklin? She hadn't seen him or heard him come out the door. Maybe security had arrested him? But that was wishful thinking, Laura knew. It wasn't going to be that easy.

A gust whistled between the containers and made Laura wince. She fumbled the hood out of her jacket collar and pulled it over her head. That helped a little, but she still wouldn't last long here. Maybe this guy was just speculating that she would crawl back in and he could intercept her at his leisure.

*A cab*, it popped into her head. She had to get away from the airport. Hopefully there were cabs around here somewhere.

Laura stuck her head out from behind the container and looked left and right. She had apparently come out the back of the airport building, where the only thing besides the containers was an employee parking lot. If there were cabs, they were at the front of the main entrance. So she would have to circle the building somehow. Fortunately, it wasn't very big.

She stood up and stepped out between the containers as inconspicuously as possible. No one was here. As she turned the corner, she saw that a crowd was forming at the front of the main entrance. Apparently her bomb threat had had the desired effect after all. Dozens of passengers were standing in front of the building, talking to each other in an upset manner. She eyed the people to see if she could see Franklin among them, but there was no sign of him.

Beyond the crowd of people, she saw a row of cabs parked on the other side. She started moving again and made her way through the people.

She was only a good ten meters away from the last cab in the queue when she felt something hard in her back. Instinctively, she stopped.

"I'd love to put a bullet in your brain right here and now," Franklin said in an icy voice. "But I'm required to deliver you alive. However, if you make a fuss like that again, you leave me no choice. So come with me now!" He drilled the barrel of his gun even harder into Laura's back. She automatically took a step forward. "Now turn around nice and easy. We don't want any accidents here."

## 28

Laura climbed the short staircase of the private jet and entered the interior of the aircraft, which was parked on an out-of-the-way position on the tarmac.

Franklin was right behind her, still ready to grab her at a moment's notice should she attempt an escape.

A half-bald man in an understated suit greeted Laura. "Welcome aboard," he said formally, pointing to the right side into the passenger area.

Laura stopped for a moment and looked inside. There was only one person sitting back there with his back to her on one of the seats. These resembled upholstered chairs rather than normal airplane seats. The remaining seven seats were empty.

"Keep moving," Franklin urged, giving her a little push.

Laura turned around and glared at him.

He acknowledged it with an amused smile. Then he murmured to the other man, "She's all yours, make sure she doesn't do anything stupid."

"She won't," the balding man replied. "After all, I still have the gun you made me carry."

Franklin now handed Laura's cell phone as well as her passport to the other man and left the plane. "Have a pleasant flight, Dr. Delille," he said without turning around. Immediately after, the stairs clanged up and the door was locked.

"You are expected," the half-bald man remarked, gesturing back to the passenger compartment.

Reluctantly, Laura started to move and walked in the direction indicated.

When she approached the passenger, he turned around in his chair and looked at her. The man was about her age, had fine features that were visibly preserved with all sorts of cosmetics, and wore an expensive-looking suit. She recognized him. His real appearance was just as sterile as in the photo she had seen on the Keller website.

In his hand he held a bulbous glass with a sip of red wine in it. "It's nice to meet you. Would you like to join me for a drink? I'll ask Spencer to pour you some of my favorite wine."

"What's this going to be? A kidnapping or a dinner?" asked Laura in a sarcastic tone.

"Maybe both? Does that have to be mutually exclusive? You are an attractive woman. The photos I've seen of you don't do you justice. But I hear you're not only beautiful, you're also very smart - and maybe a little too curious. But now it will all work itself out. Maybe this story even has a happy ending for you."

"I suppose you like to hear yourself talk?" remarked Laura pointedly.

Her counterpart only acknowledged it with a smile. "Pleasy sit down, make yourself comfortable, we're about to take off."

Laura stood there for another moment with her arms crossed. Then she heard the turbines start up. It was probably not a good idea to stand here in the aisle when the plane took off. Gritting her teeth, she now took her seat and fastened her seat belt.

"There you go, that wasn't so hard," the man said. "Now let's have a talk. I completely neglected to introduce myself. My name is Christian Keller. I think you've heard of me and my company."

Hugh woke up when the plane touched down roughly on the runway. He jumped up and hurried to gather his things, when his seatmate raised her hand in a gesture of reassurance.

"We're not there yet. This is only the stopover in Edinburgh," she said reassuringly.

"Oh, thanks. I was totally out of it," Hugh apologized and followed up with, "I hope I didn't snore."

The teenage blonde shook her head and grinned. "No, you slept like a baby."

"At least there's that. Lately, though, I've been feeling more like an old man," Hugh commented. "What time is it?"

"1:15 pm. If the plane takes off again on time, it's another two and a half hours to Reykjavik."

"Thank you." Hugh sat up straight and massaged his aching neck. For better or worse, he had to admit that it would have been better after all if he had spent a few more days recovering in the hospital. His stiff limbs told him clearly that the remark about the old man was not as far-fetched as he would have liked. He felt as if he was running on fumes at the moment. But he couldn't afford to wait for a full recovery.

At the front of the cabin door, more passengers boarded and looked for their seats. Jackets rustled, luggage compartments clattered, discussions about mistakenly occupied seats faded. Gradually, everything on the plane calmed down again, and the flight attendants began counting through the passengers.

Hugh took a box of pain pills from his jacket pocket and squeezed two pills from the blister.

"Partied last night?" the blonde asked jokingly, pointing to the sunglasses Hugh was wearing again.

"I wish I was. But no, I just got out of the hospital. Long story. And not a very nice one." He swallowed the pills.

"I see, I'm sorry. What are you doing in Iceland?"

Hugh thought about what he should answer. Of course, he couldn't possibly tell this stranger the truth. Could he tell her anything at all? After all, he didn't know himself what he would do once he got there, whether he could reach Laura or Nicole. He didn't even know if the two of them had already moved on, and if so, where to. He cleared his throat. "Yeah, I guess I'm taking a holiday there. Recreation. Bathing in warm springs and stuff," he lied, yawning demonstratively so as not to have to deepen the conversation. "Sorry, I don't mean to be rude, but ..."

The blonde nodded and smiled. "All right, I'll leave you to it."

"Thank you."

Meanwhile, the plane taxied to the takeoff position and after a few minutes the pilot gave full thrust and they zoomed down the runway.

Hugh knew he would have to try to sleep through the remaining hours to conserve his strength. He had the uneasy feeling that he would use up his reserves quite a bit in Iceland.

The full red wine glass still stood untouched on the small table in front of Laura in Keller's private jet. She hadn't spoken a word since takeoff, and she wouldn't touch that damn glass either. Not until this guy finally explained to her why he had kidnapped her.

But he made no effort to break the silence. Instead, he typed away on his laptop. Apparently, it seemed to amuse him how Laura demonstrated her dislike, which in turn slowly drove her up the wall.

"Okay, screw it. I'll start then," she said, "because I already have a question or two for you."

Her counterpart stopped typing, and now looked directly at her. "Those would be?"

"Why did you drag me on this plane and not order your lackey to shoot me right here in Iceland? Just like you did with McDouglas. Apparently you seem to like getting rid of unpleasant contemporaries. Or am I mistaken?"

"Oh, Dr. Delille, don't look at it so starkly. Of course there are obstacles on the road to success. And you have to remove them. Some in a rather discreet way and others in a radical way," Keller explained calmly, sipping his wine. "I almost feel a little sorry for McDouglas, I have to admit, he deserved differently. He was a brilliant man, but he was on the wrong side in the end. I hope it might be different with you."

"Excuse me?" blurted out Laura. "You want me to take your side? What is your side anyway? The way I see it, you've killed hundreds of people. How could I support something like that?"

"Well, first of all, I personally didn't kill anyone..."

"Only because you don't want to get your fingers dirty," Laura interrupted him.

Keller acknowledged the comment with an amused smile. "Right. I don't need that in my position. There are qualified people who can do that much better. You've met one of them, after all. But let's cut out the chit-chat and these accusations about who killed whom. That is completely irrelevant. This is about a higher purpose."

"A higher purpose? I see. And this is what you want me to join? That's why I'm not dead yet."

"Yes, I didn't think your talent should be wasted," Keller said.

"You are under an illusion if you think I am going to help you in any way."

"Oh, don't be so hasty. I think it just takes the right motivation to do it. And we've already taken care of that."

"What do you mean?" Laura demanded to know.

"All in good time, my dear Laura. I may call you Laura, mayn't I?"

Laura squinted and fixed her eyes on Keller, but didn't answer. She felt her anger at this guy growing.

"All right, then we'll stay formal for now. But I promise I'll explain everything when we arrive. It'll make it easier."

"Arrive where?" asked Laura.

"Berlin. Maybe not a particularly beautiful city, but so full of insights. There you see the state of the world very well concentrated in miniature form. The decay of manners and morals, the scum."

"Scum," Laura repeated. "That's a word that suits you."

"You see, Dr. Delille, you want to make the world a better place. And there we have something in common, because I want that too."

"Are you really as insane as you appear to be?"

"Do not confuse insanity with an unconditional will to realize a vision. And don't bother questioning my motives. The era of humanism is over. Man has had plenty of time to learn and set things right, but what has happened? We are trundling on and on downward. Why? Let me put it this way: the stupid and incompetent just don't die out. At least until now." Again, Keller smiled. "Don't worry, you're anything but stupid, you have nothing to fear."

"Yes, if I play your rotten game."

"You're joining a very noble cause. And as I said, I'm confident it will succeed." Keller picked up his wine glass and drank it empty. "You should taste some of it; the wine is excellent."

It was just before 3 p.m. when Hugh was waiting for his suitcase at the baggage carousel in Kevlavik. Iceland was two hours behind Geneva, so despite the stopover in Edinburgh, he hadn't lost very much time on the flight.

While he waited, he closely observed the hustle and bustle in the hall and examined the passengers present. He kept an eye out - on the one hand for Laura, who was probably no longer here, and on the other hand for potential threats. Especially for that guy, who had introduced himself to him in Romania as Shanks and whom he suspected he had not seen for the last time.

There was still no sign of either of them. Only inconspicuous fellow passengers of his flight gathered around the tape. His gaze kept falling on a woman opposite, whose bright red hair could hardly have been more Scottish. She, too, kept looking around the hall as if she were looking for someone.

Now a horn sounded and the belt rolled squeakily to a stop. After a few moments, the suitcases tumbled out of a hatch at the back of the wall.

Hugh looked at the passing suitcases and bags. He knew his luck, his suitcase would be one of the last, as usual. If the airline hadn't lost it.

For quite a while, the mainly gray and black suitcases passed by, some with colorful luggage straps around them, others wrapped in foil. In between, bright pink suitcases or battered backpacks. Some had name tags hanging out and Hugh tried to decipher them: Harald Reithmeier, D. Johnson, Sarah McKenzie, Ching Li, Petra Kaiser, N. McDouglas.

Hugh literally jumped at the name. Nicole McDouglas! Had she been on the same plane as him? He closely followed the path of the suitcase as it moved along the oval belt to the other side. The woman with the bright red hair grabbed the handle and lifted the suitcase off the belt.

Without waiting for his own luggage, Hugh circled the belt and latched onto the heels of the woman who was now walking toward the exit. "Excuse me, please," he addressed her.

The woman wheeled around, startled. "You startled me," she said nervously.

"I'm sorry, I didn't mean to scare you. You're Nicole McDouglas, right? I'm Hugh Stevens. Laura Delille and I work together."

Nicole eyed him, and Hugh could see in her eyes that she wasn't sure whether to believe him. Then she pulled out her cell phone and showed Hugh the last message she had received from Laura. "Don't come, it's a trap."

"Damn it," Hugh cursed. "But you don't have to be afraid of me." He dug out of the inside pocket of his jacket the card Laura had tucked into the bouquet at the hospital and handed it to Nicole.

Their features relaxed as she read. "Oh, thank God. I was beginning to think you were going to kill me or something."

Hugh shook his head vigorously. "I know exactly how it feels, believe me."

"Have you tried to reach Laura?"

"Yes, right after landing. No answer, just voicemail."

"Mine, too. Do you think ..." Nicole did not finish the question.

"I don't know what happened, but judging by this message you got, my worst fears came true. I didn't want her to fly alone, but I was in the hospital and time was running out."

"Are the same guys behind this who killed my uncle?"

"I'm pretty sure they are. And it's quite possible that they're still here. But first things first, we should get out of the airport, we're an easy target here." Hugh pointed to the baggage carousel. "I'll just get my suitcase real quick, all right?"

Less than two minutes later, the two were on their way to the exit of the security area. The sliding doors opened and closed steadily as passengers streamed out.

Hugh watched the surroundings carefully. Just before the doors closed again, he spotted him. A gum-chewing man was waiting out there - styled differently than he had been in Romania, but it was definitely the same man who had introduced himself to Hugh as Peter Shanks. "Wait," he murmured to Nicole, pulling her aside.

They positioned themselves so that they could not be seen from outside the security perimeter.

"I don't know if he noticed us," Hugh said.

"Who?"

"There's one of those guys out there. He intercepted me in Romania and knocked me out. He called himself Shanks then, but I doubt that's his real name. He's very dangerous."

"Now what? We can't get out of the security area - unless we go through that door."

"Right. And I'm sure he knows that. We have to trick him somehow, distract him. The question is whether he's looking for you or me. He definitely knows my face, but he probably doesn't know yours."

"You're not suggesting I play decoy here or anything like that, I hope?"

"No, I'd like to get you as far away as soon as possible. Put you on a plane. But you can't, the ticket counters are outside."

"So?"

"I will go out first and distract him. If he doesn't expect

me here, he may be sufficiently surprised. As soon as you notice him following me or becoming inattentive, make sure you get out and get in a cab. I've booked a room at the Dormond Hotel in Reykjavik. Let's meet there."

"This is crazy. What if this doesn't work? What if this guy has a gun?"

"This is an airport, he's hardly going to pull out a gun. That's our advantage. He'll try not to draw attention to himself."

"I feel like I'm in a James Bond movie," Nicole said.

"I'm sorry to disappoint you. I don't have an Aston Martin or a wristwatch that blows up at the push of a button. We have nothing at all, except the element of surprise."

"That's really not much. But I guess there's no point in waiting any longer. Or do you think he'll give up at some point?"

Hugh shook his head "That guy? I'm sure he won't. No, we have to go through with this. Don't forget: Dormond Hotel. The room is reserved for Stephen Humes." Then he grabbed his suitcase and headed for the sliding door. It opened and he stepped through.

The man he knew as Shanks stood unchanged a few feet from the exit, watching the door.

Hugh saw a slight frown on his face as he recognized him, but it immediately gave way to an opaque, hard poker face again.

He continued to walk directly toward him. When he was still a meter away, he stopped and put on a smile. "Mr. Shanks, what a strange coincidence to see you here again. How's your photo book coming along?"

Kruger looked at him chewing gum for a while. "You're not such a little pants-wetter as I thought, I'll give you that, Mr. Stevens."

"Thanks. And you're a bigger asshole than I thought." Hugh hadn't come up with a plan for what he was going to say and do. Besides, he had his back to the door and had no idea how long he would have to distract this guy until Nicole could disappear unseen. But he had to stand that way to block his view as best he could. It was now a matter of going on the offensive if he wanted to tie up his attention for a while. "Where is Laura Delille? I know you have her!" he said much more sharply now.

"It almost sounds like you're making demands? Who told you she was even alive?"

"You pigs want something. Otherwise you wouldn't go to such lengths. What is it?"

"Oh, Mr. Stevens, what am I going to do with you? Once again, it just goes to show that it's better to decisive action right away than to argue endlessly later on."

"Well, this is not the place for such measures, am I right? I'm sure you don't want to have security on your back and get arrested."

"Security? Don't make me laugh! These amateurs? Even if you get out of the airport, I'll still get you, Stevens. When you least expect it."

"But now I'm going to walk out of here and enjoy the evening. What else do you have planned?"

Kruger didn't answer right away, but just looked at Hugh shaking his head. "You have no idea what's going on here. You're overestimating yourself beyond measure if you think you can do anything in the little time you have left. Speaking of which, how does it feel to be an old man?"

"Quite excellent," Hugh said instinctively, at the same time pondering what the cryptic remark was intended to mean. He decided that now wasn't the time to brood over it. "Have a nice evening," he said as casually as he could and turned toward the exit. He left Shanks standing there and didn't look back. He just hoped the diversion had been enough.

No sooner had he left the main entrance than he rushed towards the cab ranks and got into the first available car.

# 29

*Secret Keller location near Lychen, evening of October 9.*

It was already evening when the beefy black SUV with Christian Keller and Laura Delille on board approached the production plant in the forest near Lychen. Due to the flight time from Kevlavik to Berlin and the time difference, the journey here had taken almost six hours in total, although only just under four had passed. For most of that time, Keller had sat at his laptop drinking wine and typing away, while Laura had racked her brains as to what he might have meant when he said he had created enough motivation to force her to cooperate.

She did not want to ask him again. Ideally, she didn't want to talk to him at all. For the life of her, she couldn't remember the last time someone had been so unsympathetic to her. But she knew that wouldn't do. There were questions she needed answers to.

The car stopped and Keller waited until Spencer got out the front to open the door in the back.

Laura didn't sit still waiting for the butler, but pulled the handle herself and opened the door. During the drive, she had thought several times about doing that and just jumping out of the car. But as a doctor she had of course realized that she would pay for such a movie-like stunt with broken bones or worse, and in the end it would do her no good at all. She wouldn't get far if she were badly injured.

Laura followed Keller to a tin-lined hall, around which were stored all sorts of stacks of wood and machinery. "This is what you wanted to show me?" she asked in amazement.

Keller just cocked his head and opened the shabby outer door with a key. A dull gray security lock came into view. On the right side was a card reader and a camera. Keller pulled out an access card and placed it against the reader. He then placed his chin on a depression below the device and peered into an opening.

Laura guessed it was a biometric retina scanner. "Okay, that looks more high-tech. Do I get access too?"

"Sorry," Keller said as the airlock opened. "You're still on probation. Besides, only the department heads have authorization to open the airlock - from the outside and from the inside. So forget any thoughts of escape, it would be in vain. Now come on." He gestured inside the facility and waited for Laura to walk in.

But she hesitated.

"You know Spencer has a gun. Don't force him to behave in an uncivilized manner. The man is English."

Laura looked to Spencer, who was standing behind them.

The latter did not make a face, but pointed forward to the entrance.

She realized that it was useless to remain here and started to move.

No sooner had the three of them entered than the airlock closed behind them again.

They entered a kind of anteroom that had been set as a buffer between the outside world and the inner production area. There were changing rooms and disinfection stations here, shelves with protective clothing and masks. There were also two narrow silver elevator doors on the left.

Keller noticed her look and pointed to the elevator as well. "Spencer will take your bag downstairs, there's an apartment recently vacated that you'll occupy while you're here. It is not particularly comfortable, but it will do. You are used to far less pleasant accommodation in Africa, I suppose."

"But more pleasant company," Laura returned. "I can look at the cell later. For now, I want to know why you brought me here."

After Keller and Laura slipped on their protective gear,

they entered the core of the facility through another two-stage airlock.

A woman with a shaved head welcomed them. Her name tag read "Dr. Rose Harding."

"Here you go, Dr. Harding," Keller said. "I've arranged for your assistance. Dr. Delille has already begun to delve into the matter of her own accord. You'd best explain the details to her."

Laura hated that Keller acted as if she had voluntarily applied for this job, but she swallowed her anger. The confrontation with Keller hadn't helped at all so far. So she decided to put on a good face for the time being. That way, she might be able to find out something useful and possibly do something on the sly. Provided she gained the trust of the staff here.

She nodded to Dr. Harding and said as kindly as she could, "I'm pleased to meet you."

"There you go. There you go," Keller said. "Dr. Harding will show you around. I shall retire. Don't do anything stupid, Dr. Delille, there are guards at the facility. Besides, we don't want you to end up like your predecessor." With these words, Keller turned and walked back towards the exit.

Laura looked questioningly at Harding.

"We'll talk about that later," the latter said, pointing in the direction of the production lines. "Let's not waste any more time, we have a deadline to meet."

"So, just to be clear: I'm not here by choice, if that's what you're thinking," Laura explained.

"I see," Harding replied curtly.

"I certainly have no intention of helping this mental patient either."

"Of course not. But you are here. That's hardly a coincidence."

"Because Keller kidnapped me, it's as simple as that. And what about you? Why are you helping him with his lousy plan?"

"Because I don't think it's a lousy plan. On the contrary. Now come on. I think, in spite of everything, you're interested in what we're working on here."

WHO Deputy Director Dr. Donata Spinoza eyed each person in the large conference room on the third floor of WHO headquarters in Geneva with a critical eye. "I ask you again, why are we now on the brink of a pandemic and didn't see this coming?"

None of the department heads and executives present dared to come out of hiding.

"Ah ha, so that's how it is? Not everyone at once!" burst out the spirited Mexican burst out. Since Engström's death a few days ago, she had been temporarily in charge of all WHO activities. Unlike her reserved Swedish predecessor, she maintained a rather gruff tone. Her demeanor perfectly matched her wildly curly auburn hair and her long bright red fingernails, which she drummed impatiently on the conference table.

"All right. Apparently, no one here can or will explain to me why we suddenly have an inexplicable number of cases of miscarriage, infertility, comatose states and unexplained flu symptoms on every continent. You all know it's almost impossible for something like this to happen overnight. There must have been cases before. I want to know where it all originated!"

Laboratory director Dr. Joseph Lang nervously slid around on his chair. Finally, he raised his hand.

"Lang! We're not in school here, dammit. If you have something to say, then out with it!" demanded Spinoza.

"If I could preface this by saying that I have always been absolutely compliant ..."

Spinoza sighed theatrically. "Get on with it!"

"Dr. Laura Delille, our study director in Mali had sent samples that may match the cases that are occurring now. I have to admit that she was on to something. Her results ..."

"Why am I just finding out about this now?"

"Engström had suspended her and declined to investigate further."

Spinoza looked at Lang for a moment, pondering. "You're saying Engstrom knew about it and deliberately delayed investigating it?"

"We had no idea it could be so damaging!" defended Lang. "Dr. Delille violated various safety regulations and overrode my authority."

"It seems to me that she is the only one with brains! Where is she? Get her here."

"It looks like she's disappeared. She can't be reached on her cell phone."

"I can't accept that! Keep trying. If it's true that Delille was on the right track and we failed to take her warning seriously, then ..."

"But Engström!" interjected Lang.

"Engström is dead!" said Spinoza much louder than necessary. "Shall I tell you what the eyewitnesses to the accident saw? That he was forced off the road on purpose. What does that tell us?" She looked from one person present to the next. "Forget it, you don't need to answer. We've wasted enough time as it is! We will immediately declare the second-highest pandemic alert level and take all necessary measures. And you, Dr. Lang, will review Dr. Delille's lab results with your entire team. I want clarification as soon as possible on what we are dealing with and what we can do about it!"

"But I've already checked the results and I don't think it's going to do much good. We simply know too little," Lang countered.

"I don't want to hear any excuses. Now get the hell to work!" Spinoza slammed the table with the flat of her hand so that the glasses of water shook, and then swept out of the room like a small whirlwind.

Hugh jumped out of the cab in front of the Dormond Hotel in

Reykjavik, grabbed his suitcase and ran into the foyer. He almost ran into an abstract art sculpture that had been placed in the center of the lobby. It roughly resembled an erupting geyser, except that the water was modeled in neon green. Hugh slowed down just in time and circled the structure in a richly inelegant manner. There was one thought above all that drove him to hurry. Hopefully Nicole had made it here in one piece.

At the reception desk, made of milky glass blocks, stood a man with a full beard in a likewise neon green jogging suit, looking skeptically over at Hugh as he approached. Apparently his near miss with the sculpture had attracted attention.

Hugh raised his arms apologetically. "Sorry, I guess I was in a bit of a rush. I had a reservation – under Stephen Hume's." He pulled out his cell phone with the booking confirmation and showed it to the man. "Has my companion arrived yet, by any chance?"

The bearded man tapped away on a tablet, then shook his head. "Sorry, Mr. Humes. No one has checked in yet. The room is ready, I'll get your keycard. Or would you prefer a digital key on your phone?"

Hugh glanced at his cell phone. "I ... no, I'd rather be traditional."

"Of course. I'll code your card, just a moment."

While the man took a bright orange access card from a stack and recorded the guest data on a card terminal, Hugh looked around the avant-garde lobby. Nowhere was there any sign of Nicole, not at the bar across the room, not in the seating areas.

She should have been here long ago. Had something happened to her? Had his bold plan not worked? What if this Shanks, or whatever his real name was, hadn't been alone? Hugh hadn't even thought of that earlier in the airport. Maybe they had already taken Nicole and he was now waiting in vain.

"Here you go. The card for room 1102 and a WLAN code. Breakfast is available from seven to eleven. If you still want something to eat, the restaurant kitchen is open until 10:30 p.m., after which we'll be happy to bring snacks," the receptionist rattled off the usual information.

Hugh took the card. "Thank you." He turned and stood rather lost in the foyer.

"Is there anything else, Mr. Humes?" the man at the front desk inquired.

At that moment, Nicole McDouglas came through the door and - much more skillfully than Hugh - walked around the neon geyser.

Hugh felt his tension ease a little. "Oh, thank God," he said. "It worked."

"Sorry, my cab driver was having a leisurely day. He was chatting and chatting and didn't exactly step on the gas," Nicole explained.

"Shall I get a second card ready for you?" the receptionist asked.

"If you had a single room for me, that would be fine with me," Nicole said, looking at Hugh. "No offense, but we don't know each other that well."

"No problem." The man behind the counter tapped away on his tablet again. "A room directly across from Mr. Humes is still available. It's a double room, but I'll charge it as a single. Right now we're not very busy."

"Perfect, thank you." Nicole took her credit card out of her wallet and handed it to the man.

"So what now?" asked Nicole, addressing Hugh. "It's definitely too late to go to the archives today. The operator told me that you can go in 24 hours a day because everything is automated and there's no one on site anyway, but I don't want to run into this guy from the airport in the wilderness at night. In fact, I don't want to run into him at all."

"We should leave in the morning. I guess we're reasonably safe here."

The man behind the counter cleared his throat loudly. "I can assure you that our hotel is very safe."

"I didn't mean that," Hugh apologized.

The man put on a weak smile and held out her credit card to Nicole. Then he gave her a Wi-Fi voucher and the room card. "Number 1108, breakfast from seven to eleven. The restaurant serves hot food until 10:30, then snacks." The man pointed to the right to a large room with "Ljúffengur" written in bright neon letters above the entrance.

"Thank you," Nicole said, putting everything in her bag. She turned first to the restaurant, then to Hugh. "I certainly can't eat after this drama. You?"

Hugh shook his head. "I feel the same way. I'm exhausted. I was still in the hospital this morning. Let's talk about everything tomorrow after some rest."

Ghostly green veils glowed in the night-gray sky above the Svínafellsjökull glacier, giving the snow and ice a demonic glow. The towering mountains bored like teeth into the delicate formations of the aurora borealis.

Kurt Kruger took note of the natural spectacle for which others traveled thousands of kilometers, but he felt nothing. Not the majesty of nature, not a sense of connection, not awe, not even astonishment. For him, the extra lighting was simply practical now that he was loading his gear onto the snowmobile. In the silver-gray steel box behind the driver's seat, he packed all the material he had previously smuggled to Iceland on Keller's private jet. Kruger regretted that there had been no room for his favorite rifle, but he consoled himself with the thought that he had more than enough weapons with him - as well as everything else he would need in the next few hours.

While he closed the box and climbed onto the snowmobile, he was still amused by that idiot Stevens, who thought he had tricked him. To do that, he would first have to know what he was up to in the first place.

Kruger was already looking forward to tomorrow. Finally,

he would draw a line under it. It was clear to him that Stevens could not be allowed to leave this island alive again. Although he also knew that Keller would disapprove if he acted against his instructions, it was time for him to take the initiative.

Keller might be brilliant at what he did, but he had no idea what it was like to do dirty work in the real world. There were always incidents and unforeseen developments. Tomorrow, perhaps, there would be a tragic accident in which Stevens was unfortunately killed. Who could have predicted that?

Kruger laughed out loud now, so that his voice bounced back umpteen times from the mountains and ice masses. Then he started the engine and disappeared with the snowmobile into the frosty darkness.

# 30

Dormond Hotel, Reykjavik, Iceland, October 10.

Hugh Stevens had had trouble getting out of bed. The cell phone had jingled for a full five minutes before he finally pushed aside the covers and got up. Likewise, he had had trouble freshening up, getting dressed, and going down to breakfast. It felt like everything took twice as long as it used to. That weighed on him the most; he wanted to hurry, but he couldn't the way he wanted. Only very gradually did he get going. He hoped that a large cup or two of coffee would help.

Nicole McDouglas was already sitting at a table for two at the edge of the breakfast room, which was just as futuristically designed as the rest of the hotel. The entire ceiling was hung full of red and gold tinsel, with Christmas tree baubles and artificial icicles interspersed throughout. The tables were oval and shiny silver, the chairs were made of anthracite wire mesh. Only the floor was reassuringly normal: large square stone tiles in a subtle gray.

Hugh quickly grabbed a coffee at the buffet and then joined Nicole at the table. "Morning!" he greeted her and sat down. "How did you sleep?"

"Pretty much not at all," Nicole replied. "I couldn't stop thinking about this guy, my uncle and what we're facing."

"That must be tough. You stumble into the middle of this plot without being able to help it. But it was much the same for me and Laura. Everything has spiraled into disaster at breakneck speed. Sometimes I can't believe this is happening myself, but it is."

Nicole nodded. "I've also been thinking about the destination of this trip," she said.

"It's still the same. We need to get your uncle's data."

"Sure, that's the plan. Only what are we going to do without Laura? Are you familiar with the medical data? I can't really help you there, I'm a biologist but not a doctor."

"We still have to get them, otherwise ..." Hugh thought for a moment before continuing. "If this Shanks guy is here, it doesn't bode well. Either he wants to prevent us from getting the data. Or he wants it for himself, or his employer."

"It's possible he's after both the data and us," Nicole opined.

"That would be the worst option. Nevertheless, we need to secure your uncle's back-up. Laura was adamant that we need this data if we are to have any chance of producing an effective antidote. We just need to get it to the right people and put a stop to Keller Pharma."

"And Laura?"

Hugh was silent for a moment. "I don't know. But I'll do everything I can to get her released somehow. Maybe we'll have to turn the tables and blackmail Keller."

"To be honest, that doesn't sound very promising. Nevertheless, I feel obliged to help, because after all, my uncle seems to be largely responsible for this disaster."

"We don't know that for sure either. Maybe his work has been abused or he's been coerced. I have seen how unscrupulous these people act."

"In any case, I need to know the truth," Nicole said firmly. "And I will!"

For a while Hugh looked at her searchingly. "I understand that all too well. But I want to suggest something."

Skepticism spread across Nicole's face, but she didn't pry, instead waiting for Hugh to continue.

"It's an incalculable risk. Maybe I should go to the archives alone and get the data."

In response, he received an energetic shake of the head. "Sorry. You can forget it." Nicole pulled a silver and black key card from her pocket and held it up. "This is a hybrid high-security key with an electronic radio transmitter in the handle.

You can't get in without this thing. And without me, you don't have a key."

"Listen, it's dangerous as shit!"

"I had a lot of time to think about it during the sleepless night today. My mind is made up. Now have breakfast and let's go. I have ordered a rental car. There are two snow-mobiles waiting at the glacier at the hiking station." She put the key in her pocket and reached for her coffee cup.

Hugh shook his head, but realized he couldn't convince Nicole. He stood up. "Why do I only have to deal with stubborn people lately?" he muttered as he walked to the buffet.

Christian Keller was sitting at his desk in his library, watching a live stream on his laptop with amusement. Just then, the interim director of WHO, Dr. Donata Spinoza, stepped in front of the cameras.

"Good morning, representatives of the press, dear citizens! In the last two weeks, we have recorded an unusually high number of presumably virus-related severe illnesses, mainly on the African continent. Initial investigations have shown that the spread of the currently unknown pathogen began several months ago, but was initially very slow. The consequences are dramatic: infertility, miscarriages, coma, death.

We have followed this development with the utmost attention and concern from the outset and have taken immediate action. Nevertheless, the number of affected countries has now increased fivefold, with cases documented in Australia, China, Europe and South America. In the days and weeks ahead, the number of illnesses and deaths is expected to continue to rise, as is the number of affected countries.

WHO is assessing this outbreak around the clock and is deeply concerned about the alarming level of spread and severity of the disease, as well as the incomprehensible level of inaction by many regional governments and agencies.

We have therefore come to the conclusion that we are now

very probably on the brink of a pandemic. Rest assured that we do not use the word "pandemic" lightly. We don't want to raise undue fears or imply that the situation could get out of control. But I want to make sure that everyone hears the alarm bell ringing loud and clear.

We know that the recommended measures could take a heavy toll on society and the economy, but they are necessary. We are collectively interested in calmly doing the right thing and protecting the citizens of the world. And I firmly believe it can be done. My colleague, Prof. Russel Waters, will now brief you in detail on what we know of the disease and the action we plan to take. Thank you for your attention." Spinoza stepped back from the microphone to make way for a gray-haired man in a dark blue suit.

Christian Keller closed the computer and leaned back in his chair. He felt a strange mixture of calm satisfaction and joyful tension. This emotion was almost grotesquely conflicted. The WHO statement had been a bold-faced lie. Neither had they found out anything of value, nor had they taken any action. They were simply clueless and, above all, powerless. It was far too late to foil his plan. No measure, no matter how drastic, could stop the spread, especially when the global rollout was about to start.

But that was only part of what explained the serene satisfaction. The joyful tension grew because Keller had completed his manifesto tonight and sent the manuscript to the printers. The machines were already running at full speed, producing his work by the hundreds of thousands. The WHO did not need to go out of its way to provide clarification. Soon the whole world would know what a turning point was at hand. Keller could already see himself standing on the big stage in his mind's eye. The Olympic Stadium in Berlin was just big enough for his presentation, which was due in little more than two days. At the thought of it, a thick dose of ecstasy was mixed into Keller's abstruse emotional mix.

Keller's secret production facility was about the most modern imaginable in pharmaceutical manufacturing, Laura had to acknowledge. The facility here offered everything needed to manufacture highly complex preparations in a highly compressed space: from research and development to active ingredient synthesis and testing to laboratories for quality control. Harding had taken her there yesterday and familiarized her with the basic procedures, but without going into too much detail about the deeper meaning of it all. Laura had stoically endured the briefing, but hadn't lifted a finger. This psychopath of Keller's and his, in her opinion no less insane, henchmen had already had to force her to help them.

After a moderately restful night in a spartan apartment two floors below ground, Laura was now back at the workstation that had previously belonged to a certain Dr. Obermeier, about whose whereabouts Harding had also remained silent. Around her, three other employees had been busy for a good two hours analyzing batches and comparing laboratory values. None of the three colleagues - two men in their 50s and a woman estimated to be in her late 30s - had spoken to her yet. They probably didn't like her. No wonder, she sat like a foreign body in this laboratory and obviously disturbed the others, although she did nothing at all.

At some point, the woman came over and sat down next to her. "It's almost lunch time, do you want to have lunch together?"

Laura eyed the woman. She had bright blue eyes that revealed she was smiling under her mask. "You say that as if this were a normal workplace," Laura wondered.

"Hardly. This place couldn't be more special. But that's no reason to forgo friendliness, nor is it a reason to miss out on food. I'm Melinda Riley."

"Laura Delille."

"So, what will it be?"

A gong sounded. Laura saw that the two men had stopped what they were doing and were walking toward the door.

"Pavlovian dogs with PhDs. I'm sure Keller likes that sort of thing," she said, but then rose and followed Melinda and the others to the cafeteria.

The dining room was small, white and sterile, as was most of the complex. It had room for about a dozen employees, and there shouldn't be much more here, if Laura had estimated correctly. In every department she had seen, there had been only three or four people. There were no staff serving food either, just three large convection ovens into which shrink-wrapped pre-made menus were pushed and heated. The whole thing was reminiscent of airplane meals, which were basically pre-cooked and only heated on board. All you had to do was peel off the aluminum foil on top and you could eat immediately.

Laura and Melinda each grabbed a serving of vegetable lasagna, and the two colleagues from quality assurance sat down with schnitzel and mashed potatoes with a group of other employees.

"Who are our colleagues?" Laura wanted to know.

"Peter Holm and Rafael Sudor. They're okay, but I'm glad not to be the only woman in the department now."

"And my predecessor?"

"Obermeier, he was in charge of quality control, which I now do on an interim basis, much to the displeasure of Holm, who thinks he's more qualified."

"Typical male problem," Laura commented, taking a bite of the lasagna. "What happened to Obermeier? Did he get tired of being part of this little conspiracy?"

"It's a little more complicated than that," Melinda said. "But I think ultimately it was probably something like that. He was trying to smuggle samples out of the facility, for what purpose I don't know."

"Isn't that obvious?"

Melinda didn't answer right away, but ate in silence for a while first. "Obermeier lost his nerve, wanted to get out, although he must have known that it was impossible."

"And then?"

"He slipped into a coma and died."

"Just like that?"

Melinda looked at her askance and put down her fork. "What are you doing here, anyway?" she probed. "Why did Keller bring you here?"

"I guess I know too much and he doesn't want me to go public with what's going on."

"As if that would make any difference," Melinda opined. "This is the same misguided assumption that cost Obermeier his life. There's nothing left to prevent."

"You always have options," Laura countered. "And you can make the right choices at any given moment." She looked at Melinda piercingly. "Why are you going along with this project, what drives an apparently fun-loving, friendly woman to participate in genocide?"

"I told you before, it's more complicated than you think."

"Then enlighten me! I'm getting tired of this scavenger hunt."

"I've been with the company for two years, Harding and some others from the beginning. You know, Keller deliberately chose us, it's not just about technical competence here, it's much more important to have the right vision of what the future should look like. And this ideal of a new world is fascinating when you first ..." She broke off and looked toward the cafeteria entrance, which was diagonally behind Laura. Then she slid sideways on the bench and pulled her tray over with her.

Laura turned to see Rose Harding and Christian Keller come in and head toward her.

"I see you're already starting to integrate, how gratifying," Keller said, taking a seat across from Laura.

"Appearances are deceiving," Laura replied tersely.

"Let's talk turkey, then. Dr. Harding has analyzed the contents of the USB stick that we found with your things. So first of all, thank you very much for the good preliminary work and the brand-new data of the real patients. This will help to further optimize our products and make final corrections. I want you to do just that. Now."

"What if I don't?" asked Laura.

"I assume the colleague told you what happened to Obermeier? What if I told you that your friend Hugh Stevens was inoculated with the same substance?"

Laura glared angrily at Keller.

"I see you understand me. You saw the symptoms yourself. In Obermeier's case, the dose was quintupled. Stevens got only twice what we tested in Africa. The effect is milder. Stevens will age and die an early death if he doesn't get an infusion of the drug you'll be optimizing. So, what's next? Motivation enough?" He didn't wait for Laura's answer, but turned to Harding, who had been standing silently beside the table the whole time. "We're starting the global rollout of Alpha. Production will be ramping up today."

"Still, I have to restate my concerns. If we ..."

"Don't talk back to me in front of the new colleague. What do you want her to think of us?" Keller asked smugly at first, then his tone became sharper. "Do it! I want Alpha added to all the drugs we make from now on, not just the new vaccines, the generics too. And deliver all prepared batches immediately. From now on, we'll be working in three shifts. Make sure everything is running." He rose and smiled at Laura. "Enjoy your meal. As soon as you are finished here, come to the research department." With these words, he turned and left the canteen.

Dr. Harding looked at Melinda. "Well, I guess we'll have to rearrange the roster a bit. Quality assurance will be down to one person per shift. Take care of that. Your team will work staggered eight-hour shifts. All available staff will go to production." She looked to Laura. "And you, Dr. Delille, follow me to the research department. We'll be working with Dr. Keller to put the finishing touches on our real stroke of genius. And I'm guessing Project Beta will be of great interest to you."

# 31

*Svínafellsjökull Glacier, Iceland, October 10*

The drive from the Dormond Hotel in Reykjavik to the edge of the Svínafellsjökull glacier via the country roads of southern Iceland had taken about four hours. Around noon, Hugh and Nicole parked the rented jeep at the end of the road, from where a path led to the hiking station.

The landscape of the island was beautiful in its own way, rough and barren, but at the same time marked by a pristine, wild harmony. The glacier tongue - gray and dirty from the debris - pushed here almost to the valley. From the white snow-covered slopes all around, black mountain flanks rose up into a cloud-covered sky. Temperatures were just above zero, but further up in the permafrost zone of the mountains, the climate might be less pleasant.

They got out and walked a few hundred meters along the path to the station, where two snowmobiles were already waiting for them. Nicole fetched the keys for them from a small safe on the outside wall of the hut, which was accessible outside the main season but not permanently manned. She had reserved the two snowmobiles from the hotel and received the code for the safe online.

Next to the safe, there was a DIN A4 sheet laminated with a rather brief instruction on how to operate the vehicles. Apparently, it was assumed that people who rented a snowmobile would be confident enough to drive it without much instruction.

With keys in hand, Nicole walked over to Hugh, who meanwhile was familiarizing himself with the snowmobiles and the weather-protected GPS unit mounted on them. "Where do we need to go?" he asked in Nicole's direction.

She handed him a key whose tag bore the same number as the snowmobile: 23. Then she dug a printout out of her pocket and placed it on her vehicle. Unfolding the piece of paper, she passed it to Hugh. "There are coordinates on the top right."

Hugh took the piece of paper and programmed the numbers into the GPS. The device calculated the distance and beeped when it was finished.

"How long is the drive?" inquired Nicole.

"Hard to say if that figure is realistic or not. The GPS says about 90 minutes. Could take longer, though, depending on how well we make progress. Judging from the map, the archive is further up in a valley between two peaks."

"Then I'd better go to the bathroom beforehand. Women don't have it as easy with peeing in the wild as you men do," Nicole said and walked towards the hikers' hut.

Hugh watched her walk off and waited patiently until she had gone through the door. This was his last chance to keep Nicole out of this. He felt bad about it, but it had to be done. From the seat of the other snowmobile, he grabbed Nicole's bag and rummaged around in it until he found the key card to the archive. Hastily, he pocketed it. Then he tossed in the rental car key and examined the front of the car, where behind a housing cover lay the car's engine. He pulled it up and began pulling out wires at random. While he had no idea what he was doing, he was pretty sure Nicole didn't know any better about these vehicles either.

After closing the lid again, he got on his snowmobile. He started it up and gave it full throttle. The engine howled and snow sprayed out the back. He steered the snowmobile directly toward the mountains.

After a few moments, he heard Nicole shouting and cursing angrily behind him. Hugh turned briefly to see if her snowmobile was indeed no longer roadworthy, and was relieved to find that it hadn't moved an inch. She waved her arms and ran after him for a bit, but was far too slow to catch up. He still felt terrible for having tricked her so badly, but he had to act that way. It was completely out of the question that he would unnecessarily expose the woman to further danger. And he also knew that if push came to shove, he probably wouldn't be able to protect her.

When Laura entered the research department with Dr. Harding, Christian Keller was already waiting for them. He was sitting on an office chair with his legs crossed and rocking with his right foot.

"You are fortunate, Dr. Delille, that you will soon be among a very exclusive circle - the initiates. Those who will enjoy the fruits of our labor. Well, at least if you prove yourself worthy."

Laura's bile started to rise again at Keller's condescending speech, but she controlled herself and only replied, "I'm already very curious about this - what did the colleague here just call it... - stroke of genius."

"Good!" said Keller, pointing to the screen of a calculator next to him. "Then I think you should take a look at these charts."

Laura stepped closer and looked at the displays. "What exactly am I looking at?"

"These are two statistical curves superimposed on top of each other. The blue one represents the development of average human life expectancy over the period of the last 100 years. As you can see, it has risen from just over 50 to over 80 years on average. The red curve shows the development of the world population. This has just exploded, from 1.65 billion around 1900 to eight billion today." Keller paused briefly while Laura skimmed the numbers.

"I have a bad feeling here," Laura said.

"You're looking straight at disaster," Keller countered. "These two curves are two sides of the same problem. People are reproducing out of control and living longer and longer. In the process, they are using up the limited resources of this planet without regard for their own offspring. And the leaders of this world stand idly by because they have no means to stem this tide."

"What do you mean? Birth control?" Laura asked.

"As an example. But it doesn't really work in practice. The only effective means of combating overpopulation is still war. But that consumes energy unnecessarily and ties up resources that could be better used elsewhere," Keller explained.

"And you found the solution, did you?"

"More than that! I found - and I admit McDouglas had a significant part in this - a way to drastically flatten the red curve and exorbitantly increase the blue. Alpha and Beta work together in this project that will ultimately change the world."

"That's sick," Laura said tersely.

"On the contrary, it is a cure. You see, people are stupid. It takes someone to nudge them in the right direction and lead them to a better future. If that doesn't happen, humanity will keep running in circles and eventually destroy itself completely. The stupid ones will also drag into the vortex of destruction all those who do not deserve it. We are now standing right on this threshold of an impending doomsday. Just look around you!"

He paused for a moment, as if actually demanding that Laura look around, but she just shook her head weakly.

"But shouldn't we give humanity one last chance?" continued Keller. "I'm going to make sure of that. I and the most capable scientists of our time. We will rescue this world from its misery and raise human civilization to a new and higher level of existence. I can see you don't believe me. You may think I am a megalomaniac, crazy, a monster. But I'm nothing of the sort is this case. I know exactly what I am doing. And I have a greater plan. A vision. Because if you don't have a clear vision, you're groping around like an amoeba, searching and wandering through a world that others are designing for you. So the question is: Do you want to swim along in the Petri dish or would you rather look down from above and observe what's happening in there?"

"I suppose you'd like to play God for a bit? That's what it boils down to," Laura said.

"I beg you, where is there room for God in this world? Man is his own god. And his own devil. I only bring these two into the right relationship, the right balance. Just as I bring the ratios of these two curves here into balance." He pointed to the screen. "Alpha makes room for a long and productive life for the chosen ones, who, thanks to Beta, will live three times, five times, twenty times as long as before. Dr. Delille, I am not asking you to participate in the extinction of humanity, I want you to do the opposite. Ensure their continued existence."

Keller stood up and smiled. "And now I'll leave you with Dr. Harding. She will show you how you can help us - and your friend Hugh Stevens."

"Don't argue, I'm taking you out of here now!" said Gozo to Kimara, his eyes betraying that he was deadly serious.

Kimara tried to shake her head, to protest, but she could not. She was too exhausted even for that. The last few nights she hadn't slept a wink, out of fear and self-sacrifice. She had nursed the wounded, trying to bring some semblance of order to this chaos. In this former refugee camp, which was supposed to be a place of refuge for those fleeing war and terror. But now a small war was raging here for the remaining resources and the power to decide who had them. They should all know that there was nothing left to decide, that they were ultimately helpless. Perhaps it was time that she herself finally accepted that.

"But...," Kimara said weakly, but Gozo put his hand over her mouth.

"No more buts. No hesitation. I know you still feel responsible, but there's nothing more you can do here. This place has become hell."

"Where are we supposed to go? The airports are closed," Kimara replied.

"West to Senegal. We'll fight our way to Dakar and try to get a ship. I know a fisherman who'll take us. You've got money!"

Kimara nodded. "But who says we'll even make it there? We only have this one last Jeep, no spare tire. No idea if we'll get enough gas on the way. People are hoarding!"

"Regardless, we can't stay here." He looked down at Kimara's belly, carefully reached out and stroked it. "Also because of our child. I won't let us expose it to any more of this madness. You know better than anyone the dangers here."

"I ..." Kimara hesitated briefly, then said all the more resolutely, "I'll quickly get my things. The jeep is hidden under a tarp behind Laura's tent. Let's meet there in a few minutes. I just pray we make it out of camp without a bloody confrontation."

"I love you," Gozo said. "It's the right thing to do, believe me!"

"I believe you. And I'm going with you. Hopefully a long way to go yet."

Gozo kissed her deeply, then tore himself away and ran out of Kimara's tent to get the jeep.

She stayed behind, took one last look at the place that had been her home for nine months, and began hastily packing her belongings into a large bag.

After a little more than 80 minutes of driving over snow-covered slopes and icy passages, Hugh approached his destination on his snowmobile. It was high time, because his fingers had become almost numb due to the icy cold and the wind. The gloves that he and Nicole had bought at short notice in Reykjavik were no good.

A narrow structure protruded directly from the partially snow-covered rock face - like a broken concrete fang. It looked rough and rugged in its own way, but nevertheless futuristic with its countless blue light-emitting diodes set flush into the surface and shining in all directions.

Hugh parked the snowmobile a good ten meters from the entrance and dismounted. Then he looked around. There was hardly a sound except the wind blowing through this narrow valley. On either side was nothing but ice, snow, and bare rocks, some jutting out of the ice as tall as houses. This was the most godforsaken place he had ever been. The best thing he could do was to get the data as quickly as possible and start back.

With his backpack in hand, he went to the entrance and pulled out the key card. At the front, somewhat set back under a small canopy integrated into the structure, was an entrance. A wide door, about 2.50 meters high, made of untreated metal that had already begun to rust extensively due to the weather. This, too, had to be part of the design. It was presumably intended to symbolize the relentless ravages of time that gnawed at the archive, but ultimately did no harm to its valuable interior.

Hugh hoped that, for all their love of architecture, they had also provided a decent heating system. Next to the door was a sign engraved in English, French, Spanish, German, and Russian: "1. Present key card at terminal. 2. wait for orange signal light. 3. insert key into lock and turn twice. 4. when signal light changes to green, access is granted."

Next to the sign, Hugh found a card reader clad in brushed stainless steel, to which he now held the key card. As described in the instructions, an LED lit up in rich orange. He inserted the key into the keyhole on the door and turned. A glance at the reader showed him a now green LED which confirmed the door had been unsealed.

Hugh pulled the handle and the massive steel door, which was about six inches thick, and swung open smoothly and almost silently. He took a step forward and went inside. Just as he was about to close the door again and turn around, he looked down the barrel of a pistol and froze. Dressed in snow camouflage, a man was suddenly standing opposite him.

"Shanks!" cried Hugh, earning a sardonic grin.

"Oh please, even a dope like you should have figured out by now that that's not my real name. But I don't want you to die an idiot either, so you may call me Kruger."

"Wonderful. I feel better already."

"I hope so, old man. We've got some plans to work on together." Kruger twitched his gun toward the interior of the plant.

Hugh did not move or answer.

"Come on. Surely you're not bothered by that little remark?"

"You motherfucker, what did you inject me with in Romania?" Hugh blurted out.

Instead of an answer, Kruger burst out laughing. "Yeah, you'd like to know that, wouldn't you? But I guess you won't live long enough to find out for yourself. Are you growing gray hairs yet, Mr. Stevens?"

Anger boiled up inside Hugh. He wanted to punch this arrogant guy right in his stupid grinning face, but he knew he wouldn't hesitate to pull the trigger. What was stopping him anyway? The door to the archive was open. Kruger was on target and Hugh was checkmated.

Kruger's smile gradually disappeared. "Well, Mr. Stevens, since you were very interested in our project, we thought it would be fitting if you could give a first-hand account of the effects of the preparations. I'm very curious myself to see how long you last with a double dose in your blood. But my client would also have you know that you can still get an antidote if you cooperate. Besides, we may let Dr. Delille live... Provided you do as we say. How does that sound? But for now, let's go inside, it's a little uncomfortable out here after all." Kruger approached Hugh at gunpoint, virtually shoving him inside the facility. Behind him, he pulled the door shut, locking out the frigid climate.

## 32

Secret Keller site near Lychen, October 10.

Laura was sitting at one of the PC workstations in the research department and could hardly concentrate. She had been trying for quite a while to get an overview of Project Beta and the drug's mechanisms of action, but she was hardly succeeding. Her mind was still haunted by Keller's words, the meaning of which she had understood, but which she simply could not digest morally and ethically. Technologically and statistically, the matter was clear. She even had to admit that Keller's project was logical in a way.

This realization shocked her the most. The dramatic increase in the world's population and the accompanying ever greater exploitation of natural resources were problems that could not be dismissed and had remained unsolved until now. And modern medicine had ensured that people lived longer than ever before. However, this combination of circumstances unintentionally aggravated the situation - even if the purpose was fundamentally noble.

Keller had found a way to resolve these contradictory developments. Only this way was paved with corpses - with millions, perhaps billions dead all over the world. This was a holocaust of unimagined proportions. At the same time, the man held in his hands a remedy that promised a multiplication of life expectancy and perhaps even immortality.

Laura suddenly couldn't help but think of the invention of the atomic bomb. The dream of a supposedly clean source of energy from nuclear fission had become a nightmare not so long ago. The development of the atomic bomb had resulted in unprecedented atrocities and triggered a seemingly endless arms race that had the potential to wipe out all life on this planet in a short time. And even the peaceful use of nuclear power had caused major disasters. All in all, nuclear fission had been a terrible invention.

Keller had now brought the biological equivalent of this to series maturity. It was incredible, but after everything she read here - and had already discovered herself - she no longer doubted that Keller had been telling the truth when he said he would change the world.

"What the hell am I going to do?" muttered Laura, shaking her head.

"Have them check the Beta batches for discrepancies and work out adjustments if necessary," she heard Harding's voice behind her.

Laura turned around and looked directly at the site manager. Again, she wondered at her so penetratingly matter-of-fact manner in the face of the magnitude of what was going on. "How can you be so hardened while people are dying out there?"

"People die. Some die earlier, others later. So far, medicine has not been able to change that. Until now. I am here to overcome that limit. And you must have realized yourself that Beta has the potential to do so. Or am I mistaken?"

Laura was reluctant to agree with Harding, but from a purely scientific point of view, this assessment was most likely correct. "At what price?" was all she asked.

"Please don't waste our time by bothering yourself with pointless remorse."

"What good is it to humankind if it lives forever but kills its humanity along the way?" Laura wanted to know.

"Dr. Delille, it's very simple. You have only one decision to make: Will you work with us and gain the prospect of a very long, contented life, or will you perish with the scum?"

"You talk like Keller," Laura commented, turning around.

She could not continue this conversation. Instead, she stared at the screen again, which showed the same lab results as half an hour ago. And the probing question in her mind was also still the same. What the hell was she supposed to do now? Could this catastrophe be prevented somehow?

As Kurt Kruger and Hugh Stevens entered the archive, the lights switched on automatically. The entrance area, which had previously been in twilight, gradually became brighter. At first, it was unclear exactly where the light was coming from; apparently, the semi-transparent, milky-white walls must be radiating it from within. Everything was white or light gray, only the floor was black and mirror-like smooth. Bushy blue fiber optic bundles hanging from the ceiling provided a bit of color in the otherwise monochromatic spectrum of the entrance area.

Hugh felt as if he were entering the interior of a spaceship that would soon begin its journey to a foreign galaxy to preserve humanity's heritage. Only the crew was missing. Or was it an unmanned mission? Futuristic was almost the wrong word for this interior design.

At the other end of the anteroom was a second door, fitted with frosted glass so that it was impossible to see behind it. A card reader had been mounted on the left side, similar to the one at the outer entrance.

Kruger pointed. "Open it," he demanded.

Hugh held the key card up to the reader, and after less than a second, a light came on from the other side of the door. The hazy layer of the glass door cleared, so that it now looked like a conventional transparent pane. Behind the door, a large, narrow room appeared that led deeper into the mountain like a tunnel. Hugh opened the door and went inside.

Kruger followed him with the gun pointed at the back of his head.

On the sides of the room, several vertical windows were set into the walls. Behind them, in the semi-darkness, rows of flashing servers and other technical equipment could be seen, the purpose of which was not apparent to Hugh at first glance. Between the windows, there were repeated steel doors that looked like they belonged to refrigerated compartments, each equipped with its own card reader. Half a dozen workstations in the empty spaces were equipped with readers, keyboards, mice and monitors. But the associated computers were not visible. They were possibly just terminals used to access the servers directly behind the glass panels.

There was no one in here either, so Hugh wondered why it required so many workstations. Presumably these were from a time when the archive had been set up and the data uploaded. That so many users regularly found their way here, on the other hand, seemed out of the question.

Hugh looked questioningly in Kruger's direction. He pointed to the first available workstation and pulled a mobile hard drive from his right jacket pocket.

"Get started and pull a full copy of McDouglas' data." He placed the hard disk on the table and moved away to take a seat in the chair at the opposite terminal.

While Hugh inserted the key card into an electronic lock at his workstation and waited for it to be released, he feverishly considered whether there was a way to catch Kruger off guard and escape. But all the scenarios that came to mind ended with him having a bullet in his head - or stomach.

A window appeared on the terminal screen with a notice: "This archive is encrypted. To retrieve unencrypted data, enter your personal access code. Or press 'Skip' to continue."

Hugh turned to Kruger. He was chewing on an energy bar which crumbled all over the polished black floor.

"What's up? Done yet?" he asked.

"We need an access code," Hugh replied.

"I know. Then enter it. That's why you're still alive, after all. Or are you going to tell me now that you don't know it? That would be downright pathetic."

Hugh shook his head. "Apparently you know more than I do. Nicole McDouglas didn't mention a code. I stole the key from her."

Kruger looked at him skeptically for a while, then threw

away the half-eaten bar and stood up. He came over to Hugh and pressed the barrel of the pistol painfully to his forehead. As he did so, he looked deep into his eyes, probably to find out if he was lying.

Hugh tried hard not to blink, but stared back into the killer's ice-cold eyes.

Finally, Kruger let go of him. "Fine, then hit 'skip' and pull an encrypted copy. I'll have to pay another visit to Miss McDouglas later."

Hugh felt sick at the thought that Kruger would continue to go after Nicole and there was nothing he could do about it.

Kruger apparently registered this hesitation and pointed the gun at his head again. "Don't try anything stupid. My fingers are itching."

After Hugh pressed the button to skip entering the code, another window appeared: "Connect disk for encrypted backup."

Hugh plugged in the hard drive and confirmed the input. After a few moments, a status bar appeared, slowly progressing. Below it, a remaining time of seven minutes was displayed.

Kruger nodded with satisfaction and picked up his backpack. "I'm sure you won't mind if I make a few preparations in the meantime." He promptly pulled out four small gray packets and a plastic bag containing several black cylindrical objects.

Hugh realized these were plastic explosives and detonators. Although it was obvious, he reflexively asked, "What are you going to do?"

"I'll make sure no one else gets the data. This is enough explosives to pulverize the whole plant," Kruger explained with an unmistakable note of glee in his voice, showing Hugh a remote detonator with a five-minute countdown set on it. He then plugged it back in and began taping the packets to various window panes and attaching the detonators.

Hugh's gaze slid back and forth between Kruger and the

status bar on the screen. He was undecided what to do - and whether there was any room for maneuver at all.

When Kruger finished placing the charges, he returned and stood some distance behind Hugh. They spent the remaining two minutes, until the copying process was completed, in silence.

When the terminal reported the successful transfer of all data, Kruger approached him. "Thank you for your cooperation, Mr. Stevens. Unfortunately, our journey together ends here."

As Kruger tried to reach forward to take the hard drive, Hugh seized his chance and shoved him in the side with all his might.

But Kruger seemed to have sensed it and parried the spontaneous attack effortlessly. He wheeled around and brutally hit Hugh on the head with his pistol.

Dazed, Hugh sank down. He fought the ringing in his ears, the shimmering stars before his eyes, and the threat of fainting. He didn't really notice Kruger putting the hard drive and key card in his pocket. But he felt Kruger grab him by the collar and drag him into the anteroom. There he let go of him, and his head hit the floor. It was freezing cold.

Then he heard shots and at first thought they were for him, but he felt no burning pain, only the same dull paralysis as before. Then white light flooded his field of vision and blackness enveloped him shortly thereafter.

Two large white area lights provided broadcast-quality illumination of Keller's place at the desk. A third spotlight behind Keller gave his head and shoulders a radiant fringe, while a fourth highlighted the bookshelves in the background.

Christian Keller sat at his workstation, turning a booklet in his hands, waiting for the recording to begin.

Now the cameraman gave him a silent hand signal that he could start.

Keller paused for a moment, gently stroked the cover of

the book with his hand, and then raised his eyes directly to the camera.

"It's amazing how often history repeats itself," he began. "And it's usually individuals who shape the course of world events. European history is full of such examples. Yet so much falls prey to ubiquitous forgetfulness in our fast-moving times. Yet we could learn so much from the ideas and mistakes of those who lived before us."

Keller pointed to the back of his bookshelf. "Let's cast our minds back to the year 1600. People in Germany and all of Central Europe felt that the world was at a crossroads. Religious conflicts were smoldering all over Europe, a split in society was running like a fissure right through the so-called Holy Roman Empire. But it was not only this conflict over the supposedly true faith that haunted the people. The signs pointed to war. There were economic crises, crop failures and climate deterioration. People were not really left with much to hold on to. The whole world seemed to be coming apart at the seams."

Keller paused and looked urgently into the camera for a moment before continuing.

"When you hear these words, don't you inevitably think of our times today? History is repeating itself. And like then, we are at a turning point. Where are we headed? Are we doomed to keep repeating the same fatal mistakes of mankind? This is the question scholars were asking themselves even back then, over 400 years ago."

He picked up the small leather-bound booklet and held it up to the camera. "The Rosicrucians will mean something to some, I suppose? That was an order of the knowledgeable. Its goal was to free people from the apocalyptic prophecies of the Church and give them a real perspective. It was about nothing less than creating a new world. And this struck a chord with those of the time. This little booklet, the Fama Fraternitatis, on which the whole movement was built, found a ready market. The work of the laudable Order of the Rosary was addressed to all the scholars and heads of Europe, to the powerful, the wise, the knowledgeable. I will now complete this endeavor to lead the world into a golden and pure future. It has taken 400 years for someone to muster the courage and the means to do this. But rest assured, I will finish what was not yet accomplished then. It is not enough to simply put your vision into words, you have to make it a reality. I will do both together. My manifesto of a new world order is only to be understood as a guide. It will educate you on what the world can expect. But I will also follow it up with deeds. They will be deeds that involve certain sacrifices, great losses, it may initially seem. But in the end, we are only throwing out ballast in order to ascend. After a difficult period of upheaval, the world will be a better place. Not for everyone. But for those who are worthy of it. It will be a golden age. Accompany me there."

Keller finished his speech and waited a moment for the red light on the camera to go out.

"That was very good," the cameraman said. "Shall we do another one?"

"Why? It was perfect. We'll move on to the next section in a moment. And after that, take care of the post-production. I want to present part of the video tonight!" ordered Keller, rising to return the booklet to its rightful place on the shelf. "Come over here with the camera, I want you to include some of these works in the presentation."

## 33

In front of the Icelandic Glacier Archive, October 10.

"Drop it!" Nicole McDouglas tried to put as much emphasis and assertion into her voice as possible. But her shaky hand, which was currently pointing a small silver pistol at the guy who had waylaid her at the airport, betrayed that she was anything but calm and confident.

The man sat chewing gum on a dull gray metal box about 100 yards from the archive's entrance, holding a cell phone-sized device. A little off to the side was a snowmobile. He turned demonstratively slowly toward her and smiled sardonically. "Miss McDouglas, it's very convenient for you to come to me, it saves me a detour."

Nicole gripped the gun tighter by the handle and tried to aim as accurately as possible. She was not used to the gun and it had been ages since she had shot. Back then it had been with a rifle - at partridges. Now she was aiming at a potentially extremely dangerous human being. "I don't want to shoot you, but I will if I have to," she stated.

"You're going to shoot me with that toy? Or rather, not shoot me?" asked Kruger sarcastically. "Well, what do you want then?"

"Where's Hugh? The key card?" demanded Nicole.

"What do you want with that? It's too late anyway. I suggest we wait here in peace for a few more minutes, then the matter will be settled. After that, we can talk about anything. Unless, of course, you do shoot me. But I think you're as much of a coward as your uncle."

The way the man talked made Nicole boil, hardened and ice-cold, yet arrogant.

"Did you kill him? You son of a bitch!" Nicole's index

finger twitched on the trigger, she could barely contain herself. Tears threatened to blur her field of vision. But she forced herself to remain calm. Something wasn't right here. Why was this guy so calm? "Where's Hugh?" she asked again.

The man nodded his head in the direction of the entrance.

Without lowering the gun, Nicole glanced briefly over at the archive. She registered in the corner of her eye, just in time, the man reach into his jacket pocket. Her instincts cried out.

She shot. Three times, without aiming.

It apparently hit, because the man flinched and toppled backwards from the crate. The device he had been holding fell into the snow. She couldn't tell where she had hit him or if he was dead, but now she had a chance!

Nicole approached the motionless man at gunpoint, ready to shoot again at a moment's notice, but it didn't seem necessary. Blood soaked the snow next to his head, and he did not move. She picked up the device and froze. It had to be some kind of detonator. A small display showed a countdown - just over two minutes left.

Nicole looked for a button to abort the blast, but nothing like that was found on it. The countdown continued relentlessly.

Now she knelt down next to the man and began to search his pockets. She found a cell phone, a heavy semi-automatic pistol and two spare magazines, a sat nav, three packs of gum, and also the key card. She promptly stopped searching and rushed to the entrance of the archive. According to the timer she had 1:30 minutes left.

Her mind objected. This was absolute madness! But she still had to try to save Hugh. She held the key up to the terminal, waited impatiently for it to be released, and then inserted it into the keyhole of the access door.

Acting WHO chief Dr. Donata Spinoza watched today's update from her crisis team with a frown. Every day at 1:00 p.m., all the latest information was brought together in the conference room, being assessed and used as the basis for any new recommendations for action or adjustments in infection control. And day by day, the outlook was getting worse, despite the containment measures already in place.

"We need to call for further restrictions. Air traffic should be stopped as much as possible," suggested epidemiologist Dr. Koharu Nakamura.

"We should be very careful with this, something like this will have massive economic consequences!" interjected crisis coordinator Winston McGowern.

"We have to do it. Or cases will explode in Europe just as they have in Africa and Asia," Nakamura stressed.

Spinoza now took the floor. "That's going to happen anyway. France will close its borders tomorrow. Germany probably will as well. If these two countries take action, the rest of the EU will surely follow. We will definitely recommend comprehensive travel restrictions," she said.

Laboratory director Dr. Lang came rushing in with a stack of papers under his arm. Half of them slipped out of his hand as he pulled back a chair and hastily sat down.

"Glad you could make it," Spinoza commented in a sarcastic tone.

"I apologize, but I had to wait for the evaluation of a second series of tests. The results are disturbing," Lang replied and collected his papers.

"Everything about the current situation is troubling."

"I realize that! It's just that none of our measures seem to be working. And I think I know why." He glanced around the room.

"Would you perhaps have the goodness to not keep us in suspense!" demanded Spinoza indignantly.

"I finally evaluated all of Dr. Delille's data and ran a second set of tests. This is not a pathogen, at least not in the classical sense. It is a hybrid construct of artificially produced mRNA and a modified viral envelope. On the one hand, the whole thing behaves like a novel gene therapy, but at the same time it spreads like the flu. Whatever it is exactly and whatever it was originally intended to do, it now seems to be reproducing and mutating. The result is an extremely unusual pattern of spread."

"What do you mean by that, exactly?" prompted Nakamura.

"I have statistically compared all the cases reported so far and cannot establish a clear incubation period, nor do any comprehensible patterns of infection emerge. It can take anywhere from 24 hours to two months for symptoms to appear, and males and females show quite different courses of the disease. And as if that weren't strange enough, this man-made pathogen seems to be reproducing in leaps and bounds at a rate that seems illogical."

"And the reason for that?" Spinoza demanded to know.

Dr. Lang was silent for a moment.

Instead, Nakamura spoke up again. "I think I know what he is implying. If this is true, it allows only one conclusion: This disease, if we can even call it that, has already affected many more people unnoticed than we think, perhaps it has even been spreading for months. The only reason this has not been noticed is because not all of those affected show symptoms - or because such symptoms happen only after a very long delay. At the same time, these latently infected persons are most likely carriers. So the pathogen can spread without a clear chain of infection being identified."

"So you're telling me the chaos we're seeing right now is just the tip of the iceberg?" inquired Spinoza. "If it is, we might as well pack it in."

"I disagree!" protested Nakamura. "We'll just have to make even more drastic restrictions."

"We have no choice anyway. We have to go to the highest pandemic alert level immediately."

Hugh had not imagined how long time could stretch when one

was waiting to die. The drowsiness had subsided somewhat, but the confusion and throbbing headache remained. He didn't know how much longer it would be before the charges went off. Kruger had taken the cell phone from him. He didn't own a watch either, so he didn't have the slightest opportunity to distract himself. He searched the dimly lit anteroom of the archive with his eyes, but it was hopeless; he couldn't get out of here.

Getting at the explosive charges was also impossible; he had neither the key nor would it be of any use, for Kruger, before leaving, had shot the reader.

The only thing Hugh could cling to was the dull hum of the air conditioner and servers quietly emanating from the archive behind him. He would die in this monotony. Sometime in the next few minutes, he would be crushed with a great thud by masses of ice and debris. He hoped it would be quick.

Suddenly there was a bang. Hugh winced. But it was not a blast. It came from outside! And it had sounded like gunshots, three of them, in quick succession.

Hugh looked at the front door. A moment later it opened. While the glaring light from outside blinded him, he wondered if Kruger would come back to shoot him after all. Actually, that would almost suit him.

Then he caught sight of bright red hair in the brilliant white. He could hardly believe his eyes when Nicole came running in. Was he hallucinating?

"Hugh!" shouted the familiar voice. It was indeed Nicole!

He got up awkwardly and went to meet her. "How on earth...?" he began, but was abruptly interrupted.

"Get out now!" screeched Nicole, holding out the detonator to him, which read 28 seconds.

"Shit!" exclaimed Hugh, and started to move.

As fast as they could, they rushed to the exit and then out into the stark white. There was still time to put about 50 meters between the archive and them, then the ground shook and they felt a shock wave hit their backs. Instinctively, they threw themselves to the ground.

Snow and ice chunks rained down and hit them painfully in the head and back. But they were miraculously not seriously injured.

When the snowy flurry slowly subsided, they turned around. The archive had been completely destroyed. Where once the entrance had been, there was a crater with smoke coming out of it, and around it lay dramatic piles of concrete, rubble and chunks of ice. The valuable research in the archive seemed to be lost forever.

Laura's shift in the research department ended around 5 p.m., and she went to the in-house canteen for dinner. Through a large-format glazed partition separating the rear laboratory area from the production line, she could see that manufacturing there was in full swing. All employees were apparently busy producing as much as possible of the devilish stuff, the theoretical basis of which she had been studying all day.

She were particularly puzzled by the fact that, unlike the Alpha preparation, no real application study had been carried out for Beta. Nevertheless, production was ramped up. Even with Alpha, which had been extensively tested, there had been significant deviations in the mode of action and distribution, judging by their findings. Obermeier, who had died in the meantime, had pointed this out several times, but had been killed before he could do anything about it.

One thing, however, seemed clear: it had obviously not been planned for Alpha to be transmitted independently from person to person. Rather, the drug was to be spread in a targeted and pinpointed manner through its hidden use in medications. Keller had obviously not been bothered by this change, because it resulted in a much faster, global spread. But he had ignored the potentially uncontrollable side effects. Now he was even forcing the spread - with unclear consequences.

Laura entered the nearly empty cafeteria and found Melinda sitting at one of the tables. She massaged her left arm while staring absently at the food in front of her. At the buffet counter, she picked up a tray, placed shrink-wrapped portions of bread and cheese on it, and then stood at the table across from Melinda.

Melinda hastily pulled down the left sleeve of her smock and put on a smile. "Good evening," she greeted her.

"May I join you?"

"Sure," Melinda said, gesturing to the chairs in front of Laura.

Laura took a seat and tore open the food ration wrappers.

Melinda now also grabbed a sandwich and took a bite.

They sat in silence for a while, eating, before Laura spoke up again. "What's wrong with your arm?"

Melinda winced briefly, then sighed. "Oh, nothing..." she continued, raising her right hand defensively.

"You're in pain, I can see that. Do you want me to look at it?"

"It would probably spoil your appetite."

Laura frowned. "I last worked in Africa. Nothing spoils my appetite that quickly."

After a moment of hesitation, Melinda rolled up her left sleeve. Parts of the upper and lower arm were pale as a sheet, and there was a brown-black discolored area in the crook of her arm, the surface of which also appeared somewhat wrinkled.

"That looks like necrosis," Laura said incredulously.

A knowing nod came from Melinda in response.

"How could this have happened? You should be treated in a clinic," Laura said.

Melinda shook her head. "Absolutely impossible. Keller won't let me go to a public hospital. I've already tried all the options we have available here. Only they don't work."

"With necrosis, the only thing that usually helps is surgery to remove the tissue. How long have you had this?"

"About two days. Rafael Sudor has it too."

Laura waited to see if Melinda would reveal more, but she already had a suspicion about where the necrosis might have come from.

"Well, so ...," Melinda resumed. "You must know that all the employees here at the site have been given an injection of Beta. In recognition of our accomplishments and ..."

"A nice reward," Laura interrupted her and immediately regretted it. "I'm sorry, I just can't believe Keller is using you guys as guinea pigs."

"We're all here by choice, at least we used to be. No one could have known that something like this would happen," Melinda defended herself.

"Of course, there was no way to know. I studied the data today. There hasn't been a decent trial of Beta, so how can you accurately estimate the real effects? The whole project seems like it was done under immense time pressure."

"Of course, there are always risks with experimental therapies, but ..." Melinda paused. "I just thought it was a temporary side effect. But it's not getting better, it's getting worse. I took a sample, but so far I haven't gotten any definitive results."

"If it is indeed necrosis, it is not reversible. At best, dead tissue detaches and can be replaced during the healing process. But dead cells cannot be resuscitated."

"I know, I know," Melinda agreed. "Let's change the subject, please."

"There's nothing else to discuss here other than this pervasive insanity," Laura said wanly. "We can't even talk about the weather because we're locked in this windowless bunker. And don't tell me you still believe in the success of this project after all this."

"I have to go now," Melinda said, picking up her tray. "I have a shift in production later."

"I can see in your face that you want to do something," Laura insisted.

But Melinda turned away and walked with the tray to the buffet, where she placed it on a dish cart and then wordlessly disappeared from the cafeteria.

"Shit," Laura growled, propping her head in her hands in resignation.

After a moment, she felt a hand on her shoulder. She looked up.

"My samples are in the quality control lab," Melinda said. "Everything is filed under Beta-MR-2/12 - if you want to take a look."

Before Laura could say anything else, Melinda turned around and hurried out of the cafeteria.

Hugh stood up and helped Nicole to her feet. After brushing the snow from his clothes, he looked Nicole straight in the eye. "I have to thank you, you saved my life. And I have to apologize. I didn't mean to put you in danger. And after you were so persistent, I just didn't see any other way."

Nicole cocked her head. "That sabotage stunt was really something. But okay, I understand why you did it."

"How did you get here? And where is your snowmobile?"

"It gave up the ghost about a kilometer ago, and I walked the rest. I didn't really fix it properly either, I just plugged cables together until it started. I'm glad I had to walk the rest, so I saw the guy with the detonator from a distance and was able to surprise him."

"Kruger! That son of a bitch. Where is he?" Hugh looked around the area.

"I shot him, three times."

"Shot?" You did that? I thought Kruger ..." Hugh shook his head. "I'm glad it was that way and not the other way around."

"I hit him at least once. He was lying bleeding next to the metal box." She, too, now looked around and spotted the crate lying under a thin layer of snow barely 50 yards away. She pointed to it.

"I don't see anyone. Do you think he's further back somewhere?" asked Hugh, walking in the direction shown.

Nicole followed him and stopped halfway. "There's a blood trail. You can't see it too well now because of all the snow, but it leads away from here. There was a snowmobile over there. Now it's gone."

"That would mean he's not dead," Hugh concluded.

Nicole shrugged her shoulders. "I don't know, it all happened so fast. In the rush, I didn't feel his pulse, but there was blood, and he absolutely wasn't moving."

They moved to the metal box and Hugh wiped off the snow. Next to it were several other objects, including a pistol and associated magazines.

"I pulled this out of his pockets," Nicole explained, picking it up. "Here's a cell phone," she said, handing it to Hugh.

"This is mine, he took it from me. Let's take everything, including the gun and the navigator. We might need those things."

"What about the box?", Nicole asked.

"Let's take a look," Hugh replied, snapping open the latches. He lifted the lid and looked at the contents.

"What else was he trying to blow up?" he asked, pondering. In the box were six more packets of plastic explosives, quite a few detonators and a remote control. "We'll take those, too," Hugh decided.

"What for?" asked Nicole.

"Don't know yet, but we shouldn't leave them here."

"You're right, of course."

"We'll put everything on my snowmobile and then let's get out of here. Knowing our luck, Kruger won't be dead. But we don't know if he's just dragging himself to the hospital or targeting us from the next hill."

"I hope he bleeds to death on the way. The son of a bitch killed my uncle," Nicole said grimly.

Hugh nodded. "Yes, unfortunately, that seems quite likely."

"We should definitely take another route back to the Jeep, just to be safe in case he ambushes us," Nicole suggested.

"Okay, very good idea. We'll drive on the western flank this time. It's a bit further, but safer. And then we'll see that we make it back to Reykjavik before nightfall. Out here, we're far too easy prey."

## 34

*Secret Keller location near Lychen, evening of October 10.*

After dinner, Laura had felt little desire to go down to her barren, underground quarters and twiddle her thumbs while a biological weapon of mass destruction was being manufactured at full speed upstairs. So around 6 p.m., she had gone to the quality assurance lab where she had worked first thing yesterday.

There, Peter Holm had sat at a PC workstation with a grim expression and had registered her arrival with a scowl, but had not commented on it with a word. He apparently tolerated her, while on the other hand she had been excluded from working in production - probably because they did not trust her and suspected an attempt at sabotage.

Laura had to admit that the thought had crossed her mind more than once. But she also knew that it would be pointless. There were guards in the hall, and besides, she didn't know the critical points of the synthesis process, nor would it make much sense to destroy production given the current situation. The additional Alpha batches were just the accelerant. The fire was already blazing meters high all around the world.

She took a seat across from Holm in front of the only screen that he could not see from his position. She sat with her back to the door and would not see immediately if someone came in, but she still hoped to be able to react quickly enough if they did.

She began looking for the analyses of recent staff samples, most notably those of Melinda Riley.

Now she had to concentrate on somehow perfecting an antidote as quickly as possible. One that didn't have fatal side effects, like the Beta drug that, according to her findings, had once been designed as the optimal antidote to Alpha, but didn't quite work as hoped.

In the meantime, it was completely clear to her why Keller had chosen such an ingeniously mean concept. Beta was supposed to protect those chosen by Keller from the artificially induced Alpha effect and also give them a long life. Laura wouldn't be surprised for a second if Keller sold the prospect of salvation to the rich and powerful for an enormous sum, forcing them into a dependency on him at the same time.

The guy pretended to be a visionary and thinker, but was first and foremost an unscrupulous businessman. In the end, however, his true motives and plans did not matter. The situation he had brought the world into was catastrophic. And should the vaunted miracle cure now fail, even if only partially, it was completely unclear how this would all end.

Laura shook her head as she realized that, in a sense, she was voluntarily doing exactly what she had been dragged here to do. But she had no intention whatsoever of making Keller as rich and powerful as no man had ever been before him. She would learn as much as she could about Beta and its potential, and then make it available to everyone to mitigate the effects of Alpha and protect the rest of humanity. But to do that, she had to get out of here somehow - with the data.

She thought of the hermetically sealed lock, which could only be opened by the department heads and next to which stood at least one armed guard. And she thought of Melinda, who had mentioned that she was now acting head of the department. If she could convince anyone to stop this madness and get them out of here, it would be her. It would ultimately be in her own best interest to be treated in a hospital as soon as possible.

Laura had just brought up the necrotic samples of Melinda Riley and the equally affected Rafael Sudor on the screen for comparison and started an algorithm-based evaluation, when she heard a throat clearing behind her.

She knew there was no point in hastily closing the current

window anymore. Instead, she turned around as casually as possible.

Rose Harding stood directly behind her and looked at her suspiciously. "What are you doing here, Dr. Delille? You're not assigned to this shift."

"Overtime," Laura said calmly.

"That wasn't my question. Everyone here is working overtime. I want to know why you're in this lab and what you're trying to do with these analyses."

"I'm sure you know yourself that there's a problem here. And I don't mean Alpha," Laura explained. "You're just too cowardly to tell Keller because you're afraid you'll suffer the same fate as Obermeier."

Harding did not respond to the attack, but remained silent.

"No answer is an answer, too. But I'm sure you know about the abnormal effects in Melinda Riley and Rafael Sudor."

"Of course I know about it. And I also informed Keller, that's part of my job."

"If so, I suppose he just didn't want to hear what you had to say to him. Is that so? Is this where the messengers of unwelcome messages get sent, out of the way?"

Harding snorted contemptuously. "You have no idea the sacrifices we've all had to make."

"I can imagine that working for a maniac like Keller is no walk in the park. But should those sacrifices have been in vain? Stop telling yourself that you have the situation under control. You're just being used!"

To Laura's surprise, Harding did not get angry or otherwise show any emotional reaction despite the attack. She pulled a chair toward her and sat down next to Laura. "Show me what you have," she asked.

"Okay, if you really want to hear it. This morning I studied your tool for AI-based compound effect analysis. It's brilliant. The simulations are fascinating. But they don't match reality -

or rather, they don't anymore. I have started another analysis of Alpha. This time based on the samples taken in Mali that preserve the mutant strain. Then I correlated the two to determine the divergence. You know yourself that the new version is much more aggressive and has learned, in a way that is completely mysterious to me, to transmit itself from person to person."

"Your finding neither surprises me, nor does it mean it's a failure," Harding interjected.

Now Peter Holm also got up from his seat and came over to join in looking at the screen.

Laura continued, "That alone doesn't tell you much, I agree. But since Alpha and Beta act as antagonists, I just applied the same principle to the second agent."

She looked to the screen, where by now a pop-up had appeared reporting the completion of the analysis process. "I'm pretty sure this confirms my suspicions." Laura opened the report and all three silently read through the results.

When she finished, Harding leaned back in his chair and stared broodingly toward the lab apparatus on the side work counter.

Laura gave her a moment to assess the significance of the data for herself and looked to Peter Holm, whose expression seemed to have become even more somber.

"There must be some kind of mistake! Alpha and Beta neutralize each other," Holm insisted. "Beta alone not only protects us, but promises immortality!"

Before Laura could respond, Harding interjected. "There's no error in the analysis. The AI would have reported that. And we took all the samples ourselves."

Holm shook his head angrily. "I refuse to accept this!" Without another word, he stormed out of the room.

Laura looked at Harding again. "You know the unlimited life plan can't succeed once you've come into contact with the mutant Alpha strain. The best we can achieve is a stalemate situation where the agents keep each other in check until we find a solution. But to do that, we would have to adapt Beta and stop the necrotic effect. Otherwise, we may be doing more damage."

"I don't know how we're going to do that. Beta will be produced in gigantic quantities starting tomorrow. We don't have time to modify anything!"

"Still, we have to try. Maybe start from scratch. I need access to McDouglas' source data, and I need to know what modifications you've made. Then maybe something can be salvaged," Laura said.

"McDouglas' data is under lock and key," Harding explained. "I can try to get Keller to make it available to us. If I can convince him with the new findings. But ..."

"He won't want to know about it, am I right?"

Harding sighed. "Keller is not the same guy who started this project three years ago. Since McDouglas dropped out, he's increasingly living in his own world."

"You have to convince him!" insisted Laura.

"I know," Harding said wanly. "I know."

Hugh and Nicole had spent the journey back to the hikers' hut together in silence. Because of the engine noise of the snowmobile and the wind, there would have been little point in talking. Because Hugh had still felt a severe headache and slight dizziness, Nicole had driven the first half of the way.

After just under an hour, they switched and Hugh took over the wheel. Another 45 minutes later, they reached the cabin without mishap, incident, or an encounter with Kruger. They parked the snowmobile, and Hugh put the key back in the safe on the outside wall. A few hundred yards down at the end of the road, he could make out their jeep.

"The car is still there," he noted with relief. "I was afraid this Kruger guy might have grabbed it."

"Thank God, I don't want to spend the night here anyway," Nicole said. "It's going to get dark soon enough, and there's no way we should be here then."

"Absolutely. We better not waste any time," Hugh said, opening the metal box in the back of the snowmobile. He stuffed charges, detonators and everything else into his backpack. In the process, the pistol fell into his hands again. He turned to Nicole. "You said you shot Kruger. With what?"

Nicole now pulled out a small silver pistol as well. "This is from Uncle Howard. I hid it in the luggage in a metal box."

"You're pretty hard-nosed for a biologist."

"I'm a Highlander!" said Nicole. "And I know how to defend myself."

"That's really good to know," Hugh replied. "We could certainly use another big helping of Highlander courage." He put the rest of the gear in the backpack, and they walked hurriedly along the trail toward the jeep.

Once there, Nicole took the key out of her pocket and got in on the driver's side.

Hugh sat down in the passenger seat.

As the hiker's hut in the rear window grew smaller and smaller and the soft monotonous engine hum of the jeep lulled him, Hugh thought about a plan. Until just now, all that had mattered was getting out of immediate danger alive, but now the question of what they could actually do was back on the table. Where might they have taken Laura? He was pretty sure that she was long gone from Iceland. If only they could somehow beat the information about her whereabouts out of Kruger. But he was who knows where, and at best long dead.

Then a completely different thought suddenly popped into his head. "Maybe we don't have to," he muttered, earning a curious look from Nicole.

"What don't we have to?" she asked.

Only now did Hugh realize that he had spoken the last thought aloud. "Oh, I'm sorry. I just had an idea. Wait." He opened his backpack and pulled out the camouflage-colored outdoor navigator that Nicole Kruger had taken off up in the mountains. "If we're really lucky, this thing will tell us where our favorite asshole has been."

Nicole pulled over on the narrow country road and leaned over to Hugh.

He turned on the device and searched the menu for saved routes and waypoints. He found all sorts of locations, many in Mali, Congo and Sudan, also in Romania, Geneva, Scotland and Iceland. Last but not least, there were two addresses in Berlin and one in the surrounding area.

"Well, there's a lot that looks familiar here," Hugh said. "I've been to almost everywhere there, except Germany. I bet those are the addresses we're looking for. Keller Pharma is a German company, after all."

Nicole slapped Hugh on the shoulder. "Good work, Sherlock. I just wonder where that leaves us."

"I'm not done yet," Hugh explained, pulling out his phone. Using his map app, he checked the locations one by one. One of the Berlin addresses was in Grunewald, a posh neighborhood with villas. That could possibly be Keller's home address.

The second location was in Rudow, in a former industrial area that looked quite run-down on the satellite images. Perhaps a secret production facility could be hidden there. The last stored waypoint was in the middle of the forest near the small town of Lychen. Only forest paths and gravel roads led here.

Hugh mused. His gut told him this location was ideal. The satellite images did not show any structures, but it was not uncommon for map services to use outdated imagery, especially in remote locations.

"This is it," he said to Nicole in a firm voice, tapping the display.

"I don't see anything there. What should be there?"

"Keller's secret laboratory, his production facility for the poison he floods the world with."

"But ...", Nicole continued. "How would you know?"

"Reporter's instinct. Believe me, the place is ideal. It's just as remote and hidden as the facility in Romania where I've been. This one fits the bill perfectly. And I know exactly what I'm going to do now, too."

Nicole looked at him skeptically. "I probably shouldn't ask what that would be, should I?"

Hugh put on a diabolical grin and pulled a package of plastic explosives from his backpack. "I'm going to blow this thing up!"

"Yes, of course, what else? Don't you think that sounds a little too easy?"

"I don't see any alternative. At least this way we can prevent them from making any more of that devilish stuff."

Nicole shook her head silently. "Your plan is an honorable one, but aren't you forgetting one small detail?"

"What do you mean?"

"You'd have to be able to get the explosives there first. How are you going to do that? I think smuggling a bomb onto an airplane is an insane idea. Besides, it will never work."

"You got your gun on board, too," Hugh replied.

"In the luggage, in an antique metal box from 1812 with walls inches thick. I was lucky it wasn't detected. But they have explosives detectors at the airport that detect the finest residue. And if they catch you, they'll arrest you and charge you with terrorism."

Hugh nodded slowly. "You're right, it's a stupid idea. But fortunately, another one just occurred to me, about how we might get around the security controls."

He picked up his cell phone, searched online for a number, and dialed.

Dr. Donata Spinoza was just leaving the evening WHO briefing when she was met in the hall by her assistant Jan Torgler - a lean young man, always in a suit, always perfectly presented. He had a cell phone in his hand and was waving it around in the air with unusual excitement.

"Dr. Spinoza, urgent call for you!" he shouted. "The man says he knows where Laura Delille is."

She stopped and answered the phone. "This is Donata Spinoza," she stated.

"Are you the current head of WHO? It's quite difficult to get you on the phone," said the caller.

"That's just as well!" retorted Spinoza. "And you are?"

"My name is Hugh Stevens, and I most recently did research with Laura Delille in Mali."

"I see. But you are not a WHO employee yourself?"

"Strictly speaking, I'm a journalist, but listen, none of that matters now. I know where Dr. Delille is. And I have valuable research. The original data from Professor Howard McDouglas, who was involved in the development of the compound that is now responsible for these cases of the disease. I would like to make them available to you."

"What's stopping you?" wanted to know Spinoza wanted to know.

"We're in Iceland, where we recovered the data from an archive and ..."

"In Iceland? That could be a problem. Borders are being closed all over Europe. There's chaos at a lot of airports."

"That's why I'm turning to you. We need transportation to Berlin. That's where Dr. Delille is. She has been kidnapped by Keller Pharma. They are to blame for this whole mess."

Spinoza silently pondered for a moment what to make of this caller. His story sounded pretty audacious. And under normal circumstances, she would have wished the weirdo a nice day and hung up. But the current situation was so convoluted and volatile at the same time that it fit with what Stevens was saying. What did she have to lose if she believed him?

"Dr. Spinoza?" prompted Hugh when she didn't answer.

"Yes, I'm still here. What you say sounds crazy. But unfortunately also logical. If you really have information about how this compound was developed, then we must have it. I will have it brought to Geneva."

"No!" objected Hugh. "I've got to get to Berlin. That's

where Laura Delille is, and I'm not going to leave her in the hands of these people. You take me there and then you get the data. That's the deal."

"I will not be blackmailed, Mr. Stevens!" retorted Spinoza threateningly.

"I'm not blackmailing you. I am proposing a trade. Please look at it this way. You know as well as I do that we are all under immense pressure."

"Fine," Spinoza said grudgingly. "You'll get your deal. But don't go to Reykjavik. I'm sure the airport is hopelessly overcrowded. I'll arrange transportation from one of the regional airports and get back to you as soon as I can." Spinoza hung up and handed the phone back to her assistant. "You heard it! See to it that this Stevens is picked up in Iceland and brought to Berlin. And you travel there personally to receive him and the data."

"Of course, I will arrange everything!" assured Torgler and hurried away.

# 35

*Laura's apartment in the basement location, October 11.*

Laura was awakened when the floor-to-ceiling panoramic screen in apartment 21F, which she had occupied for a few days, turned on, generating an image of a tropical sunrise.

She looked at the time superimposed on the picture. 6:30 a.m. How to change the alarm time or the picture, she did not know. No one had explained it to her when she arrived. It was also irrelevant - just one more thing out of her hands.

She got up and went to the bathroom to freshen up. Last night had been restless, and Laura hadn't fallen asleep until about 1:00 in the morning. She was still haunted by snippets of conversation with Harding. Had she really convinced the brittle scientist? Would she help her and maybe even manage to get Keller to at least give them the time they needed to optimize the compound? Her gut feeling told her that this was rather unlikely. The way she had gotten to know Keller, he was not amenable to arguments if they did not fit into his plans.

She couldn't help but think of an article she'd read about the phenomenon known as confirmation bias. The text had been about the extent to which the digitized world of the internet only reinforced the cognitive distortion of perception. People increasingly developed a tendency to select and interpret information in such a way that it fulfilled their own expectations as well as confirmed already established opinions. Keller would certainly be a good research subject for many a cognitive psychologist.

Still, Laura hoped that Harding could get through to him with the irrefutable facts she had determined yesterday. Keller was, despite everything, also a scientist who ought to not completely ignore objective findings.

Laura put the toothbrush back in the jar, combed her hair and left the bathroom. There was work waiting for her upstairs in the lab. And if she was lucky, there were also new results from the AI analysis. Before going to bed, she had given the algorithms an interaction analysis between Alpha and Beta, taking into account mutations and side effects.

She took her jacket from the chair and went to the door. Usually it opened automatically when approached from the inside, but today it didn't move. Laura pressed a button next to the frame. Again, nothing happened. She grabbed the handle and pulled. It didn't help, the door was locked and her apartment had become a cell.

"Damn!" exclaimed Laura, kicking the door with her foot.

So much for Keller's open-mindedness to the facts. The fact that she had now been locked up could only have had something to do with her findings yesterday. Had Harding changed her mind? Or had Peter Holm possibly seen to that? He seemed to have been very angry yesterday, and she had a lot of confidence in the dark, brooding fellow.

Laura dropped resignedly onto the bed. Behind her on the display wall, the sunrise was just turning into a colorful underwater world with lively schools of fish. As sweet as this illusion was, Laura couldn't help but hate it at that moment.

At a height of a good four and a half meters, a steel catwalk stretched around the production hall at Keller Pharma's Lychen site. Christian Keller liked this catwalk because from there he had a discreet view of the entire plant. He enjoyed the hustle and bustle down in production, as it proved that they were working at full speed on his project. The hooded security guards posted in all four corners of the hall also added to his satisfaction. Kruger had trained them well; they kept an eye on everything. Although their doubling up in the hall meant that only one man was still posted on the outside of the facility, the greatest danger currently lurked inside, and an unauthorized entry would be doomed to failure anyway.

On the opposite side of the hall, he saw Dr. Rose Harding climb the metal stairs to the catwalk and head in his direction. The satisfaction he had felt a moment ago gave way to a mixture of anger and disappointment.

He hated the idea that sand could get into the gears of his operation, that some of the cogs weren't running as smoothly as they should. And Harding was likely the messenger of such news, if not part of the cause.

The site manager reached Keller's position on a small steel balcony directly above the main synthesis chamber and stopped beside him. "The shift system is off to a good start, with all employees working overtime. The tanks are full of Alpha and we can now switch to Beta for 100 percent of the production time," Harding reported.

"I expected nothing less," Keller countered. "After all, I need 30,000 doses of Beta in two days."

"Yes, I wanted to talk to you about that demand. I don't know if we can do that. How fixed is this deadline, I mean ..."

"The appointment is worth three million euros so far. That's how much my presentation costs me. And if I can't deliver on time, it will cost me a hundred times that."

"I understand," Harding said. "It's just that we should deliver the quality we promised."

Keller felt icy anger rising inside him, but suppressed an outburst. "Save yourself the trouble of beating around the bush, Dr. Harding. I know Laura Delille has tried to deceive you. But I just can't believe you'd be stupid enough to turn on me now."

"It's not like that!" protested Harding.

"You know that this facility is monitored seamlessly. We have cameras in the labs, video analysis and also audio recording. Do you think I'd miss your little plot? I really didn't think you were that naive. And even if we didn't have all that, fortunately there are still loyal employees here."

"Holm! What did he tell you? He doesn't know all the details. I assure you, Delille's simulations are realistic. And there's really no question of any plot. All I want is a little more time to make the necessary adjustments."

"Time is currently a luxury we can't afford," Keller replied. "We're sticking to our plan. And don't try to dissuade me any further. I've confined Delille to her quarters. Don't make me do the same to you."

"I ..." she continued again.

"What else?" asked Keller gruffly.

"I was going to ask you to make the original data from Prof. McDouglas available to us. We need them to ..."

"Who is 'we'? I already said that Delille is under arrest. It was a mistake to let her cooperate with us, as it now turns out."

"I only want what's best for the project. With the data, we could possibly ..."

"The data stays under lock and key!" hissed Keller.

Harding stood there in a heap of misery, indecisive and dithering.

Keller felt that anger rising up again. Why did he still have to deal with people who were so far below his level of intellect? Why was this incompetence spreading like wildfire?

Disgust. Harding's appearance, her whole existence suddenly caused disgust. "Why are you still standing around here so uselessly?" he barked at her.

"Then can I at least take samples of all the site employees who received Beta? For quality assurance purposes. You yourself have had most of the injections so far, so perhaps it would be possible to take from you as well ..." Harding left the sentence unfinished. Instead, she reached out and pointed to Keller's left arm.

A wave of disgust flooded Keller. This inferior person wanted to touch him? Take a sample of his perfect blood? He would not allow that under any circumstances. Beta had opened him to what man was capable of. Never had his thoughts been more sublime and clear, never had his body radiated more energy. And now she wanted to interfere in it?

"Pathetic!", Keller snapped at her.

An uncertain frown crept across Harding's face.

Keller now stepped up close to her, putting on a sinister smile.

Instinctively, Harding backed away until she bumped backward against the railing.

Keller loved the look of fear in her eyes.

"I'm going to look into optimizing production processes now," she said hastily and turned aside to retreat.

"Sure," Keller replied. "Get an overview right away."

Harding took a step down the stage, and Keller sprang forward and abruptly grabbed her by the neck.

"Obstacles must be removed - consistently," Keller threatened, dragging her back to the small balcony. He felt an almost inhuman strength inside him that could be addictive.

Harding gave a meek "please," which only made Keller all the angrier.

"Of course, Dr. Harding. I'll comply with your request. What do you want? Redemption?" For a brief moment longer, he savored the feeling of absolute power over life and death and pushed her upper body over the railing. Then he eased away from Harding. "Get the hell out of here!"

Dawn seemed to drag on endlessly. In the sky above Egilsstaðir Airport in eastern Iceland, gray and dreary contourless clouds wandered by.

"Death weather," Hugh muttered, shaking his head as he gazed out the window of the foyer at the nearby Airport Hotel. "This weather is perfect for a funeral and nothing else. If there's one thing I don't miss about England, it's weather like this."

"I think it's rather Scottish weather, if that's any consolation," Nicole said, patting him on the back. "In fact, I like it; I'm a November child, after all."

"I'll just be glad when we get this out of the way."

"Somehow, I still can't believe the brazen bluff you pulled

off. And that it seems to have worked. But what if they find out we don't have the data?", Nicole queried.

Hugh shrugged his shoulders. "It's sneaky, but we have no choice if we want to get out of here."

Last night they had seen the local evening news in the hotel. They didn't understand what was being said, but the pictures spoke for themselves. The airports were in total chaos. Kevlavik airport was populated with masses of stranded tourists sitting on the ground hoping to get a flight. In addition, there were increased hygiene measures in the form of mandatory masks and sprayed disinfectant, which further unsettled people.

It was then clear why they had been sent to this regional airport and not to the international airport from which the flights to the continent usually departed.

Hugh's cell phone beeped. He pulled it out and saw a new message from an unknown Swiss cell phone number.

"The helicopter is on approach. Proceed directly to Heli-Port A on the outer perimeter. I expect you in Berlin this afternoon. Jan Torgler."

"Looks like our cab is here" Hugh said to Nicole, grabbing his suitcase.

Nicole also grabbed her luggage and they left the lobby of the hotel together. An icy drizzle began, making the weather even more unpleasant than it had seemed through the window.

After a few minutes' walk, they reached the heli-port at the nearby airport. A large bright yellow helicopter with the inscription "Luftrettung" flew roaring over their heads and touched down beyond a fence on the landing field.

The doors of the helicopter opened and two paramedics jumped out and retrieved a stretcher from the helicopter.

One of the men sprinted to the fence and opened a gate to let them in. As he did so, he eyed them skeptically. "Which one of you is the critical patient they want us to pick up here?"

Hugh and Nicole looked at each other in confusion.

Then Nicole pointed to Hugh. "Him," she said curtly. "I'm doing great."

The medic shook his head. "Well, if this order didn't come from the highest authority, I'd think we were being had. Anyway, come on. We'll refuel quickly and take off."

They walked over to the helipad.

"Fancy vehicle," Hugh said, trying to engage the paramedic in conversation. He still feared someone might try to examine their luggage with the explosives and weapons inside.

But the paramedic didn't care, instead praising the helicopter. "Yes, it's a brand new H175 from Airbus Helicopters. A modern rescue helicopter with space for a maximum of six passengers plus crew, plus a stretcher for injured people, plus comprehensive medical equipment. Sort of like a flying ambulance, except this one is about 290 kilometers per hour fast and has a range of over 1,000 kilometers," he explained as they boarded and stowed luggage. "Please fasten your seat belts, we'll be taking off in just a few minutes."

After two days of driving, Kimara and Gozo arrived in Dakar in the battered WHO jeep. Kimara had hardly expected that they would actually make it here. In fact, it was like a miracle. On the way, they had been shot at, and people had tried to steal the jeep. At one point they had so little fuel in the tank that the engine began to jerk and they had only made it to the next gas station at a crawling pace. But somehow they had always kept going, with the firm goal of reaching the port of Dakar and then leaving this hell behind them.

The capital of Senegal was located on the Cap Vert Peninsula and extended south to Cap Manuel. Thus, it was surrounded by the sea on three sides and at the same time represented the westernmost city of the African mainland. Its harbor was shielded from the storms of the Atlantic Ocean in a relatively sheltered bay. But the port was not immune to the storms of Senegal's collapsing civilization. A state of emergency had prevailed here for days, with countless people panic-stricken trying to get onto ships and boats. The fishermen had thrown everything they had caught overboard and were charging a fortune for a place in one of the hulls, although no one could guarantee that they would get far.

There were mainly small fishing boats in the harbor, painted in bright colors, but the paint was already peeling off on all sides. Only a few seaworthy ships that could make the crossing to Europe were among them. There was no sign of freighters or the larger cruise ships that usually like to call at Dakar.

"There she is, the Ramada III," Gozo said, pointing to a dark blue ship moored at the end of the pier. Dozens of people crowded onto the deck. Down on the pier, two crewmen armed with rifles stood and kept pushing back people who tried to gain access to the ship.

"I guess this nightmare never ends," Kimara said despairingly.

"But we have to go through, it's our only chance," Gozo replied. "We'd better hurry, they're planning to sail in half an hour and I don't want to risk them giving our seats to someone else." Gozo steered the jeep through the people on the docks and as close as possible to the Ramada III.

They got out and grabbed their bags. They made their way through the crowd to the armed guards defending the only entrance to the ship.

Gozo approached one of the men and showed him his cell phone, which had a message from the captain. "We are expected," he explained.

The guard eyed him and Kimara for a moment, then the man said, "Six thousand a head. Euros or dollars?"

"But ...", Gozo continued. "We had agreed on 3,000!" He pulled out the cell phone again and showed another message.

The guard shook his head. "That was two days ago. Prices are going up by the hour. Inflation, increased costs and immense demand."

"I know the captain, we had a deal!"

"The captain makes the prices. He has instructed me to keep your seats free. But only if you can pay. So, what now? Do you want to get on board?"

Gozo turned to Kimara. She looked deep into his eyes and saw desperation and determination mixed in his gaze. She shook her head. "We don't have enough money. Eight thousand is the most we have."

"Then you go!" said Gozo.

"No. We'll stay together, I'm sure there's another way."

"There is no other way, just look around you."

"I don't want to leave you!" Tears welled up in Kimara's eyes.

"You go, you and the child. You must be safe. I will follow!" Gozo wrapped his arms around her and hugged her tightly. He kissed her one last time, then tore himself away and rushed off.

Kimara was paralyzed, she knew he was right, but every fiber of her body resisted this decision. Would she ever see Gozo again? Would her child have to grow up without a father? Or did it not matter because they would all be dead in a few days anyway? All of a sudden, Kimara felt an incredible emptiness inside her – only the thought of her unborn child kept her last spark of hope glowing.

"Better make sure you get on board!" the guard said, pointing toward the ship.

Kimara turned to him and wordlessly pressed the money for their passage into his hand.

The guards let them pass.

While she was boarding, she heard the man behind her shouting to the crowd, "Listen up, the last seat just opened up! 7,000 dollars!"

# 36

*Berlin-Tegel, Germany, October 11*

The rescue helicopter with Hugh and Nicole on board approached the former Berlin Tegel airfield at around 5 p.m. local time after about five hours of flight and a refueling stop in Bergen, Norway. The airport had been officially closed for more than two and a half years, with only the northern part still in operation as a military helipad for government flights.

As an exception, the air rescue helicopter had also been allowed to land there. At the new German capital airport BER, there was similar chaos as in Reykjavik, only ten times larger in scale. The parking positions there were all occupied by aircraft that remained on the ground due to the travel restrictions and were no longer carrying passengers.

Here in Tegel, however, the situation was extremely quiet, so their arrival was discreet. It was just as well for Hugh that he didn't have to torture himself pushing through an angry crowd. During the flight, a leaden tiredness had come over him again, as he had already felt on the flight to Iceland.

Of course, the last two days had been extremely taxing physically and mentally, but Hugh realized that wasn't all. Kruger's derisive words echoed in his mind. "Old man," he had called him, amused that he had little time left. Hugh hated the thought, but judging by his state of mind, it was very likely that Kruger had not lied about that.

The helicopter touched down on the landing pad and the pilot turned off the engine. The sound of the rotor blades gradually subsided.

"Here we are," said the medic who had accompanied them aboard from Iceland, opening the doors. "I hope you had a pleasant flight."

"Thank you very much, we did!" said Hugh and climbed out of the helicopter, followed by Nicole. They took their bags, and the paramedic escorted them out of harm's way, away from the rotor blades and towards a barrier.

Behind them, a slim guy was waiting by a black sedan. He wore slicked hair and a dark blue suit. His nose and mouth were covered by a protective surgical mask.

Hugh and Nicole walked outside through a man-sized steel turnstile and toward the man.

He took two steps toward them and nodded. "Mr. Stevens, Miss McDouglas? I'm Jan Torgler, Dr. Spinoza's assistant. Forgive me if I don't shake your hand, but because of the spreading infections, we'd better refrain from physical contact. I also have protective masks for you in the car."

"While I don't think masks will protect us, I guess it can't hurt," Hugh agreed. "Thank you, too, for bringing us here. It was high time."

"I just hope it's worth the effort. Now, if you would hand over the data? Our experts are already waiting with baited breath."

"Yeah, sure," Hugh said. "Best we settle this in the car, or aren't you going to take us into town?"

"Yes, of course," Torgler replied, pointing to the black car. "Get in."

As they walked to the car, Hugh picked up his backpack and opened it. "Do you mind if I drive?"

Torgler turned around with an expression of pure confusion and was about to protest.

Hugh pulled the pistol half out of Kruger's possession and showed it inconspicuously to Torgler.

The words stuck in his throat and he turned white as a sheet.

Nicole, who hadn't said anything the whole time, murmured to him, "What the hell are you doing?"

"Relax, I'm not going to hurt him, I just need the car. I'll drop you off in town and then drive to Keller Pharma."

"You can forget that," Nicole replied. "You're not booting me out again, I'm also armed and probably shoot better than you. Besides, you're going to need me on this insane plan of yours."

"What ... what kind of plan?" Torgler timidly spoke up.

Hugh eyed him for a moment. "I'm going to blow up the plant where they make the compound that's responsible for all this," he said grimly.

"Are you serious? What about the data? We need that urgently!" demanded Torgler.

"We don't have it. We tried to get it, but someone got in the way. We're sorry. But if I had told you the truth, we'd still be stuck on Iceland. Now get on board and don't make a scene."

Torgler sighed heavily, then disappeared into the back of the car.

Laura lifted the tray with the half-eaten lunch, which had been cold for hours, and carried it toward the door. Soon another of those hooded and silent guards would have to come to bring her dinner, as they had done earlier for breakfast and lunch. Those had been the only two events of the day - apart from the animation on the video wall, whose repertoire, however, she had already seen twice in its entirety.

There was no computer in the room, no way to distract herself. On the desk, which she had to use as a dining table, there was only a telephone, which she could not use to call anyone because it was locked down.

A knock on the door signaled that the armed food messenger had arrived. Laura placed the tray next to the door and took a few steps back.

After a few seconds, the door slid open.

To her surprise, she saw that this time Melinda was holding the tray.

But she was not alone, the guard was standing right next to her, rifle raised. "Half hour," growled the masked man, taking the remains of the lunch with his free hand and going out again.

Melinda, meanwhile, entered and put on a smile. She carried the new tray to the table and waited until the door closed again. "I thought you could use some company. I have a little time before my shift at the lab starts."

"I'm so glad someone is coming to talk to me. It's awful in here. And there's so much to do!"

"I know, but Keller's not going to let you back out. He found out what you were talking about with Harding. Everybody knows, Holm spilled it all. It's all gotten a lot more complicated now. The guards in production have been doubled."

"Melinda, we have to do something! If we're lucky, it's not too late. You need to go to the lab and check on the analysis! Maybe we can ..."

"That's quite impossible!" protested Melinda. "If Keller finds out ... He's capable of anything. This morning I thought he was going to kill Harding when she asked him to postpone the rollout of Beta. I watched it from the production floor."

"One thing is clear, this man is capable of anything. That's why we have to stop him!"

"How do you imagine we do this? What do you want me to do? Overpower the guard out there and get you out of here? It was hard enough to beg for half an hour with you in the first place. Should we storm into the lab and get the data? To do what with it? We'll never make it out of here!" Melinda's voice became brittle and she fell silent. She took a few deep breaths, then composed herself. "Please realize it's hopeless."

Laura shook her head. "I can't. I refuse to surrender. I'm not asking you to mess with the guards, I just want you to continue my analysis and keep me informed. That's all. You're in the lab anyway, please take a look when Holm isn't there. After that, we'll see what we can do."

"Eat now," Melinda said, standing up and walking to the door. There she turned around once more. "Maybe I can visit you again tomorrow. If Keller hasn't killed me by then." She knocked and waited for the guard to open.

Laura watched her leave the apartment. Then she turned her attention to dinner. Honestly, she wasn't hungry, but there was nothing else to do. So she lifted the package with the shrink-wrapped sandwich and tore it open. Underneath was a folded piece of paper with handwriting that read, "Please destroy as soon as read."

As dusk gradually settled over the countryside north of Berlin, Nicole and Hugh crept up to the Keller Pharma facility in the forest near Lychen. Earlier, they had dropped off the protesting Jan Torgler at a rest stop in the province and driven on to the edge of the forest. There they left the limousine and walked the rest of the way along the gravel road.

They followed the indicated waypoints of the navigator from Kruger's possessions. After about 20 minutes of walking, they reached a clearing cut into the forest, the size of a soccer field. From the shelter of the trees, Nicole and Hugh surveyed the site. There, around a large central shed, were several tin sheds, beefy forestry machines, a Unimog, two truck trailers and several wood storage areas, as well as a large water tank.

"Are you sure this is the right place? This looks more like a sawmill," Nicole noted.

Hugh checked the coordinates on the navigator again. "It's one hundred percent definitely the location that's stored here. I can't imagine Kruger would be interested in a sawmill. It's got to be camouflage."

"It's a pretty good one, though. Still, let's be sure we don't accidentally blow up the wrong plant - which, by the way, I still think is a ludicrous idea."

"If you have a better plan on how to stop Keller, just come out with it!"

Nicole screwed up her face. She pondered for a moment, then spoke aloud what had been on her mind for quite a while, "What if Laura is in there?"

This question seemed to hit Hugh. She could see him swallow hard a couple of times. "We can't rule that out. That's why I'm going to go in and check. Maybe I can force their release."

"How?"

"I'm going to ..." Hugh fell silent.

Now Nicole heard why. A car came crunching along the gravel road. The car stopped right in front of the door of the big hall. A security guard came from the left side and checked who it was.

"The hall is guarded," Nicole whispered.

Hugh just nodded silently and they continued to watch what was happening outside the building.

The driver of the car, a stiff-looking driver with gray hair, got out, walked around the car and opened the rear door on the passenger side. The man looked like a traditional English butler.

"I don't think sawmill operators can afford a chauffeur," Hugh commented.

The guard opened the metal gates of the hall and a security door behind came into view. As if on cue, a slim man in a beige suit stepped out. The guard closed the lock behind him.

"Basement," Hugh hissed.

"Is this the guy? Are you sure?", Nicole asked.

"Yes, I remember a picture from online very well. I was researching Keller Pharma with Laura. How I'd love to polish off that slick face of his."

"Quiet, they're talking to each other. Can you make out anything?"

They listened for a moment, but could only pick up snippets of conversation. Keller shook his head and the butler shrugged his shoulders. Then Keller handed the man a silver metal suitcase. The latter accepted it, put it in the back seat and closed the door. As he walked around the car and got in on the driver's side, Keller turned to the guard and gave him instructions as well.

Now he pulled out a card and held it up to a card reader next to the airlock. He approached with his head and looked directly into an opening on the reader. After a while, it opened and Keller disappeared inside.

"There's our proof," Hugh said grimly. "Time to blow the bastard up."

"Hugh, I hate to say this again, but if Keller is here, don't you think Laura is being held captive here as well?"

"I'll find out soon enough. But first, I need to plant the charges, we need the leverage."

"And the guard?"

"That's where you come in."

"So now you want me to be the decoy after all, huh?"

"Just this once. And I know now that you can fight back if it comes to it."

Nicole shook her head. "Why did I ever get involved in this madness?"

Laura read the folded note a third time. On the one hand, to make sure that she had understood everything correctly, and on the other hand, to be able to assess whether it was possibly a trap. But this thought seemed increasingly absurd to her. Why would anyone do such a thing? She was already in solitary confinement and, for better or worse, at the mercy of Christian Keller. So why stage anything? One part of her question seemed to be answered, at least to some extent.

She tore the note into tiny pieces and threw them into the toilet. She pressed the flush and waited until the last scrap had disappeared down the drain.

The other part of her question remained: had she understood correctly that Dr. Harding was proposing to sabotage the facility? And if so, was that realistic given the armed guards and the other safeguards Keller had put in place?

If anyone had sufficient access to critical processes, it was Harding. But if Melinda's account was true that Keller had almost killed her, his trust in Harding must have suffered massively. And in that case, sabotage would truly be suicide. Moreover, Harding needed accomplices to achieve this goal, and besides Melinda, she was also supposed to participate. How that would work when she was trapped here remained a mystery to her, but presumably Harding had considered that and planned for her release. It was supposed to start during the night shift, as soon as Keller had left the facility.

Laura looked at her watch: six-thirty in the evening. The night shift had just started. Now she had to wait for a sign.

# 37

*Outside the Keller facility, evening of October 11.*

Nicole's pulse quickened the closer she got to the hall and thus to the hooded guard patrolling it. She tried to stroll as unobtrusively as possible. But inside she was electrified.

"Stop!" the guard shouted in an energetic tone when she noticed her.

Nicole stopped to the left of the hall as if rooted to the spot. "Oh God, you scared me!" she gasped, "What's wrong?"

"This is private property, what are you doing here?" the man asked sharply.

"I'm ... I'm just going for a walk," Nicole lied.

"You will leave immediately, or else ..."

He didn't get any further than that, because Hugh smashed him on the head from behind with an iron bar that he had found among the parked machines.

The man slumped unconscious and together they dragged him to a shed some distance away. There Hugh tied his arms and legs together, gagged him and barricaded the door.

Then he and Nicole set about placing the explosives. The four charges Kruger had placed on the archive in Iceland had been enough to pulverize it. Now they had as many as six packs that would surely do the same to the hall here.

Hugh helped Nicole with a leg up so she could attach a pack to a ventilation shaft. They positioned two more at the far end of the hall, where various connections and piping came out of the wall. Two more went on the right and left long sides.

They did not place any devices at the front so that it would not be discovered ahead of time. The last remaining package they attached to a large wooden trailer parked away from the hall. This they fitted with a separate detonator whose timer was programmed for 60 minutes.

Now Hugh and Nicole crept in a wide arc through the forest towards the front. Hugh was visibly exhausted from the journey and the physical exertion of the last few days and was progressing more and more slowly. Only adrenaline kept him somewhat upright. He sat down on the ground, leaned his back against a tree and took a few deep breaths. Then he set a three-hour countdown on the ignition remote for the remaining five charges and handed the remote to Nicole.

Hesitantly, she took it. "I really have an awful feeling about this, what if something goes wrong?"

"It's very simple. The timer runs by itself. And we know you can't abort it once it's started. The most you can do is pull the detonators out of the charges, but be careful doing that! You wouldn't be able to get to the charges on the vent and pipes by yourself anyway. I don't want you to put yourself in that kind of danger - Highlander or not!"

Nicole nodded. She realized that it was hopeless to dissuade Hugh from this plan or to do anything about it.

"So, if anyone other than Laura or I comes out, you detonate immediately," Hugh explained, pointing to the red button on the remote. "Otherwise, run the timer. In three hours, we're either free - or dead. As soon as the timer gets below three minutes, you make a run for it." Hugh took one last look back at the hall, as if to make sure he was really ready to enter the lion's den. He turned back to Nicole and looked at her with sad eyes.

She felt a pang in her heart at the sight, as if she were watching an innocent execution candidate on his way to the scaffold - and she realized that this thought was probably not that far off. With a sudden impulse, she sprang forward and before she realized it herself, she was kissing Hugh. Only briefly, but intimately. Then she leaned back again.

Hugh's facial expression revealed that he was completely shocked.

"Sorry, it can only be due to stress," Nicole explained. "But I had to do this now. I might not get around to it otherwise."

"What crappy timing," Hugh replied dryly. "I guess now I have one more reason to get out of this facility alive."

"That's right!" affirmed Nicole.

Hugh took another deep breath, then stood up, leaving Nicole behind in the shelter of the trees. He walked straight toward the hall entrance. There, he shot the lock out of the outer metal door with Kruger's pistol and pulled it open. He laid the gun on the floor and stood in front of the electronic access reader. He looked head-on into the built-in camera and raised his hands to show he was not armed. After a few moments, a red light next to the camera came on.

"This is Hugh Stevens, I have an offer for Christian Keller that he can't refuse," he said aloud.

Meanwhile, Christian Keller sat in the small security center of the production site, checking the video recordings and alarm messages from the last eight hours. While he had been here all day monitoring the progress of the conversion to Beta production, he still knew he couldn't have his eyes and ears everywhere at once. The intelligent video system was able to do that.

After his site manager turned out to be an easily manipulated turncoat, Keller sensed conspiracy everywhere. That may also have been due to his heightened senses. Since he had started the Beta treatment, the feeling had grown in him that his mental strength was increasing to a superhuman level and his determination was growing day by day.

But now, after more than two hours of evaluating the video, Keller was also beginning to feel the exhaustion. He thought of many of his contacts from the business world who, in such situations, had helped themselves to cocaine and ruined their bodies while jetting from Shanghai to Monaco or from New York to Barbados. He had no sympathy for such superficial nonsense. He had chosen a different path, the path of invincible health, of truth - and of genuine undivided power.

While leaning back in his chair, he reached into the inside pocket of his suit jacket and pulled out a syringe and a rubber band. He slipped down the left jacket sleeve and bandaged the arm above the elbow. Then he tugged out the plastic cap protecting the needle and placed the syringe against the vein.

He hesitated for a moment when he saw the dark discoloration in the crook of his arm, which had grown again a little since the last time. He would have to take care of that. After the presentation, when his victory march was unstoppable. There were always side effects, but that didn't mean the drug was useless. Keller could not and would not wait, even if something deep inside him shared Dr. Harding's doubt. He loathed the thought because it meant weakness and procrastination.

The needle slid into the vein and Keller squeezed the contents into his bloodstream. A pleasant warmth spread through his body.

No sooner had he put the syringe away than he heard a dull bang followed by an alarm sound. The screens in front of him showed a red flashing dot on the map. That was the main entrance. Keller switched the terminal image to the main monitor. A man stood in front of the door with his arms raised.

"Stevens?" asked Keller incredulously. "How can that be?" He turned on the audio. "... An offer for Christian Keller that he can't refuse," he heard from the speaker.

"Where the hell is Kruger?" growled Keller, full of displeasure that his specialist for dirty work had apparently proved incapable where Stevens was concerned.

Keller went to the microphone built into the control panel of the surveillance center and activated the intercom. "Two guards to the airlock, now! Take this man, but keep him alive for now," he ordered.

Still Hugh stood in front of the access reader at the entrance to the hall. He repeated his words and waited.

It took a full two minutes, then finally a green light lit up on the reader, and the airlock opened a crack. Hugh took a step back.

The airlock door slowly opened a little further, but the inside remained dark.

"I'm unarmed, but I have ..." The rest of the sentence was lost in uncontrolled groans as two taser electrodes hit Hugh's chest and sent thousands of volts coursing through his body. His legs suddenly felt like rubber, and he collapsed to the floor, convulsing. For a moment he tried desperately to somehow regain control of his body, but then everything around him was lost in deep blackness.

In apartment 21F, Laura waited with impatience and growing tension for the sabotage plan to begin. Or had it already fallen through? Had Harding and Melinda been discovered? Could they possibly not succeed in freeing her?

Laura paced back and forth between the living area and the bathroom, hoping that something would finally happen.

Then she heard a thump from beyond the door. She felt her muscles tense and her pulse rise higher and higher. What if she was about to have to defend herself? Fight for her life because they were coming to hold her to account as a co-conspirator? Laura was determined not to go down without a fight.

Finally, the door opened. What was about to appear? Melinda's friendly face, Harding's bald head, or Keller's slick visage?

When the door had slid aside, two guards dragged in an unconscious man by the arms. His head was hanging down, so that she could not immediately recognize who it was. Moreover, she was so surprised by this turn of events that she did not react at first.

As the men threw the unconscious man onto the bed,

Laura realized it was Hugh. She rushed to him. "What have you bastards done to him?" she snapped at the guards, who continued unmoved back toward the door.

"Hey! He needs medical help!" Laura shouted after them, but she got no answer. Routinely, she checked his pulse and breathing. They seemed a little shallow, but the heartbeat was strong. What concerned her most, however, was his general condition. Hugh looked almost ten years older than when she had last seen him.

"Shit, Hugh! What did they do to you?"

Dr. Rose Harding stood at Control Panel C of the production facility and glanced up at the elevated platform at the edge of the hall. Her gaze slid to that point above the central synthesis chamber where Keller had choked her this morning and pinned her to the railing. She had almost met the end of her life, expecting him to push her down over the railing at any moment. A fall from a good four meters onto the hard floor didn't have to be fatal, but it very well could be.

Then Keller had let her go. And until now she didn't know exactly why. Maybe because he needed her so close to the deadline? Because he didn't want any panic among the staff? Nevertheless, his behavior was increasingly unpredictable, even this sudden outburst of anger did not fit the otherwise so detached and elegance-conscious man. Perhaps the drug, of which they thought he had injected himself with far too much in too short a time, had even more side effects than they had been aware of so far.

Harding turned back to the displays on her terminal and checked the status of the mixtures being fed into the reaction chambers. For about two hours, she had been shifting the ratios and establishing a new process. One piece at a time, so no one noticed right away. She had secretly put the automatic production monitoring algorithms into maintenance mode. They would be offline for at least three hours and would not report what she was doing here.

While Beta was being produced as planned at maximum capacity in the main line of the plant, tying up the attention of all the employees present, she had secretly converted the sample synthesis chamber so that it produced something completely different: Nerve gas. Not necessarily a lethal one, but a highly damaging one if exposed to it for too long or too intensely.

She didn't really want to kill anyone, Keller at most, but even that seemed unnecessary. It was enough to stop him. And if the release of the gas meant that the plant had to be evacuated and production shut down, the goal had been achieved for now. What came after that lay firmly in the unknown. But it would buy her the time she needed to perfect Beta, and not fuel the spread of Alpha any further. It was only the conversation with Laura Delille that had made her realize how far they had strayed from their original course and how much Keller had deceived them all.

Harding initiated the final step to synthesize the gas. Once the tank was full, she could open the valve at any time and the contamination alarm would go off.

Lost in thought, Harding didn't notice that someone was suddenly standing behind her.

"I've got you now. Keller will finish you off," whispered a voice.

Harding spun around. "Holm!" she hissed softly. "What do you want?"

She saw a guileful glint in his eyes and sinister smile on his thin lips.

"I'm busy," she rebuffed.

Holm put his hand on her shoulder. "You're done here, come on."

Harding slowly reached into the right pocket of her gown, then suddenly thrust forward with it.

The needle of a syringe went into Holm's stomach. She pressed and quickly withdrew her hand.

Holm looked down, perplexed. But he had no time to

react, because the anesthetic took effect immediately. Another short groan, then he slumped down.

"Help, over here!" shouted Harding. "Holm's collapsed."

## 38

Very gradually, Hugh's consciousness fought its way back. He struggled to escape the deep darkness that had taken hold of him. But some instinct in him said he had to come to his senses now. At last his eyelids obeyed and opened. His vision cleared and he looked out to sea. For a moment he thought he was dead. This was the afterlife, so peaceful and idyllic everything seemed. But then his senses fully awakened and he realized it was a giant screen. The horizon was on its edge. No, it was lying on its side! With a groan, he sat up.

"Hugh!" he heard a familiar voice from behind him. He turned around. Laura was standing there.

She came rushing over, squatted in front of the bed and grabbed his hand. "Gently!"

"Laura, you're actually here," Hugh said.

"Yeah, and so are you. Nice plan, what are you doing?"

"I have come to put an end to this. And to get you out of here, if that's possible."

"But ..."

"Wait a minute," he interrupted her, "how long have I been out, what time is it?"

"Half an hour. It's now a quarter to nine."

"Shit, that only gives us fifteen minutes," Hugh said, trying to get up.

"Slow down. Explain to me what's going on first."

"Okay, but we have to hurry."

Laura sat down on the bed next to Hugh. "Shoot."

"I don't have time to explain every detail to you, but what's most important now is that we've placed six explosive charges outside that will pulverize everything in a good three hours. But before that, I want to force this facility to let us out of here. One charge will go off in as little as fifteen minutes to lend weight to my demand."

Laura shook her head in disbelief, then asked, "Who is 'we'? You said 'we've' planted explosive charges?"

"Me and Nicole. She's waiting outside, ready to set off the charges."

"Not Nicole McDouglas, by any chance? How could you drag her out here and leave her alone in the woods with half a dozen charges?"

"If it had been up to me, she'd be sitting comfortably at home - or in hiding somewhere. But that woman is incredibly strong-willed."

"And now you want to blackmail Keller?" asked Laura.

"That's right. If he doesn't want his prestige project to crumble into dust, he should let us go. We have to get to him, because in a few minutes our warning shot will go off."

"I really didn't think you were that crazy, Hugh. But now it is what it is. I'd rather blow up with this whole plant than have any more of this poison get out into the world. But you should also know that they're making some kind of antidote here. And if I understand it correctly, it's also the only chance we have to stop what's happening to you. If we actually blow up this site, that antidote is most likely lost."

"I'm fine," Hugh said. "We can worry about my health later. If things go according to plan, Keller will get involved in the deal and we won't have to go so far as to blow everything up." Hugh got up and walked as fast as he could to the door. He pounded on it with his fist. "Hey, out there! Take us to Keller, I need to talk to him."

"Shut up!" boomed from outside.

"Fine, we'll wait until the charges go off. Your call."

It took a moment for the door to open. Two guards came in and grabbed Hugh and Laura. They pushed them roughly in front of them and out the door.

The guards pushed Laura and Hugh through the entrance to the security center, where Christian Keller was waiting for them. They then positioned themselves to the left and right of the door.

"I must admit that you surprise me, Mr. Stevens. I had thought that Kruger had taken care of you. True, I had told him to keep her alive a while longer as leverage, but I know him by now. Sometimes he tends to overreact when provoked."

"Keller, we don't have time to talk about this asshole Kruger - a dead asshole, by the way. We need to talk about a deal."

Keller raised his eyebrows derisively. "You want to negotiate with me? That's cute! What makes you think you have anything of value to offer me?"

"It's like this: You let Laura and I go, and in exchange, your beautiful facility stays intact."

"Because?" continued Keller, still amused.

"Because I found some interesting objects on Kruger that are now proving useful. There's enough explosives stuck to the hall outside to blow it up three times over. If anyone other than Laura or I gets through the door first, they'll detonate."

"You better not be playing me, Mr. Stevens. That would be an awfully rotten bluff."

"You want to see my hand?" asked Hugh. "What time is it?"

Keller looked at the thick Rolex on his wrist. "One minute to nine."

"Very well. Then we'll just wait."

Keller narrowed his eyes and eyed Hugh. Apparently he was wondering if there might be something to the threat. The minute was not quite up when he got his answer.

They were one floor underground and felt the detonation more than they heard it, but it was clear to all that this had been a large explosion outside.

Hugh spoke up, "That was just a single load on one of the trailers, relatively far from the shed. But the other five are sitting at critical points along the outer walls - the ventilation, the piping, and so on. If you don't let us go within the next two hours, your beautiful plant will blow up, and you right along with it." Hugh put on a winning smile.

Keller sprang forward and struck Hugh brutally without warning. He fell to the ground in a daze.

"You goddamn son of a bitch!" Laura yelled at him, getting down on her knees next to Hugh, who was cowering on the ground.

Keller tightened his jacket and looked down at them like pathetic insects. "I probably should have listened to Kruger after all and had you killed right then and there."

He turned to one of the guards at the door. "Get Harding down here, now!" To the other guard he stated, "Stevens and Delille stay back downstairs until we have a clear understanding of the situation."

"Didn't you hear him? Everything is going to blow up here soon!" protested Laura.

"Nothing is going to happen here unless I want it to," Keller said coolly.

Nicole McDouglas' ears were ringing. She had stayed far enough away from the blast that she had not taken any damage, but the force had still been noticeable. One thing was clear to her in any case, if it came to it that the remaining five charges went off, she wanted to be far away.

She looked down at the remote detonator in her hand, whose display showed just under two hours. Hugh's words came back to her, that she should ignite if anyone other than him or Laura stepped out the door. But she didn't know if she was capable of doing that. Sitting here in the woods at night waiting for such a big bang was gruesome enough, but blowing up potentially innocent people was something else entirely. She'd had a lot of time to think in the past hour.

Surely not only Christian Keller and his hooded guards were in this large production hall, but probably also employees who were responsible for the production. Not to mention Laura and Hugh, who would inevitably be killed along with her if she pressed that wretched red button too soon.

Suddenly she felt anger. How could this Hugh Stevens impose this on her? But in a moment it vanished again when she pictured his sad face from earlier sat in front of her. Had that really just been a spontaneous overaction or did she actually feel something for him? If so, that was another reason not to press the button.

She peered over to the plant. Everything was quiet there. No one came outside to see where the noise was coming from. So Hugh must have made his threat.

Once again she looked down at the display: One hour and 55 minutes remained, then she would have certainty.

A guard appeared next to Harding at the console and demonstratively put his hand to the pistol on his belt. "Christian Keller wants to see you, immediately," the man said in a hypothermic tone and pointed with his free hand in the direction of the exit.

Harding's mind raced. Had she been busted? Should she release the gas immediately? Impossible, she was not prepared, Melinda was not in position, let alone Delille.

The guard was getting impatient. "I said immediately!"

"Yeah, sure. You may not believe this, but I have actually some difficult work to do here."

"I'm not interested in that. My orders are clear and I carry them out. Let's go!"

Harding stepped back from the console and followed the man to the airlock and out to the elevators.

They reached the security center shortly thereafter, one floor below.

Keller was on the phone now, and Harding caught the last sentence. "Then see that you get them out on the road, or I'll make an example of you!" He hung up and turned to her. His face was not quite its usual smooth facade.

Harding felt as if she was even seeing small cracks, behind which she thought she could see anger and perhaps a little fear. She was careful not to let on anything, however. Instead, she asked matter-of-factly, "You wanted to see me?"

Keller stroked his hair and straightened it before answering. Now he said in an almost casual-sounding tone, "I know we've had our differences. But now we have to join forces once again. For the greater goal." He looked questioningly at Harding.

"We will," Harding said diplomatically.

"We have to load the tanks. Everything has to be ready in 90 minutes. The trucks are on their way, waiting for my instructions."

"Loading the tanks? But that ... I mean, we have to uncover the inspection shaft to do that. That alone will take an hour, I'm sure."

"You have one and a half. And two guards will give you a hand. What's the problem?" asked Keller.

"Well, with Alpha I don't see any difficulties, but Beta is not stable enough to be transported in its current state. The compound needs to be cooled, and the tanks don't have their own cooling function; we use the facility's central system."

"I don't want to hear any excuses! You know how this ended the last time you tried to stall me. I can't guarantee that my composure will be enough a second time."

"It's not like that!" hurried Harding to reassure him. "We can't get the tanks out of here. But there is another solution. We could fortify Beta with preservatives and bottle it. I can use the sample synthesis chamber for that."

"Now we finally understand each other!"

"Yes, only it's going to be very tight. I need every helping hand for that. Peter Holm has collapsed, Sudor is feverish and can hardly get out of bed."

"So, what do you want? Take everyone still available."

"I would like Laura Delille to be involved as well, she is accomplished and physically fit."

Keller narrowed his eyes. It was clear that this proposal was anything but to his liking.

Harding, meanwhile, continued. "You can have it permanently guarded, what's the big deal? All I can say is, if you want us to get as much of Beta out of here as possible, this is the only way that might work in time."

Again, Keller stroked his hair, as if that would help him organize his thoughts. "I'll send for them. Besides, I'll personally come along to production and keep an eye on them!"

## 39

Laura reluctantly left Hugh Stevens alone in her quarters and followed the guard up to production, where she was met by Melinda, Keller, Harding, and two other staff members.

"Keller, let us out of here already!" demanded Laura. "You know Hugh wasn't bluffing. The plant is going to blow."

Melinda and Harding cast worried glances at each other.

"Didn't he tell you?" asked Laura when she noticed. "Interesting."

"We'll leave the plant before that happens. But first we have to pack," Keller explained. "You're going to help us do that. Or I'll have you shot on the spot."

Laura folded her arms in front of her chest.

"Please, it's important!" said Harding. "We have to work together." She looked at her urgently.

Had Harding switched sides again and blindly followed Keller to his doom? Laura could hardly believe that. The scientist had certainly recognized what had to be done. And something subtle in her tone told her that she was probably right about her intuition.

"All the guards in this room are armed and ready to shoot," Keller threatened. "And I'm also keeping an eye on you, so don't try anything stupid!" With those words, he turned away to climb the stairs at the edge to the elevated platform above the facilities.

"Is it true about the explosives?" Melinda wanted to know.

"Yes, you must have heard that loud bang earlier. That was a warning shot to blackmail Keller. But it didn't work," Laura explained. "And in less than an hour and a half, there's a load five times that size going off at the hall."

"We need to get out of here," Melinda demanded.

"I've been saying that since the beginning. But how?" Laura inquired, nodding her head in the direction Keller had disappeared.

"We'll be fine," Harding whispered to her. "With the agent in here." She pointed to the sample synthesis chamber, which was full of nerve gas. "Now get to work. Start bottling Beta, and I'll take care of the rest. I hope you're all good at holding your breath."

Nicole McDouglas sat in her hiding place behind the first row of trees at the edge of the clearing, freezing. The temperature had dropped noticeably in the last few hours; she estimated it was barely more than four or five degrees. Her breath condensed in the air. Staying motionless in the damp forest made it doubly uncomfortable. She knew that if Hugh and Laura didn't come out of the facility within the next 25 minutes, the clammy cold would turn to heat, namely when the countdown ended and the detonation was triggered.

A crunching sound made Nicole start up. She searched the grounds with quick glances. Her eyes had become accustomed to the darkness, and the brilliant light of the full moon was enough to make out all the objects and buildings in the clearing relatively well. But the crunching - and now an increasing hum - were not coming from there, but from the gravel road that led here. Now she saw headlights between the tree trunks, dancing ghostly long shadows across the whole area. Two trucks came slowly along the road, and behind them the dark sedan she had seen before - with Keller's butler in it.

There was clearly something going on here. Nicole looked down at the ignition remote. What was she supposed to do now? Blow it up immediately? Wait for the automatic countdown to make that decision for her? But what if it was too late then? She hated this uncertainty, hated that she was so indecisive. But she couldn't push that button.

Laura and Hugh were in the facility. And there was still

time. Twenty-two minutes, after all. Hopefully, the truck drivers wouldn't discover the explosives by then. But the drivers didn't get out, they just parked the vehicles to the right and left of the hall, while the limousine stopped in front of the building with some distance to spare. The headlights went out, and everything was again in the pale moonlight.

"Come on, Hugh!" whispered Nicole into the twilight, kneading her icy fingers.

The guards had uncovered the inspection shaft at the rear end of the hall and pushed the tank with the Alpha agent into the transport elevator created during construction. Its shaft terminated under the forest floor, perfectly camouflaged under half a meter of soil and protected by a ceiling of twelve centimeters of steel.

Harding knew it was only a matter of minutes before they would get the tank outside. Keller had climbed down from his elevated guard post and was keeping an eye on the final movements at the shaft.

Now it was her turn to act. She had continued to concentrate the agent in the tank to make sure it was sufficiently potent. Its release could cost some people here their lives - maybe even their own. But if she didn't, Keller might still get away with it, and that thought made her sick.

"Dr. Keller!" she shouted down the hall.

He turned and gave her an unwilling look.

"We can add the preservative now, but something is wrong with the lines, the valve won't open!" explained Harding.

Keller gave an unintelligible curse, detached himself from the work on the elevator and came toward her.

Harding, meanwhile, called up the manual emergency vent in the menu. Once she pressed the button to confirm, there were about three seconds before the valve of the bursting tank would open and blow the toxic contents into the hall. What exactly would happen then was written in the stars.

She did not know with certainty whether the spontaneously synthesized gas would act as intended, or how strong its real effect would be. She only knew that there was no turning back now.

She glanced over at Melinda Riley, who was standing with Laura a good ten yards away at the bottling line. She nodded to them and got a nod in response. They were ready.

Keller was now within a few steps of Harding's position.

"Could you check the sensor on the valve block, please, Dr. Keller?" asked Harding.

Keller frowned briefly, but then turned and walked to the back of the synthesis chamber.

"I'm going to start again, see if the green light comes on at the relay," Harding said, pressing the button for emergency venting. She took a few deep breaths in and out before finally holding her breath.

"I see a red flashing light," Keller reported. Then the gas burst from the valve with an eardrum-shredding hiss, enveloping Keller in a deadly cloud of gas.

At the same moment, Harding ran. Out of the corner of her eye, she saw Keller fall to the ground, gasping and blue in the face.

An alarm blared through the hall. Panic broke out. Staff and guards gasped everywhere.

Suddenly, shots rang out. One of the guards took aim at Harding, Melinda and Laura, who were running for the door, from the walkway above the production. Up there, the toxic gas had apparently not yet reached them.

By the time they got to the airlock that separated the production hall from the rest of the site, Harding's lungs were already burning. The exertion and stress made the craving for air grow stronger and stronger.

Shots again. They slammed into a steel container just next to them. Coolant escaped with a hiss.

Harding took the key card out of her pocket and hurriedly held it up to the reader. But it did not jump from red to green as expected. Then a bullet hit her in the arm. She cried out, and went to her knees. With her next breath, the gas entered her lungs. Immediately she began to cough.

Melinda and Laura dragged her aside. Harding tried to think herself through the haze and fight the paralyzing effect of the gas.

Shots again, but this time they overshot them. Presumably, the guard was now also affected by the gas.

Laura took the card from Harding's hand and held it up to the reader again. Again, the lock did not open.

With her last breath, Harding wrung out the words, "Emergency code 8833." Then she collapsed, gasping.

Laura typed in the code, and finally the airlock opened.

Together, Laura and Melinda dragged Harding out into safety. Immediately, the airlock closed again. Harding gasped cravingly for air.

Nothing was moving behind the glass, everyone was lying on the floor. There was no way to help even one of them.

"Can you stand up?" asked Melinda.

Harding waved it off. "I'm terribly dizzy, I don't think I can walk again yet," she gasped in a hoarse voice.

"We have to get Hugh!" demanded Laura. "He's down in my quarters." Frantically, she looked at her watch. "We've got five minutes, then we've got to be out of here."

"Sudor is also still downstairs. We have to take him, too!" added Melinda.

"Leave me here. Go get him," Harding croaked. "By the time you get back, I might manage to get up."

"Okay, see you in a minute," Laura said, running with Melinda to the elevator.

Hugh looked at the clock superimposed on the artificial Alpine panorama in his cell. What was he supposed to do with the last minutes of his life?

He felt incredibly weak, as if he were 80 years old. And the thick laceration on his head that Keller had administered to him was still throbbing. With difficulty, he sat up in bed and contemplated the ideal world presented in this simulation. He wished he were up there in the mountains on the lush alpine pasture, watching the clouds roll by.

But he knew that it would soon be over for him. He would be crushed by the chunks of the collapsing hall. And if the concrete ceilings of the two floors miraculously saved him from this fate, it would be completely impossible to find him down here in time and get him out. Who would do that either? No one would send a rescue team.

The ruins of this facility would rot away and perhaps eventually be overgrown by the forest again. Hugh imagined new life sprouting over his anonymous grave while his body rotted down here. Nothing would remain of him in this world. And he left the stage with a great failure.

Suddenly Hugh was jolted out of his morbid thoughts. The door to the apartment opened and Laura and another woman rushed in.

"Can you stand up?" asked Laura, in a rushed voice.

"What ...," Hugh began.

"Get up, man!", Laura drove at him, reaching out her arm to pull him to his feet.

Hugh staggered to the door with her help. He was still dizzy and his legs felt like jello.

Laura and Melinda maneuvered Hugh out the door and into the hallway.

"How much time do we have?" asked Laura.

"I don't know, a few minutes at most," Hugh said.

"We still have to get Sudor," Melinda said and hurried a few doors down. There she pounded on his door. "Rafael!" she screamed. Now she kicked the door with all her might.

Finally, it opened. Sudor appeared, sleepy, with reddened eyes and only in his underwear.

"Come on! We have to get out now! Everything is about to blow up here."

Sudor looked around in confusion.

Melinda wasted no time in explaining, grabbed him by the arm and pulled him out into the hallway.

"Now let's get out of here!" shouted Laura.

Together they helped the staggering Hugh to the elevator and got in.

"Shit, only two minutes left," Nicole cursed. Should she start running? Was she far enough away? Or would she be blown to pieces in a moment? But she couldn't leave her position, nor did she have much hope. As she did so, time suddenly seemed to race. One minute.

Finally, the floodgate opened.

Nicole squeezed the remote in her hand and peered over to the entrance.

Five people came out of the facility.

Her heart leapt.

There was Hugh, being supported by another man! Laura and another woman she didn't know were helping a third who could barely walk. They dragged her more than she could walk herself.

"Hurry up!" shouted Nicole, as loud as she could.

Laura seemed to have heard this and pointed in her direction.

The driver's door of the limousine, which was parked away from the entrance, opened. The butler got out and looked irritatedly at the people walking toward the forest. He took a few hesitant steps toward the hall, but promptly turned back and rushed to the car. He disappeared into the car with his upper body.

Finally Hugh, Laura and the others reached Nicole's position and took cover behind the trees.

Nicole saw the butler get out of the car with a gun in his hand, then she, too, dived behind a tree. "Cover your ears!" she shouted.

The countdown continued relentlessly: 3, 2 ...

In the next moment, the nightly silence shattered into a

veritable inferno. All five charges ignited synchronously and pulverized the production hall in a furious fireball. The trucks parked next to it were knocked over and pushed meters away. Chunks of concrete flew through the forest like projectiles, and a gray-black cloud obscured everything in the vicinity. Even the light of the moon seemed to die out, and darkness descended over the forest.

## 40

The dust from the explosion slowly settled, and a deceptive calm returned to the forest near Lychen. Only now and then did a chunk of concrete from the blown-up facility slide to the ground or a metal girder give way with a squeak. At the edge of the clearing, a few small fires smoldered in the undergrowth.

The detonation had been tremendous. The shock wave had gone through Laura and the others, and for a moment Laura had thought that the tree behind her back would give way and fall on her. But its roots were firmly anchored in the ground, so the trunk had absorbed most of the force and protected them from debris.

She stood up and looked around to see if everyone else had been as lucky as she had.

Sudor had put his head between his knees and wrapped his arms around them. In this crouched position, he swayed his body back and forth, apparently fearing that he might be dead after all. Next to him knelt Melinda, who tried to calm him down.

Harding leaned against a tree, dazed. Her coat was stained deep red on her shoulder and arm from the gunshot wound, but it appeared the bleeding was subsiding. It was probably just a graze. Nevertheless, it was clear that she would have to go to a clinic soon before the wound became infected.

Nicole got up and walked over to Hugh, who was apparently lying on the ground completely exhausted.

Laura also approached Hugh and examined him. His pulse was a little weak, but easy to feel, and his breathing was steady. "I still can't believe we made it out alive," she told Nicole. "Thank you for waiting and not blowing us up."

Nicole shook her head. "Those were the three most terrifying hours of my life. But I couldn't have pushed that button. Not while you were in there." She pointed to Hugh. "What about him, is he going to make it?".

"He is very weak. And I don't know how to help him. The drug they injected him with is causing him to physically deteriorate rapidly. And the superhuman exertion of the last few days has probably accelerated it further."

"But there must be something we can do?" protested Nicole.

Melinda had also joined them during the conversation and now spoke up. "There was a chance once, but the agent that could have stopped the process has just been blown up back there. Maybe we can reproduce it somehow if we can get the appropriate data, but that will take weeks, if not months."

"What a fucking irony!" cursed Nicole.

Hugh groaned and opened his eyes. "So be it," he said weakly. "But I leave knowing that this diabolical plan has come to an end."

"No, Hugh!" retorted Nicole with defiance in her voice.

"I'm sorry ..." he replied.

A cough interrupted him. It was Harding trying to speak. "Come here!" she croaked in her gas-affected voice.

Laura rushed over to her, tore a strip of fabric off Harding's gown and used it as a makeshift bandage on her arm. "It's going to be okay, you're not going to die, we're going to get you out of here."

"Hugh Stevens," Harding croaked. "He's going to die. Only Beta can save him now."

"Yes, I know that, but we just destroyed everything!" replied Laura.

"Not all of it," Harding said. "Keller has a private stash in a safe."

Hope sprouted again in Laura. "Where's the supply?"

"At his villa in Berlin. You have to get him there, now," Harding said.

Nicole pulled out the backpack Hugh had left behind hours ago and took out the navigator. She held it up. "And this thing knows where he lives!"

"Then let's get out of here," Laura decided, addressing Harding, "Can you stand up?"

"I'll be fine, I definitely don't want to stay here."

"There's a car at the edge of the woods," Nicole explained. "It's quite a distance to get there, but if we pull ourselves together, we can make it."

They helped Harding and Hugh up and, with some gentle force, also got Sudor to overcome his fearful rigidity.

When the group ventured out of the shelter of the trees, everyone saw the full extent of the devastation. Nothing but rubble and ash remained of the hall, and the trucks and machines in the vicinity had also been swept aside, overturned and demolished.

Only the black sedan parked away from the front entrance appeared relatively intact. The windows on the right side were cracked, the paint was scratched, and the car was certainly a good five meters further away from its original position, but the tires had air and it appeared ready to drive despite everything.

In front of the vehicle they saw the driver lying, apparently hit in the head by a piece of flying debris.

"Spencer," Harding said. "He was Keller's butler."

"Is he dead?" asked Nicole.

Laura knelt beside the man and looked for signs of life.

"Careful, he had a gun," Nicole warned.

Laura shook her head. "I can't see a gun anywhere, it was probably thrown off him. It wouldn't do him any good anyway because he has no pulse." She examined his jacket pockets and pulled out a set of keys. "If we're lucky, the car will still be moving. That will improve our chances of getting Hugh to the villa in time."

She went to the driver's door and got in. The engine started effortlessly.

While Nicole sat in the passenger seat, Hugh, Harding, Melinda and Sudor squeezed into the back seat.

Laura carefully steered the car through debris lying around and then accelerated when the clear gravel road was in front of them.

At the edge of the forest, Jan Torgler's car was still there just as Hugh and Nicole had left it.

"Melinda, you take the other car," Laura said. "Please get Harding to the hospital and get yourself and Sudor checked out, too. We'll get the drug and save Hugh, and we'll join you later."

Then she turned to Nicole. "I can't ask you to come with me. But if Hugh collapses on the way, I could use your help."

Nicole gave her a wry look. "If you thought I was going to back out now, you've got another thing coming."

"Hugh already said you like to do your own thing," she replied with a smile. "Then let's do it."

"One more thing," Harding said. "Keller keeps the syringes in a cooler in the library. There's a code lock. I watched it once, I think the PIN is 6996, but I'm not completely sure."

"All right, 6996, if not, we'll break it open somehow," Laura said.

Nicole handed the key to Toggler's car to Melinda, who travelled with Sudor and Harding.

They drove one after the other as far as Oranienburg, north of Berlin. As Melinda steered Torgler's car toward the local clinic, Laura and Nicole drove on with Hugh to Keller's villa in Grunewald. Now that it was almost midnight, there was virtually no traffic, and after a total of just under 90 minutes of driving, they reached the coordinates from the navigator.

The historic Kellers' villa lay dark and deserted among the other no less magnificent estates in the neighborhood.

"Everything looks quiet," Laura said.

"You mean too quiet?" asked Nicole.

"I don't know. Do you think there are guards? Dogs? Alarms?"

Nicole pulled out her pistol. "I have three shots, just in case."

Laura looked at the back seat, where Hugh had been sleeping for an hour. "We'd better get a move on. Let's get the stuff and see about getting out of here. If there's an alarm, hopefully we'll be gone before any security or police show up here."

She pulled out the car keys and examined the bunch. "One will fit."

After waking the exhausted Hugh and helping him to the door, Laura tried the keys one by one. The third one fit. She turned it and pushed the door open.

Everything remained quiet, no alarm sounded, but automatic lighting now illuminated the prestigious entrance. It gleamed with polished marble floors, wood paneling, gold sconces, and a glittering crystal chandelier on the ceiling. At the end of the entrance hall, an oval staircase with brass-colored handrails wound its way up.

"Harding said Keller has his stash upstairs in the library," Laura opined.

Nicole looked around cautiously. "I still have a bad feeling. I might be better off staying down here to keep watch. Then I can warn you in case someone comes."

Laura turned to Hugh. "Can you make it up the stairs by yourself?"

"Now don't get carried away, I'm not dead yet!"

"Okay, then the two of us will go alone. But you be on guard, please," Laura told Nicole, then took Hugh's arm. "Come along, Patient X!"

On the second floor, they found Keller's library just to the right of the stairs. The large double doors were open.

They went inside and turned on the light. It was messy here, books were on the floor, the drawers of the desk by the window were pulled out.

"I don't like this," Laura opined.

"Do you think I do?" replied Hugh, dropping into an armchair in front of the desk.

Laura searched the shelves and felt around for the hidden refrigerator compartment. She found it behind a panel with fake book spines glued to it.

"Now we're getting close," she said and typed the code on the keypad: 6-9-9-6. She confirmed the code with a green button and the compartment snapped open. "Thank God!" she exclaimed with relief.

Inside the secret compartment, which was about the size of a camping cooler, various preparations were stored. But only three syringes were among them. They all bore the label "Project Beta - Test Batch 003.

Laura removed one of them. "Let's hope it works quickly."

## 41

"Get away from the freezer!" a voice barked. It came from the direction of the door.

Laura and Hugh turned around, startled.

"That's mine. But thank you for opening the safe for me."

"Kruger," Hugh said curtly. "I was so hoping you had died in Iceland you son of a bitch."

"I'm truly sorry to disappoint you," Kruger replied sarcastically. He wore his left arm bound in a sling and a thick bandage on his head. In his right hand he had a semi-automatic ready to fire. "It takes more than that to take me out. Now put the damn syringe down and get over next to Stevens!"

Laura did not move.

Kruger narrowed his eyes. Then he shot into the book wall next to Laura. Scraps of paper splattered off.

Laura rushed to Hugh's side, Kruger tracing her path with the gun.

Hugh, meanwhile, tried to rise to stand between Laura and Kruger, but he was too weak and sank back into the chair.

"Och, hang in there a little longer, Mr. Stevens. I want to have some fun with you."

"You have what you want, why don't you just fuck off?" asked Laura defiantly.

"Because I still have to shut your smart mouth!" retorted Kruger. "But the ambience is not right here. We're going downstairs."

"Let her go," Hugh begged. "Then you can do whatever you want with me."

"No, that's not how this works," Kruger replied, waving the gun in the air. "You know what? Maybe I'll let them go once I've had enough fun with you?"

"You're inhuman," Laura said.

Kruger laughed loud and dirty. "Thanks for the compliment. Now move it!"

They went down to the wine cellar, where shelves of exquisite treasures were stored. Laura had to support Hugh, as his strength was slowly failing him again. Further back in the cellar were two large antique wine barrels.

When they arrived at these, Kruger said sharply, "Kneel, both of you!" Then he threw some thick cable ties on the ground. "You tie his arms and legs!" he instructed Laura, pointing the pistol at her.

Reluctantly, she obeyed.

Kruger took the pistol in his wounded hand and then with the other, amazingly skillfully, tied Laura's hands. He pulled out a hunting knife, put the blade to Hugh's neck and let it stay there for a few seconds.

Unexpectedly, he let go of him again. "No, we'll do it the other way around," he explained.

He walked over to Laura, who was kneeling at the second wine barrel. "I want Stevens to watch while we have a little fun."

Very closely now, he approached Laura, who pressed her back against the wood of the barrel behind her.

"Kruger, leave her alone!" shouted Hugh, but he did not respond.

"You will die one by one a long, agonizing death." He stood up, undid his belt buckle and began to pull out the belt.

A metallic click made Kruger instantly stop. He recognized the sound within milliseconds, but he had no time to react. In the next moment, a bullet shredded his skull.

His lifeless body slapped to the stone floor, and a dark pool spread out beneath him.

Behind him stood Nicole with an expression like arctic winter and red splatter across her face. "Now we're even, asshole."

It took Laura a moment to realize what had just happened. Then she picked herself up and crawled over to Hugh, who had slumped to one side and seemed unconscious.

"Hugh! Hang in there, we'll get the shot!"

# 42

*Geneva, WHO headquarters, three months later*

Dr. Donata Spinoza noted with satisfaction that all the invited participants had turned up for the final meeting in the large conference room at WHO headquarters in Geneva. She silently raised her hand and waited a few moments until all conversations had fallen silent.

"Dear colleagues, we have a tough three months behind us, and I must express my gratitude to each and every one of you. Without the unconditional sacrifice of so many of you, the situation in the world would be even worse than it already is. Today I stand before you for the last time as acting president before a new president, or presidents, takes the helm of WHO next week. They will have a difficult term - probably the most difficult yet in the history of our organization. I ask everyone to be as dedicated and knowledgeable in the future as they have been in the past."

Spinoza paused and let her eyes wander over those present. She received approving nods and occasional taps on the table.

She continued. "One of my last official acts will be to go before the press today and provide a forecast. We want to summarize the last few months and make sure that we have considered everything correctly and comprehensively. I'll turn the floor over to Dr. Koharu Nakamura."

The chief epidemiologist rose and initiated a slight bow. "Thank you, Dr. Spinoza. It hurts to repeat the hard facts, but they are part of the bigger picture. In the last four months of the peak pandemic phase, which we are now slowly exiting, some 800 million people have died worldwide, and another 750 million women are infertile, with no hope of a cure. For some 500 million men, the provisional antidote is not working or is working inadequately. Their life expectancy is likely to be around 40 years on average. The older the sufferers, the more radical the effect. But we are seeing signs of normalization. Mass application of the antidote provides very effective containment of the spread of the mutant elicitor. The forecast, therefore, is that the world population will level off at about 3.5 billion by 2030 and then remain stable. This estimate is still subject to high margins of error and depends on external factors, but for the first time, I am cautiously optimistic again." Dr. Nakamura bowed again and retook his seat.

"Thank you, Dr. Nakamura. I share your optimism. It is what keeps us going," Spinoza said, looking over to the opposite side of the table. "I would also like to use today's meeting as an opportunity once again to thank those without whom we would not have had a chance to deal with this situation. My thanks go specifically to Dr. Laura Delille, who was willing to make any personal sacrifice to make this happen."

Everyone present applauded or patted the table appreciatively.

Now Laura stood up and put on a smile. "Thank you for those words, but I didn't accomplish anything on my own. It was an effort by many. And not all of them are still with us. So before we get to the facts, I propose a moment of silence for all those who lost this battle."

The assembled group rose and remained in silence for a few moments, then Laura restarted. "Thank you, I'll be brief. You all know what has happened so far, and Dr. Nakamura has made what I think is a very solid forecast. We'll be fortunate if it actually comes to pass. The signs are good that it will. We have succeeded in amplifying the so-called Beta agent with the remaining samples from Christian Keller's possession and a backup of the original research data from Prof. McDouglas. We use it to treat severe Alpha cases. But as was just mentioned, even with this in place, the many millions of cases of infertility remain irreversible. Nevertheless, I am pleased to announce today that we have succeeded in further optimizing the compound and significantly reducing its potential for side effects. Furthermore, everything now indicates that the two substances largely neutralize each other in practice and cancel each other out in terms of effect. Does that mean all is well? Not at all. Let's not kid ourselves, we are still doing damage control. But I, too, can already see a point on the horizon where we will be able to live normally again. Let's all work together so that this point gets closer day by day. Thank you." Laura took her seat again. Again there was applause.

Spinoza waited a moment, then raised her hand. "All right, thank you to everyone present. If there are no further additions or questions, we hereby end the meeting and proceed to the press conference. Dr. Nakamura, Dr. Delille, I will see you there in about 15 minutes."

About two hours after the end of the big press conference, Laura was sitting in her favorite café on the south bank of the Rhone, looking out over the river with a fragrant cup of latte. She desperately needed some peace and quiet after the media frenzy and the countless probing questions from the reporters, which often included a hint of accusation. But that's the way it was, the press pack, always on the hunt, always a tad too much drama. Even the biggest crisis in human history hadn't changed that.

Laura took a big sip of coffee and felt the comforting warmth creep down her throat.

Little bells at the entrance announced new guests were entering, and Laura turned away from the river to see who they were.

Hugh Stevens came up to her with quick steps, a broad smile on his lips. "Laura! At last we meet again."

Laura stood up and hugged him. "Well, you've finally made it to Geneva. You look good, I'm so glad you're doing well again."

He took a seat at Laura's table.

"It's a cliché, but I feel like I've been reborn. After six weeks in the hospital and another eight in rehab, you have to feel better."

Laura nodded. "I thought I might see you at the press conference?"

"No, absolutely not. I'm done with that. My journalistic career is over. I've had a lot of time to think. And I'm not doing that to myself anymore."

"I guess that's probably a good decision, because your colleagues haven't improved one bit."

The waitress came over, and Hugh ordered a large latte macchiato.

"Since we're talking about being newborn ..." Laura pulled out her smartphone and opened a message. "Look, this picture came yesterday. You remember Kimara from camp?" Laura showed him a picture of the former nurse with her baby. "Both of them are fine. She's in Italy in a hospital. And miraculously, the father also made it out of the chaos in Africa. He's still in a refugee camp in Malta, but chances are he'll be able to see his daughter soon."

Hugh swallowed hard and Laura saw that he was fighting tears. "What is it?" she asked.

"Oh, forget it. I don't know either. Ever since I woke up in that hospital, I've been so emotional, it's not celebratory. It must be those damn pills!" grumbled Hugh.

Laura had to laugh. "Men and feelings, really."

"Let's not do that. How are you doing, what are you doing?", Hugh asked.

"Work, nothing but work. But it doesn't bother me. I know what else needs to be done to get things right - and I'm happy to do it."

"Are things coming together then? I doubted it for a long time."

"I think so. And differently than anyone could ever have imagined. Keller was a fanatic, that's undeniable. He wanted a new world order, one in which he ruled and was in control. But he was too impatient. And too megalomaniacal. He thought he could control nature. But that was a mistake."

"Where's the positive in that?"

"Well, as heinous as his plan was, he still changed the world. Just as McDouglas had once conceived. The thesis that got him kicked out of his post at the time had to do with genetic birth control. It wasn't as cruel and radical as Keller's perverted version, of course, but it was still effective. McDouglas wanted to successively reduce the world's population to create a true balance between resource use and prosperity, between conservation and innovation. To put man back in his place. Not as the crown of creation, not as the all-dominant plague of the planet, but as one part of a greater whole."

Hugh nodded slowly and thoughtfully. "And we have that chance now."

"Yes, it will be tough, there will be major upheavals. But the forecast is that the population will level off at around 3.5 billion by 2030 and then stagnate or grow very weakly. Greenhouse emissions are already at levels never thought possible. The planet is breathing a sigh of relief."

"What a crazy story," Hugh said. "A diabolical plan fails and paves the way for humanity to save itself."

"Crazy, I know. Just the fact that we got out of this in one piece is nothing short of a miracle. Well, I'll still have a lot to do. After months of processing, the German authorities have finally released the archives of the nationalized Keller Pharma. All patents worldwide have been cancelled, and the preparations may be manufactured by anyone - except, of course, for two very specific remedies. Keller's legacy will benefit countless patients around the world."

Hugh looked at Laura in silence for a while, then said, "I'm going to move to Scotland."

"What, you? I thought you didn't like Scotland, just the breakfast there. What about the weather?"

"The weather is lousy. But I'm sure you can guess the real reason."

"No, I couldn't possibly imagine. You're not moving there for a particular Highlander, are you?"

Hugh was grinning up to his ears.

"Hugh, I'm happy for you!"

"I'm starting from scratch. I'm going to write books - children's books. So many have lost their parents, they desperately need something positive in their lives. And so do I."

Laura took his hand and squeezed it, "You're one of the good guys, Hugh Stevens."

"I know I'm the best. I told you that the first time we met. It just took you a long time to figure it out." He put on a mischievous grin. "The wedding is in June, you're coming, right?"

"Sure, if the weather is right," Laura joked. "And if the best of the best doesn't serve me haggis for breakfast!"

END

Printed in Great Britain
by Amazon